A Relative Matter

A Relative Matter

A novel by
John Fallon

iUniverse.com, Inc.

San Jose New York Lincoln Shanghai

A Relative Matter
All Rights Reserved © 2001 by John Fallon

Published by iUniverse.com, Inc.

For information address:
iUniverse.com, Inc.
5220 S 16th, Ste. 200
Lincoln, NE 68512
www.iuniverse.com

ISBN: 0-595-14767-4

Printed in the United States of America

To my wife, Nancy.

Part 1

Chapter one

His most vivid early memory was of him in the back garden in his grandparents' house on a sunny spring afternoon, sitting on the grass holding his brother's bottle and soother and being told by his Granny White not to eat the daisies.

His brother had just fallen asleep in the pram, and Geoffrey wasn't eating the daisies, he was licking their middles to taste the honey the bees had put there. Suddenly there was a sharp bang like a crack of thunder and the garden shed exploded.

In and of itself, this was not a new experience for Geoffrey. He had seen the garden shed explode many times before—it was in the garden shed that his grandfather, performed his compost and fertilizer experiments. But this time, Geoffrey knew that the explosion was different from the others. It wasn't just a puff of smoke and a few panes of glass shattering, or the door being blasted open and falling off its hinges. This time the entire shed blew up—walls, door, windows and roof, all burst asunder in opposite directions. The front part of the roof rose like a rocket and crashed up through the chestnut tree. At the same time, a wall ripped across the vegetable patch and a shrivelled cabbage was shot like a smoking cannonball over the miniature privet. It rolled up the lawn and stopped near Geoffrey's feet. The chestnut tree was on fire and a thick cloud of black gritty acrid smoke climbed up into the sky.

The pandemonium was better than any film he'd ever seen. He was four years old and he had been to the flicks with his Granny Doyle, once to see Lorin Hardy and once to the Three Stoogers. But this was real, not a film. His uncle came shinnying over the garden wall in his suit, shouting 'what in the blue blazes has that man done now'. Neighbours, who previous to this Geoffrey had only ever seen behind hedges or between lace curtains, came running down the side passageway and into the back garden in full view of everyone. Better still, they were all shouting at the same time. Shouting that they had phoned the police, the ambulance, the fire brigade and the government. Uncle Bradleigh was unwinding the hose and yelling for someone to turn on the tap. Jacintha, a skinny woman who lived in his grandmother's attic, was dashing back and forth to the rain barrel with a terra cotta plant pot and calling on others to form a chain.

His brother woke up and started crying, not even crying really, but whimpering. Geoffrey plugged in his soother and looked at his Granny White and awaited instructions. But none were forthcoming. He thought she was going to say something about taking the child inside with all this commotion, and then demand that all these people leave her garden at once, but she didn't. She didn't say anything. Instead she sat silently in the green and white canvassed deckchair, her hat still on her head, and a copy of *The People's Friend* in her lap. She seemed to be staring at the smouldering cabbage. Geoffrey had never known her to do that before. Just stare.

His mother was in town shopping. It was a Saturday.

Chapter two

It was probably a year or so after Grandad White had blown himself to smithereens when Geoffrey and his mother moved out of their little red-bricked cottage and into Granny White's big house. Geoffrey wasn't sure why, or for how long, but it seemed like it was for a very long time. His school was the same but the route to it was different. And the big, tall boy, Brian, didn't bring him anymore. Instead his mother walked him there.

At Granny White's he slept in a room by himself, and his mother slept in a separate room with his brother. Lying in bed, he could hear the cars swish up and down the main road in the rain. He liked that. It was the only thing he liked about staying there.

All their furniture was stacked in the garage and in his grandmother's kitchen. At breakfast he would look at his mattress leaning up against the wall, almost touching the ceiling. Beside it was his mother and father's mattress which was twice as big. His father was living in digs for the time being, though Geoffrey had no idea what that meant. He thought maybe it meant he was in prison, but why would his father have to go to jail. His mother cried a lot and his brother was learning how to talk. Geoffrey taught him the word 'bed'. And when he wouldn't stop crying they wheeled him out to the garage and turned on his grandmother's new washing machine. That always did the trick. The slish-slosh sound sent him to sleep in seconds, no matter how cranky he was.

It was a bad time all round. His grandmother, who was always stern and seldom smiled, seemed to be more cross with him than ever. And with his mother. She disapproved of the way his mother boiled eggs or made mashed potato, and no matter how hard Geoffrey tried he never seemed able to set the table correctly.

But worst of all was the toilet business.

His grandmother's house was very big, with big high walls. Go in by the garage door with the shiny green paint breaking out in blisters, walk through the garage where his grandfather's Hillman stood on cement blocks, and where all their furniture was, except for the mattresses. Go to the far end where the new washing machine was, right beside a step and a door. Open the door and you were in the passage. The passage had a corrugated tin roof and often you could hear the branches from the tree next door scrape up and down it. There were three doors on the left, none on the right, because that was the wall shared with the neighbour. The first door opened into the scullery which led to the kitchen, the middle door was just after the scullery window. Walk on further and step down a step and you reached a third door. This had a wobbledy handle and went into the garden. If you passed that door you came to a dead end and this was the toolshed where his grandfather used to work when he wasn't working outside in the exploding shed. Now turn around and walk back to that middle door again. This was the toilet.

There was another toilet upstairs, Geoffrey could only use that at night and never for doing his jobs. This was the toilet for him, and the Jacintha lady and his mother. It was dark. Even with the light on, it was dark. And when you stared up at the light bulb, you could clearly see the curly filament, not like in ordinary lightbulbs, and then when you closed your eyes you could see the filament floating inside your head. The toilet bowl was quite high and he could only touch the floor with his tiptoes. There was never any Bronco or Izal here. Instead you had to use little squares of *The People's Friend* which the Jacintha lady had neatly cut up once a week and then speared the little squares of paper onto a sharp black spike which stuck out of the wall. When you had done your job, you had to crank the chain to make it flush, and a torrent of water would come cascading into the bowl, splashing your bare bottom, then gurgle down the hole with a horrible sucking sound.

For the first week he tried to be brave because he knew this was exactly like the digs cell his father was locked away in and he had to stay in it all day and all night. Not just to do his jobs.

That was one part of the toilet business. The second part he never told anyone about, not even his other granny, Granny Doyle, and for a long time he told her almost everything.

It was a Saturday morning. He was playing in the back garden, bouncing a golf ball he'd found, up and down on an old tennis racquet. His mother had gone to see the doctor.

"Geoffrey! Come in right away. Your grandmother wants to speak with you." It was the lady live-in, Jacintha. Geoffrey didn't much like her, so he took his time. His grandmother probably wanted him to post *The Irish Field* to his uncle in Tanganyika and there was always a big fuss about catching the midday post on a Saturday, because that was the last till Monday.

But it wasn't the silly racing paper to his silly uncle, it wasn't that at all. It was bum stains.

Beside the new washing machine was the old draining board and sink. On the draining board his grandmother had laid out his under-pants, six pairs in two rows of three. There were all inside out and they all had brown bum stains in their middles. His grandmother was hold-ing a giant pair of wooden tongs. She picked up the nearest underpants and dangled them in front of him. "Aren't you old enough to wipe your own bottom clean?"

Geoffrey was struck dumb.

"You're a dirty boy, a dirty animal," she said. "And if your mother cleans up after you, then more fool her. And she's a big enough fool already."

"In my day he would have been well whipped for that mess," said the Jacintha lady.

"And so he shall be. Take down your trousers child."

"No."

He started to make a run for the passage. He'd be in the garden in a flash. Over the wall in another and out through his uncle's side door and onto the street. Then he would find a Garda and be taken to his father in the digs. But before he'd reached the step, the grandmother had him by the shoulder.

"Either you take down your trousers or I'll take them down for you. Which is it to be?"

It wasn't the beating which was so bad—she used a long, thin stick. It was that after she made him take off his short trousers, she ordered him to take down his underpants as well, which they then checked for bum-stains, but he hadn't done a job that day and there weren't any. Worst of all, worse even than his bum being bare, so was his mickey. And the Jacintha lady kept staring at it.

They made him bend over and hold on to the front of his grandfather's car, but he didn't cry or yell out once.

"Give him the bar of soap and the scrubbing brush. He can use the tub outside." His grandmother tonged the items onto the floor and told him to pick them up, and continued to talk to Jacintha, "Don't bring him back till he has them clean."

He had to do it on the garden path. Fill the galvanized tub with the hose and then soap the brush and scrub all six middles clean. Jacintha watched and told him he'd better make a good job of it because he was a disgusting boy, and if he didn't he'd get twice the whipping.

On Monday, Geoffrey did his job at school where at least they had Bronco.

***

It was also on Monday that he put his plan into action. School had ended for the day, but instead of standing in line at the gate he had dodged down the alley between the church and the school into the Junior yard (he was in first class). His plan was to wait till everyone was gone and then sneak in behind the caretaker's house and up to bicycle sheds in the Senior yard.

It had been tricky smuggling food out of the house, it had even been tricky obtaining it in the first place. He had to creep into the pantry after supper when his grandmother was in the breakfast room listening to the BBC on the wireless because, as she told his mother, she refused to listen to Radio Eireann on principle. Except for that one time when his mother was reading her poetry.

Now the breakfast room was really the sitting room because the real sitting room and dining room were always closed off except for Christmas and Easter and special occasions. Jacintha was upstairs in her room and his mother was reading in the garden. Kevin, his little brother, was asleep by the new washing machine. It was almost dusk. He knew winter was coming.

From the outside the pantry was ordinary-looking enough except it had a noisy black latch. But once you walked inside it was like Ali Baba's cave. It was deep, dark and narrow, and when you reached the end your head touched the ceiling. Full of spicy smells and red and gold tins and glinting glass jars, it was a wonder place, as if you were in a different far-away country. Shelves were lined with jams and marmalades in jars sealed with greaseproof paper and thick rubber bands. Fatter jars with metal clamps were so stuffed with onions, carrots and cauliflowers that they squashed up against the glass like when you press your nose and lips against the window pane. Then they were the tins—square, flat tins with harlequins on the lid or paintings of Chinese people in gardens with little red bridges. Hidden inside each tin was a fruit cake, and on the outside was gummed piece of white paper with the date on which the cake had been baked neatly printed in black wax crayon. Up at the front on the floor stood stout brown paper bags with their collars rolled down, so you could see that they were full of sultanas, raisins and currants. Geoffrey scooped out a fistful of each and packed them into the front pouch of his schoolbag. Into the schoolbag itself he stashed as much as he could—a can of sardines with a picture of a trawler crashing through stormy seas, six fig roll biscuits, six Marietta, and a long thin box of dates made of wood which was so thin, it was like paper. Next he opened a razzle-dazzle round tin and tipped out eight oatmeal biscuits. His grandmother baked the world's best fruit cakes and the world's best oatmeal biscuits.

***

It was time to move. He checked to see if the coast was clear. He was hardly ten seconds out of the alley when he spotted Pines the caretaker working in his garden. He retreated and found a turning that led to the basement door of the church's boiler room. It was locked. Maybe he should have hidden in the church—it was always dark in there. But it was too late to change his mind. He could hear parents and children all over the place. Some seniors boys ran down the alley singing 'King of the Wild Frontier' but they didn't take the turning to the boiler room. Finally things quieted down. He wondered what time it was. He knew he'd been there a long time, probably an hour. He was just about to try the Junior yard again when he was shocked to hear his mother's voice coming from there.

"But he couldn't have gone home with anyone else!"

"He was in class right up to the bell, Mrs. Doyle. He and John Spifford filled the inkwells." It was his teacher Miss Lenehan, "Children have a habit of making arrangements and neglecting to tell their mothers."

His mother said that it was not so in her son's case. "Geoffrey!" she yelled at the top of her voice, "Geoffrey Doyle."

"Mr. Pines," his teacher shouted to the caretaker who was deaf in one ear, "have you seen Geoffrey Doyle in the yard since bell?"

"Do I know him?"

"Have you seen any Junior boy since bell?"

"I've seen Senior boys and I chased them the hell out. They're not meant to be in this yard. Of course it's the apples they're after. I've told that to your headmaster more than once."

"A junior boy, First Class?"

"Senior boys—yes. A junior boy—no."

His teacher dropped her voice. She was talking to his mother again. "He's probably headed home by himself. Maybe he thinks it sissy that you're walking him."

"He's only six, Miss Lenehan."

"But you'd never know what would be in their heads at that age. Tiernan Dempsey last week decided he was a spaceman and wanted to walk up to Terenure at lunch break where he planned to take a bus into the city, visit the Lord Mayor and declare himself Ruler of all Dublin."

"Then I think the school is at fault. Children shouldn't be wandering loose around Terenure at lunchtime."

"Sure he got nowhere near Terenure, Mrs. Doyle. Only got as far as the corner when he realized he'd forgotten his sandwiches."

"Geoffrey. Geoffrey!"

There was quiet for a moment, then his teacher said, "Why don't you go home and if he's not there you can ring his friends. Then phone me in the staff room—I'll be there for another hour and I'll apprise head-master of the situation."

Geoffrey couldn't hear his mother's reply.

Now that they were hunting for him, he'd have to stay put. With Pinesy on the look-out, he couldn't even go into the Junior yard, never mind up to the bicycle sheds. He'd have to wait at the boiler door for even longer now.

He had eaten the fig rolls and the Mariettas before lunch break. But he still had plenty to keep him going. He would wait until it was dark. Then he'd walk up to the Garda station in Terenure and tell them that he wanted to see his father in the digs. He decided to start on the sultanas.

For a long time nothing happened, then he heard a couple of car doors slamming, then more nothing. After he'd finished the sultanas, it started to rain. He was struggling to open the sardine can and the stupid key wouldn't work properly. At first, the rain was just a drizzle and he ignored it. Then it became heavier and he huddled in the corner of the door on the bottom step. He still couldn't get the tin open, then the tongue snapped off and cut his finger. He sucked the blood and ate the raisins which were pretty juicy. The rain was getting worse. He put the oatmeal biscuits in his pocket and placed the schoolbag on his head. He didn't care if the currants or dates got wet. He didn't really like currants or dates anyway.

A puddle started to form beneath his feet and he saw that the drain in the opposite corner was blocked with leaves and sticks and a Smarties box, discoloured and disintegrating. The wind shifted and the rain attacked him sideways, wetting his knees and running down into his socks. He moved over to the drain and pushed the gunky mess aside with his foot. The water rushed down. He wished he were back in his old house. He'd be in his back garden, floating ice-pop sticks and his two boats down the little gully that separated the path from the grass till they got caught in the fence at the ditch. Then his Ma would call him in and he'd play by the fire with his cars and stick his Belisha beacon pencil that he got in his stocking at Christmas in a lump of plastercine so the cars would have to screech to a halt and crash into the coal scuttle. Then he remembered he didn't even know where his cars were, and that some other boy was probably in his house playing with them. And now he was cold and wet like some orphan in a picture book who had no house anymore. The more he thought about it, the more he wanted to cry so he thought about the toilet in the passage instead and imagined his father living in a cell in the digs that was the same size.

The trouble with that idea was that it only made him worse because his Dad had liked the little house too and now none of them were going to live there again and he'd never see his bedroom or play cowboys in the prairie. Or walk along the garden wall till Mrs. O'Herily next door yelled at him to get down before he broke his neck or her sapling cherry tree or both. Now he was going to cry now for sure. And for a few seconds he thought he really was crying without knowing it. But it was only the rain on his cheeks. He squeezed his eyes shut and tried to think of something different...

It was very sunny and dry and he was sitting against the wall beside his grandmother's pantry with his legs stretched out in front of him all tanned and sticking out of his robe. Except of course it wasn't his grandmother's pantry because it was in Palestine and his name wasn't Geoffrey, it was Yussef or something like that. What it really was, was a cave in a long line of caves, but this cave was his own, it was his shop. The Arabs would walk along with their camels like in the bible and buy stuff from his shop before they went across the desert. And they'd pay him in heavy silver coins with squiggley curlicuey patterns on them. He had lots of these coins because he had lots to sell. He had dates and currants and sultanas; and sardines that would stay fresh no matter how many sandstorms they had to endure. He also had jams and pickled onions and spices with names that were hard to sound out. And ordinary ones like pepper and dried parsley and yellow mustard powder with a big bull on the tin. And tobacco which you put in magic pipes that looked like metal teapots—he sold the pipes too. He had them hanging from hooks on the inside of his door, along with pots and pans. And when a sandstorm was on its way, he would know it because they would all jangle against each other. Yep, he sold lots of different stuff, but he didn't sell fruit anymore because the camels would stretch out their necks and swing their heads towards his table and grab the bananas and swallow them down, skin and stalks. And then the owners would pretend that they'd seen nothing and refuse to pay. So he had to put an end to that carry-on. Then when the sun was too hot he would go inside his cave and close the door behind him and he'd lie down in the cool shadow on a mat made of rushes and look at the sun stream though the curlicue holes that were cut into the wood and he'd fall sound asleep like Kevin beside the new washing machine.

That worked pretty good for a while.

He was starting to shiver now. That was a bad sign. The only thing to do was to walk to Terenure. That would stop the shivering. It wouldn't be dark when he reached the Garda station, but nobody would see him in the rain. The rain was as good as the dark. Better, because grown-ups didn't like the rain.

Pines had gone inside and there wasn't a soul to be seen in the yards. There was no one much on the road either and hardly any cars.

It was a long walk and the road seemed to have changed. It was as if somebody had stretched it out and put in houses and buildings that had never been there before. He thought he had gone the wrong way. But he didn't want to turn back. Not now. Not after all this trouble. Then he recognized the blue house, and the shed on the corner where the old man kept his hens.

Finally he reached the main road with its buses and cars squishing up and down through the rain. He knew where he was and what to do. He didn't even have to cross the road till he reached Terenure and then he'd cross at Flood's Corner. From there, it wasn't far to the Garda station.

***

"And what would be your trouble?" asked the big red-faced man who was sitting behind a tall desk with a huge ledger opened in front of him as if he was going to take roll call like in school.

"I want to see my Dad."

"Name?"

"Mr. Doyle."

The policeman frowned at him, then decided to write it in the ledger. "Address?"

"He's in digs. But I don't know where the jail is."

***

It was Saturday morning and it was raining. He was in the garage playing handball, whacking it against the little space of wall not covered with furniture, narrowly missing the shelves of coffee tins full of fishing hooks, reels, line and tackle. His grandmother was in and out with baskets of laundry, but she didn't tell him to stop or to mind his uncle's fishing gear. She didn't say anything to him. She had barely spoken to him since the day he'd gone to the police.

Anyway he didn't care. On Monday his father was coming out of digs (which the policeman explained was just another word for lodgings) and they would move to a new house. Somebody else was living in their old house—Geoffrey had been right about that. His father was going to pick him up at school and drive him straight to the new house and together they'd wait for the furniture lorry.

The slooshing of the washing machine filling with water, was replaced with the slish-slosh of the back and forth motion of the agitator. Geoffrey liked the sound too, and without hardly noticing it, he began hitting the ball in time to it. His grandmother left.

When she came back, she switched off the machine and turned on the automatic wringer. This was the fun part to watch. Shirts, vests, socks would be fed into the rollers which would squish the first part flat and balloon out the rest, water squirting up in the air as it sucked the remainder of the garment in. Shirts were the best. Halfway through you could see the wrung part sticking straight out as flat as a board, all misshapen and funny looking like when a road-roller ran over the teacher in the *Beano*. And on the other side it would look like a bagpipes hissing water.

But he didn't go over to watch even though he wanted to. Instead he walked straight past her and went down the passage to the toolshed. He climbed onto the wooden stool and positioned himself in front of the vise—when you pushed the bar through you could pretend it was a steering wheel. He revved up his racing car and was off. He was on the second turn and about to overtake the car ahead of him when he heard the roar. It was his grandmother, but he didn't know that at first. He didn't know who it was.

The letters on the wringer badge were H-o-o-v-e-r. He recognized them, but he didn't know what they meant. The rollers were growling. They were trying to swallow his grandmother's hand. It was her left hand. Geoffrey could see her gold ring, but he couldn't see her fingers. The rollers had them in its grip like a dog that wouldn't let go. His grandmother was trying to pull them out of its jaws, but the wringer held on.

"…itch!" She was saying something. Trying to reach something with her right hand. But she was reaching across towards him. She was reaching for something near him. Switch. The switch.

O-n. That was on. O-f-f. That was off. Just like a light. Except it was bigger and it was red. He pushed the switch down to off. The growling noise stopped and the rollers stopped turning. Then the blood seeped out from between them and dribbled down into the water.

He looked at his grandmother. Her face was all twisted and one side of her glasses had fallen off her ear. He was just about to run away and get his mother or Jacintha, but his grandmother was pointing.

Beneath the switch was a lever. U-n-l-o-c-k-e-d. L-o-c-k-e-d. He looked up at her. She was moving her head up and down. She was telling him "yes." Yes, push the lever. But the lever wasn't like the switch. It wouldn't move. It was stuck. He tried it with both hands. It budged suddenly, and with a loud metallic snap the wringer sprang open.

He saw her hand. He saw it for a long time. Then he ran screaming upstairs.

Chapter three

Granny Doyle was a very different kettle of grandmother from Granny White. She was smaller and she always wore her hair chopped short around her ears and she had little black eyes that seemed to twinkle behind her spectacles. Grandad Doyle said that the twinkle meant trouble.

Mostly Geoffrey would see Granny and Grandad Doyle on Sundays after lunch. He and his brother Kevin would scramble into the back of the Austin Somerset and be driven right into town, past the Lord Mayor's house and down to the bright red door with six doorbells and a fanlight beside Fodges & Higgis bookshop.

Getting up to their flat was scary. Very scary. His Dad would pull back the black gates on the lift and they would walk inside. Then with a crash, he would close the gates, but you could put your hand right through them, like being in a cage, only you didn't because it would get chopped off for sure when his Dad pulled the long brass lever and the lift lurched into the air, rising higher and higher. Then the dusty, crumbly bricks and the cobwebs would descend from above and pass under them, then a door, more bricks, a door on the opposite side, more bricks, and so on, never stopping till they jolted to a halt at the highest door. His father would push the lever down, roll back the gate and ring the bell on the door in front of them which Granny Doyle would open just a crack and shout out, 'Friend or foe? Answer now, or down ye go,' and Geoffrey and his brother would shout back, 'Friend. It's us, Granny Doyle.'

But what was even scarier than the lift was the dumb waiter. This was in the corner of the flat near the sink. Granny Doyle would hoist it above their heads so that he and his brother could stare directly down into the black abyss—like when he had had the whooping cough and his father brought him to the gasworks on the quays and held him by his ankles over a tar pit.

Having stared into the void his brother would drop at least three marbles so that they could count as they fell. At eight or sometimes nine you would hear the little ping-ping-ping as each hit the bottom. After that, they would sit up at the long kitchen table with the drawers in it, and swallow scone after scone slobbered in butter and sticky raspberry jam and wash it all down with scalding hot sweet tea.

Sometimes Grandad Doyle would take them into the lift, this time all the way down, past the hallway, down as he told them, 'to the bowels of hell'. Then the clatter-rattle of the gate and they stepped out into a dark tunnel. The next thing you knew you were underneath Dawson Street, looking up at the pavement through glass that was a foot and a half thick, watching the wavering shapes of people walking over your head.

Visiting Granny Doyle's was different from anything else in the world. You could never be sure what might happen to you. Granny Doyle didn't like rules. And as far as Geoffrey could tell she never did things in an ordinary way. One Saturday when his mother was giving a poetry reading in town in her red dress and pearls, she dropped him off at Granny Doyle's. It was early and the bookshop was open. There were lots of people right there, standing beside the door to his Granny's home picking up books at a shilling or one and six, flipping through the pages, reading bits, then putting them back again. His mother had to ask a man to please move aside so she could open the door. Going up in the lift was tricky too, because his mother hadn't driven it before, but in the end they got there and Granny Doyle shouted 'Friend or foe? Answer now or down ye go.'

His mother didn't get out because she was running late. She told Geoffrey to be good and explained to Granny Doyle that he had coloured pencils, paper, fourteen soldiers, two tanks, and a *Topper*, so he wouldn't be getting under her feet.

"You know," Granny Doyle said to his mother as she shut her back into the lift, "if I were to pass you in the street, my dear, I'd never pick you for a poet. Just goes to show you what little imagination I have. I expect my poets to be excessive and outrageous, or intensely restrained and neurotic. But you, my dear, are a perfect lady and quite respectable. It just goes to show you—you should never judge a book by its cover."

They locked his mother back in the cage and away she went down to the centre of the earth.

"Well," said Granny Doyle, "we've a lot to get done this morning and precious little time in which to do it, so you'd better get yourself over to the table and polish off that bit of breakfast I cooked for you."

"What is it we have to do?" Geoffrey asked in mid-sausage.

"First the ducks, then eleven o'clock Mass at St. Valentine's, some pork chops for your grandfather's dinner. Then we'll pop in and have a look at Paddy Mac and see how the world is treating him, then down Nassau Street, around by the College and we'll be back before your mother can iambic her pentameter."

"Who's Paddy Mac?"

"A man with a generous heart, God bless him. Eat your breakfast."

"I can't go to Mass, Gran."

She looked at him strangely and then poured them each out a cup of tea, "why not?"

It was odd when you had to explain grown-up things to grown-ups. "You know why not, Gran."

She leaned over and whispered, "do you mean because you're not a Catholic?"

"Yes Gran."

"Sure neither am I. But we'll keep it a secret and say nothing to nobody."

That was the way of it with Granny Doyle. Once she had the bit between her teeth there was no holding her. That was another thing his grandad said about her. Geoffrey looked to see if there was a twinkle in her eye. He thought there was, but she had her roundy glasses on and he couldn't really tell for sure.

"Where's Grandad?"

"At the races, thanks be to God."

***

He couldn't properly enjoy the ducks or hanging over the bridge, with this Mass thing bothering him. Dekko was a Catholic and he said Mass would scare the living bejasus out of any mortal sinner. He said that priests were wizards and used blood and magic smoke to cast their spells and turn objects into living people. 'You see that bicycle there,' he had said to Geoffrey once, 'a priest could turn that into a walking man with just a few words of mumbo-jumbo. Now that's wizardry for you.'

There was no mumbo-jumbo in Geoffrey's church. Just a lot of thees and thines, potted jam sales and mother's unions, and old Mr. Emmet who was always forgiving trespassers while everyone else was hoping not to be delivered into evil.

Finally they left Stephen's Green, though at the archway his Granny decided to stop to talk to a beggar and chat about the importance of wearing warm underwear on cold concrete. She gave the man sixpence.

It was five past eleven when they reached St. Valentine's on Aungier Street. "Do as I do," said his Granny, dipping her hand in the granite wall basin at the top of the steps and then blessing herself. "Up down, left right," she instructed.

He followed her through the high heavy door which nearly batted him back down the steps. Now he was inside and in the dark. The aisle was a mile long—he could see the priests and the altar boys tiny and faraway in a bright light like actors in a play. The service had started and already people were pushing behind him, anxious to get into the seats.

His Granny knelt on one knee and briefly blessed herself again, then marched up the aisle. He tried to copy her, but someone walked past him and he couldn't see where she'd gone. He stood up. The person who blocked his view had slipped quietly into a seat nearby. So had the people who were behind him. But his Granny was still going on up the aisle. He wanted to call to her, tell her there were empty seats right here close to him, that she didn't need to go to the very front, but it was too late, and not once did she look behind her.

Suddenly one of the priests sang some words and everyone stood up and answered him, but they didn't sing. Then the priest sang more words—Geoffrey didn't understand them, but the people did and they spoke back to him all at the same time. The priest was talking the mumbo-jumbo part right away and although Geoffrey still couldn't make hide nor hair of it, he knew well enough that it was about him. About him and his Granny being Protestants and not being in seats.

His Granny had stopped. She was waiting for him. Then everyone knelt down. This was the worst of all. Now he and his Granny were the only two people standing. Step by step he started to tip-toe up to her. The kneeling people were praying out loud. Then the priest looked at him. Geoffrey prayed he wouldn't yell at him and order him to leave.

His Granny pointed to the row of chairs beside her. Hardly anyone was sitting there. Everyone would be staring at the two Protestants with the bare-faced nerve to sit right up at the front of a church they shouldn't even be in. He hurried into the row and knelt. She knelt next to him. He closed his eyes and wished he was back with the ducks.

Throughout the Mass she whispered to him. Things like, 'That's Latin, the priest is talking in. It's the language of the ancient city of Rome and all of the Roman Empire.' 'See the smoke? That's called incense.' 'This bit is the transubstantiation—the crux of the business.' 'Now the bread and wine have been changed into flesh and blood.'

The two priests came down the steps from the altar and stood at the top of the aisle. Each carried a gold plate heaped with little round pieces of white paper. The same priest as looked at him before was looking directly at Geoffrey again.

"What age are you?" his Granny asked him suddenly.

"Seven, Gran. I'm seven."

"But you're very tall. Are you sorry for your sins?"

He could hear the scratching of the chairs on the stone floor. People were pouring into the aisle and lining up in front of the two priests.

"Are you sorry for your sins?" she repeated.

"Yes Gran."

"Then get into the queue. When we reach the priest, stick out your tongue and he'll place a wafer on it. Then swallow it and bless yourself, just like they're doing."

***

When it was all over and most people had left, she took him all around the church to follow the Stations of the Cross. They stopped at every picture and she made him look closely at all of them, even the ones he didn't want to—the pictures of Jesus being whipped and bleeding, and the soldiers hammering the nails in his hands and feet and making fun of him before hanging him high on the Cross and leaving him to die. "While they sat there getting drunk and playing cards," she said. "Nothing changes."

After the stations, she had him sit in an empty Confession Box for three minutes to think about his sins. And when he came out, they went over to the candles, where they paid money and lit a candle for the girl his granny said she had once had, but who died before she could see her third month. "She would have been your aunt had she lived. And it was not right that she wasn't allowed to live. Poor mite at my breast, and too congested to suck."

They were outside again in the sunshine, dipping their fingers in the holy water and blessing themselves. "You know Mutton," she remarked "being Protestant is fine, but we miss out on a lot of powerful stuff."

He smiled to himself, he liked it when she called him by his nickname.

They walked down Aungier Street. A horse pulling a coal wagon stopped outside a pub. "I think it's time to have a look in at Paddy Mac," she said.

***

Now they were in a pub. His mother did not go into Catholic churches. And she did not go into pubs either. Sometimes she drank sherry in the Shelbourne Hotel. But Paddy Mac's pub wasn't posh like that. It was dark, but friendly dark, with warm shadows like a fireplace—the brightest part was the farthest from the door. That's where the men were sitting in a line. It was called the bar. He could hear their gentle murmur of conversation.

Geoffrey thought they might sit at one of the little round tables, but Granny Doyle made straight for the bar and perched herself on one of the stools. Geoffrey climbed up on a stool beside her.

"Ah Mrs. Doyle, it's yerself at last. I almost despaired of seeing you again. Is that husband of yours not with you?"

"He's at Punchestown, Paddy, getting his tips straight from the horse's rear."

"And who might this be?"

"My grandson, Paddy. Geoffrey Doyle. He's seven."

"Geoffrey," the man pondered the name, as if he'd met him before, but couldn't quite recollect where, "that's a grand name altogether." Then he shook Geoffrey's hand firmly and formally, "you'll be wanting a whiskey and red so."

"He will Paddy," said his Granny before Geoffrey could protest, "but without the whiskey. That will be for me."

And as he sat high up on his barstool, sipping his red lemonade, with his Granny beside him sipping her whiskey, he studied the long lines of fabulously labelled green bottles and tawny bottles glittering on the shelves and photographs of hurling players and little books of raffle tickets tucked in between bottles, he decided he liked this pub place.

And he liked Paddy Mac, despite Paddy telling him that the red lemonade would put hair on his chest, and that having a name like Geoffrey would make a man of him.

"It's not the boy's name I'm concerned about," said his Granny prophetically, "it's the blood lines he's inherited that trouble me."

"How so?" asked Paddy.

His Granny didn't answer at first, and then she smiled sort of to herself. "Well Paddy, you have the fatheaded Doyles who suffer from perpetual illusions of wealth, married to the pigheaded Whites—that's his mother's side—who suffer perpetual delusions of grandeur."

"But you're neither Mrs. Doyle, except by marriage. And I think he has the look of you about him."

"It's good of you to say, Paddy. But what use is that to him? Just look at me. A Lenny. And what have the Lennys ever done but emigrate. Before, during and after the famine. And who got left behind? Me, the runt of the litter—"

"Never the runt Suzy…" Paddy whispered fiercely, "the prize. And if that wasn't recognized, then it was pig ignorance on their part. They took advantage of your kind heart," he added quickly and turned to see to another customer.

His Granny didn't say anything for a while. She took a handkerchief out of her black handbag and blew her nose. Then she asked him if he was enjoying his red lemonade. He said he was, but in the back of his mind he couldn't help wondering whether he was going to grow into a fathead or a pighead. And what was the matter with being named Geoffrey?

Chapter four

Uncle Bradleigh looked exactly like Humphrey Bogart. He had a craggy, serious face, seldom smiled and was often sarcastic. Nearly always he wore a brown fedora with matching suit, and was under constant pressure from his work. He smoked Capstan Plains, sometimes one after another, and often came in to Granny White's kitchen to check if his underpants had dried. With her twisted fingers, she would reach up over the Aga stove, pinch down a pair from the long row of underpants, turn them inside out, push her hand through the front pouch and say that they were still a bit damp and that it was better to be safe than sorry. There was never any mention of bum stains.

"Jesus Christ," snorted Geoffrey's father through his tea at hearing the latest outrage from Oakdale (that was the name of his grandmother's house), "the man must be nearly forty if he's a day and he still has the mother washing his underwear. Is it any wonder he hasn't a wife. Sure what woman in her right mind would put up with that carry-on. Living next door to his Mammy, I ask you!"

"Shush Mattie," said Geoffrey's mother, "you'll upset the children. Sure you know poor mummy's heartbroken these last years since Daddy…since Daddy was sent up to Heaven."

Then she said she was going to lie on her bed to rest, but Geoffrey knew it was really because she was sad.

"Your Grandfather White was a good man, his fertilizer infatuation not withstanding," his father announced when she'd left, "but the rest of them Whites, excepting your mother of course, can go take a running jump."

It was round about this period that Geoffrey became more actively involved with his extended family. He was eight years old, brave and skinny, patient and long-suffering, the last two qualities being invaluable in his dealings with Granny White and Uncle Bradleigh and his wretched four year old brother, Kevin.

Rumour had spread that his Uncle Bradleigh had expressed a spark of interest in a certain woman of Protestant stock and marriageable prospects and the entire family had been put on alert.

"Oh my God," said his father, "the poor woman. What do you think, June, should we warn her off now and give her a chance to die happy, or should we let her discover a dimension of Hell not even Mr. Alighieri could have dreamed of."

"She attends church regularly," continued his mother, "which is more than Bradleigh ever did. Until now that is. She is in the choir. And she helps run the Girl Guide troop. So you see there's great hope. And I expect you all to cooperate. That includes you too Geoffrey. Your grand-mother insists on meeting her before anything gets out of hand. And I think Geoffrey should go along to tip the balance in Bradleigh's favor."

"How do I do that?"

"You don't have to do anything Geoffrey except behave. It's what you represent that counts."

"Well what do I represent?"

"Misrepresent more like," said his father.

"What do I misrepresent then?"

"That your mother's family is halfway normal," his father answered, "and you Mutton, are their only hope."

"Your Uncle is going to take you down to Enniskerry tomorrow as a treat," said his Mother.

"Why?" demanded Kevin, who as usual was refusing to eat his dinner, "he never gives us treats."

"Not both of you Kevin, just Geoffrey. And it's not true that he never gives you treats, it's just that his work keeps him very busy, that's all."

"Why can't I go?"

"Because you talk too much and you'll upset your Uncle Bradleigh."

"He could take Kevin for a treat instead of me," suggested Geoffrey.

"No!" insisted Kevin, "I want to go with you."

"Maybe next time," their mother ruled, "when the lady has got more used to your Uncle."

"And your Granny," added his father.

His mother sighed, "Yes, I'm afraid so."

Geoffrey was catching on. "What sort of a treat? Is Uncle Bradleigh going to be walking down some beach with this lady Girl Guide, and me and Granny White walking behind them making sure they don't go kissey-kiss-kiss, and Granny White saying 'stop throwing skimmers into the sea Geoffrey' and 'don't pick up that massive whale jaw Geoffrey— you don't know where it's been.'"

"Uncle Bradleigh going kissey-kiss-kiss?" Kevin was amazed. "What's a Girlguy?"

***

This trip, the first of more than one, took place the next day right after supper. Geoffrey was duly dispatched on his bicycle to his Granny White's. Jacintha was waiting for him at the front door —this fact alone forebode ill—only Uncle Bradleigh ever used the front door. Geoffrey's mother, his Aunt April, his cousins, friends and visitors, tradesmen and deliverymen with the sole exception of the postman (and that was only because he might have news of Uncle Hugh in Tanganyika), all were trained to use the side door. As did Granny White herself. Geoffrey's father never went in any door. 'And never will—not front door, side door nor down the chimney.' When Geoffrey asked his mother about this, she explained that there were 'differences' between him and her family.

"Wouldn't darken that door if they came out on bended knee and begged me," his father had said another time when they were by themselves. And when Geoffrey asked him why, he had told him, 'time enough to be burdened with that history, and by then you'll have found burdens of your own.' Geoffrey already considered himself to have burdens—his brother Kevin mainly, but Granny White was his first. Uncle Bradleigh was the latest.

"You're late," Jacintha told him, in her curt voice, "your uncle came in to get you and your grandmother over five minutes ago."

He had made a gobstopper and aniseed ball stop on the way. It was his personal opinion that since his uncle had pressganged him into service, then the least he could do was stuff him full of gobstoppers. But Geoffrey doubted if his uncle even knew what a gobstopper was, and even if he did, he certainly wasn't going to fork out and buy some.

His grandmother was wearing her hat and coat. "Put your bicycle in the passage." It was a warm May evening and he was sweating.

Together they walked down the driveway, out onto the pavement and into his Uncle Bradleigh's driveway. There stood Uncle Bradleigh waiting beside his Ford Zodiac, its body sleek and shiny black, like a cat's, and its chromework glinting like a cat's eyes.

"Why does he always look like that?" his uncle was staring at him with an irritated expression.

"Hello Uncle Bradleigh," said Geoffrey very politely to remind him of his manners.

"Comb your hair before you get into your uncle's car," said his grandmother, "and wipe your face—you're perspiring, child."

Quickly he ran the back of his hand across his forehead.

"With your handkerchief," snapped his uncle, "doesn't the boy own a handkerchief?"

His Uncle Bradleigh might look like Humphrey Bogart, but he certainly didn't act like him. Geoffrey was sitting in the back seat on a rug, under edict not to touch the upholstery. His grandmother was in the front. They had driven as far as Dundrum at a steady twenty miles an hour —and it was only through Geoffrey's willpower that they went that fast—while his uncle muttered about the state of the roads and the incompetence of the County Council and the waste of hard-earned taxpayers' money. Now for the second time, they'd pulled over and his uncle was outside again, wiping the windscreen free of dust and a dead fly. It suddenly dawned on Geoffrey that this was a peculiar way to get a lady to fall in love with you. Humphrey Bogart would not bring his mother and nephew along if he was keen on a woman. No, if there was any woman stuff involved, he'd just steer straight through swamps and deserts, with crocodiles and snakes on his windscreen for all he cared. And then the woman would think he was wonderful and mush all over him.

They were off again, racing at twenty-seven miles an hour past a row of slate-roofed cottages in Kiltiernan, and coming up fast to the Scalp. Geoffrey liked the Scalp. One day when they were ten, he and Johnner and Dekko were going to climb it. The giant boulders were terrific. It was as if in biblical times, the boulders had been avalanching down both sides of the valley, when suddenly Moses raised his staff and froze them dead in their tracks. So now they just hung there yards above the road, waiting to be released at any second and come crashing down on black Ford Zodiacs now doing only fifteen miles an hour because the road was twisty.

Twelve for a penny, thirty-six for thruppence. Geoffrey counted out a penny's worth of aniseed balls and lodged them in his cheeks. That would keep him going till they reached the Girl Guides' camp. That was where they were going. A beach would have been okay, there'd be even something to do in a forest, but to Powerscourt for a Girl Guide Camp! He'd been to Powerscourt before for Boy Cubs, and when he became a Boy Scout he'd get to camp in a tent, but it would be nowhere near the Guides' site, and being the sissies they were, the Guides slept in a wooden cabin. He probably wouldn't even be allowed to wander off to the river. He'd be stuck in this wooden cabin for the next hour, maybe more, with a bunch of giggly Girl Guides.

By the time they emerged from the Scalp and began the daredevil descent into the village of Enniskerry, now at the breakneck speed of eleven miles an hour, with twenty thousand cars, tractors, buses and combines on their tail and blowing their horns goodo, Geoffrey spat out five aniseeds into his palm to see if they'd turned white yet. But they'd only half-turned, so he put them back and wiped the colour off his hands with his handkerchief, which he did own and he had brought.

"Senseless…reckless…irresponsible!" grumbled his uncle, peering in the rear view mirror at the impatient parade of vehicles behind him. "And what in God's name is the matter with that boy? Is he bleeding?"

His grandmother swivelled round in her seat and stared at him. "Are you eating sweets in your uncle's car?" she demanded.

Geoffrey nodded, and some wine-coloured spittle dribbled out.

"Wipe your mouth, child. Your chin is covered in dye."

"I don't know why we had to bring him," said his uncle.

"He was your sister's idea," replied his grandmother, "it gives the impression of family. And an interest in children. Though why you're throwing yourself at this woman that you hardly know is beyond me."

"I know Thelma quite well, mother" his uncle asserted, "from church."

They were in the village. His uncle pulled up at small hotel and sent Geoffrey in to wash his face. When he returned, his uncle demanded the remainder of his 'disgusting sweets' and Geoffrey gave him a gobstopper and two aniseed balls.

"Honest, Uncle Bradleigh, they're not disgusting, they're delicious. You should try them. Really."

"Don't be absurd," said his grandmother, and his uncle rolled down the window and threw them into the gutter. Then they prepared for the ascent out of the village and towards Powerscourt. This part really was exciting. Massive revving, then into first gear and stay in first till the engine screaked, then jolt into second gear for an eternity, screeling their way up the hill's steepness, sounding like a pterodactyl stuck in a gorse bush.

And then they were at the summit. The car gasped for breath. Geoffrey even heard his grandmother breathe a sigh of relief. It was an odd thing, but Uncle Bradleigh never seemed to notice that he was the only person in Dublin, not even in Dublin—in the whole world, who drove a car so badly. Of course, the problem as Geoffrey's father had pointed out more than once, was that Uncle Bradleigh considered himself to be the only person in Dublin and the universe who knew how to drive a car properly.

The Zodiac crawled into the camp site, Uncle Bradleigh beep-beep-beeping so that Girl Guides with their handcarts and elaborate craft projects and kit bags and cooking utensils would have time to clear the path for the royal visitors.

Uncle Bradleigh got out of the car and surveyed this new territory.

It was obvious even to Geoffrey that Thelma was taken off guard. "Bradleigh, I never expected to see you here."

"Well you said drop down anytime and…well it being such a beautiful evening, I thought I'd take my mother and nephew out for a spin."

"Your mother?"

"Ah, yes, well my mother felt it was time she met you and we were in the area…"

Geoffrey and his grandmother were still in the car. Thelma, whose name was Miss Fitzpatrick, came over, shook their hands through the open windows, commented on the loveliness of the evening and invited them in for a cup of tea. She was skinny and tall with thick blonde hair chopped off at her ears and she wore the blue Girl Guide uniform with seventeen badges, a whistle and a knife. She wasn't very pretty and her front teeth were sort of rabbity, but she didn't look like the back of a bus either and she didn't goo-goo over Geoffrey. In fact she ditched him pronto.

"The senior girls are building a raft by the river," she told him, "you can go down and watch if you'd like."

"Okay." He walked down the track she had pointed to, kicking the ferns on either side as he went. He wasn't too thrilled with this arrangement, but at least it got him away from his grandmother and uncle.

The girls by the river were much older, they must have been sixteen. 'Who are you?' they demanded. And, 'Is your uncle trying to court Miss Fitzpatrick?' 'What does he look like?' The jungle telephone was certainly working.

"Humphrey Bogart."

"Yeah, but what does he look like when he's not dreaming about himself?"

For girls, they weren't so bad. The bossiest one sort of reminded Geoffrey of his babysitter who was a beatnik. Their raft, however, didn't look too riverworthy. Like other scouting rafts he had seen, it consisted of a variety of empty containers—petrol cans, oil drums, a butter barrel, a milk churn—all strapped to an assortment of branches crisscrossed with each other.

"So do you want to help?" asked the bossiest. "Or are you just going to stand there like a dope?"

They had about ten different kinds of rope and string and every branch must have been the most crooked they could lay their hands on. The raft was supposed to be finished an hour before he'd arrived and was to be launched in front of Miss Fitzpatrick and Mrs. Walpole the other woman in charge. If it stayed afloat for ten minutes with two on board, they'd all be awarded a badge for shipbuilding or somesuch.

Geoffrey had never done this before. Not even down at the Dodder with Johnner or Dekko. It would be coolo if they did. It would be like Tom Sawyer and his pal Huck. Floating down the Dodder and out to sea. The waterfalls, he could think of seven including the huge ones in Ballsbridge, would be a problem. And the gurriers in Ringsend would probably feck stones at them. Still they could at least go the length of Dodder Park. It was worth trying out. August would be a good time to do it because the river would be very low.

After about twenty minutes of frantic tying, untying and retying of branches, the raft was declared ready for launching. He helped them overturn it, drums and cans and churns face down, and tether it to a tree. Two of the girls—the smallest and lightest—went back to the cabin to change into their bathing suits. They returned with Mrs. Walpole who had a clipboard and a stopwatch, Miss Fitzpatrick who had two life-rings, all the other guides, plus Uncle Bradleigh and Granny White. The sun was setting and the midges were biting.

The test started well enough. The raft was dragged to the edge, the passengers positioned themselves in the centre without too much difficulty—one of them got her foot caught in the branches, but the other extracted it. The rest of the team then pushed the raft into the water until they were up to their knees. It lifted and began to float lazily down the river towards midstream. Everyone cheered and ran downstream except Mrs. Walpole who was watching the rope. The raft picked up speed. It was only a few more yards to the end of its tether and it was merely a matter of seconds in reaching it. The rope snapped tight and held.

"Eight minutes remaining," boomed Mrs. Walpole who had a huge voice.

Geoffrey was running after the others when he heard the short, sharp snapping sounds ricochet through the air.

In the tug-of-war between the river's current pulling in the one direction and the tether holding firm in the other, the raft was being ripped in two. Branches flew up in the air. One of the girls was toppled backwards into the water. The milk churn separated and tore away about half of the structure and carried it downstream. The girl, sitting on what remained of the tethered part of the raft, was screaming. Geoffrey watched to see the first girl surface, but she didn't.

Miss Fitzpatrick dashed into the water and waded out with the life-rings around her shoulder. Somebody saw the girl's foot sticking upside down through the branches, the toes pointing upstream.

"Her foot, her foot!" People were yelling.

Then Mrs. Walpole saw it. "Miss Fitzpatrick," she boomed calmly across the stream, "Mary is underneath the raft. Her foot is caught."

Miss Fitzpatrick reached the raft and rammed one of the life-rings over the screaming girl's head and flung the rope back to Mrs. Walpole. Then she reached down, grabbed the protruding foot with one hand, and set to ripping a path out of the branches with the other. When the foot was freed, she began to walk upstream with her back to the current, pulling the foot, then lifting it to bring first Mary's knee and then her torso and lastly her head to the surface so that it appeared she was floating on her back. She gripped the girl round her waist, stood her up and thumped her on the back several times. By now Mrs. Walpole and a team of Guides had hauled the other girl and the wreckage back to the bank. Suddenly Mary was coughing and kicking and punching and flailing all at once. But Miss Fitzpatrick held her tight and wouldn't let her go. She didn't even take the life-ring off her shoulder to put round her. She just held her and kept talking to her but nobody on the bank could hear what she was saying.

After a few minutes, she relaxed her grip and the girl stood by herself in the water. Miss Fitzpatrick was saying something to her and the girl was shaking her head. Miss Fitzpatrick said it again. This time the girl dunked under the water, swam a few strokes upstream, turned, swam back to Miss Fitzpatrick and stood up again. They both waved to say that everything was all right and together they walked ashore.

***

It was dark when they boarded the atomic-powered rocketship and Uncle Bradleigh fired up the engines.

"You'll have to leave him off at your sister's," said his grandmother, "he can walk over and collect his bicycle tomorrow."

The black Zodiac descended into the depths of Enniskerry darkness at a never-ending nightmarish crawl, demon eyes of speeding oncoming cars flashing in and out of its windows. Then painfully it re-emerged from those same depths and ascended on the opposite side of the twice-tortured village in the single continuous screech of the

Banshee. At the Scalp, his uncle mercifully changed into third gear, and finally, at Kiltiernan, fourth.

"She's all wrong, Bradleigh."

"What's all wrong?"

"She is. Of course you realize that yourself by now."

"Who are you talking about?"

"Your Miss Fitzpatrick woman."

"Thelma. You didn't like her? I thought she was admirable. She handled that raft crisis very competently."

"Humph. Mrs. Walpole confided in me that the entire rafting idea had been your Miss Fitzpatrick's. A ridiculous display. Misguided enthusiasm at best, downright irresponsibility at worst. And look at the outcome! Two young children almost drowned. And what's more the woman obviously can't cook, because if she could she'd certainly teach those girls to come up with something other than mud for tea and oatcakes as dry as tinder."

"Oh!" said his uncle quietly. "You didn't like her."

"It's not a question of liking someone, it's a question of suitability. And that woman would be an inappropriate choice for you. And for your career."

"Oh!"

When they finally reached his house, Geoffrey said that it had been an interesting excursion, and a great deal more exciting than he had expected.

"And Uncle Bradleigh…"

"What?"

"I liked Miss Fitzpatrick."

"You did?"

"Yes. She was very nice and she was very brave."

Chapter five

June—that was Geoffrey's mother's name—was the youngest of four, his Uncle Bradleigh being the eldest. Next to Uncle Bradleigh came Uncle Hugh who lived in Tanganyika because he couldn't abide Uncle Bradleigh. Then came Aunt April. She lived in Manchester with Uncle Brendan who was from Tipperary and had been a dentist in the British army during the war, but was now a dentist outside Manchester and spoken of in low tones by Geoffrey's family because he was really an IRA spy and insisted both his daughters be baptized Roman Catholic like he was. The girls' names were Maggie and Kathleen. Maggie was eleven—two years older than Geoffrey—and Kathleen was fourteen. Geoffrey liked them. He liked his Aunt April. She and the girls came to Ireland every summer and stayed in his grandmother's house. He had never met his Uncle Brendan.

But now he was about to.

***

It was almost Easter and Geoffrey was going on an aeroplane, not on the ferry, to Manchester, so that his mother could have the new baby in peace and quiet. At the airport, his father gave him to a lady in a green uniform. She was the air hostess.

"Best of luck to you, Mutton." His father shook his hand inside the terminal. "Behave yourself and there'll be a big surprise for you when you come back."

Then the air hostess lady took him by the hand and led him through several doors, past a long queue of people all holding their overcoats and newspapers and their tickets. Through another door and they were outside.

And so began one of the most exciting and horrifying holidays in Geoffrey's entire life.

The plane was 'dynamo'. To get into it, you had to walk across the concrete where the planes were parked. His was a DC-3 with a green flash down the side and its name was St. Finbarr. You climbed up little metal steps and the air hostess had to duck to get in the door. Inside everything was tilted like you were walking up a hill. The air hostess seated him by a little square window with green curtains where he could see the wing, the engine and the propeller—there was another engine and propeller on the other side as well. She reached behind him, and then like a magician, she stood back with the two ends of a belt in each hand as if they had been hidden up the back of his jumper. Next she gave him two boiled sweets and told him not to open them till they were in the air, but that as soon as they were, he was to suck on them like the divil.

"Why?" asked Geoffrey.

"It's the only way to prevent children's eardrums from turning inside out."

For a long time nothing happened at all. Then a man sat down beside him, glared at him, and opened up a newspaper. Geoffrey copied him and pulled a joke book out of his jacket. He read a pretty good joke about soldiers and a donkey. He looked out the window again. Still nothing was happening. He was getting bored with the joke book and decided to concentrate on what he had to buy in England. First and foremost was bangers. They were against the law in Ireland, but not in Northern Ireland or England. He needed bangers, Chinese jumping jacks and H-bombs. He could sell them in class for twice as much, maybe even more. It'd be 'wildo'. Old Clarkey would flay him alive with the strap, but it would be worth it. He spent a long time imagining Old Clarkey lepping out of his skin and the girls screeching blue murder while the jacks jumped every which way around the classroom. Everyone would know that it was him that did it. And Spiffo. He couldn't leave Spiffo out. And anyway it was partly Spiffo's idea.

He looked out at the propeller and still nothing. He also had to get the English sweets—Spangles, Rollos, Mars bars, Milky Ways, the works. And comics: particularly *Lion* and *Tiger* which you'd only find in the shops once in a blue moon, and *Eagle* hardly ever.

He must have looked at the propeller a hundred times by now. He heard doors banging below him, but he couldn't see anything except a man walking backwards and away from the wing. Then the air hostess came up to the front and spoke to them in Irish, but Geoffrey only heard "a cairde" and "eitilt" because the engine outside took a violent fit of spluttering, immediately followed by loud coughing, belly belches and great puffs of oily black smoke. He saw the propeller lurching, then spinning round and round, faster and faster. Really fast. So fast you could see through it, like it wasn't there at all. The din was pure noise torture—instead of the Japanese putting water hoses up your nostrils, they would have been a lot better off putting propellers in your eardrums. He wondered if he shouldn't be sucking the sweets right away. And then the second engine got going and the whole plane began to shudder.

When both engines seemed ready to burst, the plane jolted forward, swung around in a semi-circle and set off. It was odd but the noise seemed much less now and it was quite cosy bouncing up and down as the plane lumbered along the concrete. He saw a hare running through the grass, and a bunch of black and white cows looked up at them.

Another big semi-circle and the plane stopped. They were at the end of the runway. One at a time the pilot revved the engines to boiling point and when both were screaming to be let go, he released the brake and the plane began to drive down the runway. The man closed his paper and blessed himself. Cows, sheep, houses and a woman hanging out her washing whizzed passed the window. Faster and faster. His seat lifted up and stayed level, but they still weren't in the air. And then they were. The aeroplane leaned over to his side and suddenly he was looking down on the roofs of a bunch of houses, then he saw some tinkers' horses which looked so close he felt like he could jump down and land on their backs.

Gudunk, gudunk.

"That's the wheels coming up," the man yelled across at him.

The air hostess reappeared. "Start sucking your sweets now and keep swallowing," she shouted across to him.

＊

Lots of things about Aunt April's house were wonky. The front door was at the side, there was a bedroom next to the dining room which was going to be his, there was a church organ on the landing, a dentist's office and waiting room in the garage and the living room was upstairs. It was to this upstairs living room that his aunt brought him in order that he might be introduced to his uncle. It was a long, narrow room with a fire burning in the long side and a big, beefy man in an armchair. There was a TV set—Geoffrey only knew of one person in Dublin who had a TV set and you could hardly make out what it was showing. This one was showing films of horse races—and the film wasn't fuzzy at all. His cousins were not yet home from school.

"This is your Uncle Brendan," said his Aunt sweetly, "his bark is worse than his bite."

The big man reached for the TV set and turned it down and then dislodged himself from the armchair. His hair was jet black and Brylcreemed straight back.

"So this is the first fruit from the loins of June and Mattie, is it. And what's your name?"

"Geoffrey," said Geoffrey and put out his hand.

"What class of a name is that?" he demanded as his massive hand crunched Geoffrey's. "Never heard of a true-blooded Irishman called Geoffrey." He glanced at his wife, "Never heard of an Irishwoman with a name like April either. It's a good thing you and your sister weren't born in the winter." He turned back to Geoffrey and let go of his hand.

"You're not one of these Protestant pansies are you? You have the build of a pansy and the handshake of a fish."

"My father calls me 'Mutton'," said Geoffrey.

"'Mutton,' why 'Mutton'?"

"From the 'Mutt and Jeff' comic in the *Evening Mail*."

"Alright Mutton, let's see the cut of your teeth."

"Your Uncle Brendan is a dentist," said his Aunt reassuringly.

***

There was a pond in the back garden with a statue of a naked boy in the centre and he peeing into the water like he was in the middle of a Roman mansion or a museum or something. "What do you have that for?" he asked Maggie.

"I don't know. It's meant to be a famous sculpture or something."

She'd grown taller and her red hair was a lot longer. But she still smiled nice and still had her nice way of looking at him.

"We have other guests staying, did you know that?"

"Who?"

"Wait till dinner and you'll see."

"Where are the shops? I need to buy stuff."

"What sort of stuff?"

He could tell Maggie, because he knew she wouldn't tell Aunt April. "Bangers."

"You mean fireworks, don't you? Sure you can't get them till October. For Guy Fawkes. The Cooper boy might know where you'd get some, but they won't be back from Scotland till Easter Sunday. C'mon and I'll show you the surgery."

"Won't there be patients in there?"

"It's Holy Thursday. He doesn't see patients on holy days. But of course, we still have to go to school."

He followed her inside, past his room which was the one next to the dining room, and down the passage. Maggie took a penny out of her dress pocket and squealed it over the bumpy glass in the door. They went inside. This was the waiting room, but it wasn't like any dentist's he'd been in before. There were huge coloured pictures of rotting gums and decaying teeth all along the walls and a big, red, capital-lettered sign which said 'EITHER YOU BRUSH OR THEY FALL OUT'.

"I wrote that," she told him, "and Kathleen copied the pictures from a medical book. Pretty good, eh?"

"Pretty scary, you mean."

In the surgery she showed him all the picky pointy dentist instruments, and the wadding and the mop in the cupboard for the blood. She pressed the pedal of a large white bin and the top flew open. This she explained was the sterilizing machine so you wouldn't get the germs from the mouth of the patient before you. She ran the water in the spittoon, reached up and steered the drill over to her, turned it on and off, told him to sit in the chair and she'd give him a check-up.

"Not on your life."

"Cowardy custard."

"That's not true. And even if I was a cowardy custard, I'd be a cowardy custard with my teeth safe from the likes of you, Maggie McNamara."

She laughed and took him up to her sister's room where she was also sleeping because the two guests were in her room.

"Where are they now?"

"In there, asleep and probably stinking up the place."

"Why are they asleep at four o'clock?"

"Because they were travelling all night and only got here after breakfast. Do you think Kathleen's a good drawer?" she asked, pointing at all the pictures on the wall. They were all of girls in frocks and ladies in evening dresses, but he said they were 'brillo' anyway.

"You still say things with 'O' on the end. It's neat. She wants to be a fashion designer when she leaves school."

"'Neato,'" said Geoffrey.

"She also wants to be a tennis player. Is Spiffo still your best friend?"

"Yeppo."

***

The guests came to dinner in mud-brown uniforms and fully armed. One had a revolver, the other a rifle which he leaned up against the wall next to the sideboard. The one with the revolver was a sergeant, the rifleman was a private and had the face of a ferret. They were both from Wales.

"Soldiers of the Free Welsh Army," his uncle bellowed, "an honour to have them under our roof."

"Yes dear," said Geoffrey's aunt, "would they like some shepherd's pie?"

Wait till Spiffo heard this one. Armed to the teeth and sleeping in his younger cousin's bedroom. He wondered if they had grenades. They didn't say much and what little they did say he had difficulty understanding. Their voices sounded nice though, soft, but not like a woman's. After dinner they lit up their Navy Cut fags and went with his uncle into the surgery to discuss strategy.

Kathleen came home. She'd been playing tennis at school. She acted really different to Geoffrey—not nearly as friendly as she'd been the previous summer.

"See, her cherries have ripened," Maggie pointed.

"Shut up, you little brat," said Kathleen.

"Can we watch the TV set?" asked Geoffrey.

***

They wouldn't be allowed to watch TV on Good Friday, his aunt said, so they watched it till bedtime. There were an awful lots of ads, mostly for Daz washing powder. And the programme was just a lot of singing and dancing and most of the jokes Geoffrey already knew. Then more Daz ads. Free this and free that with every packet of Daz for bluer whiteness. Maggie started to run up to the set and cover it with the hearth rug every time a Daz ad came on, but her mother told her to stop. At nine o'clock his uncle and the soldiers came up to watch the news on the other 'side' which meant the BBC which had no ads at all. The Navy Cuts came up with them. And the guns. Geoffrey wanted to hold the revolver, but he didn't ask. He'd ask tomorrow. Then Aunt April took him and Maggie downstairs into the kitchen where she heated them cups of milk. In bed he read bits of *William* books and *Billy Bunter* until Maggie crept down the stairs, made ghost sounds through the door and scuttled back up again.

His uncle and the soldiers were out in the city most of the next day and Easter Saturday as well, meeting 'key personnel within the organization' and discussing more strategy. Kathleen spent her time at friends or at the tennis club. Maggie and Geoffrey were left to their own devices. Her friend Marjorie Cooper, who was the older sister of the boy who might know about the fireworks, was away till Sunday so she showed Geoffrey where the shops were, and the park, and then they went to the flicks together and watched *Flubber*. They also played hide and seek and soccer and searched the soldiers' room for grenades and tried to play the organ on the landing.

"Do you want to see something you're not supposed to?"

"What?"

She ran into Kathleen's room, which she was sharing and locked the door behind her. "Don't come in till I call you."

Geoffrey waited. Whatever she was up to was taking a long time. He could hear drawers being opened and shut and her saying 'damn' and 'blast', but when he tried to look, the key was blocking the keyhole. So he just waited. Then he heard the key turn.

"You can come in now, but if you ever tell anyone what you see, I'll…I'll…I'll cut your mickey off. So there!"

"First you want to pull the teeth out of my head," he shouted back, "now you're going to cut my mickey off. You'll die a grisly death hanging by your neck, Maggie McNamara, and nobody will come to your funeral."

"That's because there'll be nobody left. I'll have murdered them all."

He didn't have an answer to that so he didn't say or do anything. He'd never met a girl like Maggie. Certainly not the ones in his class. Maggie would make minced meat out of them. Except maybe Susan O'Brien. She was kind of a holy terror like Maggie. Though Maggie was quieter at it.

"Are you coming in?"

"No."

The door opened a crack and her face popped out. "You had better come in here right now, Geoffrey Mutton Doyle after I've gone to all this trouble."

"What will you cut off if I don't?"

She thought for a moment. "If you refuse to come in, then I'll tell Kathleen that it was you who took out her underwear and flung it on the floor and she'll tell my mother and my mother will tell my father."

This was serious. He gave in.

"Close your eyes, I'll have to lead you in now, and don't even peek until I tell you to."

She took him by the arm and walked him far into the room. She let go of him, whispered 'not yet' and walked ten paces away and then he heard her locking the door again. "Turn around," she instructed, and when he did, she said, "Now. Open your eyes now."

Whatever he'd been expecting, what he now saw standing in the middle of the room was not it. First of all, Kathleen's underwear was not on the floor. It was on Maggie. She had taken off all of her own clothes and was wearing Kathleen's white brassiere which was hanging down her front, and a white garter belt thingamajig loose around her waist and sort of attached to baggy black stockings. And her feet were in Kathleen's black shoes with the tall heels. But worst of all, she had no knickers on, and had put black crayon or paint or something just above her you-know-what.

"Jaysus!" said Geoffrey.

"Wait, wait a min." She made a little fake cough and began strutting in the shoes and sang a song, acting out the words as she sang.

"On top I've cherries, down below I've hairies, I'm a big girl now."

***

Easter Sunday there were no Easter eggs. Only porridge, tea, toast and marmalade. Kathleen, Maggie and his uncle had already been to Mass.

"I suppose you two Prods will be off to pray for the good health of the Queen," remarked his uncle referring to Geoffrey and his aunt.

"Don't we get any eggs?" Geoffrey whispered to Maggie, but his uncle heard him.

"Eggs. On Easter Sunday?" he bellowed, "There'll be no pagan customs celebrated in this house, boy."

Geoffrey was more or less used to the bellowing by now, but he could never be sure whether his uncle was serious or not. This time it was really bad, because his uncle went on and on.

"That's the problem with the world today. Obsessed with sex and fertility. Greed and materialism. Motor cars and lawn mowers. No concept of self-sacrifice. Protestantism in its essence! They'd have you believe the crucifixion was a spiritual symbol. Just a symbol. That the body and blood consecrated during the sacrament are nothing more than an appetizer before lunch. They don't want to have anything to do with the real blood of Christ's martyrdom. Might offend their genteel sensibilities, might be somewhat beyond the Pale. 'Have a nice chocolate egg little boy. It'll take your mind off our Lord's suffering.' Is that real religion? Of course not. It was never anything more than a manoeuvre to permit Henry VIII to add another officially sanctioned notch to his shotgun."

"He's only nine. He can't help that he's a Protestant." Kathleen spat the words at her father.

Geoffrey didn't know what to do or where he should look.

"Can't help it..." repeated her father, "can't help it...the great excuse of the indifferent, the panacea that relieves all qualms of conscience.

Right up there with ' it's not my fault' and 'there's nothing I can do about it'. And what would you know about it? With your Elvis Presley and the lipstick you tart yourself up with and think that I don't know about, prancing about the place very pleased with your new woman shape and your new woman breasts, but you can't help that can you? It's not your fault is it? And I suppose it won't be your fault when you arrive in the door with a baby in your belly. Oh no, you wouldn't have been able to help that either."

Geoffrey scrutinized his toast. He wanted to look at Kathleen. He wanted her to know that he would fight for her. From the corner of his eye he could see she was gripping the fork, her knuckles dead white. He looked across at her. It was as if she'd squeezed all the blood out of her body and forced it up into her face. It was her face that told him she was going to do it, she was going to kill her father, she was going to stab him between the eyes with the fork.

She started to speak, but her red, raw rage suffocated the words and her mouth remained hanging open. Then she did something Geoffrey hadn't foreseen. She dropped the fork and bursting into tears, she ran from the room. The ferret-faced soldier sniggered.

"Crybaby!" his uncle called after her and then muttered with exaggerated frustration as if he were the injured party, "Daughters! What did I do to deserve daughters! No wonder yer man Lear was always whingeing."

"You shouldn't upset her like that," said Geoffrey's aunt. Then she also left the room, but returned a few minutes later with a plate of sausages and rashers. "You'll have to help yourselves," she announced and took off her apron. Geoffrey and I need to get ready for service."

***

Sitting in the dark, half-empty church with his aunt, Geoffrey could hardly control his anger. He was angry at everybody and everything. He wanted to get up out of the pew and smash the colourful stained glass window nearest him and knock all the angels and shepherds into smithereens. How could God give Kathleen and Maggie such a mean father. It wasn't right that He allowed him to talk about Kathleen's cherries and about babies in her belly in front of everyone. But Kathleen shouldn't have started blubbering, she should have stood up to him, or just said nothing. And his Aunt should have told him to shut his dirty mouth and get his arse down to the shops and buy some Easter eggs.

Everything about this Easter Sunday was wrong, everything should have been different. He should have been different. He should have done something. Kathleen's father had only been mean to her that way because she was defending him. And what had he done in return— 'sweet damn all,' as his own father liked to say. 'Sweet damn all.'

At least Jesus had done something. Letting himself be killed like that so people's souls could be saved. He almost couldn't go through with it, but fair play to him, he stuck with it nonetheless and changed the world from that day forth. It probably wasn't the jeering or the beating that had him tempted to call on his angels to rescue him, but the nails. The nails would have been the killer. And the spear in his side. Sure who could blame him if he were to change his mind! But he didn't. He didn't give in even though he could have.

The minister was saying what a happy day it was, a day of rebirth and rejoicing, a day of hope, a confirming of belief. Geoffrey began thinking about when his mother would have the baby. He hoped it would be very soon and then he could go home. He had wrapped his green and cream Dinky bus in tissue paper for its present and had written the word 'baby' on it in blue and pink and had hidden it under his socks. It was a double-decker and even had all its tyres—if his wretched brother hadn't got his hands on it by now.

"We're having goose for dinner," said his aunt on the walk back, "but it will be a while. Maybe you and the girls could play in the garden, it's such a glorious day."

***

A sheet over the clothes' line acted as the net. The rockery and the statue in the pond marked the sideline nearest the house, the vegetable patch was one baseline, a flower border the other and the path the other sideline. Kathleen had wanted to play tennis. Geoffrey wasn't great at tennis, but it was the least he could do. It was him and Maggie against Kathleen. Maggie was okay —better than him—but she giggled all the time especially when she missed. Kathleen was really good, her serves were massive. She had her black hair tied up and wore a baggy cardigan so you couldn't see the outline of her cherries. Geoffrey was picturing them in the brassiere Maggie had dressed up in. Kathleen would kill her dead if she ever found out.

"Love thirty," she called out when he sent the ball into the rockery.

"No you don't," tittered Maggie, "you only love Paul Hanson."

Kathleen ignored her and proceeded to beat the pair of them hollow. They were starting the second game when the soldiers came out with their deckchairs, and their newspapers and their guns, and their Navy Cut fags. They seemed to pay no attention to the tennis, but Geoffrey knew that they were only pretending. He'd bet they were disappointed about the cardigan.

"Fifteen love," announced Kathleen as Geoffrey's second serve walloped into the sheet. The first had beheaded a tulip.

"Who are you kidding?" shouted Maggie. "Not even Paul Hanson loves you."

"Shut up you little creep or I'll come over to your bed in the middle of the night and cut off all your hair."

"She tries to draw pictures of Paul Hanson with no clothes on," Maggie whispered quickly, "I know, 'cause I've seen them. They're on the top shelf of her wardrobe."

The soldiers were watching him now. He'd have to pull the finger out. They were the last two people on earth he'd want seeing him being bettered by two girls. He concentrated on his next serve—he had to at least get it over the sheet and 'in'. He aimed it carefully and hit it hard, but not too hard. It was a good shot. Kathleen barely returned it, and when she did Maggie reached it easily and sent it over her head.

"Fifteen all," she declared and then giggled.

A little more confident this time, he tried to ace Kathleen with his next shot, but he hit it far too hard and too low and it thudded sickeningly into the sheet. He was certain Ferret-face made some sort of a guffawing sound. He'd show them.

Like before, he didn't rush the serve and landed it pretty close to where he'd intended. Kathleen had to step right back to hit it. He expected it to go to Maggie, but instead she knocked it back to his side. It was going to bounce just before the rockery. He'd have to run like mad to get to it.

He could just make it. He stretched out, barely clipping the ball. But it was enough. He was watching Kathleen race to it in vain, when his right foot stumbled on the stone and he knew he was falling, falling like a fool into the rockery. The next thing his head banged against stone and he was drowning. He was underwater. He was upside down and he was underwater.

It wasn't until he surfaced that he realized what had happened. He had fallen into the pond. The soldiers were up out of their deckchairs, buckling at the waist with laughter. Something was pounding at the back of his neck. Like an eejit he turned round. The little stone boy caught him straight in the face.

✳✳✳

When he'd stopped crying over his embarrassment, he started crying because he had cried and run away just like Kathleen had at breakfast. Running and hiding in his room like a blubbering girl. Then his aunt coming in with a towel and being nice to him—that had made him cry even more. When he was finally cried out, he began to plot his revenge. He had no idea what it would be except that it would be sweeter even than that of the Count of Monte Cristo. He was going to do something that was for sure. He was not going to do nothing anymore. His aunt came back in to see if he'd changed out of his wet clothes and to tell him that dinner was ready.

"I'm going to get them," he told Maggie, when she came hurtling down the stairs. "I'm going to get those soldiers."

"Let's put something in their beds. We can get frogs. There's dozens of them 'cause of the pond."

The door to the dining room was locked. Kathleen came down and tried it for herself.

"You'll have to wait," his uncle barked from the other side.

They waited.

"Mutton says he's going to get even with the soldiers," Maggie reported to Kathleen.

"Why? They didn't throw him in the pond. He was showing off."

"You were the one showing off," Maggie asserted, "and we're the ones that's going to put frogs in their pyjamas. And maybe we'll put some up your nightie—so there."

His uncle opened the door. "All right, you can come in. One at a time. Are your hands clean? Teeth scrubbed? And I don't want any whingeing because there's no eggs and that's an end to it. You'll eat the meal that's cooked for you and be thankful."

Geoffrey had never seen anything like it. The table was piled high with eggs of every dimension and description. On his plate was a giant Aero egg with a Sabre jet sellotaped on top. Beside it were half a dozen other eggs including a Smarties—his favourite—and a marshmallow egg in a tipper truck. Kathleen's egg was shaped like a tennis ball and it was stuck to the strings of a brand new Dunlop tennis racquet. There were five more chocolate tennis balls in a box. Maggie got a Smarties egg too, but she also got a ballerina on a music box. The ballerina was holding up a crystal sphere and moved in circles when the music played. Even the soldiers had eggs, Ferret-face's was taped to a Saracen armored car, the Sergeant's to a Churchill tank, but Geoffrey didn't pay any attention to them. His aunt's egg was a whopper though! Black Magic containing a half pound assortment.

"Thank you dear," she said, but that was before he told her to open it and she discovered the gold necklace hanging around it. Then she said, "Oh Brendan! Oh my!"

"Put it on," said Uncle Brendan.

Geoffrey noticed that his aunt was blushing.

"Go on, Mum," urged Maggie.

Carefully she lifted the necklace from the egg and after a little fussing with the clasp, she arranged it round her neck, patted her breastbone lightly, and smiling, she looked up at them. They all clapped.

"Jewellry for my jewel," his uncle whispered, and leaning over, kissed her on the cheek.

It was the only time Geoffrey had anything like a warm feeling for this man.

***

"My toast is a toast to the brave, the unselfish, the patriotic, to the soldiers of vision and the men of action." His uncle had pushed back his chair and was standing with a glass of whiskey in his hand. Geoffrey had a glass of ginger beer, he'd never drunk ginger beer before. It burned his throat even more than ginger ale, but he liked it. The Sergeant had unstrapped his revolver and placed it beside his dessert bowl. He was pouring a bottle of Newcastle Brown Ale sideways into a glass, the way Geoffrey's father poured Guinness. Ferret-face was doing the same thing, tilting his glass the same way, nodding at the same points in his uncle's speech—it was almost as if he were mimicking the Sergeant. Kathleen had wanted to go to a friend's and Geoffrey and Maggie were all set to walk down to the Coopers' house, but his uncle said that they could do that any day of the week and how often was it that the family had such important guests to dinner, that this day, Easter Sunday, represented a resurrection in more ways than one. It represented the resurrection of Christ, a resurrection of the Irish nation, and one day it would represent a resurrection of Welsh national pride, a resurrection of a nation whose identity was long thought to be dead, a resurrection both spiritual and physical.

Geoffrey resigned himself to the fact that there were going to be a lot of resurrections and that he'd have to wait till tomorrow to ask the Cooper boy about getting fireworks.

"It has been both an honour and a pleasure to have these true heroes as guests under our roof, men who sacrificing all, carry the torch of freedom ablaze once more. It is these men, and the men and women like them, whom we now both toast and salute." He raised his glass, set it down and snapped his large body into a military salute. The Sergeant and then Ferret-face stood up, clicked their heels together and returned the salute.

"Very eloquent dear, and quite stirring," said Geoffrey's aunt when the men had sat down. In response his uncle nodded his head and then requested the Sergeant outline the non-classified activities of a Free Welsh Army soldier.

Free Welsh Army soldier with every box of Daz, Geoffrey smirked to himself imagining his mother opening up the washing powder and a miniature Ferret-face climb out complete with rifle.

"It would be no harm," his uncle pointed out, "if our young people had a more in-depth understanding of the daily activities of soldiers such as yourselves. For instance, explain to us why it is necessary you are armed at all times."

The Sergeant consulted his Newcastle Brown Ale then folded his arms. Geoffrey tried to concentrate on his words. As with his uncle's bellowing he was becoming accustomed to their accents.

"It's the fear you see. Fear of capture. Correct me if I mislead, Private, but our capture would be a tragedy to the cause. For who knows, despite all resolve, what may be divulged under interrogation and torture—I am not talking of the old- fashioned torture through mutilation of the body, mind you, for a man can endure any pain. But no man can defend himself against the mental torture which distorts and disfigures the brain cells with drugs and serums and chemicals."

"Brainwashing," said Geoffrey. He and Spiffo were experts.

"Exactly," replied the Sergeant, "there's hope for you yet, boyo." When he said this, he grinned widely. So did Geoffrey's uncle.

Geoffrey scowled, but the Sergeant didn't notice, he was continuing with his speech again.

"And the worst of it is, is that even if nothing is learned despite all their truth potions, can our comrades be sure, can our families feel safe, bearing in mind now that the authorities would have already spread the rumour that names had been named, and plans for their overthrow divulged, though such were not the case? The answer I tell you is 'no'. They cannot. And all who were known to our unit must go into hiding, all plans to which we had been privy must now be cancelled. So you see then, why we must be armed at all times of the day or night, and ready to shoot our way free at a moment's notice." He unfolded his arms and addressed the Ferret. "Private, am I misleading our good friends in any shape or fashion."

"No sir, that is my reading of the situation in which we are placed, exactly."

"Well now," said Geoffrey's uncle, "could you outline some of the army's general strategies and tactics. Give them an insight."

The Sergeant consulted the Newcastle once more, then rolled up his sleeves. "There'd be the bridges and the police station, clandestine activities but not classified, I'd believe I'd be correct in saying that Private Jones."

"That would be my clear understanding, sir."

Geoffrey learned that a propaganda campaign was conducted by daubing the words FREE WELSH ARMY in Welsh on the bridges along a main railway line between two important towns. START COLLECTING YOURS TODAY, Geoffrey imagined to himself and then he pictured mothers all over Wales driving under bridges, seeing these signs, and then hurrying off to grocery shops and buying Daz washing powder by the ton. Once they'd got home, they'd open their Dazzes, and little armies of soldiers would jump out and run amuck in their kitchens. It was such an hilarious image that he began to burst out laughing, but he knew the story was being told seriously, so he converted his chuckle into a cough like he always did at school with Old Clarkey.

The Sergeant explained that the bridge daubing was performed at nighttime under cover of darkness. On one such night, an hour after the go-ahead had been received from headquarters, the weather turned foul, rain poured from the skies, the cold was wicked. But they pressed on regardless and approached a key bridge which spanned a certain valley. Ladders were set up, the whitewash prepared and the work began. They were barely halfway done when Fate dealt them a cruel blow and tragedy struck. A gale force wind rushed down the valley whipping the ladder from beneath the feet of one of the men who fell onto the road below and sustained a broken ankle in addition to a concussion from the paint pot.

That clinched it for Geoffrey. If the armies from Daz could be subdued, the whitewashers from Wales could not. He laughed, coughed, laughed, gulped his ginger beer, burned his throat, choked and coughed. Maggie thumped him on the back. He recovered his composure, but was aware that the men were all staring at him. He fiddled with his Sabre jet while the Sergeant resumed.

The next story was not as good. It involved a police station. In a different valley, mind you. The raid had been coordinated for some time. It was late at night when they got the word. The diversionary car left first. It sped up to the station, guns firing into the air. When the constable came out to ascertain the cause of the commotion, a second car from the opposite direction approached and from it an object was tossed through the window of the station. Glass flew in all directions. The constable dived for the ditch. More shots were fired from the first car, then both vehicles accelerated from the scene. The constable remained in the ditch. When nothing happened, he emerged and thinking the danger had passed, he re-entered the station.

"And do you know what he found by the broken window?" the Sergeant asked. "Do you know what he found?"

"A time bomb!" guessed Geoffrey's uncle, thrilled at the ingenuity of it all. "And he had thirty seconds to get the hell out of the place."

"No sir," replied the Sergeant with a grin, "not a time bomb."

"Well what then?" asked his uncle. "Don't keep us in suspense Sergeant. What was it?"

A box of Daz. Geoffrey didn't say it, but just thinking it started him off again.

"A brick!"

"A brick?"

"And do you know what was painted on the brick?"

"What?"

Buy Daz and get your free army today—Geoffrey believed all his organs would seize up, the pressure of the imprisoned laughter was so intense. He attempted to sip his ginger beer.

"'Next time 'twill not be a brick, 'twill be a bomb!' It was a warning you see."

Geoffrey exploded. Ginger beer erupted through his nose and fountained onto the wing of his jet. He snortled, gurgled, choked and spluttered. He could hear his aunt telling him to excuse himself and go to the bathroom. He started to get up, but his uncle interrupted, dictating that the boy would stay where he was.

He wiped his face with the napkin and all his laughter stopped.

Ferret-face spoke first, not to Geoffrey, but to the Sergeant. "I believe our tennis star and deep sea diver here finds our activities to be a source of entertainment."

Geoffrey didn't say anything.

"So what precisely is it that amuses you?" his uncle demanded.

"It's all right dear," his aunt intervened, "the ginger beer went down the wrong way, didn't it Geoffrey?"

"No it isn't all right. Tell us what you found so funny, Mr. Smart aleck."

"Nothing," answered Geoffrey.

"That's a lie!"

"The stories just reminded me of a joke." The minute he said it, he knew he'd dug himself into a hole so deep he'd never get out. He wished he'd just kept his gob shut. He knew what his uncle was going to ask him to do next. And he was right.

"What class of a joke?"

Then it shot into his brain like lightning. The joke he'd read on the plane. "It's about army soldiers and a boy with a donkey."

"Then you will at least have the common courtesy to share this joke with us."

There was an uneasy silence. His uncle broke it by smashing his fist down on the table. "Tell the joke."

Geoffrey cleared his throat. "There were these two soldiers…"

"And what type of soldiers would they be now?" asked Ferret-face.

"Free Welsh Army soldiers," said Geoffrey knowing he had said it deliberately, "yes they were Free Welsh Army soldiers. And one day they were…they were smoking cigarettes by the roadside when they saw a young boy coming up the road pulling a donkey by a rope…"

He paused, but nobody said anything. It was as if he were telling the most important joke in the world."

"Go on!" his uncle ordered.

"So one soldier says to the other, 'Let's have some sport with this yahoo and his ass.' 'Okay!' says the other."

He could hear his own voice as if it coming from a wireless or a TV set in a different room. Now the voice had stopped. He couldn't give up. He'd have to see it through. The voice started talking again.

"So when the boy reached the soldiers, the first soldier called out to him and said, 'Hey young fella, why are you pulling your brother around by a rope?' The boy looked at the soldiers and then looked at his donkey and then looked back at the soldiers again. 'Why am I pulling him around by a rope? Because I have to, that's why.' 'And why's that?' asks the second soldier.

He paused again, but he knew there was no stopping him now.

"'Because if I don't,' said the boy, 'he'd probably run off and join the Free Welsh Army.'"

Nothing happened. Nobody yelled at him or banged the table or called him names. He looked at his uncle straight in the face. He could see his jowls red and quivering like raspberry jelly.

"You are no longer welcome at my table," said his uncle, "you will leave it now."

***

Maggie and he wandered down to the Coopers. They were a big family with two dogs and a cat. Everybody shook his hand. Maggie and her friend Marjorie went off some place together. He talked to Ken Cooper who was twelve and went to some public school called St. Albans, which really meant it was private. At any rate he was mighty pleased with himself and with St. Albans which had the best soccer team, the best rugby team, the best cricket team and so on.

"Where can I buy bangers?" he asked him.

"Do you mean sausages or fireworks?"

"Fireworks. What would I want to buy sausages for?"

"I don't know. I thought you had a big famine in Ireland."

"That wasn't even in this century. Maggie says you can't buy them till before Guy Fawkes."

"Maggie's right for once. Do you keep a pig in your kitchen? "

"No, but I'd love to see yours. Would you show it to me?"

Ken stared at him very strangely.

Geoffrey was really scoring some beauts today. Too many for his own good. He decided to shut up and let Ken talk about St. Albans.

They went up to Ken's room where Ken had a huge train set. And it wasn't banjaxed like Geoffrey's with missing bogeys and buckled train tracks. Ken's was like brand new, all laid out with Plaster of Paris mountains and lakes, and little sidings and four stations with porters and newsstands and the express whizzing out of the tunnel every thirty seconds, just as the local was pulling into the second station and the goods train shunting down a siding. Of course nothing ever crashed and you couldn't really rig it up for a crash since everything was nailed down to stay in one place. But Ken was happy enough with it anyhow and Geoffrey didn't pass any comment. He even resisted the temptation to change one of the points when Ken wasn't looking.

They played some Three-and-In soccer with the girls when they came back and with Mr. Cooper who wore brown corduroy shorts and looked like a scoutmaster. He was nice though. Then they had tea and sandwiches.

Geoffrey realized with a horror that they'd have to go back to his aunt's house very soon. He really didn't want to go back. He asked Ken to show him his train set one more time. Maggie told him not to be too long. Geoffrey lingered over each locomotive, praised the attention to detail when the goods train unloaded, anticipated the repeated arrivals of the express, and browsed through a neat stack of backdated *Eagles*.

"Can't get *Eagles* in Ireland," he hinted.

"Do you have Inter-Galactic Rockets in Ireland?"

Geoffrey wasn't sure if he was poking fun at him or not, but he was determined not to be a smart aleck and said that they didn't.

"You can buy them here anytime. It doesn't have to be for Guy Fawkes. And they make a pretty good explosion. Not as good as Earthquakes, but pretty good. And they last till you lose them. Make sure you get Fat Caps for them. Fat Caps are best. And if you eat the hundreds and thousands in the tail, then replace them with sand or clay, they'll still fly right."

"C'mon Mutton," Maggie called up, "we've got to go."

"Why does she call you Mutton?"

"You know—'Mutt 'n' Jeff'…Geoffrey…in the newspapers."

"Do you like it?"

"Yeah. My Dad invented it."

"Okay then Mutton, it was nice meeting you," and he shook Geoffrey's hand.

He wasn't so bad thought Geoffrey as they walked back, bit drippy, but he'd met worse.

"I don't think we should do the frogs," said Maggie.

"No," Geoffrey agreed.

Just before they reached the house she said quietly, "Perfecto."

"What's 'perfecto'?"

"That joke you told at dinner."

"Yeah, it was perfecto all right."

★★★

His aunt was sitting in the armchair in the living room upstairs, listening to the wireless with her eyes closed. There was no sign of his uncle. Or the soldiers. Maybe they had gone out. Maybe they had more strategy to discuss somewhere else and wouldn't be back till after he was in bed and fast asleep. By tomorrow the whole thing would be forgotten. Maybe. Geoffrey wondered if he'd have to eat breakfast by himself in his room. Perhaps he should just apologize to his uncle and get it over with.

"Where's Dad?" asked Maggie.

"He's at the station."

She didn't open her eyes. Was his aunt angry with him too?

"What station?"

"The railway station, Maggie. He's taken the men to catch their train. Is Geoffrey with you?"

"I'm right here Aunt April."

She opened her eyes and peered up at him. "I was dozing," she explained. "Your Dad phoned when you were out, Geoffrey. Your mother's in the hospital—we should have some news anytime now. So stay close to the house and don't go wandering off."

He was about to say that was great or something like that, but Maggie was more interested in the soldiers. "That means I can have my own room back. I hope they didn't stink it up with their smelly socks and their smelly fags."

Geoffrey had imagined a more furtive form of travel than the train. He had pictured them in the boots of cars or in the back of a lorry under a tarpaulin or something like that. "They just get on the train with their guns and everything?"

"No dear, they travel incognito, in their suits."

"But what about the rifle?" How could you travel with that he asked himself. You could hardly disguise it as a fishing rod or a flagpole. And it wouldn't fit in a suitcase.

"I'm sure it can be dismantled dear."

"Oh." He was thick not to have thought of that.

Uncle Brendan didn't return until after supper. Geoffrey was brushing his teeth in the downstairs bathroom when he heard the key in the door. He had told his aunt that he was tired and she had said that he had done a lot in one day and should try and get a good night's sleep in case there was any news by the morning.

When he'd finished in the bathroom he walked up to the living room to say goodnight. They were all watching the TV set. He could see his uncle's big face white in the glow. He kissed his aunt goodnight and then stood in front of his uncle. "I'm sorry I was rude to your soldier friends when I told that joke."

"So am I," replied his uncle, "but it's a bit late now isn't it. 'Err in haste, repent at your leisure.'"

"Yes uncle," but he didn't know what he was saying 'yes' to.

***

He didn't know. What time was it? All he could see was that it was dark and not even the hall light was on. He could tell because his door was open, but he didn't know who had opened it. He wasn't even sure why he was awake, he didn't need to go to the bathroom. He could make out the moon through his curtains. It wasn't a very bright moon. He decided to roll over to face the wall and go back to sleep, and just as he was rolling over, he realized he had seen a figure standing by the wardrobe. His heart turned to stone and dropped down into his stomach. There was noise now. The figure must be coming over towards his bed. Geoffrey wanted to turn round and look, but his mind didn't have the courage to instruct his body to do it. His mind wouldn't do anything. It had stopped, just like his heart. It wouldn't let him yell for help, it wouldn't let him jump out of bed and run for the door, it just did nothing. He was going to be murdered in his bed, and his mind understood that he was going to be murdered in his bed, and still it refused to function. All that remained was part of the dim shape of the wallpaper pattern in front of his nose.

"Get out of the bed and keep your mouth closed if you want to live through this night."

It was his uncle's voice. Why was his uncle in his bedroom?

"Get out of the bed, now."

Without him telling it to do anything, Geoffrey's body slowly sat itself up and his head turned round. His uncle was fully dressed and he was pointing something at him. Then Geoffrey saw that it was a revolver, one like the Sergeant's.

"It's time," said his uncle. "Your hour has come." He wasn't speaking loud, or angry or even pretend angry, he was speaking matter of fact. "Go out into the hall."

There was no noise in the hall, no sign of his aunt or his cousins. Then he knew that he was the last of them. The only one who was still alive.

"Walk down to my surgery."

That's where the soldiers were. In the surgery. They hadn't gone back to Wales. Maybe they were only going to kidnap him. Maybe that was all it was.

The door was straight ahead at the end of the passage. He could see the frosted glass pane and the black outline on the gold letters that read 'Surgery'. They were in there and they would chloroform him so that he wouldn't start crying and take him to a certain valley, till his father sent them money to buy more guns.

"Open it."

He wasn't going to mess around. Being kidnapped was one thing, being shot dead for not opening doors was a lot worse. Geoffrey opened the door. He entered the waiting room, but nobody was there. He heard his uncle gently close the door behind them and turn the key in the lock. "Go on through."

Now they were in the surgery itself. The moon was shining in this window. The circular porcelain tray seemed to hover above the silhouette of the dentist's chair, its neat formation of dental instruments glinting at him. There were no soldiers.

"Make one sound and it will be the last you'll make. Now get onto the chair."

Hardly without him noticing, his wrists were strapped to the armrests. The drill was hanging over him like a crane. His mind was working better now, it was urging him to keep quiet for this part, not to scream if the drill was turned on to drill a hole in his head, because that wasn't what was going to happen. It was going to be chloroform or gas, it wasn't going to be the drill. When they gassed him and taken him to a certain valley, his mind would help him to escape then, but not now, not until this part was over.

For a little while, Geoffrey was left untouched. His mind had been right. His uncle hadn't gone near the drill or the tray with the tools. He was in the corner behind him, fiddling with something. Then Geoffrey heard a single hiss of air or gas. Then it stopped. Then two more short hisses and then a steady deeper flow. Suddenly his uncle was leaning over him, holding a long hose with a mask attached to it like jet pilots wore.

"Now you will know what it's like for a soldier to sacrifice everything in the fight to free his country."

He could smell the gas, and his eyes followed the mask coming over his mouth and nose. His mind had been completely right. He wondered if it would be a nice green valley and if the women would be hanging out their white washing, the sheets and shirts billowing in the wind.

***

When he woke up, the moon was gone, the sky was brighter and a few birds had started their singing. But though at first he thought he was, he wasn't in the valley, he was still in the dentist's chair and his uncle wasn't there and his wrists weren't strapped down anymore. They must have changed their mind about taking him hostage. He clambered out of the chair and walked cautiously into the waiting room. The door wasn't locked. Then he walked to his room and climbed back into bed. In moments he was dead asleep. When he woke again, it was because Maggie was pulling his toes and telling him to get up for his breakfast.

Everything seemed as normal, nobody questioned that he was with them in the dining room, eating at the table. A family picnic in the country was being planned on account of it being Easter Monday, and his uncle was quite cheerfully lopping the heads of the boiled eggs in his twin egg cup.

"Morning Mutton," he bellowed, "you slept well I trust?"

Geoffrey wasn't too sure what to say, so he said that he did.

"No one coming to take you away in the night?"

"Sure who'd want me, Uncle Brendan?" This was exactly the right thing to have said, and his uncle laughed heartily.

"Ah, you're not the worst Mutton, not the worst. Nothing wrong with you that a good night's sleep couldn't set to rights. April," he bellowed over his shoulder into the kitchen, "is there a bite of breakfast for this man. He needs to put a bit of weight on him."

His aunt brought him fried bread, rashers and an egg. His uncle considered it to be a good start, but warned her to have a couple of sausages at the ready in case more was needed. "Any sign of that sister of yours doing the business at all?"

"I'll phone Mattie before we go out."

"Good woman yourself. Tell him to give her a bit of encouragement, otherwise she'll forget what she's in there for and think she's on her holidays."

As it turned out, his Dad phoned before he finished the rashers. Geoffrey now had a second brother and his name was to be Michael. "Bald as a coot, he is," his Dad said.

***

Six days later, the Sunday before school started, Geoffrey was sitting by a little square window in the aeroplane again, armed with his boiled sweets and a new joke book. All in all, he had done well. He had twenty-eight Atomic Rockets in his suitcase, plus a half ton of Spangles, Rollos, Mars and Milky Ways. Ken Cooper had even sent his sister down with an old *Eagle* annual, which was pretty decent of him.

The plane roared and whined, then whizzed along the runaway and the next minute they were up in the air and gawping down at the ships in the Manchester canal.

"Perfecto!" said Geoffrey aloud and popped the boiled sweets in his gob.

Chapter six

For the second time in his life, terror raced through him, incapacitating him to the point that he had no longer control over his body or his brain. His will had no power, he was becoming paralyzed and he had no means to prevent it. It was if someone had pulled the plug and all his systems were closing down. Fear screamed silently in his brain.

This was like that night in Manchester with Uncle Brendan, except now he was much older—almost thirteen—and he had been given weeks of warning in advance. An hour previously the butterflies had begun emerging from their chrysalises, stretched their wings and then beat them, slowly at first, then frantically, till they created a frenzy within his stomach rendering him helpless, a physical and mental cripple. He couldn't talk to his friends or to the others or even look at Duffy—it was as if his stomach had drawn all the energy from the rest of his body to fuel the butterfly frenzy.

Mr. Furlong came into the room and beckoned to him and Duffy to follow him. Suddenly all the flapping abated. Only now it was replaced by an overwhelming heaviness that pervaded and permeated his insides like a enlarging rubber cloud. His eyes could only see his bony knees pumping up and down as they trailed Mr. Furlong and Duffy into the noisy, crowded hall, too dark to see where his father and grandfather were sitting.

Obeying Mr. Furlong's instructions, his legs climbed up and stood in the corner. Mysler was there. Then he heard his name over the loudspeaker and Mysler gave him a shove. Unbidden, the legs walked him into the centre and stood him beneath the blinding lights. A man he'd never seen before, a man in a white shirt with a black bow tie was talking to him, but Geoffrey couldn't make sense of his words. It wasn't until Duffy hit him in the face, that the machinery in his brain unseized, and his body came back under his control.

The bell rang for Round Two. Geoffrey knew he had lost the first—Mysler made that plain and told him if he didn't get on the offensive, he'd never make it to Round Three. "Use your left, Doyle or you're dead."

Duffy was his own man and had his own style. Smaller, but heavier, he came at his opponents like a whirlwind. He was afraid of nothing and no one, least of all the long lean rasher of a kid like Geoffrey. But Geoffrey had two advantages. One he could dodge and weave like a willow in any whirlwind, and two, he had a very long reach. By dodging and feinting, he had survived Round One, now he had to use his left to break through Duffy's barrage, move in and follow it with a right. And his brain had to convince his body to do this.

Right from the bell, Duffy was on him again. The first left grazed against his cheek, the follow-up right, Geoffrey managed to deflect, but in doing so left himself open to a second left as Duffy backed him onto the ropes. It was that second left cracking him across the mouth that did the trick. In a millisecond, it triggered all Geoffrey's brain cells, and a new picture flashed into his head. Now he saw the third left coming and at the same time realized that a right would be fast on its heels. He ducked the left and came back up with his own left before Duffy's right was even launched. Geoffrey's left was only a jab and it caught Duffy not cleanly, but glancingly on the chin and cheek. It was enough though. Duffy recoiled and already Geoffrey was stepping in with the combination right. It connected solidly with Duffy's nose, and the force of it knocked him back.

Geoffrey could see everything. The motes had been lifted from his eyes, the rubber cloud had burst. He could see Duffy's right hand drop, and his brain told him that this was the opportunity, and to go, go, go. Left, move in, right, move in, left, move in—Duffy was stumbling backwards. Go. Go! Another left, right, advance, left—three of his salvo hit home, the third on the nose again. Blood was seeping down from it.

Duffy countered wildly. Geoffrey sidestepped to the right and connected with a ferocious left, not a hook or a jab, but a simple straight left—lean, long and lethal. He had him now. Keep going. Go!

But Duffy wasn't there. The referee was. His arm braced across Geoffrey's chest, blocking him, his face shouting into Geoffrey's, "Neutral corner, neutral."

He had done something wrong. He must have fouled Duffy. He felt the referee's spit land on his forehead and then the referee was gone.

He turned to his own corner and saw Mysler pointing him to the third corner. He was yelling at him. But what had he done? Geoffrey walked to the corner he was pointing at.

The referee was talking to Duffy. Then he pointed to the three judges seated on the different sides of the ring and began counting really loud, counting each numeral with his hand. It was a standing count. The referee was giving Duffy a standing count of eight. The blood was streaming down Duffy's mouth and onto his singlet. Geoffrey also saw that Duffy was crying. The referee held his hands up and crossed and re-crossed them at the wrist. It was over.

That he had won was fantastic. That he had won by a technical knockout was sensational. For the next few days, boys in the third and even the fourth year would thump him on the back as they passed him on the stairs or in the yard and say that he did a hell of a job. On the way home that night, his grandfather had given him half crown and his father had bought him two large singles of chips with extra vinegar and a large bottle of 7-Up at the chipper. His mother hadn't come to see him because she simply could not condone outright and premeditated violence.

***

Secondary school was still strange, still daunting, and by June he was eagerly awaiting the summer. Maggie and Kathleen and Aunt April were all coming over the first week in July. Uncle Bradleigh had bought two holiday cottages in Ardaroe in Wexford and they were all going to stay in one of them for two weeks, Geoffrey, Kevin and their mother included. Little Michael was going to a special home in the country for children who were the same as him. But before Ardaroe, there was another month at school, plus the exams.

One of about ten Protestant all-boys schools in Dublin, Geoffrey's secondary school had the reputation for having the looniest staff. It wasn't until years later when he read the novel *Decline and Fall* by Evelyn Waugh, that he was aware of a teaching staff that came even close to approximating his. Although occasionally prone to sudden losses of temper, it was not a violent staff like Dekko had with the Christian Brothers. The staff at Geoffrey's school didn't come armed with straps and tawses, nor with canes like Old Clarkey. Instead they were equipped with an overabundance of eccentricity, quirkiness and unbelievable idiosyncrasies.

Eyeball for example.

Eyeball taught Irish and had written books in Gaelic, and been a consultant on translating the New Testament of the Bible into Gaelic. He also put the fear of God and Gaelic into every boy from First to Sixth year, and of course of the three teachers of Irish in the school, Geoffrey's class—the 'B' class—had to get Eyeball.

"You realize sonny, that you're nothing but an umadawn, that's idiot in Gaelic, you umadawn." Eyeball always spoke in a low, guttural growl which curled the toes in your shoes and pushed the porridge in your stomach back up to your throat. He reminded Geoffrey of his Uncle Brendan in Manchester.

The class was declining prepositions, and Eyeball was critical of Dilton's pronunciation. Dilton sat beside Doyle because in first year you sat in alphabetical order. Now Dilton was up at the blackboard having his head banged against it.

"The word sonny, is 'agam' meaning 'at me', and not 'a-gum' meaning the pink fleshy mass which holds the teeth in your head.

"Agam," spluttered Dilton.

"Continue boy."

"A-gut…a-get…eggy…"

"Agat! Agat! Dear God above! Agat! At you," bellowed Eyeball. He had Dilton by the scruff of the neck. "'A-gut' is what you should have inside you, you gutless gobshite! And eggy is what your Mummy made you for brekki." He released his grip. "In the name of God, si sios."

He scrutinized the roll book as Dilton returned to his seat beside Geoffrey.

"Doyle."

Geoffrey braced himself and made the journey up to the blackboard.

"'Orm', Doyle. Ta tuirseac mor orm. There is great tiredness on me. 'Orm' and not 'orum' as your neighbour Mr. Dilton would have us believe."

"Orm…ort…air, aici, orainn, oraib, ortu." He'd done it.

"Mait an fear. The boxing must be more of a benefit to the brain than previously supposed. Si sios."

"Please sir," said Geoffrey, "my uncle says that were it not for the Treaty, the entire country would be speaking Irish all the time, and English would be as foreign to us as Swahili. Is that really true sir?"

There was a skill to sidetracking Eyeball. What was required were nerve, detail, and a quality question. Fall down on either of the last two and he smelled a rat. Fall down on the first and you sounded like a blithering eejit.

Attitude was also vital. Too ingratiating and he despised you, too cocky and he'd kick you out.

Of the three ingredients though, the nature of the question was the key. Hook him with an irresistible one, and you earned the admiration of the whole class and spent the rest of the period listening to Eyeball's infamous stories. Because like the tributaries of a river, every good question ended up at the same place. And that place was the Civil War.

Eyeball was anti-Treaty and considered Michael Collins, if not a traitor, then a misguided hero who lacked the fortitude to hold out for the whole shebang and permitted opportunity and a united Ireland to slip through his fingers.

"Your uncle, Doyle, is not a man lacking in insight. Take deValera for example. After the Rising of 1916..."

He was nicknamed 'Eyeball' because his left one was made of glass. And no boy in Class 1B would ever forget it. It happened in the third week of first term during poetry by the patriot Padraic Pearse. Masterson had made some smart aleck comment derogatory of the poet's handiwork. Eyeball went for the jugular. He accused Masterson of being arrogant and superior and ordered him to stand up.

"And what might you have done to feel so superior about?" Eyeball had growled. "Is this conceit born of a lifetime of endurance and achievement, literary or otherwise? Or is it merely the product of overcoddling by parents labouring under the yoke of suburban expectations? Do you know what I think, sonny boy?" His growl descended an octave and he took his handkerchief out from under his black gown. "I think you know nothing of the world, and probably never will." He paused and placed his index finger to his left eye and neatly popped it out so that it dropped onto the handkerchief. "I think you know nothing of suffering or sacrifice." He spat on the glass orb. "I think your opinion of a man who was both a poet and a patriot lacks critical validity." He was polishing it now, polishing his eyeball with his spittle and handkerchief. "I think that Daddy having a nice government job and Mummy being on the Ladies' Committee for God-Knows-What does not warrant your current high opinion of yourself." Now he held it up to the light, studying it with his good eye. Geoffrey was vaguely aware of a dull thud behind him. But Eyeball paid no heed. "I think Masterson, that you need to be a little more exposed to the world and all that therein is, and to have achieved substantially more than the acquisition of suitably middle class parentage before you can afford to affect a swagger. And in the meantime, I believe you would be better served taking your nose-in-the-air, better-than-thou attitude and parking it outside of my classroom." Satisfied with the shine, he thumbed up his left eyelid and popped the glass ball back in the socket. "Do you get my drift, Masterson?"

But Masterson was no longer with them. He was slumped over his desk, out cold.

That was Eyeball for you.

Then there was Itch. Itch's room was on the fourth floor of the main house. He taught them Irish and European History. He was a younger man, very tall and lanky with a mop of flaming red hair and a temper to match. But dramatic though his temper was, it was his rigamarole of physical habits that fascinated 1B. The man was perpetual motion in action. He paced the room almost constantly, and when he was talking he was also picking, touching, rubbing and scratching. All these tics and gestures could be relied on to occur, but not always in the same cycle or with the same frequency. To keep count of them, various class tallymen were self-appointed. Connaughton did the nose tweaks; Dilton—the hand through the hair; Geoffrey—the armpit rubs; Goldstone—the ear lobe tugs; Major—the trouser crotch readjustment; Leahy—the arse yank; Sullivan—the stork stance.

"The battle of Agincourt,"—two nose tweaks—"was more than a surprise victory for the English longbowmen,"—one hefty arse yank—"the result of climate interacting with French military-issue clothing and armour."—one ear lobe tug, one armpit rub—"it represented a watershed in the histories of both nations. In what ways did it represent a watershed?"—one hand through the hair, a second armpit rub. "Take the English first, um…um…"

Geoffrey duly picked up his pencil and noted the second armpit rub on the upper right-hand corner of his jotter.

One long and hefty wooden pointer crashing down on Geoffrey's desk and smithereening the tip of his pencil. "Doyle!!! What are you writing, boy?"

Then there was Eoinstein who taught science. His classroom was in the inner yard, next door to Eyeball's. He was elderly, but not as old as Eyeball who was the oldest of them all. His silver hair stood out like Einstein's, only straighter, and his Christian name was Eoin, hence Eoinstein. In addition to his hair, which by common lore, was attributed to his experiments with electricity, Eoinstein was the quintessential eccentric, the archetypal absent-minded professor. His notoriety had spread the length and breath of Dublin's Protestant secondary schools. On learning where Geoffrey went to school, people would inevitably ask if he had Eoinstein and were the things they heard about him really true. What made it even better, was that most of them were. Some days Eoinstein really would be wearing unmatched shoes. The morning he had two ties on, one on top of the other, he almost caused a riot in assembly as the word spread through the ranks. But it was his behaviour, rather than his being oblivious as to how he dressed, which truly placed Eoinstein among the Immortals in the ranks of memorable mentors.

By nature, Eoinstein seemed to be mild-mannered, ineffective at keeping discipline, and to many of 1B, a pushover. And you could get away with a lot. Just as you could sidetrack Eyeball onto the Civil War, you could easily distract Eoinstein with any halfway feasible question relating to science. It could even be a question you'd asked and he had answered two days previously. The static electricity one was famous.

"Please sir, when I take off my shirt at night, sometimes it crackles and sparks shoot all around the room Why is that sir?"

"It would be a nylon shirt, would it not, Sullivan?"

"I think so sir. Should I look at the label sir?"

Then some gink, probably Saunders would grab Sullivan by the collar, try to read the label upside down, declare it indecipherable owing to grime, and question in a loud voice whether Sullivan knew the meaning of the word soap.

But Eoinstein would already be off and running, talking about the attraction and repulsion of bodies electrified by friction, and low levels of air humidity.

"A phenomenon I have observed on occasion when my wife removes her nylon nightgown."

By now the class would be in a state of silent, hysterical seizure, interrupted only by whispered bursts of speculation as to which of the two bodies involved was the repulsive one.

"Sir, if I do it slowly, it doesn't happen as much. But if I take it off really fast, then it sparks. Do the sparks fly only when your wife takes off her nightie really fast like I take off my shirt, or if she takes off her nightie slowly sir, will there be sparks then?"

You had to hand it to Sullivan. He had neck beyond neck.

"Velocity, Sullivan, is the factor which causes the friction…"

The only snag with Eoinstein was knowing how far you could go. He was easily duped, but if he caught on, or if your behaviour was blatantly disruptive, or you thought you had licence to run riot in his class, you were in dead trouble. Once with a single blow to the side of the head, he had knocked Masterson clean off his laboratory stool for messing with the Bunsen burner. Another time, when a bloke from 2C was outside in the yard rubbing a farthing back and forth along the frosted glass on Eoinstein's door, Eoinstein picked up a broom and shoved it right through the panel, smashing the glass and scaring the living daylights out of the boy. But the best known instance of Eoinstein's incurred wrath took place outside of the school altogether.

They were learning about the conductivity of water and Eoinstein decided to give them an example of its practical application. He had an older brother, he told them, who lived near the football field at Dalymount. And when the matches were over and the crowds poured out, many of the male spectators would relieve themselves up against the corrugated iron fence at the back of his brother's garden. This distressed his brother, so Eoinstein decided to do something about it.

"I ran a small current through it, which by means of their urine was instantly conducted to the source of the problem. And that put an end to the bladder-emptying activities of those too lazy to take care of the matter at the facilities provided by the Dalymount authorities."

As soon as they came over from England, Geoffrey had planned to tell Maggie about his school, and about Eoinstein, and this beaut he was going to save till last. She'd love it.

***

It was two weeks before the exams when Granny Doyle announced that she and his grandfather were going to take the boys to the circus. It was a Saturday morning and his father had driven them out to Cabra where Granny and Grandad Doyle now lived on a small cul de sac in which all the houses had been built especially for Irishmen who had enlisted in the English army and fought in World War I. And Grandad Doyle had joined up to be in the cavalry when he was seventeen, but a friend had told him to be a fusilier instead, because horses were easy targets.

What was nifty about the street, was that at the entrance were two giant stone pillars shaped like cannon shells. Granny Doyle was very happy with the house. It was the first house they'd had since Geoffrey was born, and even though they could never own it, it was theirs for as long as they wanted. Granny Doyle had polished up the brass knocker and put crispy, white net curtains in all the windows. His grandfather had planted spuds in the garden.

Chipperfield's circus was coming over from England and his grandfather was friends with the elephant trainer.

Unlike Geoffrey's parents, Grandad and Granny Doyle knew a lot of very interesting people. His grandfather knew two tiny cobblers who looked like leprechauns and who had a cobbler's shop on South King Street opposite the Gaiety Theatre. They also had season tickets to the theatre and the keys to a private door. Once, when he was about nine and his grandfather was minding him (Granny Doyle had been sick that day), he had taken Geoffrey to the cobblers and one of them had brought him inside the theatre to show him the opera rehearsals. Up a thousand steps in the dim and the dark, up to the Gods, and then plunging down the extra steep steps between the wooden benches and into the very front row, so that when you looked over the edge you thought you were going to fall off and die for sure.

And there for over an hour, until his grandfather and the leprechaun returned from the pub, Geoffrey sat open-mouthed and wide-eyed, staring down at the figurines strutting and restrutting across the stage and stopping and singing and then being shouted at by a foreign man in the dark, who Geoffrey couldn't see even when he leaned over as far as he dared.

Of course Granny Doyle knew the elephant trainer as well, but he was really his grandfather's friend.

They had planned to go to the three o'clock show in the Big Top in the Phoenix Park, but first Joey (that was the trainer's name) was to take them behind the scenes and let them see all the animals being fed and meet the performers, and perhaps give them a ride on the elephants. Kevin was insistent that he be allowed to watch the tigers having their teeth brushed. He was also determined to get the autograph of Carla the Cannon Girl, who, according to the posters on the buses, was shot three hundred feet across the ring daily and twice on Saturdays and Sundays. In the posters she wore a black swimsuit and helmet each painted with a red lightning zig-zag flash. Kevin also wanted to ask her to go to a film with him. Kevin was eight. Geoffrey asked if they could bring Michael, but his mother didn't think it would be appropriate. "He wouldn't understand it, Geoffrey. It would just frighten him."

Michael was a Mongoloid baby, and though he was five years old now, he couldn't really talk or eat or do anything properly. He couldn't even manage the toilet part very well. But he liked Geoffrey. And he liked very bright things. And he was quite good at drawing, considering.

Geoffrey had read a book of his mother's which said Michael would probably die before he was twelve. He had asked his father about it.

"I'm afraid that's the way of it, Mutton."

After their father had dropped them off at the Cabra house, Granny Doyle had cooked up a super breakfast 'just to keep them going'. Then they took a short ride on the number 12 and got off one stop before the Park and walked up a long hill, Geoffrey taking Granny Doyle's arm and his grandfather holding Kevin by the hand.

"Where are we going Grandad?" asked Kevin. "The sign says the other way to the circus."

"We have to meet Joey first."

No doubt he's in some pub, Geoffrey thought to himself. He also thought that Granny Doyle was wheezing a lot and asked her if she wanted to rest, but she declined his offer saying that she'd have plenty of rest in her coffin when her Time came.

"You shouldn't say that Gran."

"Why not? Does it scare you?"

"It's not that. It's just…morbid."

"It's not morbid at all. It's realistic. You're young and I see me in you and everything to hope for. But when I stand at the mirror to put on my hat, the person I see is my own mother and I know all the hopes and dreams have been used up."

At the top of the hill was a pub, but there was also a great view of the park and about a quarter of a mile away and almost level with them was the circus itself. You could see the trucks and caravans in a semi-circle around the back of the big top. The elephants were out exercising.

"That'll be how we get in," his grandfather surmised, pointing up ahead at a large open gate in the wall.

Joey was about the same height as Geoffrey. He had been a jockey before he became an elephant trainer. He wasn't very friendly either, at least not to Geoffrey and Kevin. Geoffrey asked him about the elephants and he said that the big fella was acting up, but he didn't say they couldn't ride on them. He was a bit more chatty with Granny Doyle, but for the most part he spent his time at the bar, sipping his stout and muttering and mumbling intensely with the grandfather as if they were planning to rob a bank or hobble a horse in the big race. Geoffrey and Kevin sat with Granny Doyle at one of the small tables. Kevin had finished his red lemonade and was getting impatient.

"Gran, when are we going? Gran? What time is it Mutton?"

It was almost half one. There was buckets of time. They had an hour and a half before the show started.

"But I want to see the tigers. I want to see Carla the Cannon Girl and get her oughtergraph. Tell Grandad, to tell the man we want to go now."

"The more you hurry them, the slower they'll be," she observed.

There was a lot of noise outside.

"Everybody's going already."

"Stop whingeing Kevin," said Geoffrey.

"I'm not whingeing."

Granny Doyle opened her purse and gave Geoffrey half a crown. "Go up and order for us. We'll be a while yet."

"Lions, tigers, elephants and darkies, that's what you'll be seeing," a woman was explaining to her two daughters at the table closest to the bar. "And orientals jumping on top of each other and swinging from their trapezers."

The girls obviously weren't interested in Carla and her oughtergraph, Geoffrey smiled to himself, and stood tall in an attempt to get the barman's attention. But before he could, something else did.

There was a ferocious thud behind him, the whole room shook. Dust fell out of the ceiling. Geoffrey saw the barman's face register astonishment.

"Jaysus," the man mouthed the word.

Geoffrey turned around. There in the doorway was the front half of an elephant. Its trunk curled up to the ceiling, it just stood there, jammed in the frame, the door itself bent off its hinges and flat against the wall and inches away from Granny Doyle and Kevin.

The two girls were screaming crying and everybody was shouting at once.

Joey muttered something to the grandfather, put down his pint and walked towards the beast. Then everyone got quiet and watched to see what would happen next.

As Joey approached, the elephant tried to back away. And there was more creaking and groaning and dust falling on Granny Doyle and Kevin. Joey stopped where he was and raised his hand slowly for everyone to stay calm. Then he talked to it. Nicely, yet sort of sad.

"Ah dear God, Calcutta, sure you're a terrible trouble altogether, you'll have me heart broken." And then in the same voice, he said, "Now Mrs. Doyle, be a good woman and stay put with the boy, till I settle Calcutta here. Nod your head now, nice and aisy, Mrs. Doyle if you get my meaning."

Geoffrey watched her black hat go up and down and saw her take Kevin's wrist.

"That's grand Mrs. Doyle. Grand altogether. Sure, poor Calcutta had a hard time of it crossing the sea on the big boat. It's no wonder he's a bit out of sorts. I hope you didn't hurt the lad."

"I'm here Joey," a young man whispered who had sneaked in from the back. "He'd just wandered off to go looking for you. Not even the stick would keep him back."

At the sound of the young man's voice, the elephant trumpetted a huge long cry and cast its trunk in a great sweep about the room, knocking over an empty table in the middle and then walloping Geoffrey's stool straight across to the other side, dashing it against the wall. The customers scattered and crowded up to the bar at the back of the room. Everybody seemed to be screaming and shouting and crying. The door frame made a splitting noise and lumps of plaster dropped onto the tables. Someone yelled, 'Dear God, he'll have the place down on our heads!' Two of the men climbed over the bar, and the barman opened the flap to let others in behind. A few of the men, and the woman with the two girls scuttered out the back, but the rest of them just stood out of range.

Granny Doyle, white with the dust, sat still, her grip clenched around Kevin's wrist. Geoffrey pushed a man out of his way so that he could see them.

Joey was still talking and the elephant began to listen again. People started telling each other to be quiet.

"Ah now, Calcutta. Sure we can't be having that activity at all. Sure you'll get us both fired. And then what would we do?" He paused, but didn't look away. "Now Mrs. Doyle, I have a lump of bread here in my jacket pocket which I'll feed to Calcutta and when he takes it, I'll give you the word. Don't say anything now Mrs. Doyle, just nod your head again nice and aisy like you did before."

The elephant was still swinging his trunk from side to side, but not violently. He was definitely listening to Joey.

"Well Calcutta, it's a good thing that I always keep a lump of bread in my pocket." He held it out and the trunk began to nuzzle the bread, nudging it in Joey's hand it as if it was checking to be sure this wasn't a trick of some sort. Then its snout rested on it and Joey patted the top of the trunk with his other hand.

"Now Mrs. Doyle, like the good, brave woman that you are, take the child and move slowly along the wall up to the bar. Nice and aisy, while I have a word with Calcutta here. And when you reach the bar, be sure to tell the barman not to let anyone in the back door, for there's a crowd of people out front already. And you might also inform him we'll be needing the guards to clear the people from the front and that he should dispatch his wife with all speed to the circus and get the carpenter, for I fear Calcutta here is well and truly wedged. But sure if we all keep our heads, then we can avoid further commotion."

Now that they were safe, Geoffrey joined Granny Doyle and Kevin behind the bar. Joey stood with Calcutta and the barman brought him a whiskey and Calcutta a large sliced pan. An hour later they were still there. The Guards had come and they were waiting for the carpenter. The barman was serving drinks again.

"Begob," said one of the customers, "An elephant stuck in a pub doorway. Now that's not something you see every day. I wonder if it'll be wanting stout or whiskey."

"Have you any potatoes?" Joey called back to the barman.

"I've a sack below in the cellar, but sure they're not cooked."

"He doesn't eat them cooked."

You could tell there was chaos out back and people kept coming round to get in and have a gawk. But the Garda stood his ground, and when a newspaper man yelling 'Mail, Mail, make way for the Evening Mail' tried to barge his way in and take a flash photograph, the Garda grabbed the camera and told him in no uncertain terms, that making flashes in the eye of a trapped pachyderm was not a wise course of action.

Geoffrey and Kevin were on their fifth red lemonade and Calcutta halfway through the potatoes before Joey and the carpenter finally freed the door lintel from his back.

"We're not going to get to see Carla, are we?" asked Kevin.

"Not today," said Granny Doyle, " I think we've had enough excitement for one afternoon."

"I knew it," said Kevin. "I knew it wouldn't happen."

Chapter seven

Ardaroe was a gas. They went down in two cars. Uncle Bradleigh and Granny White in his new black Ford Consul, Aunt April, his mother, Kathleen, Maggie and himself in his father's Morris Oxford—Aunt April at the wheel. The Oxford was so far ahead of the Consul that they stopped in Gorey for lunch so that Bradleigh could catch up and lead the way the next ten miles to Ardaroe, which of course was more like ten thousand.

The 'chalets', as Uncle Bradleigh called them, sat side by side at the top of the big field like twins with only one another for companionship. They were both cream-coloured, but one had green trim and the other brown. The green one, the one reserved for Granny White was called Corsica—it had a bigger garden. The brown one—the one they were staying in for two whole glorious weeks was Sardinia, or The Sardine as Kevin termed it. Names, plot-size and the paintwork apart, the houses were identical. Each had a wooden gate (one green, one brown with the appropriate name screwed on in individual brass letters) and a pebble pathway that in a hop, skip and a jump led you to three wooden steps up to the front door and the verandah where you could sit out at night and count shooting stars by the zillion. What was funny was that although there was a gate, there was no need to use it. There was no fence or wall around either house, just a narrow border with baby privet hedges no higher than cabbages.

"June, tell that boy to use the gate. Those hedgelings cost money and I don't want him trampling them."

"Kevin, Uncle Bradleigh says to use the gate."

"Why?"

"Because you'll trip over his hedges."

"What hedge. I don't see any hedge. Can we go swimming?"

"Let's see if he makes us go in the back door," said Maggie.

"April, June, tell the children to use the back door."

"The hell I am!" growled Kathleen under her breath and pushed past Uncle Bradleigh with her suitcase.

There were only two bedrooms, one containing two sets of bunk beds, one with a double bed which Geoffrey's mother and Aunt April agreed to share. There was also a tiny living room with a fireplace, a kitchen and bathroom.

Uncle Bradleigh gathered everyone in the living room. There were rules, a lot of rules. First of all, Granny White would be staying in the Corsica where he would also spend the night if he was ever staying over, but probably wouldn't be since he was very busy. Secondly, The Sardine was being rented after their two weeks so it had to be kept in good condition. No jumping on the beds, no eating except in the kitchen because of the field mice, no painting or crayons indoors, no climbing the tree in the back, no playing ball in the garden—they had a whole field, no sticky sweets or fizzy drinks in any room except the kitchen. The cooker, toilet and bathtub must be cleaned after each use, the windows were to be shut when the lights were on—to avoid attracting the insects. The curtain rod and the curtain in the bunk bed room were to be used only for purposes of privacy and not for swinging off, on or from. He looked at Kevin and Geoffrey. Lastly, he might bring Thelma down for a day trip the following weekend, but he wasn't sure.

Kathleen said that she had brought her oil paints and her easel in addition to charcoals and sketch pad, and that since she was taking 'A' level Art next year, with the hopes of getting into art college in London, she trusted she would be exempted from the painting rule. Uncle Bradleigh looked at her strangely and told Geoffrey to go take his grandmother's suitcases and bed linen out of his car and put them on the steps of the Corsica.

As he unloaded the Ford Consul, Geoffrey took a good look around him. It was a spectacular panorama. Being the only houses at the very top of the hill, Ardaroe was laid out beneath them. The sea was less than a mile away and it glittered at him in the sunshine. He counted four fishing trawlers and no yachts. There seemed to be one yacht in the harbour, but a big barn at the bottom of the field blocked most of the harbour from view. He could see a windy road and two churches in the distance, and beyond them sand dunes. There were three caravans in the field, and up in the far east corner an old double decker bus painted pink, with a white rose trellis around its platform, pink curtains on every window, upstairs and down and more trellis fence around the bottom and around the front garden. The caravans were locked up and he couldn't see any sign of life. Then he saw a lady working in the bus's garden. She waved and he waved back.

It was going to be a great holiday. Uncle Bradleigh would be gone before teatime and Granny White would be in the Corsica. After tea, they could walk down the hill to the harbour and explore the village.

As it turned out, Ardaroe was more of a small town than a village. The harbour had sixteen fishing trawlers and most evenings around seven, Kevin would act as look-out and espy the boats heading for home. Then, as they had done that first evening, they would all walk down into Ardaroe, measuring their progress against that of the trawlers'. At the final leg, Kevin, Maggie and Geoffrey would hurry to the edge of the pier just in time to wave to each boat as it entered the harbour. They even knew the names and which ones were late and which had come in early. Twice Aunt April bought fresh cod which the trawlerman beheaded and gutted right there on the deck.

Inside the harbour was a tiny island shored up with massive granite boulders. The river flowed on one side of it, the sea lapped against the other. There was a footbridge on the river side decorated with cockles and mussels which you crossed to reach the island and to reach the pub—the Harbour Haven—with its tables and chairs and umbrellas outside on the grass. After conducting the same discussion three evenings in a row, Granny White finally agreed to cross the bridge and to have a lemonade outside at one of the tables. Geoffrey wanted to say that it would be fine inside as well and that Granny Doyle often took him inside pubs and that making such a fuss about this whole pub thing was silly. But he knew better. Instead, he whispered to Maggie that with a bit of luck there might be an elephant at the bar who would take a shine to Granny White.

There was a conspicuous lack of elephants at the Harbour Haven, indoors or out. Just boring people. At least the view was interesting. It took a while till he spotted their field, the Corsica, the bus and the front of the barn. It looked totally different from the island, as if their field wasn't important, just part of the scenery like the other fields with other houses leading up to the headland where you could see the cafe with Popeye on its roof.

"Would that tickle your fancy, June?" said Aunt April. She was pointing at a poster in the window advertising that the Harbour Haven featured traditional Irish music on Wednesdays and country & western on Fridays. "What do you think, June? Might be worth a try. Might meet some handsome fiddlers."

His mother laughed, but didn't say anything. Kathleen wrinkled her nose, and Granny White, like Queen Victoria before her, made it evident that she was not amused.

"I think you should go Mummy," said Maggie. "You and Aunt June. It would be fun for you both. And you're meant to have fun on your holidays."

Ardaroe had a lot to it. A bunch of shops, four bed and breakfasts, one hotel, one garage, eight other pubs, one pitch and putt, two crazy golfs, one real golf links and a tiny cinema with wooden benches for seats. The best of the shops was Uneeda which sold everything, and where Kevin bought a torpedo boat and Geoffrey a black widow which he put between Kathleen's sheets and was very sorry that he ever did.

Every day was busy. Every day they went to the beach in the afternoon. Aunt April bought Granny White a straw hat at Uneeda's and she actually wore it. The sea was always cold, but the sand was soft and warm. Kathleen stayed with Granny White when they went in swimming. Kathleen never went swimming and wouldn't even change into her bathing suit. Instead she sketched. She sketched all the time. She sketched Granny White in her straw hat sitting in the deck chair. She sketched a fella nearby only she didn't put any swimming trunks on him and she drew the cheeks of his bottom nude.

At night, Aunt April taught them how to play poker and they used Batchelors dried marrowfat peas for stakes. On Wednesday night she said that she had a little bit of news.

"Over the Christmas, I wrote a story, a short story which I submitted to *The Listener* and just before we came over, they wrote back saying that it would be published in their August issue. And they enclosed a cheque for fifty-five pounds." She puffed out her chest and placed one hand on top of the other. "And that's my little bit of news."

"Coolo, Aunt April," said Geoffrey, who still sometimes lapsed into the 'oh' language.

"I hope you told Daddy. Did you?" asked Maggie.

"No dear, of course I didn't."

"Why not. This is very important. Why didn't you tell him. He should be told how clever you are."

She thought for a while and then said, "He'd probably think it was silly."

"Is it a silly story? I bet it's not. Not if *The Listener* is publishing it." Kathleen asserted.

"No it's tragic." She turned to her sister. "Not happy or a celebration, like your poems, June."

Geoffrey noticed that his mother didn't really say much except that if April was going to pursue writing as a career, she might consider getting an agent. But that night the two of them did go to the Harbour Haven. And when they came back, it was very late and Geoffrey could hear them in the living room giggling.

The next morning a family arrived from Waterford to stay in one of the caravans. They had two boys, one who was the same age as Kevin, which was great because it meant Kevin wasn't hanging around him and Maggie all the time. He and Maggie walked up to Popeye's on the headland while his mother and Aunt April drove to Wexford town. For the umpteenth time, he told Maggie all about school and Eyeball and Itch and Eoinstein, and about Joey and Calcutta.

"You lead an amazing life, Geoffrey Doyle," she said. "My school is so boring, you could die and not know it. And no one else would know it either. And when they finally did, they'd say 'Oh Maggie McNamara is dead. We ought to bury her right away and then hurry back before algebra starts.'"

There was to be a dance in the barn on Friday night and Maggie wanted to go, but Kathleen absolutely refused to bring her. "Fifteen is far too young. I wasn't allowed to go to a dance till I was sixteen." Maggie retorted that that wasn't true. And Kathleen pointed out that this was a real dance, not a school dance. "Either I go by myself or I'm not going at all." Geoffrey's mother said that there might be a Teddy Boy element present at such an event, and added that she was glad she didn't have the extra burden of worrying about daughters.

By Friday afternoon, Aunt April agreed that Maggie shouldn't go. Maggie went into a funk and it wasn't until after Kathleen had got dressed up and put on her make-up and lipstick that she finally came round.

The band had started playing long before it was anywhere near dark and you could hear the music all over Ardaroe and especially in the field. Hundreds of people came from other towns in buses, lorries and tractors, but they weren't allowed to park in the field. Kathleen wouldn't go down till it was ten o'clock. She said that she wasn't going to stand on her own like a dope waiting for the dancing to get going. Finally she decided to go at half nine and Aunt April escorted her down and Geoffrey's mother told her she looked very pretty.

Lying on the top bunks, Geoffrey and Maggie speculated on either side of the curtain as to what the dance was like and they listened to the band till sleep drowned it out.

On Saturday, everything happened at once. The farmer who owned the field, mowed it with his tractor and blader right before breakfast. Kevin and his friend from the blue caravan found a dead frog that had been chopped in two by the blader. They brought it into the kitchen to show Geoffrey. But Kathleen who was eating her cornflakes saw it first and got sick all over the table and was in the bathroom for the next half an hour so everyone else had to use Granny White's in the Corsica.

Two other families in cars piled high with luggage on their roofs came to two of the other caravans. Then, when Kathleen was still in the bathroom, and Geoffrey and Maggie were sitting on top of one of the farmer's newly made haystacks, Uncle Bradleigh's Consul crawled into the field.

When it had successfully made it up the hill and come to a welcome halt outside the Corsica, Uncle Bradleigh stepped out and opened the back door. An older woman emerged. Then Thelma got out from the passenger side.

"It's Thelma and her mother," Maggie clapped. "You know what that means don't you Mutton?"

"No. What does it mean?"

"It means they're engaged. Mother meets mother. They must be. It can't go on any longer. It isn't natural. I bet you two shillings she's wearing a ring."

"You mean a diamond ring?"

"Yes Mutton, a diamond engagement ring, given to her by Uncle Bradleigh because he finally, finally asked her to marry him."

"And she wants to marry him? Why?"

"That part I don't know. Come on, a shilling."

"You'd think that going out with him for years and years would be boring enough. Now she'll have to live with him next door to Granny White. Sixpence."

Maggie was right.

When the entourage, now appropriately accompanied by Granny White, trouped to The Sardine, Kathleen—under threat of immediate death by execution—came out of the bathroom, and everyone admired the wonderful ring and ooohed and aahed, and Uncle Bradleigh beamed proudly and patted Kevin on the head and didn't even mention that the children were using the front door or that there were seventeen lumps of raw potato on the living room ceiling courtesy of Kevin and his spud gun.

But what was even more amazing than Uncle Bradleigh, was that Thelma's mother looked like the identical twin of Granny White only younger, but not much younger. And just like Granny White, she too didn't take off her hat when visiting someone else's house. It had a long, blue and red feather in it.

Aunt April suggested that they all take a walk to the beach at the dunes past the two churches, but Bradleigh insisted that it was too warm and that he'd drive the mothers and Thelma.

When the rest of them caught up, the mother was already ensconced in a deckchair and reading a library book. She was still wearing her black Sunday hat with the feather. Beside her in her deck chair was Granny White. But at least Granny White had her straw hat on. And, Geoffrey noticed, seemed to be wearing it with a slight tilt of defiance.

Uncle Bradleigh and Thelma were in their swimming togs. Not even Kathleen could remember seeing Uncle Bradleigh in swimming togs before.

Amazingly, Bradleigh proposed a race to see who would get into the water first. Kevin was first with Thelma, Bradleigh, Maggie and Geoffrey right behind. Then a splashing fight broke out initiated by the paddy lasts—Aunt April and his mother. Geoffrey splashed Thelma on her back to see what she would do. She turned, called him a horror and splashed him for all she was worth. It was at that moment he decided that he really did like her, despite her poor choice of a husband. Then she bent over to splash him again and suddenly he realized he was looking at her breasts.

✳✳✳

The next day, Sunday, was very bad. When they returned from the church for lunch and to get their things for the beach, Geoffrey's Dad was standing waiting for them outside the Corsica, and everybody knew something bad had happened. He had taken the train to Wexford town and got a bus to Ardaroe. They had to go to Ratheden in Wicklow right away. Michael had died.

✳✳✳

The Wicklow mountains lay back and stretched themselves out in the sun, letting their wet green fields and farmland soak up the warmth for all they were worth. Michael's coffin was a little one, only half-size, its plain pine shining in the morning light. They buried him in a pretty cemetery which sloped gently towards the Protestant church that stood guard nearby. Two of the Roman Catholic sisters who had minded him, had obtained special dispensation to attend the service and burial. The round red-faced rector said the Twenty-third psalm and 'Unto God we commend thee Michael Doyle' and an old man and a boy lowered Michael into the damp earth. Geoffrey held Kevin tightly by the wrist, the way he had seen Granny Doyle do when Calcutta endangered him. And then everyone turned and walked away.

He remembered Maggie's description of her school and applied it to Michael. When they noticed he was dead, they thought, 'Oh, we'd better bury Michael Doyle before he starts to stink the place up.' And then, 'now that we've buried him, we ought to be getting back to class.'

Well he was under the clay now, and somehow, Geoffrey didn't know quite how, but somehow, in some way, he knew that it hadn't been done right.

✳✳✳

Getting from Ardaroe to Ratheden the day before had been horrible. At first everybody was very quiet, there wasn't much traffic and they whizzed along the main road towards Dublin in the Morris Oxford. His mother was quiet too. It wasn't until they turned off the main road to go in towards the mountains that she began.

"Tell me Mattie, what they said."

"I told you everything."

"Tell me again."

But his father didn't.

Then she uttered a low curdling growl. "Tell me."

Kevin started to cry.

"Tell her Dad," Geoffrey had urged him. "Tell Mum again."

So his father said that on Friday night the Mother Superior had telephoned and said that Michael hadn't been eating—"

"She was lying. He's always had a good appetite."

"…and that the doctor thought he might have a touch of pneumonia—"

"You know perfectly well what they did, don't you? They killed him and they're trying to cover their tracks. He was only there four months so they thought they would get away with it. And you're not going to do anything about it, are you Matthew Doyle? You'll just let them off the hook scott-free. While they lie through their teeth at you. What other lies did they tell you? That I hadn't cared for him! That he had been a neglected child! That I didn't want him in the first place! Is that what they told you? Is it? Answer me, you! You who always have to have your way with me!"

"I have answered you. They said nothing of the kind."

Outside one village where there was a traffic jam and people walking down the road to a hurling match, she banged at the passenger window, shouting for the people to get out of the way and then crying that they were liars and murderers, lying to her, they were all lying. That none of it was true and her little boy hadn't died.

"Dr. Whitmarsh said he wouldn't die till he was twelve," she screamed through the glass. "And he was just five. And you all thought you could get away with it. Well, I'll summon the authorities and we'll have an autopsy performed and then the whole world will know that you are nothing less than murderers, nothing but evil incarnate."

Kevin started crying again.

"Dad!" said Geoffrey.

"There's nothing I can do, till we get there, Mutton. She gave him life. She'll not accept that he's taken in death. Not yet. Not for a long time."

If only Aunt April were with us, thought Geoffrey, she would know what to do. But his mother had said no, there was no need. And when Granny White had asked if she should represent the Whites and pay her respects, his father had told her that since she never wanted anything to do with him when he was alive, there was no point in visiting him now that he was dead.

At the gate of the field where the hurling match was to be held, there was a Garda directing traffic. A coach bus was in front of them and the Garda was saying something to the driver. His mother was screaming again, shouting crazy things. Geoffrey had his arm around Kevin who was frightened. Some boys in the back of the coach bus were banging the window at his mother and sticking out their tongues at her.

His father blew the horn repeatedly. People walking by thumped the top of the car and told them to have a little patience and wait their turn.

"Dad, the policeman, ask the policeman."

The coach pulled into the field and his father rolled down the window.

The Garda looked at the Dublin license plate and then looked at his father. "Out for the Sunday drive are we? Sure we're very sorry our little match is delaying your progress."

Geoffrey heard his father say 'death', 'Ratheden', 'hysterical', and 'doctor'.

The Garda pointed to a turn up past the field and told him to pull in there and wait for him.

It was much better now. There was only traffic on the far side now and his mother didn't shout at the people walking towards them. "You don't know where we are, do you Mattie Doyle? You've got us lost again. Poor little sheep who has lost its way. Always lost. Lost and alone like me."

"The Garda is bringing a doctor, June. Then everything will be all right."

"That's good Mattie. He'll arrest the nuns that killed Michael and the judge will hang them by their necks till they're all dead. And the doctor will see that Michael gets proper treatment. And we'll be sure to do something nice for his birthday. Maybe even take him to the zoo. He'd like that, wouldn't he Mattie?"

"Yes, he'd like that surely."

The doctor sat in the back with Geoffrey and Kevin and directed their father to his house. Then the three grown-ups went inside and Geoffrey pointed out to Kevin the ducks in the driveway and how they followed each other in and out of the pond. Waddle, waddle, waddle. Quack, quack, quack.

As they drove the doctor back to the match, their mother drifted off to sleep.

"She'll be out cold till you get there. Then give her another after dinner. O'Hanlon knows you're coming, so telephone him when you've decided where you're staying. Your mother's going to sleep now, lads. She'll be right as rain in a day or two. I'm sorry for your loss, Mr. Doyle."

The Guest House they stayed in was old and musty and the people in it were old and musty and didn't like children, and the food was old and musty and there were piss pots under Geoffrey and Kevin's beds. When the second doctor came, it was raining. And in the morning it was raining. And when they walked into the church it was raining. And when Geoffrey saw the two nuns there, he prayed his mother wouldn't get started again about killing and murdering and hanging them by their necks. But she didn't. And she didn't say anything at the Rectory afterwards when they had lunch with the round minister and his round wife.

***

At the convent, the head nun handed his father a suitcase. And a box with his toys. It was the toys that set Geoffrey off. He could barely look at them, but he couldn't not look at them either. The book with the pictures of the red and blue aeroplanes and ocean ships that Kevin had given him. His stuffed dog that they had had to take the ribbon off. His blue blanket all chewed at the ends. Even the Dinky double decker bus was there. With all its tyres intact.

They should have buried them, he thought. Should have buried his toys with him. Just in case.

Chapter eight

It was the first Tuesday of the Christmas holidays and Geoffrey was sitting on the top of a double decker bus en route to Cabra. He had been promised to Granny Doyle to help her with her Christmas grocery shopping—the bulk of which was to take place at a nearby supermarket called W. Hillions. The particular attraction of W. Hillions was that, on Tuesdays, it issued double Green Stamps to pensioners who entered the emporium before eleven.

"Don't let her take you into any pubs," had been his mother's last words of advice. But it wasn't pubs he was bothered about, it was pensioners in their plenty, and all of them prepared for plunder. He had done this before and he knew the ordeal which was ahead of him.

He arrived at just after nine o'clock. He had half-expected a roaring breakfast to fuel him for the fray, but it was not to be. Granny Doyle was at the door, coat buttoned, hat pulled down, walking stick at her side, four string baskets in her pocket. She was ready to do battle. The stick had become necessary after her hip operation, and though she had fought against the idea of depending on a crutch as she described it, once she accepted it, she accepted it wholeheartedly. It was as if it had imparted new power to her, and she wielded it with vigour and authority.

In recent years Geoffrey had become aware that what he had on his hands was a real Dub granny—no airs, no graces, no nonsense. He was also realizing that that was part of the problem. For a large proportion of the people living in the Cabra vicinity felt that their suburban status put them one step higher on the social scale than inner city grannies whether they be Protestant or no. And Granny Doyle had no time for their high-faluting front-garden fancies. Although she had a few friends in Cabra, they too were displaced inner city grannies, and they had sought each other out. But they were few and far between, and for the most part Granny Doyle was still a round soul in a square suburb. And she had been getting progressively rounder ever since the hip. And shorter.

But her face hadn't changed any. It was as mischievous as ever. In the flash of an eye, it could still switch from a soft, warm, grandmotherly expression to an at-the-sound-of-the-bell-you-come-out-fighting glare. And he noticed her Dub accent was becoming more and more pronounced. On top of that, she was, of late, more outspoken than ever.

The stick, the accent, the new-found power—it was a dangerous combination. If she'd been in the Wild West, Ma Barker would have sat up and taken note.

"Thank you for coming, Mutton."

"No prob, Gran."

"Your grandfather would be worse than useless, not that I'd trouble myself to ask him."

She handed him the key to lock the front door, and off they set, her arm in his, the four string bags swinging awkwardly between them, and the niggling tap-tap-tap of the walking stick interrupted by the occasional swish as she lopped the closed heads off dandelions or the kneecap of anyone feckless enough to be in their line of progress.

'Jaysus! What the...Oh. Sorry missus. Didn't see you there.'

Cars, lorries, policemen—nothing fazed her. It was a nightmare of embarrassment: holding up the traffic while she beat her stick on the front of some innocent motorist's car because he failed to screech to a halt the very instant she decided to launch herself and Geoffrey into the road. Once she stood in the centre of a pedestrian crossing and refused to budge until traffic in all directions obeyed the sweeping instructions of her stick. And the people would shout at Geoffrey. Not at her.

It was mortifying. The entire population of Cabra seemed to be staring at him. 'Yer wan, there—the tall gink with the unfortunate grandmother. God love him, but wouldn't you think he'd have more sense than to lep out into the road like a kamikaze.'

And of course his face was lit up in a scarlet string of acne eruptions, just in time for Christmas.

They were getting closer now, closer to W. Hillions Supermarket and the dreaded Pensioner's Double Stamp Bonanza.

"What time is it?"

"Ten to ten."

"We're all right so, except me ankles are killing me. How is school these days?"

"It's okay, I suppose."

"Have you got yerself a girl yet?"

"Aw Granny, don't be asking me that."

"Sure they must be in bud by now. What's wrong with you?"

"I'm going to a dance tonight."

"Good, good. Now if only we could do something about those volcanoes on your face."

"Aw Gran, please."

"I know they embarrass you, and there's no point in me telling you you'll grow out of them. Turpentine—that's what's I used on your father. Just a little, mind."

"Did it work?"

"It did…I think. It was more the side effects I was worried about."

He didn't want to ask, but he had to. "What side effects?"

"He started courting your mother."

"Jesus Gran, that's dreadful," he was laughing though, imagining his father smelling like a paint brush and going for long walks with his mother, "you shouldn't say things like that about my mother. Or me father."

"I suppose I shouldn't. And you shouldn't take the Lord's name in vain. Now stand up straight, because we're going in here."

'In here' was Flood's Fishmongers, a smelly pokey shop inhabited by a Mr. Flood, his dour white-faced daughter and three women customers. Granny Doyle reconnoitered the day's offerings and announced loudly that the mackerel was too pricey for what mackerel should be. Geoffrey stood in the corner. Granny Doyle picked up a haddock and held it aloft.

"This haddock has had it. Should have been given a decent funeral weeks ago."

"That haddock," said Mr. Flood quietly, his purple veins rising in his bulbous nose, "that haddock ate sprat for breakfast this morning. And you'll not find fresher, Mrs. Doyle."

"Must have choked on it then! Maybe that would explain its colour."

Geoffrey clung to the corner and prayed that this purgatory might soon cease.

"I'll take a bit of cod. I should be safe enough with the cod. Perhaps your fish-faced daughter would be civil enough to serve me."

"Serve the woman," he hissed at the unfortunate girl and turned to deal with the other women.

Geoffrey attempted to smile at the girl as she weighed and wrapped the fish, but she wouldn't look up at him.

"What time is it now?" asked Granny Doyle as they left.

"A quarter past ten."

"Grand, we'll head for Hillions so."

W. Hillions, which had several stores around Dublin, considered itself very modern—a shining light of hi-efficiency 1960s shopping. In addition to its stainless steel and bright lights it boasted a heart—and Double Green Stamps to pensioners who entered their premises before 11 a.m. on Saturdays was the manifestation of this heart. They also had a slogan, 'the heart of shopping.' However this particular W. Hillions was not the jewel in the grocery king's crown. It was narrow, oddly-shaped and poorly laid out.

"Brace yourself!" She warned him as they entered and were handed the Double Green Stamp Heart as proof of timely arrival.

The place was swarming with them—pensioners accompanied by all their paraphernalia of winter coats, gloves, scarves, umbrellas, handbags, shopping bags, black hats, walking sticks, pencils, shopping lists, green stamp books, supermarket baskets and trolleys. Most were fairly well-to-do reflecting the tenor of the neighborhood, but financial solvency was not related to the all-consuming desire for Double Green stamps.

Geoffrey equipped with basket, Granny Doyle with trolley, they marched boldly into the battle.

Fresh veg was first. The old biddies buzzed in bunches around the bundles of celery and carrots, reaching across to scrutinize the scallions, criticize the cauliflower, pummel the potatoes, grabbing the green beans. Granny Doyle plucked out a limp cabbage by the stalk and thrust it under the nose of the girl at the weighing scales. "What do you call that?" she demanded.

"It's a cabbage, missus."

"Get me the manager."

The girl called out, 'Mister Reilly' and a man strutted up with the officious air of authority. "What seems to be the problem?"

"Yer wan here tells me that this miserable thing is meant to be a cabbage."

"It is a cabbage, Ma'am," the manager asserted.

"It is not. You couldn't even call it an apology for a cabbage. My opinion is that it should be arrested and sentenced for impersonation."

"Give it to her for half price," he snapped at the girl and walked off.

And on they went. Celery, peas, potatoes. Nudging, bumping, banging. People tripping over each other and going round the wrong way. Tomatoes rolling onto the floor. Then to the fruit: oranges, tangerines, bananas, dates, figs—'what Jesus had on his birthdays as a lad'.

They stopped in front of a woman contemplating a pre-packed dinner at the frozen food counter. "You're wasting yer money on those," Granny Doyle informed her, "they'd make a cat sick."

She was forever doing that. Talking to people she didn't know, shouting, complaining, advising, dismissing.

And so it continued. Butter, cheese, jam, eggs. "There's that Mrs. Murtoch," she pointed down the third aisle, "would you just look at her! Fussing among them tins wondering whether she'd save a penny on one or get an ounce extra in the other. And her with money to buy and sell us all, and wouldn't even spend the same penny in the public lavatory to save her knickers."

"Yes, Gran. Do you have to get biscuits?"

"Five hundred and twenty-three books of Green Stamps. That's how she got the fur coat, you know."

Biscuits, flour—a five pound bag (she had a bit of baking she needed doing before the Christmas), porridge, sausages (the meat, she would buy separately at the butcher's where she had a nice spiced beef on order for Stephen's Day), washing powder, toilet paper (the soft stuff for his grandfather's piles), steel wool (which she considered a more suitable remedy for the piles), Vim abrasive cleanser (Geoffrey mentally steeled himself for a suggested application of this, but mercifully she didn't comment), mustard, tins of sardines, herrings and Jack mackerel, Chef brown sauce, Lea & Perrin Worcester sauce, Bovril, Lyons Green Label tea, four pounds of sugar.

A three-day wait to reach the cash register, and at last they were there. Face to face with the pasty-faced girl behind it. Clash, crash, clang went the cash register. Clash, crash—the flour had no price label on it.

"That's four and tuppence," the girl decreed.

"Three and tuppence," his grandmother countered.

"Una," the girl shouted to a compatriot, "four and tuppence for the five pound of McDougals. Am I right."

Una concurred.

"Three and tuppence," his grandmother reasserted.

"Dear God," muttered Geoffrey.

"Three and tuppence!" said the woman behind them. "You're quite right Missus."

"There you are!" Granny Doyle proclaimed victoriously. "This woman agrees with me. That bag of flour retails at three and tuppence only!"

"Mister Reilly!" the girl yelled, then sat up very straight and averted her gaze to the lopsided asbestos tiles in the ceiling.

While they waited, the subject of debate travelled down the queue.

"How much did she say they're charging?"

"Rampant scandal, that's what it is."

"Four and tuppence, would you believe that? Exorbitant."

"Of course, that Reilly jacks everything up on account of the season that's in it."

"Three shillings in Mulveys. And not a penny more."

"Is she trying to barter? Is that the cause of this delay?"

"Thinks she's still buying off the stalls in Moore Street."

"Should have stayed in Moore Street, if you want my opinion."

"That lad with her doesn't look too well to me."

"Very red in the face."

"A plague of pimples."

"Bicarbonate of soda."

"They're charging how much for bicarbonate!!"

Years later the manager arrived. He eyed Granny Doyle and her stick warily. Having capitulated on the cabbage, the pride of W. Hillions demanded he fight for the flour.

"Madam," he pronounced, "that bag of flour has been retailing at four and tuppence since Christmas last."

"In that case," replied Granny Grady, "it'll be none too fresh then," and handed it to him.

Five more minutes and they were out. On the street in the open air again. The shopping bags were full to overflowing, double stamps duly awarded, and the sun shining.

"We'll just pop down the road to Mulveys to get the flour and then we'll cross the road for a wee one," she said with a wink. "There'll be no need to mention it to your dear mother."

Mulveys was a ordinary grocery shop where you requested an item and a shop assistant went and fetched it from a shelf behind the counter. None of this self-service malarky and it didn't deal in Green Stamps. The flour wasn't three shillings, but it wasn't four and tuppence either. It was three and eleven.

Carrying two of the bags between them, and Geoffrey with the other two on his left arm, and she with the walking stick on her right, they staggered through the swinging door of Sweeney's public bar. Granny Doyle chose a corner by the fire, sat herself down and arranged their baggage at her feet. "Get up there now and I'll have a hot Jemmy, two cloves, no sugar," she rummaged around in her purse and uncurled a pound note. "What age are you now?"

"You know I'm fifteen, Gran."

"You'd pass for twenty. Get yourself a lager."

She was wheezing. He didn't like the sound of it.

"Go on with you."

He had to wait some time before he could catch the barman's eye. And when he succeeded in getting his order in, the man gave him a skeptical sort of look. "And what age might you be thinking you were?"

"He's with me, Frank," his grandmother called over from the corner.

"Very good Mrs. Doyle. I didn't see you there. How are you keeping?"

"Fine, right down to me ankles."

"Bad weather for ankles right enough. " He turned to Geoffrey. "You'll be eighteen I take it?"

Geoffrey nodded.

"You'll not have read the notice then."

Geoffrey looked up at the printed sign above the barman's bald head. It read: PERSONS UNDER THE AGE OF 21 NOT SERVED INTOXI-CATING DRINK ON THESE PREMISES.

Geoffrey felt the suffusion flood into his face. He was flummoxed. Then he thought of something. "Mrs. Doyle needs it to wash down the whiskey. I'll just have a glass of water for myself."

The man nodded. He gave him a bottle of Harp, an empty glass, and a glass of water. "You'll have me in 'The Joy' yet. Tell your Grandmother I'll bring her over the whiskey when it's ready."

***

He was lying in bed thinking, but thinking too much. And some of it was dreaming, the falling asleep type of dreaming, like when he believed he was crossing the road with Granny Doyle and he tripped on the curbstone. And then he was awake again.

He wasn't sure what was troubling him, but he knew it was connected with Granny Doyle and Michael. Michael was dead more than two years, and although Granny and Grandad Doyle sometimes drove with them on their Sunday drives up the Dublin Mountains to the Feather Bed, she didn't really know him. Nobody did. Not even him or Kevin, or the two nuns. Granny Doyle had a daughter who died, but she was only a baby.

He tried to imagine Michael in Heaven where the angels minding him would be like the nuns. In Heaven though, Michael would be an ordinary boy. Probably be playing soccer or hurling with the saints. Or tennis. Playing tennis with the saints was a nice thought. Running and laughing in the sunshine, the clouds soft and bouncy. He'd go asleep now, thinking about Michael with the saints.

But he didn't go to sleep. Why did Granny Doyle always talk about her ankles and never her hip or her chest? He had actually studied her ankles when they were in Sweeney's and they didn't seem swollen at all. It was odd. And it was odd with Grandad Doyle too. Geoffrey couldn't decide if they liked each other or not. It was almost as if Grandad Doyle didn't really care much. He didn't seem to worry about her. Not even with the hip. And Granny Doyle was the only one in the whole family with a bit of heart to her.

Geoffrey's father had grown up in a big house. And Grandad Doyle had owned four shops then. So what had happened? Nobody ever said exactly. And Granny Doyle never mentioned it. Or even seemed sad or bitter that she didn't live like that any more. As far as he could make out, it was connected with gambling and horses. Once his grandfather had said he owned three race horses, but at the time Geoffrey had thought he was only codding him. But he was forever going to the races and the elephant man had been a jockey.

His father didn't gamble except on the Grand Nationals, and everybody in the whole world bet on those. His father didn't really do much of anything. He played the tin whistle sometimes with a traditional Irish band and sometimes he played golf. And he read books and he was always worrying about his job and he was always worrying about money. And of course he couldn't abide the White family. Excluding Grandfather White whom Geoffrey didn't remember except for the exploding sheds.

He considered the turpentine again. He wondered if he should mention Lesley Williamson to Granny Doyle. Maybe she might have an idea. He had asked her up twice at the dance, and both times she had said 'later'. And then later, she was dancing with some creep who was at least seventeen and who thought he was Mick Jagger. And of course, Moocher, Leahy, Major and Sullivan and the rest of them were standing around like dopes waiting for a girl to fall out of the ceiling and land on their heads. And even if one did, they'd probably start discussing school and the first fifteen rugby team or something equally fascinating to girls. At least he had danced. Even if it was only with Dorothy Patchwater who looked like a tall matchstick with skinnymalinks shape and her pageboy thatch of red hair. And anyway she had a bit of life to her and danced pretty well. It was a lot better than standing like a daw talking about prop forwards and wingers. Thank God she said 'yes' when he crossed the floor and asked her up. That would have been grim. Standing like a fool in front of the girls after he'd been turned down for the third time. Bad enough the first two with Lesley

Williamson—his chin glittering in the reflected light of the spangled globe spinning in the ceiling.

Dorothy Patchwater must have felt sorry for him, or didn't care what he looked like, or reckoned no one else would ask her. Or maybe, strange though it might seem to his peers, maybe she just wanted to dance.

The chin was by far and away the worst ever. He'd do a test area with the turps. There was some in the garage. If he were Lesley Williamson he wouldn't want to be seen dead dancing with him either. Maybe when she had said 'later' she had really meant 'ask me ten years from now when you don't look like the surface of the moon covered in luminous paint.'

That was another thing bothering him. President Kennedy was coming to Dublin in a couple of weeks. And now that all the Cuba thing was over and done with, and they didn't have to pray for the Third World War to be averted anymore, Geoffrey was waiting for the Yanks to get cracking. The Russians were still beating the pants off them in the space race. They'd be mining the moon for salt if the Yanks didn't get going. He could remember years before one late afternoon when he and Dekko and Singer and Mad Malley had stood on Dekko's wall with the binoculars, watching for the satellites to pass over them like it had said in the *Evening Press*. First it was chimpanzees and dogs. Next they tried real men but they came back to earth dead men. Then came Yuri Gargarin and he made it. Not just up and down. But complete orbits, five of them. And when he got home he told the Communists about flying over Dublin and seeing Geoffrey and Dekko and the rest of them standing on the wall in broad daylight with Dekko's brother's binoculars. And the Communists would fall about laughing at the gormless Irish and drink another vodka.

If the turps did the job and kept working, he could ask Lesley Williamson to go and see President Kennedy with him. Maybe he would also have conquered the guitar by then. There were only a few chords in 'Little Red Rooster'. He was also halfway there on the James Bond theme tune. And Lesley Williamson was far sexier than Ursula Andress.

He would think about her undressing, and then he might dream about her. Her and him. Not in the crowds waiting for President Kennedy, but in a field on a summer's day, on a hillside looking down at the fields below them, and the sun shinning. And bar a few sheep, not a living sinner in sight. A day like the day when they buried Michael.

Michael and his Dinky bus. Michael playing tennis with the saints. Michael laughing. Not just smiling or sort of smiling like he used to sometimes do, but laughing, actually laughing out loud. Laughing because he was happy now.

***

His mother was shaking him by the shoulder. It was Sunday. He had to teach Sunday School class—the four year olds. He hadn't prepared their lesson yet. Four boys and three girls. He was very strict with them. But he enjoyed teaching them. One boy, David, had drawn a picture of Adam and Eve and God in a big car. Adam and Eve were in the back seat. And God was driving them out of Eden.

"You have to wake up Geoffrey. Granny Doyle died in the night."

Chapter nine

It was Geoffrey's last year at school and in many ways it was his best. He was captain of the boxing team, and in early February, under his leadership, they had beaten the bejasus out of the snotty Antrim High, winning eight bouts out of nine, his own included. Because he was captain of the team, Geoffrey was in his school's corner as the second for all the fights, except of course his own. This meant he had to coach Kevin. And miracle of miracles, Kevin actually took his advice, fought a strategic fight and won it unanimously. Geoffrey's own fight was seventh on the bill—Alko and Moocher representing the heavier divisions. His opponent was a similar build to himself, but stiff, inflexible. It made for a difficult fight and it took Geoffrey until the third round to open it up and really start to mix punches with him. One good left staggered him, a rapid fire follow-up stung him into life—Geoffrey had to play the aggressor, had to be less cautious. It was a style the opponent was uncomfortable with, and although he caught Geoffrey a good left cross on the cheek and a right on the nose, Geoffrey was able to dance around him and pick him off. Seconds before the bell, he almost floored him with a text book left-right combination to the chin. Eileen, whom he had only gone out with twice, had come with her friend Alice to watch him.

Afterwards they all had gone for a pint in Rice's on the Green. His father, mother and grandfather, Kevin and Moocher included. His mother under duress from Kevin had actually attended the boxing as well. She explained that had she been a Catholic she could have cherished the suffering she experienced and then offered it up for the souls in purgatory. But since she wasn't a Catholic she had no recourse but to close her eyes during the bouts and settle her thoughts on a more elevated plane.

"You didn't even watch me?" Kevin took umbrage and took it in high dudgeon. "After all the bother I had getting you to come. And then I win. And you didn't see me. You didn't look once. How could you not watch me?"

"I did dear. I watched your fight and Geoffrey's. You both acquitted yourselves with dignity." Then she reached round and tickled Kevin. "And you both won! And I am very proud. So there I said it."

She also congratulated Moocher.

Kevin, who was now thirteen, and pleased as punch with his first victory, sneaked some of Geoffrey's Harp into his red lemonade and squeezed himself in beside Alice at the table. Eileen put her hand on Geoffrey's thigh and performed some light roaming.

"Well Geoffrey, you have the world at your feet," his grandfather was actually proposing a toast. "Victory, the fair maiden, and youth are on your side. May you have the brains in your head and the testicles in your trousers not to squander any of them. Your Granny Doyle would have been very proud, proud of the both of her grandsons, God rest her long-troubled soul."

It was a happy evening. His mother drank three Camparis, Kevin drank a third of both of Geoffrey's Harps, and Alice turned down two dates, one with Moocher and one with Kevin.

About a month after this, Geoffrey became aware of a ruction between his father and Grandad Doyle. Since Granny Doyle's death, Grandad Doyle had upped and outed from the Cabra house without a word to a soul. Since then he had lived in a succession of unusual lodgings usually related to whatever job he was working at, at the time. Every so often, generally on a Wednesday which was his half-day at school, Geoffrey would bicycle to his grandfather's newest place of employment, check that the man was sound in body and mind and then report all the details when he got home. Father and son, Geoffrey learned, were not on speaking terms, and coming to the boxing in February had been a temporary concession on his grandfather's part.

The issue had something to do with his Granny Doyle's funeral, beyond that Geoffrey knew nothing.

The last Geoffrey was aware, his grandfather was still in the Presbyterian church on Parnell Square where he had three tiny rooms near the boiler. He was the sexton, and the first time Geoffrey visited him there, he had brought him on a tour of all its nooks and crannies. It was like a haunted house: with passages that led from the basement meeting rooms up to the narthex; concealed doors to the nave, a tunnel beneath the choir pews that journeyed all the way to the presbytery; steep stone spiral stairs up to the belfry where pigeons sat fat and safe and looked down on O'Connell Street as if they were its squires.

His grandfather seemed pleased enough, though he had a poor opinion of Presbyterians and of the curate in particular. So Geoffrey was taken by surprise when he was summoned out of class to the school secretary's office for a phone call. His Dad was on the other end of the line.

"I've just learned that your grandfather has changed his job and place of residence. Have you got a pencil and some paper?"

"Hold on." The secretary handed him the necessary.

"He's at 168 Harcourt Street, that's at the Stephen's Green end. It's a place called the Overseas Students' Boarding House. Can you go after school and see what he's up to now?"

"Okay."

"You're not in detention or anything."

"No."

He'd intended to meet Eileen and go for a walk through the Green and with a bit of luck a decent smooch in the bushes, then on to Robert Roberts for a cola. They'd pass 168 Harcourt Street anyway. And Eileen had already met his grandfather at the boxing. Plus it wasn't raining.

Eileen was a girl the likes of which he had never quite encountered before. She was wild but not reckless. She was smart, but she never did a tap of schoolwork. She was pretty, had real shape and she worked wonders with a simple school uniform.

Her navy overcoat open, her satchel over one shoulder, the tie loosened and the top three buttons of her white shirt undone combined to have a noticeable effect on Geoffrey. What's more, by rolling her skirt at the waist, she shortened it so the tips of the pleats bounced on her upper thighs as she walked. The only disadvantages to Eileen were that she talked almost nonstop and that Alice usually came attached.

"Good thing you're not in detention, Geoffrey Doyle. I wasn't going to wait for you."

"Where's Alice?"

"In detention. It was my fault really, in French class, but I got Alice to own up because I am tired of getting blamed for every itsy thing that goes wrong during that wretched woman's class. Like the fact that her precious book *L'Enfant et la Riviere* had a little glue on it. The French are so damn superior. It's just a cog of *Huckleberry Finn* anyway. Except it has more irregular sentence constructions, which owing to the glue business, she was unable to read to us. Are you asking me to the Rathgar dance on Saturday? I'm going so you might as well invite me. I've decided to wear my new blue dress—you haven't seen me in that— well you hardly know me and I've never worn it before, so you couldn't have. And anyway I only bought it last week. But it will blow your slow-witted brain, Geoffrey Doyle."

"The expression is 'blow your mind.'"

"Thank you for taking the time to correct me. Why are we stopped here?" Geoffrey explained.

"Well it's a shame Alice is in detention, that's all I can say. She's rather attracted to black men."

"Why do you think they're black? They could be Welsh or Norwegian. There mightn't be any Africans there at all."

"It clearly says 'overseas.'"

"Well Wales is overseas. So is Norway."

"It's a, a you thingamajig…"

"A euphemism? No it's not."

"Yes it is. But that has nothing to do with what I was saying. What I was saying was that personally I believe all men are the same, black, white, green or blue. They're all trouble and they all want only one thing."

"Are you speaking from a lifetime of experience, Miss Bardot?"

"It's what my mother says. And she had loads of boyfriends before she met Daddy."

"And you've no interest at all in that one thing, have you?"

"Don't be such a smart aleck."

They walked up the steps, pushed open the door and entered the hallway. A tall African man was reading a newspaper behind a wooden reception booth. He slid the little window open. "Can I help you?"

"I told you," Eileen whispered. "Now Alice will be ticked."

"I'm, we're here, to see Mr. Doyle."

"Mister Doyle..." he was consulting a registration book.

"He works here."

"He does? Ah, you mean Alfred. Yes Alfred. He's not signed out and he's not on duty till 4 o'clock, so he's most likely in the attic. Most likely."

It was six flights up, with the stairs becoming increasingly narrow at each flight. But it was a lot more elegant than the Presbyterian church basement. In fact the view was of the Green, even better than the pigeons enjoyed in the belfry.

His grandfather had two rooms, plus a kitchen and a toilet. Everything was painted white and the furniture was bamboo. Eileen loved it, "One day I will have a studio like this. I will paint, or write, or compose, or do something. Because if I don't do something I will die."

"What do you do here Grandad?"

"Mail and tradesmen in the mornings, door duty at nights. It didn't take you long to find me."

"Dad phoned me at school. Are these Trinity and UCD students?" Geoffrey had applied to both.

"Most are College of Surgeons."

"Are any of them women?" asked Eileen.

"Five. An Indian, a Kenyan, an Indonesian—she's some class of a princess—and two orientals—one Chinese and I'm not sure what the other one is. Oh, and a Norwegian." Geoffrey kicked Eileen under the table. "...six women. Thirty-eight men including the management buckos. Two cooks, two morning cleaners and myself. I suppose you'll want a cup of tea."

"Sure. Must be like the United Nations."

"Humph."

"What's wrong?"

"Nothing."

"You don't like it here, do you Grandad?"

"I don't feel at home here." He was rummaging around in the kitchen. "All this fecking bamboo and coloured people everywhere I look. Giving me orders too. It's as if I weren't in my own city where I was born and bred and the only coloured person you'd see would be in the circus."

"You're lonely Mr. Doyle," said Eileen, "you need a lady friend."

"Grandad, your Dublin is right there at the doorstep. You're only a stone's throw from Camden street and that pub you used to go to."

"It's not just the coloureds. Everything's changed. Dublin has changed and the old ways are going and the people I knew are going with them."

Eileen broke in again. "I'm only saying one thing Mr. Doyle and it is this. You're a handsome man. You stand straight in your shoes, and there is no reason on this earth or in this city, why you shouldn't be out there making the most of it, Mrs. Doyle's death notwithstanding."

"That was quite a speech you gave him," Geoffrey commented on the way down.

"I'm not my father's daughter for nothing."

"I thought he worked for the government."

"He does. He the Labour party representative for Southwest Dublin. And he's a barrister."

***

Easter brought Aunt April and Maggie to Dublin—Kathleen couldn't take the time off. It was her first year out of Art college and she was supporting herself.

As soon as he'd heard that they'd arrived, Geoffrey got on his bicycle and was over at Granny White's within fifteen minutes. He hadn't seen Maggie since the previous summer, just before she moved to London to study to be a primary teacher. She would know everything there was to know about the London scene. Geoffrey wanted to go to London for the summer, but he hadn't told anyone yet. He wondered if she'd changed.

She hadn't. The same old Maggie. Huge hug and lots of laughing about how tall he'd grown. He was taller than her now. Her hair was longer and redder than ever and her freckled face as impish as always. Geoffrey didn't like the eye shadow though. His grandmother said they were making too much noise.

"Making too much of life," whispered Maggie, "it's unseemly." They walked out to the garden. "I hear you're going steady. That's unseemly too. What's she like?"

"She's like you, Maggie," he said without even thinking.

"You mean red-headed and gorgeous, talented and charming, engaging and enraging?"

"And bold as brass."

Quite suddenly he became overwhelmingly embarrassed, but he didn't understand why. They were walking hand in hand past the flower beds of late tulips, pansies and anemones, up the flagstoned path towards the privet hedge and the vegetable garden.

"Are you leading me up the garden path, Geoffrey Doyle?"

He laughed and said he didn't think he was.

"What about you?" he finally asked. "Are you going steady?"

"Sort of. Well two fellas really. Kathleen is living with a fella. Of course we're not supposed to know, but Mummy does. And I found out in September as soon as I got to London. You can't breathe a word. If Daddy ever got wind of it…" She squeezed his hand.

Without any warning whatsoever he burst into tears.

"Mutton! Whatever's the matter?"

"I missed you," he blurted.

She squeezed his hand. "I know," she said simply.

They had reached the herb plot which had been planted years ago to replace their grandfather's shed. Geoffrey always thought that they should have moved the compost heap there. It would have been more fitting, but when he mentioned it, his mother said the opposite, that even though compost was his grandfather's livelihood, it was also the cause of his death.

"Mike works as a session guitarist with different bands," Maggie chatted, "he was on Top of the Pops once with his own band, but they broke up."

"Who's Mike?"

"The fella Kathleen's living with."

But Geoffrey wasn't interested in Kathleen's romances. His brain was hop-scotching all over the place. He was sad for the grandfather he didn't even remember, he wanted Granny Doyle to be back, he wanted to know if Michael was happy, he wanted Maggie to move to Dublin, he wanted to be with her always.

"Is your friend Moocher still head-over-heels in love with me?" She had met Moocher once.

"Yes," Geoffrey laughed through his tears. "There's an airshow out near him on Easter Monday. I'm bringing Kevin. Moocher wants to know if you'll come. We'll have a picnic."

"Will your girlfriend come too?"

"Maybe. She's in Spain with her parents."

★★★

He had the week off school. A week with Maggie. In town, at the zoo, ten-pin bowling, going to the flicks. He asked her a thousand questions about London, but mostly she talked about her professors and the training college and her flat mate Suzy and about the boyfriends. One of them was writing a play or something.

"How's Uncle Brendan?" he asked.

She told him that he had been appointed an honorary Grand Marshall by the Ancient Order of Hibernians and had led the parade through Manchester on St. Patrick's Day and that Aunt April had been given a seat of honour on the viewing stand. And that now her father was planning a St. David's Day parade for the Welsh and was also involved in the Free Cornwall Movement.

"And guess what the latest is?"

"What?"

"He's bought a hundred acres of land. Guess where."

"Ardaroe."

"No, but good try."

"I give up."

"In the Bahamas. On an exotic island called Great Exuma."

"Wow. Is he taking you there?"

"When I graduate. So he says."

By Good Friday, the Easter Sunday dinner was becoming the family bone of contention. Who was eating with whom and where. His father wouldn't go to Granny White's house. His mother didn't like to cook, she didn't like Easter as a religious observance anyway, believing the crucifixion to be an unnecessarily brutal precursor to the resurrection. But out of the blue, Uncle Bradleigh phoned and announced that Thelma would cook the dinner and that everyone would eat at his house. His magnanimity and largesse was also extended to Grandad Doyle.

"The man's either tanked or manic," judged Geoffrey's father, "or both."

"Please don't talk about Bradleigh like that at the table," his mother reprimanded him. "It was a nice offer, although a little unusual. And I'm sure it was kindly meant."

"June, are you telling us you've accepted?"

"Certainly I accepted. It will be very pleasant."

The father and both his sons groaned.

"We will make the best of it," she said angrily, "and you'd better phone your father."

There was silence while she beat the Birds Instant Whip for dessert.

"Moocher and I were thinking of going to work in London this summer."

"Were you?" his father was being sarcastic.

"The money's very good."

"Is it?"

"It's far too dangerous," his mother responded. "Beatniks banning bombs and Mods fighting Rockers."

Geoffrey was about to say that that stuff was years ago, but he didn't. All he wanted to do was introduce the idea, not get into World War III about it.

"And mind-warping psychedelic stimulants," continued his mother.

"I think female stimulants are what's on his mind," his father finished off.

"I could go with him," suggested Kevin.

***

After church service the five Doyles, decked out in their Easter finery, assembled in front of Granny White's house. Maggie bounced out the front door in a floppy straw hat streaming yellow ribbons and a long flowery button-front dress. "It has been decreed," she announced, "that the day of resurrection shall be a 'front door' day."

Next came Aunt April who went right back in because she had forgotten her hat, came out again and went back in to get her bag. Then came Jacintha who was more nervous and jiggy than usual. She wasn't sure if her dress was quite appropriate and hoped no one would think her daisy hat too silly. Granny White told her to shut the door and be sure to turn the key round twice to double lock it.

"Yes of course, Mrs. White," she almost curtsied. Then she removed her little white gloves, performed her task, dropped the key when handing it back to Granny White, apologized and picked it up and put her gloves on.

"Where is April?" inquired Granny White, anxiously surveying the entourage.

"She's getting her bag, Gran," Kevin called out.

When Aunt April started banging on the inside of the door, Granny White instructed her to go round the side and through the garage, but Aunt April didn't hear her and kept banging. Led by Kevin, a chorus of shouting erupted, "Go through the garage."

Clearly irritated, Granny White took the key back out of her bag, "Jacintha, reopen the door."

Then the shouting changed to a cacophony. "Wait there April" and "Hold on Aunt April" and "Don't go through the garage" and "Jacintha's reopening the door Mummy," and "Stay put Mrs. MacNamara, in the name of God, stay put." This last cry was from Geoffrey's grandfather who was wheezing with laughter at the scene and then at his own acerbic wit.

"It won't open," said Jacintha.

"That's because you haven't turned it round twice," his grandmother snapped and pushed her aside, "let me do it, you stupid woman."

It was at this point that Aunt April, hat and bag, emerged from the garage door, "I was locked in. Can you imagine? And I couldn't make out what you were all saying. But here I am."

"Resurrection or ascension, we'll all be using the garage again before this day is out," Maggie remarked to Geoffrey.

And then, with Granny White to the fore, the eight of them filed down the driveway, turned right onto the pavement, walked the breadth of the front garden walls of the two houses and turned right into Uncle Bradleigh's driveway.

As bidden, Jacintha pressed the bell.

Thelma opened the door. "Happy Easter, everyone!" She shook all their hands and ushered them into the sitting room, told them to sit down and where, "Mrs. White and Mr. Doyle either side of the fireplace now, as there's a chill in the air despite the glorious sunshine. Shall I take your hat and coat, Mrs. White?"

"No."

"Where's Uncle Bradleigh?" asked Kevin.

Thelma cleared her throat and addressed them as a group. She explained clearly and precisely that Bradleigh was sick in bed with stomach cramps and diarrhoea, caused by a virus which, as they probably knew, was rampant throughout the city (there were nods and murmurs of recognition and sympathy for poor Bradleigh). She herself had suffered from a milder version earlier in the week. So although he was unable to join them, she wanted to assure them that he wished them all a happy Easter and wished her to direct their attention to the pyramid of Terrys of London chocolate eggs displayed on the corner table, all of which Bradleigh had purchased himself in London on business the week before last, and which she would now distribute.

And having said all that, she proceeded to take the smallest egg from the top and presented it to Jacintha who immediately took off her white gloves and fluttered with excitement as if she were at the Czar's court and had just been given Faberge's latest model.

"And for you Kevin...and Geoffrey. Next I believe, yes, is Matt. And one for Mr. Doyle senior—couldn't leave you out, now could we Mr. Doyle...or should I call you Alfred?"

As the presentation continued, the pyramid got smaller and the eggs got larger till finally she reached for the centerpiece—a whopper with its chocolates spread out in front of it for all to see. "And last, but certainly not least, for Mrs. White."

Thelma lifted up the egg like a trophy.

"My, my!" said Geoffrey's mother.

Geoffrey noticed that where the sleeve had slipped down to Thelma's elbow, there were two thick vivid stripes across her bare arm.

"You could feed an army on that one Mrs. White," said his grandfather as Thelma presented it to Granny White. Kevin clapped. His mother, Aunt April and Maggie joined in.

"Now," continued Thelma, "sherry before dinner, minerals for the children of course. Please excuse me while I go to the kitchen. April, perhaps I could ask you to do the children."

When the two women left, there was a difficult silence among the guests, but Kevin, true to form broke it. "Maggie," he proclaimed loudly, "is so beautiful today that we should phone up a portrait painter and have him come right over."

Maggie thanked him and took up the theme, by telling them about Kathleen completing art college and how she already had three of her illustrations published in different magazines. With her name on them.

"Bradleigh," Granny White snapped "was always a very talented painter. And," she underlined, "still is."

"I know what you mean Margaret," said Grandad Doyle as if the two were old pals. "Given a bag of bull's eyes, Matt here could distemper a wall in a morning before he was out of short trousers. Give him two bags and you had the woodwork to match."

"Mr. D." Geoffrey's mother scolded, "you are quite outrageous. I've been trying to get him to do the kitchen for months."

"Inspire him June, he's probably outgrown bull's eyes. Try a different incentive. When all fails, look for another carrot."

"I am his inspiration, as he is mine, Mr. D." She closed her eyes. "Poetry is the soul in blossom."

Aunt April had returned. "Speaking of blossoms, I see we have the Easter Lilies on the front of the city buses," she chirped. "Very seasonal."

"Commemorating that 1916 is a national disgrace," said Granny White.

"Hard to believe," said Grandad Doyle, "that half a century has passed since that Easter. I was in Ypres then, chewing mud and blood for breakfast to keep the empire alive. And all the while, the buckos back here were shoving crackers up its arse. I'd been in school with a couple of them too. But while I took the King's shilling and spent it, they smelted theirs for bullets."

"That's ancient history Mr. D.," said Geoffrey's mother. "Now surely we don't want to discuss politics on such a lovely and happy day."

"No June, it's recent history." Grandad Doyle stood up and positioned himself with his back to the fire. "I fought for the empire when I should have been fighting against it. Your sister's husband did the same twenty years later and, from what I hear, he's been spending the rest of his life trying to make amends."

Geoffrey wanted his father to say something, anything, but he didn't. Nobody said anything. This time, even Kevin kept his mouth shut.

Aunt April got up and opened the door, then returned with Thelma and the trolley.

"Sherry on top," Thelma directed them, "minerals on the bottom. Perhaps Matt, you could later oblige me by carving, Bradleigh being out of commission so as to speak."

"Yes, certainly," his father said. The only damn thing he had said so far.

"Turkey," decreed the grandmother, "should be carved by separating the entire half breast from the bone and then cutting it horizontally. The extremities should be given to the dog." She was still wearing the hat and coat.

"Like many of the infamous monarchs of England, I'm an extremities man myself," said Grandad Doyle and sat down again.

"Of course," agreed Thelma, "drumsticks for the men, quite in order."

To his embarrassment and discomfort, Geoffrey caught himself studying Thelma, and as he watched her, he sensed a kindred feeling for her. And when he thought about it, although he tried not to, she wasn't half-bad looking. In a prissy, bossy sort of way. He also noticed Kevin had poured most of Jacintha's sherry into his own red lemonade. This kid was destined to be trouble.

Sherry in hand, Maggie came over to sit with him.

"Am I the only one drinking the soft stuff?" complained Geoffrey.

"You and Granny White. It's going well, though, isn't it. If we haven't all murdered each other by dessert, it will be a miracle."

"I'm sorry about my grandfather."

"Well you shouldn't be. He speaks his mind. He and Granny White are two of a kind."

"They are?"

"Well he's a bit crude, suggesting Aunt June look for another carrot. At least he didn't say cucumber."

"What are you talking about? He meant carrot like carrot and stick, a reward, didn't he?"

"Double entendre, cuz. Think about it. Anyway that's not what I came over for. What do you make of our Brad and Thelma? How many years are they married now? Four? It must be. Four years and no fat, baby-filled belly. So much for marital bliss and the fruit thereof. Do you know what I think?"

He would have said that he didn't, but he had no chance to.

"I think he's still sucking at Granny White's teats. And she doesn't want to wean him."

Chapter ten

Geoffrey and Kevin bickered over the merits of Vampires and Viscounts, one preferred a Scimitar, the other espoused the design lines of a Javelin, they both agreed on the Dagger, and both fervently hoped that the weather would hold out and that all the planes would actually be flying as advertised, since they weren't all on view.

It was Easter Monday and they and Maggie had taken the bus to the Baldonnel Army Aerodrome for the greatest flying display in Ireland's history. Eileen had returned from Spain on Good Friday, but she had to go to the races with her parents. And his great love for Maggie notwithstanding, Moocher had cried off too. Had to visit an aunt in Carlow. Easter Monday was that kind of a day, a day of family obligation.

A twin-decked Douglas Globemaster in United Nations markings lumbered up to the runway while the commentator narrated its history, the number of Irish troops it had carried to the Belgian Congo and its flight back to the Arizona Desert where, like the noble workhorse it was, it would be put out to pasture to enjoy the rest of its days in sunshine.

"Very grandiloquent, considering it's just a big old, noisy plane," said Maggie, but she took a photo of it anyway. Geoffrey had forgotten his camera.

It wasn't even lunchtime and already he knew it was going to be a terrific day. It was sunny, warm but not hot, and a rich blue sky with tubby white clouds allowed you to see for miles. Even Kevin wasn't a pain. He actually conceded that Geoffrey knew the different planes better, and knew more about them. And he didn't hang on to him and Maggie like the annoying little puppy dog he generally was. In fact the opposite was true. He would wander off from their spot alongside the runaway and explore different sections of the static display and then return to report that the queue to get into the cockpit of the Viscount was too long, or that the helicopters were in the second hanger and that he got fourteen brochures on guided missiles.

"Be back here in an hour," Geoffrey instructed him as he set off on yet another foray into the crowd, "and we'll have lunch then. The fighters are flying at two."

He was glad Eileen couldn't come. He was annoyed at her. She hadn't even phoned him when she got back. He had to ring her, and she had completely forgotten about the airshow. Anyway she would have been bored to death. And she probably wouldn't have liked Maggie.

"So Geoffrey, did you eat the golden egg yet?" She tickled his nose with a daisy as he lay on the blanket. Her hair was shining like copper in the sun and he tried not to stare at her breasts, which though usually inconspicuous, were now defined in outline by her yellow-ribbed sweater.

"No, it'll only give me a rash of acne. I'll let Kevin have it. Maybe." He had intended to give it to Eileen since he hadn't thought to buy her one, but decided to wait and see.

"Do you think Uncle Bradleigh really had the stomach flu?" Maggie was tickling him again.

"Well I don't suppose you do. You'll probably tell me he was hung over."

"That's what I'd tell you. The White family facade is cracking to its foundations and what lies beneath it is decay—worm-squirming, weevil-ridden and rotting. The dynasty is dying and you and I Geoffrey will be the spectators at its deathbed agonies."

"Now who's being grandiose."

"Norm wants to be a playwright. I try to impress him with my dramatic sense."

"Which is Norm?"

"The one I'm really going with, I think."

"What do you mean you think?"

"He wants me to do it with him, you know—go all the way."

"Does he now." It wasn't a question.

He was inextricably torn between wanting to know everything and nothing about these so-called boyfriends.

"I'm not sure if I will or not. But everyone else is doing it. At least in London."

"How do you know about the vegetable stuff, like you were saying yesterday?"

"You should see the magazines Norm shows me. They do it with everything. And Norm calls his thing his banana. Like Mae West. But it's really more like a carrot."

"Is it." That wasn't a question either.

To change the subject, he started to talk about the dinner again and how she had suggested that Grandad Doyle and Granny White would be good for one another—he told her about the Overseas Students Place and what Eileen had said, and Maggie agreed that he was a handsome-looking man. Then they tried to calculate everyone's age, but got stuck on Thelma.

"I can't tell," Maggie said, "she must be at least thirty. Getting a little late in the day for children."

"I thought you'd worked out that the lack of offspring was due to his not being weaned yet? That's what you said yesterday."

"Did I?"

"Yes you did."

"Well it could be an either-or situation or a combination of both. The fact of the matter is that we have no evidence of fertility and so are left to conjecture like idle fools huffing and blowing. I've also been reading Shakespeare, can you tell?"

"You've been doing a lot of things."

"What about Jacintha?" she asked. "We forgot about her. Did you see how squiffy she became on the Madeira?"

"When she dropped her fork down the front of her dress."

"And then reached in to pull it out. And couldn't because it had become entangled with her undergarmentry. I never heard anybody use that word before. It's a great word. I thought she was going to ask your grandfather to help. And she ended up excusing herself from the table and having to go to the bathroom to extract it."

He laughed but Maggie detected something else. "You don't like her do you?"

"Not particularly."

"Why?"

"No reason. She's just weird, that's all."

"You know she was arrested years ago, Mummy told me once."

"You're joking."

"No I'm not, but you'll never believe what she was arrested for?"

"What?"

"You won't believe me."

"I probably won't, but tell me anyway."

"For loitering."

"For loitering?"

"Yes loitering. Now ask me where she was loitering?"

"Where?"

"In the men's public toilet in Rathmines, I swear it, Mummy told me."

"You're right, I don't believe you."

"Mummy said it was because she never had a chance to know a man, and she wanted to see what the, you know, their vegetables looked like. The judge fined her ten shillings."

"You've definitely got vegetables on the brain." He tickled her waist and she screamed and tickled him back till he got her again and they were wrestling on the blanket. And even as they were tickling each other she told him that all the planes were streamlined to look like giant vegetables and that the delta winged planes were women's skirts spread wide and that the pointy noses were the vegetables which had gone right up them.

"You are a lost cause Maggie MacNamara, and if you do decide to do it with Norm, make sure he puts a frenchie on his carrot first."

***

Before lunch, three Aer Lingus Viscounts arrived from Dublin airport and instead of landing, flew in formation just above the crowd. They made four passes and the people cheered. Lunch itself was a delicious mish-mash of things they had each brought: gurr cake, hard-boiled eggs, Calvita cheese and onion sandwiches which were Kevin's contribution, apples, oranges, a melted Cadbury's Dairy Milk, eleven sticks of celery, three sticks of rhubarb, two bottles of ginger beer, and a large bottle of Taylor Keith Orangeade. Kevin asked Geoffrey if he'd take him to the hanger with the Dagger so that they could get the pilot's autograph. Geoffrey warned him that they'd never be allowed in, but that he'd take him anyway after the Javelin demonstration and before the helicopters.

The commentator announced over the loudspeakers that he had finished his lunch and he had half a chicken sandwich remaining which anyone was welcome to. Also a bag of knitting had been found and a child's roller skate, but he couldn't determine if it were the skate of a left or right foot. A second commentator, Michael O'Hehir from Radio Eireann could be heard on numerous transistors giving the warm-up for the big football match at Croke Park.

The afternoon started with an Etendard jet from the French navy. It stretched out its nosewheel so that it stood lean and tall like a stork at the end of the runway, and then amid the roars and cheers of the Croke Park spectators on the transistors mingled with the oohing and aahing of the airshow crowd, it blasted down the runway like the divil and flung itself into the sky.

It climbed, it spiralled, it dived and rocketted over their heads with an ear-splitting roar that reverberated throughout the countryside. Babies were crying, people were yelling, cheering, laughing. The jet shot upwards again, performed loops, levelled out, disappeared between clouds, dashed from north to south, east to west, heaven to earth as if the whole blue sky were its playground and it could play for ever. And every man, woman and child set their giddy spirits free to fly along with it.

When it had landed and its engine subsided to a whine, the pilot flung open the canopy and blew the crowd kisses with both hands. Everyone went wild, jumping up and down, cheering, applauding.

Geoffrey glanced across at his little brother. His mouth was open but no words came out.

***

The other acts were good, they were great, the helicopters which hung eerily in front of them, and the parachutists, and the Scimitar and Javelin flying side by side, but the best wine had been served too early.

Kevin clutching at his program and a pen, shouted at his brother to hurry up. Maggie stayed with the blankets and the bicycles. Geoffrey had been right about the hangars, they were fenced off, although you could easily see into them. Two or three soldiers were standing in front of each. The Delta Dagger sat broadsides in Hangar 3. It was white. A red lightning stripe ran from the top of its tailplane through the words Convair Aviation and along the fuselage to the edge of its needle sharp nose cone. A triplet of Irish Army Vampires swung over the hangers and the national anthem played on the loudspeaker. The soldiers came to attention and saluted.

"I don't think it's going up today, Kev," said Geoffrey. "I think this is the end."

"It's on the program."

"Programs change. The woman didn't do the trapeze act from the helicopter either."

But Kevin walked on. Past Hangars 4 and 5 and towards the perimeter fence.

"Where are you going, Kev?"

"Round the back, see if I can get in at the back."

"Jaysus, Kev, you'll get us arrested."

"So go back and sit with your lovey-dovey cousin Maggie."

Geoffrey watched him go ahead, knowing that not accompanying him would do nothing to deter him. They were about a quarter of a mile away from the hangers now. Kevin doggedly walked through the long grass, climbed over a drystone wall into a field, bypassed an assortment of grazing sheep, made a wide semi-circle behind them and started back towards the hangers. The whole circuitous route took about ten minutes. At the rear of the hangars there was nobody to pay any attention to either of them. Geoffrey shrugged his shoulders and followed him past the first hanger.

Even though he knew Kevin would do it anyway, he still couldn't believe it when he saw his brother open a small door at the back of Hangar 3, walk in and close it behind him. Jaysus, he'd kill him when they got home.

He ran to catch up with him, expecting to have to extricate him from the Military Police. He reasoned that since Kevin was small for his age—he didn't look thirteen—he could play the big brother tact. Trying to keep an eye on the little bother who had wandered off by himself and got lost—it sounded convincing. Anyway, he was limited for choice. Steeling himself, he opened the door and went inside.

At first he thought he had the wrong hangar for there was no sign of the Dagger or Kevin. There was an aeroplane engine slung from the roof with gantries underneath it, but it was a propeller engine not a jet. And he couldn't see the front of the hangar which he knew was open. Then he spotted another door beyond and opened it slowly. Now he could see the Dagger. The pilot was beneath the wing, checking something. He had his helmet tucked under his arm. Kevin was standing at the bottom of the cockpit steps, with his pen and his program, waiting.

Geoffrey edged up the side of the hangar keeping in the shadow as much as possible. There was a mechanic in white overalls with Convair

Aviation on the back and he walked over to the pilot and said something and then went to the front of the plane and started to hitch up a tow bar to an Army tractor.

The pilot finished what he was doing. The Vampires taxied by out front. The mechanic shouted, "You're on in ten minutes, they have a Brit bomber coming in from Wales."

Then the pilot approached the front and saw Kevin.

Please give him the autograph and don't have him arrested, Geoffrey prayed, just give him the autograph and we can get out of here and back to where we're allowed to be.

They were talking but he couldn't making out what was being said. He edged closer. Talking was fine, talking was not calling for the soldiers to take his brother away. What the hell were they talking about?

Geoffrey was opposite them now, not ten yards away.

"It has two seats." Kevin seemed to be insisting.

"I can't, kid. You shouldn't even be in here."

Geoffrey couldn't believe it. He watched Kevin as if he watching a film in the cinema.

Now Kevin was talking again.

"Before you were a test pilot and before you ever flew a plane, when you were a boy like me and the only thing you wanted to do was to be up in the air, out of the gardens and fences and streets and doors, did you ask a pilot just like you to show you what it was like?"

"You're really something else, you are."

"But did you?" Kevin persisted.

The pilot paused. "This ain't some two-bit cropduster kid! A big company owns this plane, and believe me, it cost a hill of beans. Listen, you could pay money and get up for a spin. They do that in Ireland, right. Sure they do. Probably doing it now, right here at the show."

"Not in a jet. Not in a Delta Dagger."

"I'm sorry kid, I just can't."

"Please mister, this is the only time I'll ever be this close to a Delta Dagger. This is the only time I will get to talk to the test pilot of a Delta Dagger. No one will ever know that you took me up. But I will know, I will know it for the rest of my life.

"Jeeze! Where are your parents anyway?"

"I cycled here by myself. Nineteen miles. Just for the Delta Dagger." Kevin turned and walked away. Then he looked back and gave it one final try. "That pilot didn't say no to you when you asked, when you were a boy. And you wanted to fly."

The mechanic had come over to the cockpit. "What's the problem?"

"Ed, get the second helmet and strap him in. And don't ask. Convair will rake my ass over the coals if they ever get wind of this. Goddam kid knows every button to hit. He'd sell sand to the Arabs."

***

By the time Geoffrey had made his way back to Maggie, the Dagger was already airborne and the commentator was describing its service with the NATO forces.

"Where on earth were you?"

"I'll tell you later."

"You missed a huge bomber, it landed five minutes ago. But you'll like this one. It's the dagger you and Kevin kept talking about."

"Coming in now from the south at an altitude of 1,000 feet and a speed of Mach 0.75, the F-102, Convair Delta Dagger, vanguard of NATO, protector of democracy…" the commentator read from the script.

"Where is Kevin?" asked Maggie, "He'll miss it."

"He'll be here any second. He's coming in from the south at an altitude of 1,000 feet."

Chapter eleven

Pyjamas. Underpants. Socks. Handkerchiefs. English money. Aeroplane ticket—his mother was superstitious about the sea although she considered it a poetically superior way to pass from this world. Notwithstanding, she insisted that he and Moocher apply for student union memberships so they could qualify for the student charter flights. His cousins' addresses and phone numbers. Ring Moocher to ensure he's on time and has the boarding house address which Geoffrey had not yet clapped eyes on. Letter-of-work-offer from the factory stating terms of employment and wages—four shillings and fourpence an hour, time and a quarter for the first two hours overtime, time and a half after that, time and a half for any hours worked on Saturday, double time for any hours worked on Sunday. Report for work Monday morning 8 am at Personnel office on the first floor, Signed Michael Hart, Personnel Manager, Lindus Frozen Foods, Covent Garden.

Work trousers. Work boots. Sneakers. Underpants. Socks, Toothbrush. Toothpaste. Wash cloth. Alarm clock. Bell bottoms, jeans, hipsters, flower tie, button-down denim shirt, green paisley corduroy shirt.

Geoffrey's mother supervised as together they ran through her checklist. His father furnished the address of a traditional Irish fiddler who was a pal of his from the old days and now owned a pub in Epsom. Although Geoffrey protested that he and Moocher had every detail taken care of and that neither thirteen pairs of underpants nor fiddlers in Epsom would save him from the vicissitudes of London living, in truth he was scared. He hadn't admitted, even to himself, that he might be scared, at least not to the degree he was now. As the hour of departure drew nigh, everything about the trip was suddenly intimidating. He'd never been to London, and although Kathleen and Maggie now lived there, they were nowhere near Covent Garden. And except for a school tour around Jacobs biscuit plant off Clanbrassil Street, he'd never set foot in a factory. And to top it off there was Moocher's unpredictable and irresponsible behaviour to deal with. He almost wished he weren't going. But it was too late now. The disgrace at funking out, not even giving it a try and the subsequent embarrassment that would be visited on his head was still greater than the fear of the unknown city.

He phoned Moocher. Moocher said yes he would be at the airport on time, yes he had the address of their digs in Tufnell Park (a friend of a sister of his mother's had made the arrangements), yes he was packed and he was just baking a fruit cake. Now would Geoffrey stop fussing like an old woman and get off the phone.

Geoffrey decided to stop fussing like an old woman. He had gone on trips with Moocher before, just camping for a weekend and the likes, and Moocher inevitably forgot some essential item or other. Like the tent. Or his sleeping bag. And yet more often than not, their expeditions turned out to be a lot more fun because of, not in spite of, Moocher's lackadaisical approach. Moocher embraced adventure, and Geoffrey suspected he deliberately tempted fate by not adhering to the prescribed plan.

Of all the boys in his class at school and of all his other friends, only Geoffrey and Moocher were setting off for London. It was 1968 and they were both seventeen and both hoping to get two honours in the Leaving and go to "uni" in October, having visited France and Spain in September using some of their earnings from the factory to finance the trip. It was a great plan, none of his friends were doing anything close to it. None of them were even going abroad let alone working in London. But he and Moocher were. And the whole world knew that London was the only place to be. His mother who had earlier cautioned him on bomb-banning beatniks now also advised him to be wary of female beatnik poets whom she was sure would fall quickly in love with him. Kevin noted that Geoffrey need only concern himself about the blind female beatniks as he was in no danger of being abducted by the sighted ones. Geoffrey was going to retort by pointing out that beatniks were no longer the thing in London, but didn't. And that was that. He was off to the airport.

A Student Union charter flight meant that you flew at night in an unidentifiable aeroplane belonging to an unheard-of airline, whose check-in desk was not in the main airport lobby. But Geoffrey's father had already sussed all this out and together they joined the guitar and kitbag queue standing in front of the handwritten cardboard sign. Moocher was not one of them. A half hour crawled along the clock.

"There are too many of us," said the man in front of him. "They'll bump us."

This comment gave birth to a discussion nurtured by numerous speculations and it gathered momentum as it travelled up and down the queue. How delayed was the flight? Were they flying Icelandair again? What airport were they landing at anyway? The ticket was non-specific. Geoffrey learned that London had at least four and all of them were contenders.

An airline official and a student union person emerged from a secret door in the wall and began processing the passengers. The queue was moving. He went for a phone while his father held his place, then changed his mind and asked his father to make the call because he didn't want to get bumped. At the same time he didn't want to go by himself. This choice of airports was rattling him. He looked around so hard he realized his eyeballs would no longer recognize Moocher if he came in. Would the others let Moocher join the queue with him? He'd have to shout out "hey Moocher, I've got your ticket" which was true. And what would he do with Moocher's ticket if he didn't turn up? He would give it to his father he decided. The bumping discussion started again. Maybe Geoffrey would be bumped. Come back again Saturday night.

"Ticket and card."

"I have my friend's ticket, but he's not here."

"Are you going to London?"

"No answer," said his father, "so he must be on his way. Give the woman your ticket."

She examined his student card, took his kitbag, stamped and stapled his ticket to his boarding pass and gave him a leaflet about foot and mouth disease.

"What about my friend?"

"We're boarding in five minutes."

"Who goes first, us or the horses?" asked the man behind him.

"The livestock is already boarded. Ticket and card."

The five minutes expanded to ten, but it made no difference. Everyone was checked in. Geoffrey kept running the scene through in his mind. Already Moocher's Dad was driving up to the door, Moocher was rushing in. He'd spot Geoffrey and say 'Are you still here, I thought you'd be halfway across the Irish Sea.' But no matter how much he'd rerun the scene, it still didn't make it happen.

The airline woman said boarding was commencing and everyone filed through the secret door.

"Go on," his father instructed, taking Moocher's ticket from him. "Ring me when you get there and I'll fill you in."

It was raining and the plane stood waiting for them far out on the tarmac, its huge clamshell at the front stretched wide to expose a dim, gaping mouth.

It had been a lie about the animals. One blindfolded racehorse was being led up the ramp while two bulls—one was a Black Angus—waited restlessly below with their owners. At the top of the ramp, the racehorse shied, then whinnied and backed down, pulling with it its trainer and several men in white overalls.

Inside the plane was a partition separating students from livestock and that was where Geoffrey ended up. Face to face with the partition which bore a scratched Aer Turas (Ireland's foremost charter airline) logo. On the floor was a coffee-stained laminated sheet which informed him that he was about to fly in a Bristol 170 Wayfarer with four emergency exits as illustrated. It also explained that a slight discomfort may be experienced during take-off and landing due to changes in outside air pressure.

The passenger beside him strummed a guitar, behind him a long blonde-haired girl was necking with her boyfriend. Geoffrey proffered the laminated sheet to the guitarist, but he shook his head. "We're all dying anyway man," he philosophized in a Tipperary accent.

Geoffrey waited for an air hostess and a boiled sweet, but neither were forthcoming. He just stared out the window at the lights and the rain and the darkness. This was a high-winged plane and the left engine was just over his head. He waited for it to stutter into action and start the propeller spinning. He hadn't even left Dublin and already the great expedition to London was a fiasco. What was he to do when he arrived at whatever airport and there was no message from Moocher? What if Moocher had changed his mind at the last minute and wasn't coming at all. Day one, Geoffrey would be phoning Maggie asking if he could sleep on her floor. Little boy lost in London. It was mortifying. Nothing less. He strained against the glass to see Moocher, bags akimbo, dashing across the tarmac. But all he saw was the rain running down the window and all he heard was the guitar strumming and the horse neighing on the other side of the partition. Then the engine overhead coughed into life and he knew there was no going back. It was all or nothing now.

The flight didn't land at Heathrow. Or Gatwick. Or Luton. Or Stansted. It didn't land anywhere near London. At least not initially. Owing to a shifting of freight in flight—i.e., the Aberdeen Angus breaking free of its tether and putting a hind hoof through the partition causing the entire shebang to collapse on Geoffrey and the guitarist—the plane was forced to land at Cardiff. In the terminal, Geoffrey nursed his bloody nose—the navigator had supplied him with a damp cloth—while the other passengers dozed. At 5 a.m. they and the bull re-boarded—the guitarist demanding recompense for his instrument—and almost three hours later descended painfully on the great city of London without an air hostess or a boiled sweet in sight.

The airport the plane had chosen didn't seem to have a name. The only other plane in view was a fellow Aer Turas machine though this one boasted four engines and an absence of barn doors. His ears ringing and nose throbbing, Geoffrey trudged to the tin Quonset hut that acted as the terminal. Sitting on the first bank of seats, sipping a cup of coffee, chewing a lump of fruit cake and reading the *London Times* was Moocher. "Jaysus Doyle, what the hell kept you?"

***

Day One at the factory turned out to be Tuesday and not Monday. This was owing to a confusion in addresses. The corporate headquarters of Lindus Frozen Foods was in Covent Garden, the factory was not. It was in Hammersmith. Consequently the digs at Tufnell Park, which Moocher's mother's sister's friend had booked them into, was over two hours and several different tube lines away. And that did not include an extra hour trapped in an inescapable Escher-like predicament that kept them perpetually circling on the Circle Line unable to figure out how to switch to the Earl's Court line, successfully disembark at Hammersmith and locate the factory.

By the time they did finally reach the factory, it was 3 p.m. and they were tersely instructed to report back the next day 6 a.m. sharp.

Next, they walked to a newsagent's and wrote down the names and phone numbers of available bedsits on the back of Geoffrey's hand. Then followed the hullabaloo of trying to get the English sixpenny bits to drop into the phone when it went bip, bip, bip, bip indicating that the other party had picked up. And then the inevitable responses. 'Taken not 'alf an 'our ago mate.' 'Call back after tea.' 'No students.' 'Not here till after seven.' 'The Missus don't hold with you Paddies.' Till finally…

"Well you'd better get yerselves round here then, 'adn't you." Her name was Izal and she had a bedsit for two people which would be six pounds ten shillings a week, two weeks deposit.

"We can't afford it. She's even dearer than the bat in Tufnell Park. We only get thirteen pounds a week basic. That only leaves us six pounds ten. Less, they'll take tax out of our wage packet."

"We'll get overtime," said Moocher. "What sort of a name is Izal. Sounds like a fortune teller. 'Izal from the mysterious East will reveal your future. Izal knows all. Izal the toilet paper and disinfectant lady will keep you clean and free from all household germs.' What's Izal's address?"

"102 Settrington Road."

They found Settrington Road in a labyrinth of terraced redbrick two-storey streets lodged between Settrington Crescent, Settrington Drive, Settrington Grove and Settrington Way. 102 was the corner house. A yellow tipper lorry, a bulldozer, and a red-capped gnome had the postage-stamp front garden to themselves.

"We won't get our deposits back from Tufnell Park," Geoffrey announced.

Moocher rang the doorbell.

Izal was in her thirties, plump and pleasant. Her son was six, and the owner of the tipper lorry and the bulldozer. The bedsitter was upstairs, had a kitchen, bathroom, and a sitting room with two couches that doubled as beds. The door had its own lock.

"You boys can have it," said Izal after she had established their pedigree and Geoffrey had shown her their letters of employment. "Two weeks in advance."

"Six pounds ten a week?" asked Moocher.

Izal nodded. "English money. You have English money?"

They said that they had but that they'd have to think about it.

"Cheerio," she said at the front door. "And don't take too long."

"Cheerio," mimicked her son, "you're too long."

They were at the beginning of Settrington Road when Moocher suggested they return to Izal. "We could ask her if she would reduce the price."

"I don't think she will."

"We won't know if we don't ask."

They walked back to 102.

"Sorry boys, it just wouldn't be worth it. Six pounds ten is very reasonable for what you're getting."

They thanked her. It was half past four and they had accomplished nothing. This was a real mess. They'd never find another place today. Which meant they couldn't look again till Saturday. Which also meant that for the rest of the week they were stuck out in Tufnell Park, almost two hours from the factory. They would have to get up at four in the morning to be there at six.

For the third time they were back at the beginning of Settrington Road. The bat in Tufnell was charging them five guineas apiece for separate rooms with no locks, and a toilet they had to share with the other lodgers. Meals extra. Now Izal wanted an additional one pound five because they would have a lock and their own toilet. And a kitchen. Geoffrey supposed it was standard, but how could he and Moocher possibly make any money at those prices. The thing was he liked Izal's place. It was a ten minute walk to the factory. No tube fares. And they'd have some privacy. They could even bring girls in on the weekend. Because it was separate. Because it had its own lock. It was a bedsit. It wasn't digs.

"Moocher."

"What?"

"I don't think Izal is charging six ten a week each."

"You know bloody well she is."

"No. It's six ten for the bedsitter."

"What's the difference?"

"Three pounds five shillings. We each pay three pounds five shillings. It's a bedsitter, not digs."

***

"Mum, it's the long boys again."

Izal was not friendly. "Listen ducks, there's no use keeping coming back. I've told you the price. If you bother me any more I'll call the coppers I will."

"Izal," said Geoffrey. "It's six pounds ten a week for the bedsit, right?"

"I've told you once, and I've told you again and that's the end of it."

"It's not six pounds ten for each of us. It's six ten total. That's three pounds five each."

She was eyeing them now as if they were trying to be comical or trying to pull some mathematical wool over her eyes. "I don't care which of you pays me, so long as I get six pounds ten in my hand every Sunday. And the two weeks in advance."

"We'll take it," said Moocher. "We'll give you the money now and go get our kitbags."

"Do your mothers know you're over here?" she asked.

That night just before ten, having successfully returned to Tufnell Park via the Green Line, the Circle Line (only twice) and the Northern Line and unsuccessfully attempted to retrieve their deposit from the bat—"That's why it's called a deposit, so that if you leave me 'igh 'n' dry, I get your money"—and successfully returned to Hammersmith via the Northern, the Circle (once) and the Green lines, they stood triumphant on the doorstep of 102 Settrington Road prepared to live there forever.

Izal invited them in to the parlour for a cuppa. Moocher whispered that she was going to read their leaves.

There was a girl watching telly. She was the boy's sister. There was also a husband. He said he didn't much hold with Paddies, but if it was alright with Izal, then it was alright by 'im. And anyway Paddies were better than Pakkies because they weren't always cooking those bloody curries of theirs, "stink the ruddy 'ouse to 'igh 'eaven."

"Just open the windows and keep your door shut if you boys are cooking cabbage," added Izal, "it'll 'elp keep the 'ouse fresh."

"Do you know," said Geoffrey when they'd finally settled into their respective couches and were chewing on knobs of fruit cake, "do you know what Izal's name really is? It's Hazel. And your ruddy socks, Moocher, are stinking this ruddy 'ouse to 'igh 'eaven."

***

"Paddy, you come with me."

"Geoffrey," Geoffrey politely corrected him.

The foreman looked at him as if he had a smart aleck on his hands. "As I was saying Paddy, you'll be in Braised Beef, Slicers One and Two with Eamonn."

They had separated him from Moocher. He was on his own now. At least Eamonn sounded hopeful. He might even be a student.

They were on a freight lift—the foreman in his white coat and green cap, Geoffrey at sea in giant white overalls, a white paper hat jammed on his head, plus a third man—old and toothless—leaning against an eight foot high trolley packed with empty metal trays. He looked Irish, but he didn't say anything. The foreman crashed the gate shut, punched the button for 4 and the lift lurched upward. Floor One came and went as in a dream, leaving only clouds of hissing steam and the image of a little red electric lorry whizzing by. Floor Two flashed past them with ear-threatening clattering like an army of jackhammers run amok, but all he could see was a large black lady in a hairnet standing waiting. A new rush of noise and a moving rack of frozen pig carcasses swept them through the third floor. Then came the heat.

It was quiet heat. They were in a different world now. The lift shook itself like a tired old horse. The empty trays bounced on the toothless man's trolley. The foreman crashed open the gate. " 'ome sweet 'ome, Paddy."

Through thick black rubber double doors, dodging trolleys of meat. To his left, a giant fridge door being opened, a trolley entering, puffs of frosty smoke escaping into the heat. More rubber doors. More noise. Heavier, damper, thicker heat.

They were standing in a long, long room. Down its length ran a conveyor belt carrying open metal boxes which spat and sizzled atop continuous jets of blue gas flames which flared to yellow with every spit of fat. Parallel to this were a dozen caged slicing machines being opened, shut, started and stopped. Metal trays were slid into metal trolleys and pulled out again. The whole effect was a physical assault of searing heat and splitting noise. The foreman pointed him to the first pair of caged slicers, Slicers One and Two.

A very tall man was working both slicers.

"Eamonn" shouted the foreman, "I've got you your Paddy."

Geoffrey walked over and proffered his hand. Eamonn was not only six foot six tall, he was also very black and came from Jamaica, and Geoffrey didn't think he had an Irish grandmother. He peered at Geoffrey for a moment, not in an intimidating, or for that matter a friendly manner, but neutrally or a shade or two below, as if Geoffrey were yet another small, bothersome detail in his life that needed to be addressed.

Then he bared the biggest, whitest teeth Geoffrey had ever encountered.

" 'ey Paddy, you were supposed to be 'ere yesterday." His accent was a peculiar blend of rich Caribbean and high-pitched Cockney which cleared its own space separate from the din of the machinery and the sizzling.

"It's Geoffrey, Eamonn," said Geoffrey, "and I'm sorry about yesterday."

"You're from Ireland, ain't you, mon?"

"Yes, but just because—"

"Then you're Paddy."

Geoffrey wanted to say that even though Eamonn was from Jamaica, he was called by his own name and not "Jammy" or whatever people from Jamaica were called, but he didn't. Instead his brain remembered to warn him that this might be a good time to hold his tongue. He heeded the warning, and trying to block out the noise and the heat, he concentrated on what Eamonn was showing him.

As the open metal boxes of braised beef reached the end of the conveyor belt, they were stacked in tall carts like the toothless man had in the lift. The beefs were than distributed among the six sets of slicers by a very grumpy Pakistani called Whitter, not Pakki.

Eamonn forked the meat out of the pan and onto the butcher's block. Then he took the carving knife and with it he deftly topped, tailed and trimmed the beef, tossing the nubs into a bin. Next he picked up the beef and locked it up against the slicer blade, slammed the cage door shut and switched on the machine. As the slices dropped down, Eamonn inserted a square of wax paper on every fourth and placed the completed pile on shallow tray which he called a wire. Then he told Geoffrey to do it.

"You do it now, mon."

After four solo runs, Eamonn adjudged Geoffrey sufficiently competent. More beefs arrived and the wires of sliced beef were removed. Now both men worked their individual machines. There was a certain rhythm to the routine—chopping, trimming, lifting, inserting, locking, slamming, switching, waxing, piling and wiring. Then repeat.

Geoffrey smiled to himself. He wondered how Moocher was doing. He wondered what his friends would think. Even his brother would be impressed.

" 'ey mon!"

For a second, Geoffrey thought somebody was shouting for Eamonn, before he realized that it was Eamonn who was calling him.

"I go piss mon. Ten minutes. You work both machines" And without waiting for Geoffrey's reaction, Eamonn was gone.

Panic set in instantly. For that next ten minutes he was like the speeded up comedians in the silent films, like a Harold Lloyd or a

Charlie Chaplin, zipping and whizzing from one machine to the other, skidding and sliding on the beef drippings, over to the butcher's block, across to the slicers, back to the wires—one beef fell off the fork and skeetered across the floor under Eamonn's cage. Then Eamonn's machine wouldn't operate because Geoffrey hadn't locked the meat up against the blade properly.

" 'ey Paddy, where's Eamonn?" It was the foreman in his green cap.

"He's gone for a piss."

"Where? In bloody 'yde Park?"

And then in the fullness of time, Eamonn ambled in, checked the wires, told Paddy that he had 'done good mon' and resumed his post. Pride and a sense of being accepted through initiation swelled in Geoffrey's breast. And now with Eamonn back again, things calmed and relief replaced the panic.

Another twenty minutes passed. Courtesy of the surly Whitter, beefs came, were cut and were taken away. And so the process of producing an end product entitled "4 Slices of Beef in Brown Gravy" to feed the populations of England, Scotland and Wales was well under way.

"Hey mon," Eamonn called over. "you go piss now. Ten minutes."

Geoffrey smiled and shook his head. "Thanks Eamonn, but I don't need to."

This response evidently angered Eamonn. He crossed over from his machine. "You go piss now. Ten minutes."

Not knowing why, Geoffrey found himself sitting in the men's locker room adjacent to the toilets reading the *Daily Sketch* and smoking a Players Gold Leaf. Nine other men were doing much the same. Geoffrey speculated as to what they would say when the foreman walked in. When the ten minutes had passed he took the staircase instead of the lift to the fourth floor, didn't recognize where he was, turned left and ended up in Mousse. A cluster of ladies in white hairnets were at the end of a deafening packaging machine. Each would gather the boxes ten at a time into a row, and then lift the row and stack it on a tray. A black lady beckoned him over, gave him a mousse and told him to 'clear orf' before he got her in trouble. He thanked her and asked her for 4 Slices of Braised Beef in Brown Gravy.

It took two further wrong turns before he accidentally stumbled on the Braised Beef section and reassumed his new role in life. Eamonn tapped his watch. A day late getting to work. Ten minutes late on his piss break. His opinion of Geoffrey's punctuality remained poor.

A half hour passed. The surly Whitter came round every ten minutes, would deposit the hot beefs, then scowl and go away again. An old man arrived with a mop and bucket and washed down the floor. He was the toothless man from the lift. Geoffrey said 'hi' to him, but he didn't respond. By contrast, the tall young Indian who took the full wires away talked all the time. He was studying law at Oxford. Told Geoffrey his father was a prince and had ordered him to stay in England for the summer and work in a factory to learn how the common man lived. He rolled up the arm of his overall to show Geoffrey the cufflink on his shirt. It was gold with a fat ruby setting.

Next to Eamonn and Geoffrey were Slicers Three and Four. They screamed a lot at each other and the taller of the two kept throwing the beef nubs in the other's face. The student prince told Geoffrey that both were from Nigeria, but one was Biafran. With the civil war still going on and the mass starvation of the Biafrans, it seemed madness that the foreman would have these men working side by side.

"He's evil and he's a sadist," explained the prince. "He won't let me wear my rings."

"Paddy!" It was Eamonn.

The prince hastily removed the wires. Geoffrey turned around.

"I go shit mon. Twenty minutes. You work both slicers."

Geoffrey went into his silent comedy routine again. By Eamonn's return, he was dripping with sweat. A klaxon sounded. "Tea break mon," said Eamonn, "fifteen minutes."

John Fallon

Back in the locker room, he unbuttoned his overalls and peeled off his jumper and shirt, then he went in search of the cafeteria and Moocher.

"I'm on the fourth floor doing 4 slices of braised beef in brown gravy. Where are you?"

"On the third," laughed Moocher, "doing 4 Faggots in Brown Gravy."

"That conjures up quite a picture. Do they pair off and actually do it in the gravy after you put them in?"

***

Back at Izal's they flopped into their couches. It was after midnight. The whole day had been one of the most exhausting he could remember. He had been in Braised Beef and Moocher in 4 Faggots till 4:30. Half-hour break, then from five till ten on the Mousse, filling the trolleys with wireloads of strawberry mousse, and hauling them into the refrigerator while Moocher worked on Sealed Sandwiches. From 10 till 11 they had both been on 'Ose Down which meant washing all floors with a vile disinfectant and steam cleaning the machines. The steam cleaning was dangerous to say the least. Holding the hose in one hand, you had to turn the hot tap on full with the other, but keep the nozzle shut till the pressure built up. This caused the heavy hose to leap and buckle like a mythical dragon. Opening the nozzle was not the simple operation Geoffrey had anticipated. More Harold Lloyd antics as Geoffrey attempted to wrestle the beast into submission till the night-shift foreman took the dragon in hand and quelled it by gently depressing a button on the nozzle which permitted the dragon to spew forth its steam, and deflate itself in the process.

"You know Eamonn from Jamaica who I work with?" Geoffrey mumbled through oncoming waves of slumber.

"What about him?"

"I've just realized his name isn't Eamonn."

"So why does everyone call him Eamonn?"

"It's 'Hey Mon' with a cockney accent, ''Ey Mon!'"

"You should introduce him to Izal."

***

The factory had its own circadian rhythm which started to simmer mid-morning and by early afternoon reached boiling point. Then tempers calmed down again and the pressure didn't start to build up till the following day. But as the week progressed, the simmering started earlier each morning and became more insistent. By Friday, everybody seemed on edge. Even before the first tea break they were asking 'Arrold—that was the foreman's name—when the pay packets were coming. Geoffrey already knew that he wasn't getting paid till the following Friday so he wasn't anxious. But the others were. Very. Eamonn was slamming the meat onto the block. Whitter emptied and reloaded their trolley with added venom. Even the beef on the braising belt seemed to sizzle with a viciousness.

After Geoffrey returned from his 'shit-20-minute-mon', he could sense the tension reaching a higher pitch. The Nigerian and the Biafran who had been bickering nonstop like Kilkenny cats now turned their mutual animosity up a notch. The Nigerian began to toss the scrag ends of meat at the Biafran. When it was the Biafran's turn to top, tail and trim his meat, the Nigerian came up behind him, poking him and criticizing his way of doing it. The Biafran turned and swung the cleaver across his antagonist's face, bring it to a halt millimetres from the tip of the man's nose. Undaunted, the Nigerian spat at him. The Biafran said nothing. Then, with the quickest flick, he nicked the Nigerian's nostril. A single drop of blood splashed onto the red tile floor. The Nigerian stood rigid, horrified and incredulous as a prey hypnotized by a snake. A second drop formed and fell.

Suddenly Eamonn was with them, pushing the Biafran aside and ordering him to get on with his work. Then he thrust a wax square at the Nigerian, told him to hold it to his nose and report to the nurse.

'Arrold came round with the pay packets at ten to twelve. The slicers were quickly switched off. A bell sounded at far end of the braising belt to signal no more meat was to be sent through. 'Arrold was fumbling through the packets, trying to get his departments sorted and telling the assembled group to " 'old orf" and " 'ave some patience." Whitter, who had pulled his trolley stacked with the empty trays up to the group, was muttering ferociously. Somebody told him to shut up. Sensing the man's agitation, 'Arrold called his name first, but even this didn't seem to please him. Whitter pushed his way through, snatched the paycheck, stepped back to the trolley and gave it a vicious kick that sent it careening along the passageway.

Somebody yelled out "Paddy" to warn him, but the toothless old man didn't see it until it was too late. He scrambled to move his mop and bucket out of its path, but the trolley knocked the bucket sideways, caught the mop and jammed it against the his chest, forcing him over the conveyor belt. The old man reached back to support himself, pressing his hand against one of the metal boxes as it rode over the flames. Instantly, the hot metal burned him. He screeched, and lunged forward with both hands grabbing at an empty tray in the trolley. But the tray slid out, pushing him further back over the conveyor belt. The last of the metal boxes had passed by, and although he didn't know it, the old man was now desperately reaching into the naked flames. His paper hat dropped off and descended as a small fireball. Flames erupted on the back of his head, dancing around the edge of his bald pate. 'Arrold was shouting to turn off the gas. Geoffrey and the man from Slicer Six got to him first. Slicer Six shoved the protruding tray back into the trolley and leaned over to assist Geoffrey tug the old man out of the flames by the front of his overalls. Varoomph—the flames sank and disappeared back into their black jets. The intense heat dissipated. Geoffrey stretched to get his arm around the man's back and scooped him out. Somebody else smothered the last flames on the back of his neck.

The man wasn't making any noise. His face was rigid, his toothless mouth locked open in a noiseless scream.

They sat him on the floor as the crowd circled. 'Arrold sent the student prince to fetch the nurse. Slicer Six caught Whitter by the arm and started to yell at him. But Whitter shoved him aside and stomped off without a second glance.

Chapter twelve

She was in his bed under the blankets, lying on her side facing him. She had long dark hair. And pretty brown eyes like Eileen. But she wasn't Eileen. He didn't know what her name was, and she didn't have her clothes on, just her underwear. He could see her soft breasts sloping into a starchy patterned white bra which felt prickledy against his bare chest. His hands were tracing her hips now and he could tell she was wearing a girdle or something. And her hand, her hand was reaching between his legs, rummaging discretely in his underpants. "Bingo!" she whispered when she reached his erection. Her fingers outlined it and she smiled to herself. Somebody was banging on the door, but she didn't seem to hear them. This was it. This was really it. She really wanted him, wanted him to do it to her. He had a frenchie in his jeans. A pack of three in fact. He'd have to get out of the bed to get them. And to answer the door. He was a bit concerned about the girdle thingie —should he ask her to take it off or should he do it himself. He could start with the bra. The knocking on the door was louder now, but still she kept her hand there, exploring every inch with her long thin fingers.

"Geoffrey."

It was Izal's voice. The girl became startled. Her hand froze. Why didn't Moocher open the door and find out what she wanted.

"Geoffrey."

The girl withdrew her hand. Geoffrey put his finger to his lips signalling her to be quiet. Izal would go away in a moment. And he was right. The knocking ceased. He could see her beautiful thin shoulder relax. He felt her hand find him again. He slid his beneath her bra strap and gently pulled it off her shoulder and down.

"Geoffrey. Your uncle is here to visit you."

The girl glared at him and abruptly returned the strap to her shoulder. She wasn't holding him anymore. And the knocking didn't stop.

He climbed out of bed and into his jeans. Which uncle? And why would either of them be here to see him? His brain was jumbled like a puzzle, only some of the pieces were false and didn't belong to the picture. He could see Moocher in the other bed. That was a real piece. He felt the money in his left back pocket and the frenchies in his left side pocket. Those were real pieces. Izal and his uncle couldn't be real. He would discard that piece and keep trying to assemble the puzzle. It was daytime.

"Geoffrey!!!" The Izal piece was real.

He turned to check that the girl had pulled the blanket back over her, but she wasn't there. She must run into the kitchen or gone to the toilet. That was smart. He didn't want any trouble with Izal.

When he opened the door, his Uncle Bradleigh was standing in front of him. He too was a reality. But he looked different, askew. He was wearing one of his timeless brown three piece suits alright, but his tie was crooked and there were stains on the suit. Plus he hadn't shaved and his hair was matted. And he had a suitcase. But why was he here? And how did he find him? Something was wrong at home. His parents or his brother were sick. Or had been in some sort of an accident.

"Well luv, is it your uncle? 'e said 'e was."

"Yes Izal, he's my uncle."

"Well then," she concluded, "I'll leave you to get reacquainted."

"What took you so long?" His uncle demanded.

"What took me so long what?"

"To open the door."

"What are you doing here?"

"Ah. You're surprised. Over on business, just for a few days. En route to Heathrow. June, your mother, asked me to stop by, see how you were getting on. Worried about you. Young pup in the big city. Drink, drugs, loose women. Mothers always worry about these things."

It was then Geoffrey noticed the smell of whiskey.

"Well, let's see what sort of an arrangement you have here." He picked up his suitcase. "Move out of the way Geoffrey and let me pass."

Geoffrey turned, but the girl was still in the kitchen.

"And who's that?" he asked indicating the blanketed body of Moocher.

"That's my friend Moocher."

"Well why is he asleep at half-three on a Sunday afternoon? And why aren't you dressed properly?"

"We worked the night shift," Geoffrey lied. "What time is your flight?"

His uncle ignored the question. "Well," he exclaimed summing up the room, "is there somewhere for me to sit down?"

Geoffrey pointed to his couch-bed. He couldn't see the girl's clothes anywhere. She must be changing into them. Although he couldn't remember what she'd been wearing. Except of course her bra, and whatever that was she had on below.

"Aren't you even going to offer me a cup of tea? Or a sandwich for a spot of lunch? I could do with something after the difficulty I had trying to find this place. Why is there a shoe on the dresser?"

"It has my pay packet in it."

"That's what banks are for."

"We don't have time. We work seventeen and a half hours a day. In a factory."

When he'd reached the kitchen, he knew the girl was the only false piece in the puzzle. The only piece he had wanted to be real. He fished a half crown out of the Heinz tin and fed it to the gas meter. He found the flint, lit the front ring, and then the oven. He filled the kettle, got out mugs and milk and sugar. He opened the fridge, took out the milk and 4 Faggots in Gravy (four of the four hundred Moocher had stashed in case of thermo-nuclear war). He tore the top off and flung the foil tray in the oven.

When the tea was brewed he called his uncle, but there was no answer, no sound of movement. If only he dreamt the uncle part and had woken up to find the girl. He called him again and then went in to get him. The man was stretched out on Geoffrey's couch, dead to the world and snortling like a pig.

Back in the kitchen, he poured himself a cup and lit up a Gold Leaf.

"Elsie, I'm stuck with a drunk uncle, the father figure of the White family and respected by all," he announced to Moocher's bare-breasted pin-up girl on the wall. "What on earth am I supposed to do with him now?"

But the eminently suggestive Elsie had no suggestions that would resolve his predicament.

He gazed out the window at the park at the back and idly watched an assortment of men and children kicking a soccer ball about. Izal's husband was there. And the little boy and his sister. Playing in the park—he and Moocher were supposed to be in Hyde Park for the Spencer Davis concert. What time did they come home at anyway? He didn't remember coming home. They had gone to the Duck and Dandelion near Neverin Square. Armstrong and the gang hadn't turned up, so after closing time he and Moocher had toured the Square, scouting out the parties. They'd even brought the gin and vodka bottles filled with water as their admission ticket. The party they'd got into was fairly decent. A lot of women. He had been dancing with one. No, he'd been necking with her, in the corner, even had his hands up her sweater, though she didn't really have much to write home about up top anyway. But she kissed deep and tight. He remembered now. She was studying to be a gym teacher. He liked her. But then he and Moocher were thrown out because of the phony spirits and because they didn't 'ave any 'ashish with them, like Moocher had said they had. Somewhere, at a street stand or a cafe car, they'd eaten chips and huge pickled onions, but that was all he could retrieve of their virginal night on the town.

Moocher ambled in, in his pyjamas, poured himself a cup, removed the faggots from the oven, started in on faggot number one with gusto and began to cast blame on Geoffrey for their missing the concert. "I see I returned home empty-handed as usual. You were obviously more successful, though I should warn you on your change in direction or taste or whatever, when it comes to bed partners. It's a disturbing development and I don't think your parents would approve."

"Har de har-har."

"Well who is the old geezer anyway?"

"He's my uncle Bradleigh, my mother's brother, the one I told you about."

"There are so many. But nice of him to drop by. How long is he planning to sleep with us?"

"Have you any tanners. I've got to go and ring my cousins."

"Try the dresser. And since you're going out, I'll give you a list. I think I'll bake a fruit cake. In honor of your uncle's visit."

At the corner shop, he called Kathleen first. No answer. Then he tried Maggie. No answer either. He rang both numbers again, but no luck. He bought raisins, sultanas, glaced cherries, flour and called a third time. Still nothing. He bought the Sunday Times, The Observer, News of the World and Men Only and then phoned one last time. But they were either out, or in Kathleen's case, still asleep—World War III could begin and end without disrupting Kathleen's sleep. Probably inherited it straight from him, Geoffrey speculated, as he studied his uncle back at the bedsit.

"What time is his flight anyway?" Moocher inquired as he tossed some butter into their largest saucepan which he was using for a cake bowl. "Did you get butter?"

"It wasn't on the list. And I don't know what time his flight is."

"Well you'd better wake him up."

Geoffrey shook the man, shouted, patted his face. No reaction beyond the sonorous snortling.

"He's out cold, he must have been drinking all night," Moocher concluded. "You'll just have to let him sleep it off, flight or no flight. He's not your responsibility anyway."

But Geoffrey wasn't so sure. He could too easily imagine how this incident would be depicted back in Dublin, and what his mother would have to say about it. 'I can't believe that you could be so thoughtless, Geoffrey. What sort of a host lets his guest miss his aeroplane, let alone his own flesh and blood, his uncle. So irresponsible. And after he had gone out of his way to visit you, see how you and your friend were doing. Bradleigh says you didn't even offer him so much as a cup of tea. And the state of your lodgings, he said was appalling—clothes everywhere, dishes not washed and you asleep at four o'clock in the afternoon. That's not how your father and I brought you up. Your first time living by yourself in a strange city and just look how you conduct yourself. Your grandmother says that there were pornographic pictures strewn everywhere, pictures of naked women plastered on the wall. No wonder your uncle was horrified. And to let him miss his plane just tops it all. I really don't understand you Geoffrey. And I surprised at that Moocher too. His mother is so refined.'

"I don't know," said Geoffrey, "I've got to do something."

"Pour some cold water on him, then. That should do it."

The cold water was a bad idea. In addition to landing on his face, it went down his nose and throat causing Uncle Bradleigh to have a fit of coughing and choking. Quickly they sat him up. The coughing subsided into a gurgle and his face turned rapidly from white to red to puce.

"He's having a seizure," Geoffrey yelled.

"No he's not," Moocher thumped his back, "it just went down the wrong way. He has to catch his breath."

Gradually the gurgling eased and the vivid colour faded, but there was no sign of a return to consciousness. "Uncle Bradleigh, you have to wake up, you'll miss your plane."

No reaction. Nothing.

They watched him for a few minutes. Moocher picked up the saucepan and resumed stirring. Then he stopped.

"Moocher, I don't think he's breathing."

"Hold on," said Moocher. He took the saucepan into the kitchen and came back with the shaving mirror.

They held it an inch from Uncle Bradleigh's lips. Although the exhalations were silent, the mirror fogged over, slowly and completely. Then the snortling returned.

"Back to square one," Moocher sighed and stood up. "I'll have to use half butter, half marge, and I've only three eggs."

Geoffrey was revising his uncle's playback of this in Dublin. Now it would catalogue near-death-by-drowning as another highlight of his nephew's hospitality.

"Give me ten minutes to get this in the oven," Moocher called out, "and we'll go for a pint. Locally mind you. And you can try your cousins again."

***

The Goose and Garter was a Whitbread house which meant the bitter was marginally less insipid than in most competitors' establishments. But it was a dull pub, peopled mostly with patrons of their parents' vintage who sipped in virtual silence at their 'alf pints of mild and bitters and nibbled industriously on zesty bacon-flavoured cheese and onion crisps.

"They don't talk much," commented Geoffrey, "beats the hell out of me how they ever got an empire together."

"Go ring your cousins," Moocher advised.

He tried Kathleen first. Someone else answered, but yes, Kathleen was in. Extra tanners in fist, he waited for the roommate to fetch her. He was glad he had got through. Kathleen was eight years older than him, and had her own job as a fashion artist, so she should be able to advise him. She had shown him some of the illustrations she had published in women's magazines. She was definitely more worldly wise than Maggie.

"He was here last night. I was out, thanks be to God. Penelope said he was looking for money, that his wallet had been stolen and could she lend him something to tide him by. But she didn't believe him, and her boyfriend was there, and he sent him packing."

"So what am I to do with him? And what if he asks me for money?"

"You don't give any. Let him sleep it off. It's Monday tomorrow. His bank will be open and he can sort himself out then."

"But I've to be at work at five-thirty. They've changed my shifts. I'm the first stage on the mousse now."

"Well you'll just have to get him up, or go in late."

"What if he wants to stay till the banks open, or if he wants to come back and wait for his flight? I can hardly throw Uncle Bradleigh out on the street. My mother will have a canary. With Granny White it will be even worse. I'll never hear the end of it!"

"Don't be so green, Geoffrey. They both know the old fool's a raving alcoholic. That's why Granny refuses to give him any more money. Thelma's virtually running the business now or what's left of it. Don't you know any of this? You live over there for heaven's sake."

Geoffrey didn't know any of this. Or if he did, he only knew that all was not 'quite right' as his mother put it, and Granny White certainly never said a bad word about her first born and sole heir to her deceased husband's fertilizer fortune. Quite the opposite.

"Kathleen, I can't just throw him out."

"Please deposit another sixpence or your call will be disengaged."

Geoffrey dropped three tanners on the floor, but succeeded in getting one in the slot.

"Listen Geoffrey, just tell him that your landlady doesn't allow guests and that you're already in trouble because he stayed over. And don't lend him more than a half crown for bus fare."

"Are you at home tomorrow?"

"Phone me tomorrow night. You and your friend can come over next weekend, Penelope and I will take you to the club in Richmond where the Stones got started. That's where I was last night with Mike. You'd love it. We'll bring Maggie and Norm. Mike's going on the road next

Wednesday. Five weeks in Spain, Italy and Turkey with the Kinks. And you know what he'll bring back from Turkey, if he doesn't get it in Spain via Morocco."

"Yep, I know."

"Good luck with Uncle Bradleigh. Phone me tomorrow night."

He wasn't sure exactly what he had expected from Kathleen, but somehow he sensed he was really on his own in this.

"But she told you what to do. Makes sense to me," insisted Moocher.

"I know, but it's easier said than done. This man is the patriarch, the whole White family stands to attention at his every word. Only he can enter my granny's house by the front door. Every one else has to come through the garage. Even my mother and Aunt April. My father refuses to set foot in the place. So look at the repercussions if I throw him out on the street. My grandmother still washes his underwear and irons his handker-chiefs for Christ's sake. And the man is four or five years married."

"He also lives next door to your Granny, right?" Moocher countered. "He still hasn't left home."

"But I don't see how I can deny him help if he asks for it."

"Look, give him ten bob, say that's all you have and explain that although you'd like to accommodate him further, he can't stay with us."

Geoffrey didn't bring up the matter of his uncle asking Kathleen's flat mate for cash or about Granny White not lending him any more money or what Kathleen had said about the family business. He didn't tell him because he didn't know what to make of it all. There was a lot more going on with his uncle than he had realized.

Moocher went up to the bar and ordered them each another pint. "Tell you what," he announced on his return, "if we can't get him up and out before we leave in the morning, then I'll stay."

Geoffrey didn't understand. "What does that achieve?"

"You can get the mousse started so there'll be no trouble. There are three of us on the faggots and we interchange jobs all the time."

"Yes?"

"I can explain to your uncle that you had to go to work, that no one could cover for you—which is true. But more importantly, he's not a sacred cow in my family. I can give him ten bob and, without ruffling any family feathers, make it plain that he can't stay at our place."

"Oh."

"Of course you would pay me for the hours or parts thereof I miss, and you would be beholden to me for the rest of your natural days."

This answered everything. It was the perfect solution. They had one more pint and headed back.

"And if he's awake by now, you'll let him stay over, but he has to be out with us in the morning."

"Agreed," said Geoffrey. "And thank you."

"You're welcome."

***

But Uncle Bradleigh was more than awake when they got back. He was gone. So also was the remainder of Geoffrey's pay packet in the shoe on the dresser. No message, no note, no nothing.

"Thirty-eight quid at least. Thirty-eight quid. He stole thirty-eight pounds from me."

"Good thing I keep my boots under the bed," muttered Moocher and went to check the oven to ensure the cake wasn't also among the missing.

Chapter thirteen

On his return to Dublin he felt like the conquering hero. He had fended for himself in a different country, worked unbelievable hours in a real job, earned more money than any of his friends or peers had earned their lifetime, seen the Hollies and the Yardbirds in concert at Hyde Park, smoked 'ashish, partied in the trendiest areas in the western world, seen bits of France and parts of Amsterdam (Spain was too far, he and Moocher had agreed)—and all before his eighteenth birthday.

Somehow, coming home was not as much fun as he'd anticipated. He was all set to tell his friends his tales of derring-do, but now that he was no longer at school there was no pre-assembled audience and no big reunion. He couldn't even cobble together enough friends, school or non-school, to host a halfway decent booze-up. Some, like Dekko were already in full-time jobs, permanent and pensionable. And Trinity College didn't start till October so new blood was not yet forthcoming. His only consolation was a batch of pints with Moocher one night and that was fun—Moocher had opted for Business Studies at UCD so he wouldn't get to see much of him for the next four years—but what he wanted was a new audience, a party. And he wanted to show off.

He had to ring Eileen four times before she called back. They went out to a film, but when he'd put his arm around her, she smiled and informed him of what he had already guessed, namely that she was sort of interested in some other fella, and that anyway her father had made it plain that since this was to be her last year at school, she'd better put her nose to the grindstone and get the honours necessary for college. "Maybe, this time next year, we'll both be at Trinity and you could take me to Bewleys for tea."

One nice surprise though was his brother. In Kevin's ladder of esti-
mation, Geoffrey had clearly risen a rung or two. Kevin seemed one of
the few who really wanted to hear all about London. He was also quite
taken with the 1/33 scale F-102 Convair Delta Dagger that Geoffrey had
brought him.

A week had passed before he saw Uncle Bradleigh. Up until then, there
had been no mention by anybody of the London incident. In fact, it was
dawning on Geoffrey that Bradleigh probably hadn't even told anyone
about dropping in on him at Izal's. He was having a cup of tea and three
oatmeal biscuits with Granny White and was telling her about Kathleen's
sketches and how she was trying to establish a name for herself with the
different magazines, and how difficult it was, and how much competition
she was up against. He had brought a London *Sunday Times* colour sup-
plement and had opened it out on the table to one of Kathleen's illustrations with her name creditted. She seemed pleased and called Jacintha
down to look at it, but Jacintha asked too many questions about London
and was too impressed with his factory anecdotes that Granny White told
her to go back upstairs to take down the curtains in Hugh's room. There
was word that he would be in Amsterdam for a few days and might fly
over. Since the man hadn't set foot in the house in over twenty years,
Geoffrey thought this doubtful. However it gave him an opportunity to
segue to his own very recent Amsterdam experience. He was just starting
to relate (Jacintha who had surprisingly stayed put, was his chief audience
now) some of his less sordid doings in that same city, when they all heard
the key in the front door turning twice. Geoffrey braced himself and
Jacintha scurried upstairs.

Bradleigh walked into the kitchen, seemed startled at the presence of
Geoffrey, kissed his mother on the cheek, commented on the weather—
he had heard on the BBC that it was raining across much of England—
pulled two pairs of underpants and a pair of socks from the rack over
the Aga cooker and told her he'd drop by again in the evening to say
goodnight. Then he started to walk out without so much as a word to

him, not an ah, yes or hello, not even so much as a 'I'll catch up with you later Geoffrey,' or 'why don't you call by next door when you're finished your tea.'

"Uncle Bradleigh." Geoffrey heard his own tone and it was angry.

"What is it?"

"It's thirty-eight pounds, Uncle Bradleigh, that's what it is."

Bradleigh stared at him.

"From London, Uncle Bradleigh."

"Have no idea what you're talking about," he snarled and left.

Geoffrey listened to the key turn in the door twice.

A tornado of fury swirled up inside him. He wanted to chase after him, hit him in the face, turn him upside down by his heels and shake the damn money and the gall out of him. How dare he not even acknowledge him. Never mind acknowledging the fact that he had rudely imposed himself on his nephew in Settrington Road. How dare he outright deny that he knew nothing about the money. Moocher was right—he should have done something at the time. He should have phoned his mother, his grandmother, Thelma, Aunt April—each and every one of them—and cause the biggest family furor in living memory. But Kathleen had said not to. And Maggie had agreed with her. So he had played the game. And anyway, he didn't want to embarrass anyone, cause a stir, be seen to be petty and sordid over what would eventually be construed as merely 'a misunderstanding.' Didn't want to embarrass himself. Didn't have the confidence to assert himself. Just follow their rules.

And yet, somewhere in the back of his mind he had honestly, naively believed that on his return, Bradleigh would pull him aside man to man, excuse the incident with a nudge-nudge, wink-wink, got into a pickle with the gee-gees, and then do the decent thing and square up with him. He had even half-expected to receive a postal order in the mail when he was still in London. Kathleen had said that he'd got off lightly and that at least he knew where matters stood.

Well he knew well enough now where matters stood. And this time he was not going to stand for it.

***

That night his parents were out at some social function and having no girlfriend and no-one free for a jar, he was helping Kevin assemble the retractable undercarriage arrangement of the Dagger jet and playing Jimi Hendrix on the record player while Kevin pointed the plane at the ceiling and sang, ' 'cuse me, but I've kissed the sky.' The phone rang and Kevin, as was his wont, danced into the hall to answer it.

"Uncle Bradleigh's on the line and it's you he's looking for."

At last. Although since supper Geoffrey had been experiencing further misgivings about the exchange in Granny White's kitchen.

Bradleigh's voice was seething. "Don't you ever mention money in front of my mother like that? Do you hear me?"

He heard him. But he didn't have the words to answer him. He wanted to say he was sorry if he had upset him in front of Granny White, but that Bradleigh should have paid him back weeks ago and should have apologized. That's what he wanted to say.

"Do you hear me. Don't you ever bring this matter up again."

Now he found the words. "You owe me thirty-eight pounds and I want it back."

"I owe you nothing. How many times have you stayed at my chalet house in Ardaroe? How many times have you played in my mother's house, been fed, sheltered and minded. How many? You are an ungrateful, money-grubbing, social-climbing, ill-bred, Doyle. No better than your father and grandfather. And you dare to call me to account for a couple of pounds."

"It was thirty-eight pounds," was all Geoffrey could manage to get out. "And you stole it."

"You'd better think twice before you accuse me with your gutter mouth."

Geoffrey hung up.

***

Other things were happening that month. Grandad Doyle had now taken up residence at the Elderly Gentlemen's Asylum in Ranelagh. Apparently there had been some trouble at the overseas student place and the Guards had to be called. When Geoffrey asked his father for specifics about the incident, he said that he had it up to the eyeballs with that man, but gave no further details. When he questioned his mother, she explained that she could not bring herself to discuss it since it involved a woman of ill-repute and therefore did not constitute a suitable topic of conversation between a mother and her teenage son.

College started and he and two others with him in school went to the Freshers' Dance where he met a stunning girl called Monique, who was not from France but from Sutton, and who was not studying at Trinity but her older brother was. She danced with him all evening and led him to the Provost's Garden afterwards. They necked voraciously for ten minutes and he got under her blouse, but no further. Still it was a hopeful start and she was a pretty good kisser. When he asked her would she go out with him the following week, she declined because he wasn't her type.

***

Trembling with nerves, he pressed the bell. Its buzz echoed through his body.

There was no answer. But he knew they were in. Then he heard her footsteps descending the stairs and saw her peer at him through the red-petalled stained glass pane in the front door.

"Hello Geoffrey," she seemed to whisper, ushering him in, "I heard you were back from London. How do you like college?"

"It's alright so far," he followed her into the kitchen. "I came to talk with Uncle Bradleigh."

"I'm making some tea," she said softly, "would you like a cup?"

"No thanks. Where is he?"

"He's upstairs Geoffrey." She was talking very softly, as if there were an infant sleeping in the room. "He can't be disturbed right now."

"I really do need to talk to him Aunt Thelma, could you let him know I'm here."

"Geoffrey, your uncle is asleep."

"It's three-thirty in the afternoon."

"I know that Geoffrey, I know what time it is."

She was definitely not herself. She somehow didn't seem to be in charge of things, and she looked tired. Although, as he studied her arranging the crockery for tea, he saw that it wasn't fatigue exactly, but something else, surrender, no not surrender, resignation.

"Is he drunk?" he asked quietly. "He was drunk when he came to me in London."

At first she said nothing, just turned off the whistling kettle and poured the water into the pot, which she stirred three times to the left, three times to the right. Then she reopened the cupboard and took out a second cup and saucer. "He's beyond drunk, Geoffrey."

He didn't ask her any more questions and he politely accepted the tea she had poured him. He was wondering if 'beyond drunk' meant something similar to the near coma he had been in in Settrington Road and without any big decision on his part he started to tell her about it very matter of factly as if he were describing someone neither of them knew.

He related the whole story except the money bit, and she listened politely, as if she had heard it many times before. When he stopped talking she thanked him for telling her and then he asked her.

"When you said, 'beyond drunk' is that what you meant, what I described?"

"No."

"Well what then?"

She stood up and beckoned him to follow her out into the hallway. They went up the stairs and she slowly opened the bedroom door.

Whatever Geoffrey pictured, and images of murder and suicide were racing through his brain, this was not it.

One curtain was partially drawn, the other hung by a single hoop. A huge mirror on the dressing table was smashed, a dresser was over-turned, clothes and toiletries were on the floor, and a sheet slashed with vomit and blood lay bundled at the end of the bed half covering a man's shoe, his uncle's shoe. Uncle Bradleigh was on his side shivering in the middle of the mattress, fully dressed in his suit, except for his tie and the one shoe. Across his body were three rows of belts knotted with ties and ropes strapped to either side of the bed.

Geoffrey didn't speak, couldn't. He just stared at his uncle as if hyp-notized. Finally he looked away and turned to her.

"He thought there were monsters in the room, Geoffrey."

"We'll have to get a doctor."

"The doctor's been. He gave him an injection."

"Holy God."

"It's delirium tremens, Geoffrey. Dr. McCarville is having St. Patrick's send an ambulance. They're taking him for rehabilitation."

"You mean, 'to dry him out.'"

"Yes Geoffrey. That's what I mean."

Back in the kitchen she poured another cup of tea for each of them.

"Does Granny White know?"

"She doesn't want to know."

"She'll see the ambulance."

"Probably."

"When is it coming?"

"Soon, before teatime."

"Do you want me to tell her, do you want me to phone my mother?"

"I'll explain to your grandmother he was taken in with stomach pains and that Dr. McCarville didn't want her upset. The rest will come out later. You can tell your mother whatever you think is right."

"I'll wait with you till the ambulance arrives."

"No, there's no need. He won't be conscious for hours."
"I'll stay just in case."
"No Geoffrey."

∗∗∗

For the next week Geoffrey heard a lot about 'poor Bradleigh' and his stomach ulcers. The only person not to stick with this approved script was his father who said that drying Bradleigh out would be equivalent to drying out the Liffey on a wet day, to which Geoffrey's mother responded by saying that he should be more compassionate and understanding of the pressure Bradleigh had been forced to deal with after the sudden death of their dear father. And Geoffrey's father retorted that the man had had thirteen years to acclimatize.

But by mid-week Bradleigh's hospitalization had been upstaged by another event which had been waiting in the wings—Geoffrey's mother's poetry fest. The Evening of Poetry & Prose was to be held on the Friday night and necessitated furious preparation, organization and confusion. This literary bash was to generate funds for the restoration and preservation of recently discovered literary manuscripts, or as his father disparagingly referred to them, 'funds for the restoration and preservation of recently discovered dead poets'.

The function was to take place in the Guild Hall for the Society of Indigenous Roomkeepers on Capel Street which had a club license to serve alcohol. Geoffrey's mother was chairwoman of the ad hoc fund raising committee. Famous poets and novelists and short-story writers were to read from their own and others' works, but who-reading-what was the source of fierce juggling and contention. Three hundred and seventeen tickets had been booked and thirty-seven paid for. His mother, who by Thursday, was permanently attached to the telephone, made repeated references to 'that wretched man Kavanagh'.

Geoffrey was to be no idle spectator at these proceedings. He had to assemble eight barboys of which he and Kevin were to be two.

Remuneration would be from tips only. However his friends at school or college, all being flat broke, jumped at the opportunity.

The Guild Hall for the Society of Indigenous Roomkeepers was impressively tall with a vaulted wooden ceiling much like a church's. When Geoffrey, Kevin and their father arrived at seven sharp—the evening was due to begin at a quarter to eight—there were few guests. His mother and presumably fellow committee members had already set up folding tables and covered them with a variety of white and coloured linen tablecloths. On the instructions of a formidable lady in tweed, Geoffrey and Kevin erected the chairs—four per table, and their father distributed candles in saucers—one per table. An ongoing discussion took place across the hall about how dim the lights should be, the whereabouts of the programmes which should have been mimeographed an hour previously, the house of liquid refreshment in which Mr. Kavanagh would be most likely located at this hour, the estimated time of arrival of Eulick O'Connor who was attending a soiree in Ballsbridge, and the identity of the little man who was taking in the money at the door.

It suddenly struck Geoffrey that his mother was nervous and he made a deliberate effort to mentally switch from his naturally cynical and mocking mode to something more constructive. He actually walked up to her when he saw her still fretting over the programmes.

"Mum, even if the programmes don't get here on time, or if they're not right, we can still give them out and you can just announce the changes."

"Geoffrey, it's twenty-five past seven and no one's here—no guests, not even the artists. And where are your friends for the bar?"

"They're coming Mum. Everyone will come."

"That's all your father can say. What if they don't? I'll be the laughing stock of the city."

"Then we'll make the best of it. It will just be a smaller, more intimate gathering—more your style anyway Mum. So long as you cover your expenses, everything else is gravy."

"Hmm," she replied, but she looked at him differently as if she hadn't seen him for some time, or wasn't quite sure who he was, "keep your eye on that little man at the door. I think he belongs to Mrs. Wilkinson, but needless to say she's not here yet. And one doesn't want to offend by asking."

By twenty to eight, people were arriving in talkative clumps, bamboozling the little man at the door who furiously consulted one sheet of paper for unpaid reservations, a second for paid reservations and a third which the unreserved had to sign to get on the mailing list. The tweeded committee lady came to his assistance and admitted two of Geoffrey's barboys whom he was holding ransom for the student discounted rate.

Things speeded up from there on in. Tickets were bartered, tables were filled, chairs rearranged, coats hung, territories mapped out, people noted, spotted, hailed, and confabulated with.

Right from the start, the bar did a brisk business. Lots of Gs & Ts, Vs & Ts, Bs & Gs, sherries and Dubonnets—the barman limited one ice cube per drink. Not so many beers—the Guild only had bottled—a sprinkling of lager & limes, and Britvics in all five flavours. As Kevin pointed out to one of Geoffrey's friends who was complaining about the lack of tips, the root word for tip was 'tipsy' and urged him to serve with all speed.

Armed with banjo, bodhran, fiddle and uilleanns, four of his father's friends who had been press-ganged into service on Thursday night, now assembled on the tiny stage to provide traditional music as a backdrop to the proceedings. His father joined them with a penny whistle for the first number—a mild jig of their own composing.

Geoffrey's mother, looking very much the poet in her long black dress and patterned silk shawl, cleared her throat into the microphone, and made her opening remarks. These included a warm welcome to all, an apology for the lack of programmes and the delay in starting and an invitation to enjoy the fine traditional music of the...the..."

"The Streetboys," his father supplied from behind.

People were still queueing for admission. Geoffrey, his Time Ale tray in hand, was amazed to see two of his lecturers from Trinity in conference with the man at the door. He was even more amazed to see his grandfather arm-in-arm with a woman behind him. She was wearing a red coat, but before Geoffrey could get a decent gander at her, another committee-type lady—this one thin but also betweeded—was thrusting a stack of programs in his face, and a table was calling him over to take their orders.

All in all, about a hundred and twenty paying guests turned up. His mother tested the microphone again. This time she apologized for the confusing announcements in the papers—entries had listed contradictory times and dates—and having dispensed with the formalities, officially opened the evening by reciting two poems, one by Katharine Tynan and one by herself. She bowed her head modestly and Geoffrey led the applause by banging on his tray.

His grandfather was waving him over, Incredibly he was actually seated at the same table as Norris and Browne from Trinity. Mercifully neither of the lecturers recognized Geoffrey when he approached.

"I'll have a small Powers and a bottle of Phoenix if they have it, Smithwicks if they don't," his grandfather informed him.

"Where's your ladyfriend, Grandad?" he inquired, seeing the red coat on the back of the empty chair beside him.

"Powdering her nose. She'll have a gin and tonic. And Mutton…"

"What?"

"Whenever she orders a gin and tonic, you're to make it a double, have you got that?"

"I didn't think this would be your scene, Grandad," he answered, ignoring the instruction.

"It is not my 'scene' as you call it. But it is the kind of 'scene' that appeals to my 'ladyfriend' as you call her. Now have you got that about the double?"

When Geoffrey returned with the whiskey and chaser and the double G & T, the ladyfriend was still absent. A novelist was reading an extract from *Finnegan's Wake*. His grandfather paid him and whispered that the quality of the end-of-evening tip would be dependent on his ability to fetch doubles on the double. Geoffrey turned to take the orders of his lecturers, but out of the corner of his eye, he was aware that the ladyfriend had returned from the ladies' room and was about to take her seat beside his grandfather. He glanced over and saw her pat him lightly on the shoulder. It was Jacintha.

"Dear me, Alfred," she was saying, "fancy my having to go to the loo right in the middle of Mr. Joyce."

***

The Evening of Poetry & Prose dominated the conversation at breakfast the next morning. The event was deemed a roaring success, financially as well as socially. Both the *Press* and the *Independent* had given a write-up, the latter under the banner RARE LITERARY MANUSCRIPTS TO BE SAVED FROM DESTRUCTION, and the *Times* featured a photograph of his mother standing beside 'that wretched man' whom the caption identified as Patrick Kavanagh, one of Ireland's greatest living poets with June Doyle, poet and organizer of the Save the Manuscripts Fund. The phone was still ringing every two minutes, but this morning it was with messages of congratulation and praise.

Only Kevin mentioned Grandfather Doyle and Jacintha. Their mother immediately dismissed as 'too ridiculous to even contemplate'.

"Stop the lights!" said their father and he wasn't joking.

Kevin winked at Geoffrey and closed the subject.

As prearranged, Geoffrey cycled over to Granny White's, ostensibly to work on the garden—the last gardener having given his notice after a disagreement over the pre-winter pruning of the pear trees—but also to check on how she was doing since Bradleigh's convalescence for the ulcers. As they drank a cup of tea, he couldn't decide if he was noticing a change in her because he had anticipated one, or whether in fact there was any change at all, but she seemed to him to be not quite herself, a little tired, as if some of the stuffing had been pulled out of her. He was also surprised to find that he was being bolder and more assertive.

"Any news on Uncle Bradleigh?" he asked straight out, while staring at the omnipresent socks and underpants dangling over the Aga.

She jolted in her chair, then considered her response. "His doctor says it will take time."

"Can you go in and see him?"

"Next week. I will see him next week."

"Do you want Mum to bring you?"

"There's no call for your mother to be involved. She…" she indicated next door by inclining her head towards Bradleigh's house, "will take me."

"Who's running the business while Uncle Bradleigh is convalescing?"

"Geoffrey, I will not tolerate an interrogation. Your impudence is unbecoming. None of these matters concern you or are any of your business. What should concern you, and for which I have contracted to pay you ten shillings no less, is the left border which has not been weeded in over three months. You will start at the patio and take care not to uproot the spring bulbs."

Having gathered the trowel, fork, mat, wheelbarrow and transistor, Geoffrey set to work. As had been his habit since adolescence, when weeding on that side of the garden where, for the first part he was shielded from the kitchen window, he began tossing every second clump of weeds over the high wall and into Bradleigh's border. He had already done it several times; 'one for the barrow and one for Uncle Bradleigh' when it dawned on him that next week he would be eighteen years old, and that clandestinely lobbing weeds into his uncle's bed was a feeble attempt at revenge or gesture of frustration or rebellion or whatever the hell it was supposed to be. Puerile—that was the word for it.

He tip-toed to the wall and jumped up to see if Thelma was in the garden—that would have been even more humiliating—but there was no sign of her, except a long cotton flowery dress hanging on a hanger from the clothesline, blowing backwards and forwards in the late autumn breeze. He decided he would call in on her after he was done with his grandmother.

It was a pleasant morning with still a lingering of summer warmth in the wind. He thought about his eighteenth birthday and whom he'd invite and about how he didn't have a girlfriend of his own to ask, and about how his life was not evolving, and the motor bike he wanted to buy, and how he would never get his thirty-eight pounds back. He was working faster. Bindweed, followed chickweed, grasses and dandelions into the barrow. He stood up and used the foot fork to uproot a patch of stubborn dockweed when he heard her rapping against the glass. He hadn't realized that he had come into her view already.

"No fork. You'll impale the crocuses."

He gave her the thumbs up sign and put the fork to the side.

Almost eighteen years of age and here he was weeding his grand-mother's garden like he was still a boy scout. Grandad Doyle had been fighting in the trenches in Ypres when he was eighteen. And Geoffrey considered himself a big shot because he had worked in a factory. He was pathetic.

***

At one o'clock his grandmother rapped on the window again and beckoned him in for lunch of mashed potatoes and mince and cabbage, during which they listened to the BBC Home Service on the wireless, learned about the Queen and Princess Margaret, what was expected to be said and not said during the Prime Minister's question time in the House of Commons, and, of course, got the weather for England, Scotland and Wales which, as always, was highly useful. Then he had custard with some of her bottled pears and went out for another two hours and finished the border all the way to the vegetables. When he'd put everything away, they shared a pot of tea and she cut him two slices of fruit cake. The brown envelope containing the ten shilling note was on the table and he popped it in his pocket without opening it. Ten bob wasn't bad, considering.

"Thanks," he said.

"Mind how you spend it."

They talked about college and the Evening of Poetry & Prose—Jacintha had filled her in on most of the details and had already cut the articles and photo from the papers. Jacintha, she informed him, was in town today. No mention was made of his grandfather and Geoffrey guessed that Jacintha had not made any.

For some reason he felt furtive about going next door. He didn't even know if Thelma was in or not. He didn't even know exactly why he was going to visit her, but he was glad of the high bushes and walls which prevented Granny White from witnessing his treachery.

His aunt appeared neither pleased nor displeased to find him on her doorstep, bicycle in hand. He stood there, awkwardly silent. Then she said hello Geoffrey and he said hello Aunt Thelma and she asked if he'd been at his grandmother's and he replied that he had and that he thought he'd just call by, "after you know...last weekend."

She said he should come in, she had just put the kettle on and he propped his bike against the porch and followed her through to the kitchen.

He inquired after his uncle and she replied that his treatment would take a long time, possibly as long as two months and that Dr. McCarville had said she could visit him on Tuesday and that it would be very hard for his grandmother to come to terms with it.

Then he asked about the business and she explained how the manager was a good man and how in recent months she had been becoming more involved and, how, till his uncle's return, she would be going into the office in the city, not to the factory in Meath, at least once or twice a week.

Then he sat down at the table and asked her what he really wanted to know. "What about you Thelma?" He hadn't intended to leave out the 'aunt' prefix, but he did and he liked the way he sounded.

She was pouring the kettle. "What about me, Geoffrey?"

"What are you going to do when he comes back?"

"What are you asking me?"

"Are you going to stay with him?"

"Are you being impertinent, Geoffrey?"

"He's a drunk and he beats you." He was being impertinent. He hardly knew himself why he was talking to her like this. He didn't even recognize his own voice. He didn't know what he was doing or why. But he did know that he had to come out in the open and say these things.

She started to get angry and to question how he dared come into her house and talk to her in this way. But he didn't answer her. Then she protested and told him that what he had been saying was absolute nonsense.

"Why would that even enter your mind? That he beats me."

He wasn't stopping now. "I saw the marks Thelma. I saw them on Easter Sunday."

She put the lid on the pot and sat down, automatically adjusting the hem of her navy blue dress so that it covered her knees. "That only happened once Geoffrey," she spoke the words softly, matter of factly, "I had poured his whiskey down the sink. A whole bottle. Right in front of him."

Geoffrey nodded that he believed her.

She got up again and set the table with the same cups and saucers as his last visit. She took a packet of Bourbon Creams out from the cupboard and arranged them in a tiny circle on a matching plate.

"Don't stay with him Thelma," he heard himself saying aloud.

Now he had gone too far. Her face was taut and she gritted her teeth to control her rage. Then she let fly.

"Don't you presume to tell me what to do with my life. Don't presume to know what is in my head or my heart. You have no idea what you're talking about. None of you do. All too busy dancing attendance on him. Bradleigh the firstborn. Son and heir. But where is my son and my heir? Where is my daughter so fair? Where are my children? There aren't any, are there? Look around you Geoffrey, do you see any upturned toys or tiny shoes or baby clothes strewn higgledy-piggledy around my home? Do you see a pretty girl running up to me in her Brownie uniform, proudly showing me how she has learnt to weave, or a cheeky-faced boy climbing trees, a strong older sister cycling her bicycle and smiling, laughing. You don't see any of them, do you Geoffrey? You don't now and you never will. And do you want to know why? You who wants to know everything. You who demands answers. I'll tell you. That's what I'll do, I'll tell you why. Because your Uncle Bradleigh's manhood doesn't function, Geoffrey. It doesn't do what it is supposed to do with a woman. And that's not because of the drinking. It never did function. Not even on our wedding night. Not even then."

Calmer now, she stood up and re-stirred the pot, three times clockwise and three times counterclockwise. She brought the pot to the table and sat down again.

"Geoffrey, I'm a thirty-five year old woman, married five years to a man who's almost fifty, a man who courted me for another five years. And despite all of that I'm still a virgin. I am so shamed I could never leave him. And who would ever want me now? I might as well have been a spinster."

"I want you Thelma. And my manhood functions." It came without warning. He didn't know how the thought even got into his head, let alone out of his mouth.

"What did you just say to me?"

He had started now. There was no point in holding back. "That I want you, crave for you. That even though I hardly know you, I know how attractive you are. That you are in my head all the time since Easter. That I'm still a virgin too."

She was staring at him in shock, in horror, in amazement. She seemed unsure of what to do or say. He was afraid she would tell him to leave. Then, in a quiet, matter-of-fact voice, she asked him what precisely he meant by saying that she was in his head.

He might as well be hung for a sheep as a lamb, so he told her everything, things he didn't know himself. And all the time he looked directly at her as he told her. "Kissing your face. I think about kissing you, your lips, about my tongue discovering your mouth, your neck, your shoulders. About watching you undress in front of me, taking off your sensible shoes and your sensible dress, unhooking your brassiere, showing me your naked breasts…

She covered her face with her hands. She wanted him to stop, but he didn't. He couldn't. It was as if his mouth had been locked open and an unseen, unknown force were pulling the words out in a never-ending torrent.

"…watching you lower your panties down over your garter belt, then lifting your leg to step out of them and looking up to see me naked with my penis jutting out in front of me, leading me to the fulfillment of its desire—the wet, warm place between your thighs—"

"Stop it Geoffrey, stop it now, right now." She said it calmly, but firmly and his torrent of obscenity ceased.

Her face was red, but not with rage. And not with lust. He had humiliated her. He had humiliated himself.

"I want you to leave, Geoffrey. I want you to leave now. I think we've both disclosed far more than we intended today."

Chapter fourteen

It had been a five hour odyssey, Moocher on his newly-acquired three-year old Heinkel scooter, Geoffrey on his four-year Suzuki 80. Together they had crossed the Curragh, ascended the Curlews, driven through sun, wind and rain, wet and cold and finally arrived at Moocher's aunt's country cottage outside the village of Lullaghan on the northern tip of the Sligo coastline.

The cottage was in total darkness and it had no electricity. Moocher ran down to the neighbours to let them know they were staying there and came back three-quarters of an hour later with a pot of tea and a plateful of ham and cheese sandwiches. In the meantime Geoffrey had, after four attempts, successfully lit the Tilly lamp, figured out how to connect a new Ergas tank to the cooker, had heated up two packets of Maggi beef barley soup and was now on his knees in the front room, patiently nurturing some miserable flames up through the damp wood and turf.

They decided to eat in the kitchen, and keeping the cooker and their coats on for warmth, they dined heartily on the sandwiches, soup and tea.

After washing the dishes, (the cottage did have running water) they returned to the front room. The fire had taken beautifully and filled the enormous fireplace, its flames licking up at the overhanging cooking hooks and bathing the room, its two half-stuffed armchairs covered in a variety of rugs, the plain oak settle under the front window and the narrow bed on the side wall, bathing everything in a wombwarm red glow scented with the sweet smell of peat.

"Can I take this bed?" Geoffrey asked, dumping his knapsack on it anyway.

"Sure, for tonight," Moocher answered and stepped into the tiny bedroom off the opposite side where he flung himself on a wrought iron bed which squeaked and pleaded to be spared. Or at least oiled.

"Don't lie down Moocher, or you won't wake up till tomorrow. C'mon it's only eight o'clock." He had hardly seen him since London. Moocher hadn't even been able to make his party.

They took off their coats and hung them up in the tiny porch, being careful not to upset a variety of potted plants which were lined up along its narrow windowsills. The rain danced on the panes and Moocher pointed to where the ocean was, and the path through the fields down to the rocks, and the grassy headland which was the perfect spot for a picnic with the girl of your choice. And even though it was as black and thick as pitch, Geoffrey beheld every feature and cherished it.

They opened their knapsacks, extracted and lined up the goodies. Between them they had eight pint bottles of stout and three open packets of cigarettes—a total of seven Major, four Carrols No 1 and six Players Navy Cut. Moocher fetched two glasses from the kitchen, a bottle opener and an oil lamp, Geoffrey lugged a night's supply of turf from round the back which he carefully stacked at the foot of the fire to dry out.

Each then settled into an armchair, poured their first stout, lit a cigarette, stretched their legs into the fireplace, leaned back and sighed.

"Did you ever get that money back from your uncle?"

"Well yes, sort of."

"There's 'no sort of' with 'borrowed cash'. Did he pay you back or not?"

"My grandmother did. She slipped a cheque in with a ten bob note she was paying me for gardening."

"So some honor remains within the White clan. Good. Still don't understand why your cousin doesn't find me as adorable as I do her. And that Norm bloke. What a waster! He's using her, you see that yourself, don't you?"

"How's Business Studies?" Geoffrey changed the subject.

"Not good."

"How so?"

"Failed my first term essay. Missed half the lectures. Don't ask. I don't want to talk about it. The cheque didn't bounce, did it?"

"Don't want to talk about it." Nor did he. Didn't talk or think about why he hadn't cashed the cheque, and if by not cashing it, he had somehow absolved himself for his indecent proposal to his uncle's wife, his grandmother's daughter-in-law, his aunt by marriage. Didn't speculate if his uncle was a drunk because he couldn't perform or because, as Maggie had diagnosed at Easter, he had never weaned himself or been weaned from his mother's breast. Didn't question if the entire White family fortitude was, as Maggie had also suggested, nothing more than a papier-mache facade collapsing from within. Didn't worry whether Thelma would be sucked into the implosion and swallowed up by the void. Instead he slammed the door on the cell section of his brain marked 'The White Family', tossed the key over his shoulder, put another sod of turf on the fire and poured out the remainder of his first stout.

They talked. They talked of London, the factory, the parties, the pot, the concerts, the women they could, should and almost did make love to. They talked of their futures, their ambitions to be independent, their need to avoid corporate ruts and civil service stagnancy. They talked through eight large stouts and seventeen cigarettes. They talked till the turf was gone and till all that Geoffrey could see were the lingering embers of a glorious fire and the final fleeting moments of one of the most satisfying evenings he was ever to experience.

***

Lullaghan was small even by west of Ireland village standards. It didn't so much as constitute a crossroads, but a fork in a side road which itself was a branch off the main Sligo-Donegal thoroughfare. At the apex of the fork was a triangular pub, aptly named The Triangle, and behind that a second pub called The Dew and which doubled as a grocer's. Proceed on the branch road and you were led eventually back to rejoin the main road in the seaside town of Bundoran. But take the fork and it took you up a hill past the miniature post-office and a shop, past six ascending whitewashed terraced cottages, trimmed in brown, green purple, red, blue and purple respectively, each sporting a tiny front garden with a dog, cat, hen or child soaking up the sunshine for all its worth.

Continue, and the hill dropped as steeply as it had risen, teasing you with dramatic glimpses of the Atlantic, not five hundred yards away, crashing against the rocks. And when you were levelled out, you were taken past the rectangular whitestone church standing alone in a field sprinkled with sheep, holding high its cross in Virgin Mary blue. Walk on and the road undulated before you, meandering alongside the coastline, never more than a field or an occasional farmhouse separating it from the ocean.

Another mile, during which you encountered sporadic traffic—an Austin Cambridge with a bale of hay in the boot, a red tractor with two red-faced boys perched on the rear mudguards, a farmer and two heifers, a girl with a donkey and cart—and you were finally back at Moocher's aunt's cottage.

It stood solidly at a high point on the inland side of the road, not quite brave enough to tempt the ocean. Diagonally opposite was the grass-muddied, tractor and bovine-rutted path to the cove. You couldn't see the beach or the rocks where he and Moocher had collected the driftwood, but you saw the water and the grassy hump of a headland that seemed to be making a fist at the distant mountains of Donegal some twenty miles across the bay.

Turn away from the sea, turn inland, and beyond the cottage you beheld Ben Weskin, twisted into a peak like the Matterhorn, the vanguard for Ben Bulben which stretched its long, cloud-dappled, sheep-dotted back across the horizon from west to north east.

This was Lullaghan on a sunny October day, and this was Geoffrey walking back from the Dew bearing oilcloth bags packed with groceries, cursing and blessing the fact that he had not made the trip on the Suzuki. They had one day left here and they had only started the kitchen ceiling.

Having taken out eight sausages, eight rashers and four brown eggs, Geoffrey wrapped the remainders in cheesecloth and placed them in the meat safe circa Moocher's aunt's childhood. Then he washed out two frying pans, found the lard, threw the neighbour's hen out of the kitchen and started the breakfast, yelling at Moocher on the stepladder to lay off showering the table with paint chips.

By four o'clock that afternoon, the ceiling had had two coats and the kitchen walls were prepared. Moocher tossed a chicken and eleven spuds in a huge black pot, put the lid on and hung it over the fire in the front room. Three hours later, the kitchen was finished, their deal with Moocher's aunt honoured, and the dinner roasted to perfection.

By nine o'clock they had taken their positions on two barstools in The Triangle. Waiting for their pints to be fully pulled, Moocher chatted with a pair of farmers, one of whom knew his aunt personally, and who promptly told the barman who the aunt was, but the barman claimed he had been made privy to that information the morning after they had arrived when he had met the neighbour by the bog over Callaghan's way. And furthermore, didn't they all know it since the aunt had sent a message by phone to the post-office so that the neighbour wouldn't be alarmed by the sight of them, long hair and all. Meanwhile Geoffrey contemplated the amazing range of merchandise on offer behind the bar, and filled in five Mr. Perri Potato Crisps Mystery contest forms to win a mystery house somewhere in Ireland, noting with satisfaction that he was qualified for entry, being the requisite age of eighteen years or above. In the spirit of generosity, he completed another two forms using Moocher as his first name, since Moocher had another month to wait before he could qualify and so would have missed the deadline.

"Back to the big smoke tomorrow, eh lads!" announced the barman. They nodded.

"It might be tricky. There's something of a storm blowing in from Donegal."

They drank quietly. It had been a great four days. They had amassed tons of driftwood for the fire, walked miles over beaches and rocks, cut barrows of turf from the bog, climbed Ben Weskin in the rain, painted the kitchen, slept the sleep of the righteous, eaten as they needed, and when the day was done, they had quaffed the nectar of the burned hops.

As they walked the winding, hilly road in murky darkness back to the cottage for the last time, and as the wind howled from the black-inked ocean across the unseeable fields and on towards the distant blackness where the mountains slept in the blanket of night, God slowly withdrew the unseen curtain and revealed his treasure of a trillion diamonds and their diamond dust cast on his ebony sky.

**

He was adapting to college life well enough, but sensed impending disaster academically. French in particular, was slipping, at first slowly, and more recently with alarming momentum, through his fingers. Racine's *Phaedra* and Moliere seemed to be out to get him. He could barely follow them in English let alone in their native tongue. Philosophy and English were just so-so. But with any of these disciplines, he found himself constantly misled. He'd think he'd be getting the gist of things, only to discover he was on the wrong track entirely. The year ended with him scraping through his first term.

On the social front, things were faring better. He had grown to almost six foot, his hair was down to his shoulders, he had purchased an army greatcoat, and was sort of seeing an English girl, who advocated political, but sadly not sexual, anarchy. He had also made a few new friends, but one in particular was gaining his ear. This was a long, loafy bloke called Flanagan, who, on initial meeting struck him as being the most laid back and carefree person imaginable. He might attend lectures, he might not. And he had no qualms about sleeping through them if he did. At the end of November, in Trinity's front square right after a French seminar, Flanagan casually asked him where one might consult literary criticism on Moliere.

"You mean the '37 Reading Room?"

"I do?" he seemed surprised. "And where might that be, Sir Geoffrey?"

Almost since they had first met, Flanagan had called him 'Sir Geoffrey', though Geoffrey had no idea why.

Geoffrey pointed to the prominent rotunda on their right.

"That's a library?"

"It's the Arts library. Our library."

"I often wondered what it was…I suppose you've been going there all this time."

"Virtually every day. And not just me either."

"You mean the others doing Arts use it as well, don't you?" He smiled at his own innocence.

"Flanagan, you've been attending Trinity since October. You actually have rooms here. You live here, for Christ's sake. Are you on something or what?"

"Attending Trinity since October…" he mused, looking up at the sky as if for confirmation, "but since October of last year, Sir Geoffrey, not of this year."

"You're repeating first year?"

"Owing to a misunderstanding with a certain professor, yes. And to address the latter inquiry, while I may dabble occasionally, I am not 'on something' as you quaintly phrase it. It is women, Sir Geoffrey, the pursuit and ravishment thereof, that is my downfall. Women and agriculture."

Geoffrey knew about the agriculture part and that Flanagan's father wouldn't spring for the fees to send him to Gurteen to study animal husbandry. He wanted Flanagan to go into law, ultimately specializing in corporate law like himself. But Flanagan hadn't qualified for Law school (Geoffrey suspected deliberately). The women thing, however, was a shock. If anything, with his tall skinny frame, pasty white face, blotchy freckles, sleepy eyes and Einstein coiffure, Flanagan came across as being vaguely philosophical, eccentric and sexless like some imitation of a P.G. Wodehouse character, or at best, a philatelist with low hormonal activity. Geoffrey now had to consider if what he beheld were, in fact, the symptoms of debauchery in an advanced stage.

On the home front, things were happening too. Thanks be to God, his path and his Aunt Thelma's had not crossed since the proposition. Not that he had stopped thinking about her or what he had said to her. Uncle Bradleigh was back in the picture with a good prognosis on his ulcers which were sometimes interchanged with his liver. Geoffrey hadn't seen him either and was content to keep it that way. He had cashed his grandmother's cheque to fund a reconditioned carburettor for the Suzuki.

The big story though, was with his grandfather, who having been expelled from the Gentleman's Asylum for conduct unbecoming, was now living at home with Kevin, himself and his parents despite a lot of opposition from his mother. His father also made it plain that he was there on sufferance. It was not a happy household and Geoffrey contrived to be out of it for as much of the day as possible. To cap it all, Kevin's room was given over to the grandfather, and Geoffrey was forced into sharing with him.

"What's conduct unbecoming?" Kevin asked him at one in the morning."

Geoffrey didn't know, hadn't been told, nor did he want to be. "Go to sleep, will you!"

"I bet it's something to do with a woman," Kevin revelled, "probably doing the dirty with Jacintha in the games room on the billiard table."

It had always been Geoffrey's rule not to talk of anything related to women or sex with his incorrigible brother and not to rise to any of his endless taunts and questions as to how experienced or inexperienced

Kevin judged him to be in such matters, so as his policy dictated, Geoffrey deflected the issue.

"It's nothing to do with Jacintha, Kevin. Get that into your thick head. He probably instigated a riot in the dining room over the stale rolls and the rice pudding he was forever complaining about."

"You're just jealous because you can't get a mot and he can." The sheen had obviously dulled on Geoffrey's post-London lustre.

Four days later, their grandfather disappeared. Left the house sometime before lunch and never returned. It was Christmas week and there were no big horse meetings on, and the usual haunts drew a blank. By the third day Geoffrey's mother was starting to get frantic. Geoffrey was suspicious that it was not so much concern for the man's welfare that rattled her, but rather what people would say.

"He's out there somewhere telling Heaven-only-knows-who that his daughter-in-law evicted him on Christmas week," she said to his father after the Jack Benny Show. "The man's a menace." She switched off the telly. "You'll have to do something Matt."

"Phone that crazy dingbat who lives with your mother."

"Don't be ridiculous. What on earth would she know?"

But she phoned anyway. "Jacintha is down in Cork at her sister's for the Christmas," she reported and then realized that this was odd because Jacintha had never taken Christmas off before. If anything she went down after New Year's. And for two weeks in the summer.

"Told you so," Kevin stuck his tongue out at Geoffrey.

"You keep your tongue in your head and mind your own business," said their father.

The next day, a postcard arrived featuring a colour photograph of the harbor at Youghal, Co. Cork. The message read: 'Spending Christmas here. See you in the New Year.' It was signed 'Doyle.'

"'Doyle!'" his mother exploded. "'Doyle!' Not Dad, or Mr. D. or even Grandad, but 'Doyle'" She read it aloud again. "'See you in the New Year…Doyle.' This is beyond the Pale. Had us all worried to death. It's a good thing we didn't ring the Guards. I'm going to ask Bradleigh if he has any clout with the board at the Asylum."

"I've already talked to McFadden," said his father, "this afternoon. There's a chance they might let him back on a provisional basis. The Board is meeting the second week in January. He's promised he'll bring up the matter then."

Christmas came. Geoffrey had bought his mother a pewter brooch of a quill pen, his father sheet music from Walton's on Clare Street and his brother the *Observer's Book Of Aircraft 1969 Edition*. It was three o'clock and they were finishing Christmas dinner when the phone rang. Kevin answered.

"It's Uncle Bradleigh."

"We're not going!" said his father.

His mother glared at them and got up to take the call.

When she returned, she said they were. They were going over to his house at seven. They were all going and there would be no arguments. Her brother who had been so ill, was now much, much better, and the least they could do is provide moral support. It would only be for an hour and it wouldn't kill them. Furthermore they should all bear in mind just how much she had gone through to accommodate the Doyle side of the family in recent weeks.

Over the next couple of hours Geoffrey rehearsed it in his head a thousand times and a thousand different ways. What he would say to her, what his tone and manner should be. Should he speak at all? What if she didn't speak to him, what if she ignored him? Or if she was rude to him? His mind went into automatic mode and painted alternative scenarios one on top of the other. What if she drew his parents aside to talk to them in confidence; what if she refused to let him into the house—she may not even be aware that Bradleigh had rung. What if she made remarks during the conversation which were directed at him and none too veiled in their distaste for him, and when they came home his parents would ask, 'Did something happen between you and your Aunt

Thelma. Her comments seemed very pointed. All about 'teenage boys today' and 'boys growing up'. You didn't clonk her on the head when you were weeding, did you?'"

"Happy Christmas, Geoffrey," was what she said. She was wearing a charcoal gray cableknit jumper with a Santa Claus brooch and a red skirt. Her hair was longer, but still chopped above the shoulder. And she looked him straight in the eye as if nothing untoward had ever passed between them.

There were a lot of people in the living room. Her older sister and brother-in-law and their two boys. Granny White. The manager from the business and his mother. A friend who had been Thelma's bridesmaid. Thelma's mother. Plus the biggest Christmas tree in Dublin barring the Lord Mayor's.

Uncle Bradleigh was effusive. He kissed and hugged his sister, pumped Geoffrey, Kevin and their father's hands like all three of them were his long, lost friends. Geoffrey wanted to scream 'No Uncle Bradleigh, we're the Doyles, not worth wasting your spit on!' and 'How's your little pee-pee keeping, you pompous bag of shite?' Then his Uncle would come right back at him by saying 'Listen to the guttersnipe—the guttersnipe nephew with his guttersnipe mind, who weaseled his way into my house when I was ill in hospital so that he could make dirty, sordid suggestions to my wife.'

But what Geoffrey said was "Happy Christmas" and all his uncle said was "By God Geoffrey, you've grown into quite the man." Then he directed him and his father into the kitchen to meet a bunch of his old pals, whom he knew they probably remembered from the tennis club.

More hearty introductions followed and Geoffrey heard his father mumble that the EST had surely worked wonders. Then came the what-will-you-haves and his father said that he wouldn't say no to an ale, and Geoffrey replied that he'd have one as well, to which his uncle gave an exaggerated nod and a wink and Geoffrey pointed out that he was now eighteen and in college, and his uncle said "By God!" again.

"What's EST Dad?" Geoffrey whispered.

As an answer, his father turned to face him, placed his index fingers at either side of his temple and went "Bzzzz!"

"Wow."

"More pow than wow, Mutton."

Uncle Bradleigh, still jovial, poured them each a bottle of Celebration, the new ale which was being advertised on the telly a lot. He rapped the kitchen table with a spoon and announced that he had an announcement to make.

"As you all know, I've been in the hospital with liver problems. But I'm back now and in one piece and thank you all for your good wishes. You'll notice that I have a beer glass in my hand and you may think to yourselves 'This is not the Bradleigh we know, where's his Black Bush? Sad to relate, the docs have ordered me off the whiskey for good. Not even a wee one to toast the day that's in it. No spirits of any calibre for me—the docs say they aggravate the liver condition. So it is without my favourite tipple that I am obliged to toast you and wish you all a happy Christmas and a prosperous New Year."

Geoffrey was stunned, flabbergasted. He had never ever seen his uncle so gregarious, so full of life. It was impossible to believe that this was the same man he had seen tied down to his bed, the same man whose mouth he and Moocher had held a mirror to not six months previously.

As they were leaving, Geoffrey wished his Aunt Thelma a happy Christmas once more and she shook his hand. "You must call me Thelma from now on Geoffrey. I think you've outgrown the 'Aunt' part."

That night he lay in bed listening to his brother gurgling in his sleep—their father had stated that they weren't going to shift the damn beds only to have to shift them back again next week— and wondering what Thelma was doing now, and if, with the arrival of the new, improved Uncle Bradleigh, she was still a virgin.

Chapter fifteen

Nine o'clock at night and he was waiting in the rain for a bus. The Suzuki was out of operation—it needed a new gasket. He had left it off at nine o'clock that morning in Harry Balkley's shop on Ship Street, and was informed that it would be at least three and possibly five days before he saw it again. Not half soon enough, because the first thing he was going to do, when he got it back, was sell the damn thing. If there was anybody fool enough to buy it. At least the bicycle was reliable. What he wanted was a car, but it would be another year and another summer in London, or maybe America, before he'd have enough money or even close. And with the current state of his love life, a car would be wasted on him now anyway. Valentine's Day had been and gone. And so too had the English anarchist. Gone off to some bloke on the College newspaper—someone who was more 'politically alive' as she described him.

The antithesis to Geoffrey certainly. Politically dead, intellectually dead, sexually dead. What was he doing taking Arts anyway? It wouldn't get him a job. Unless he became a teacher, and then he'd have to go on and do an extra year to get the education diploma. And he didn't even want to be a teacher. Not that he had an iota of a clue as to what the hell he wanted to be. Or do. This Arts thing was merely a way of postponing the inevitable evil day of decision. And he knew his father wasn't go to pay for him to repeat the year if he failed. And his mother would say 'I'll give Bradleigh a call and see if he can fit you in somewhere in the firm. Give you a start.' A fate worse than waiting for the number fourteen bus in the dark and the rain. With no umbrella. And a greatcoat that absorbed water like a sponge.

He had time, but not much. If he really wanted to be a writer like he sometimes claimed, then he'd better get writing. Submitting two short poems to college magazines, being rejected and taking offense, did not constitute being a writer.

Fifty yards up, a car had pulled out of the traffic and seemed to be beeping at him. It was a red Mini, a new one. He didn't recognize it, but since he was the only person left in the queue, he ran up to it. The passenger door opened and his Aunt Thelma was leaning across from the driver's seat.

"Geoffrey, may I offer you a lift?"

He was so surprised that it was her—various friends and neighbours and the identity of the cars they drove had been scrolling through his brain—that he didn't answer.

"Geoffrey?"

He climbed in.

"I thought it was you," she said, "when I was stopped back there at the light. I recognized the coat. But what with the rain and the dark, I wasn't sure. Not till I drove past."

She reminded him to fasten his seat belt, and when he'd done so, she checked her rearview mirror, signalled and pulled back into the traffic again. As they drove around Stephen's Green she asked him how he was and he said he was fine. Her hair was even longer than at Christmas. It came down to her chin now and curled in at the edges. She was wearing a gray businesswoman's suit— skirt and matching jacket. And a white blouse. He asked her how she was keeping, and then instantly remembered that he had heard a few days ago that Uncle Bradleigh was back in the brig.

"Busy," she replied. "Bradleigh has had to go back into St. Patrick's."

"Was it like last time…?"

"No. Not like that."

"So why did they put him back in."

"To prevent it becoming like last time."

When they reached Rathgar he said she should drop him off at the lights and not go out of her way.

"Geoffrey, it's teeming. You'll get drenched."

He thanked her and they drove down towards the Dodder river. But at the waterfall, she pulled in to the side. He dreaded what was coming. He knew it wouldn't be kept swept under the carpet forever.

"We have to clear the air on a few issues, Geoffrey. So we might as well do it now."

He had intended to apologize straight out, to say that he had lost his head, that he had had no right to speak to her in that way, but instead he just muttered 'okay' and steeled himself for the recriminations.

"When you said those things about me, were you trying to make a fool of me, to make me into some sort of joke?"

This was not what he had anticipated. He wasn't even very sure what she meant exactly.

"Well Geoffrey?"

"It wasn't a joke, if that's what you think. I was wrong to have talked to you like that. I should never have said any of those things. But I did-n't say them as a joke."

"Or to make fun of me to your friends. A bet of some kind?"

"Of course not Aunt Thelma. I haven't told anyone. I'd be mortified with embarrassment."

"Did you honestly find me attractive? Did you really fantasize about me?"

"Yes."

"Do you still?"

"I can't help it."

The wipers slapped themselves from side to side across the screen. A car drove past, splashing through the puddles.

"Are you still a virgin, Geoffrey?"

"Yes."

He could hear the rain and see it spatter on the windscreen and he watched the wipers continue to slap back and forth. Why had she asked him that? Why wasn't she saying anything? Maybe she hadn't heard his answer. He wanted to look at her, but he was afraid. He decided to say it again.

"Yes, Aunt Thelma. I'm still a virgin."

No response. And he couldn't bring himself to look at her.

Finally, she reacted. "I am too, Geoffrey." Her voice was soft and it was also sad.

"I'm sorry," he said. "I'm sorry it isn't working out for you and Uncle Bradleigh."

"I think the time has come to do something about it."

He was unable to determine what she meant or where this conversation was heading.

"You're planning to separate?" he hazarded his best guess.

"No Geoffrey."

"I don't understand."

"I meant it's time to do something about our virginity status."

***

First he phoned home and said that he was staying over in college at Flanagan's again. Then they each had a glass of sherry in the kitchen and she smoked two of his cigarettes. He explained that he hadn't any frenchies.

"I'm on the Pill, Geoffrey."

"You're on the Pill?"

"I'm on it because my periods were so heavy. It has other uses apart from contraception. Are you nervous Geoffrey?"

"Yes," he admitted.

"So am I. Are you sure you want to go through with it."

For an answer he leaned over and kissed her lightly on the lips. "Yes."

They used one of the four spare bedrooms in her house—the double room at the back. She didn't seem to know how to French kiss very well. She sort of just opened her mouth and let him insert his tongue, but she didn't reciprocate with her own or even tease his with hers. And then later he rushed things. He pushed it into her before it was really ready. He knew it wasn't really ready, but he was afraid he would lose it and the opportunity. And then once he was in, it was all over in a matter of a minute.

"I think we need practice," she said, as she rolled out from beneath him, but she didn't rush to put her clothes on. Instead when he lay down, she stretched out beside him and ran her fingers across his chest. It was nice being naked with her. It was nice the way she was studying him, just as he was her.

"You're much hairier down there than I am," he noted.

She blushed and covered her pubic area with her hand. But even then her thick black patch of hair stuck up and peeked out between her fingers.

He gently moved her hand away. "I like it," he assured her, "it's very sexual."

"It's not curly like yours is."

"I like it 'not curly.'"

He also liked her breasts. They weren't anything close to what he had imagined. Not voluptuous, but he hadn't expected that. But they weren't just small and plump either. They were kind of skinny, sort of, and very pointy, with nubs for nipples which pointed up like little electrical switches waiting to be turned on. He sucked the nearest one into his mouth and gently rolled it between his tongue and teeth. It responded by stiffening and she uttered a little 'oh' sound. He repeated the procedure with the other one and again she made the little sound, only for longer. Now he felt himself stirring, stiffening like her nipples, coming back to life. He guided her hand down to him.

At first she just held it, but as it continued to rise and assert itself she said 'oh' again and began to explore, her long thin fingers so cool on him.

The second time worked better. He let her steer him in, and he stayed still for a minute before he started pumping. And when he did start she immediately shut her eyes and lay very quiet. He had thought there would be a lot more groaning and thrashing around, but all she did was get red and say 'oh' in a whisper.

Afterwards she set the alarm clock and put out the bedside light. He parted the curtains and they lay naked, she curled up against his chest. It was still raining outside. Listening to the raindrops and the ticking of the alarm clock, and feeling the warmth of a naked woman against him, he fell into a deep sleep with his hand over her breast.

He woke and saw that his penis was now a pole, the dimensions of which he often sported in the early morning, the sort of pole that could support a tent to sleep six. But there had never been a place to put his pole. Up until now, maybe. He stood up on the bed and caught sight of himself in the mirror. He decided to wake her.

"Thelma."

She opened her eyes. He was standing astride of her.

"Oh," she said softly, then her eyes focussed, " oh, oh dear."

"Do you want it, Thelma?"

Closing her eyes again, she put her hand between herself and then opened her eyes and nodded to him.

And when he entered her, she said 'oh dear me', and clenched her fists. Then once he was all the way in, he pushed himself up on his arms and watched his penis withdraw and enter, in and out, in and out. He cradled her head with one hand and then lifted her head gently to show her.

When she realized what he wanted her to see, her eyes opened twice as wide and she fell back on the pillow. He stayed up on his arms and watched her breasts jumping as he drove into her. And when he finished, he stayed inside her, until it became small again and quietly slipped out.

She kissed him in the car before dropping him off at Trinity. "I think," she said, "I think we're getting the knack of it."

The sun was out, the wind whistled down College Green, they had arranged to meet on Friday night, and he strolled into class confident and clear-headed. A new man had been born.

***

Over the next three weeks they were giddy like puppy dogs, over-come with curiosity and shyness alternatively. Just knowing they were free to touch one another's bodies, to explore the nooks, crannies and appendages without let or hindrance was in and of itself, the thrill of a lifetime.

She was more bashful about showing him herself, particularly between her thighs. She did let his hands wander around 'down there' as she termed it, but didn't want him to look and wouldn't tell him where exactly to touch or how. "Next time Geoffrey, I promise."

But she wasn't shy whatsoever about his 'down there'. On the con-trary, she was fascinated. She loved to stroke his penis, to concentrate on moulding it to its full potential with her long slim fingers, like a potter absorbed in shaping her creation. Then, when she had it standing to her satisfaction, she would sit back and admire her handiwork. She named it her 'obelisk', like on Killiney Head with the big stone cannonballs at the base. "It would be fun to go there for a picnic. You and me."

"And then do it, right there in the grass."

"Yes. Do it in the open."

She wanted to learn everything about it. What it felt like when it was growing. If he knew beforehand when it was about to enlarge itself. Why it was bigger some days than others and how it could start off tiny and go to huge, or start off thick like a curled up snake but not be so tall when it was upright. And did its size determine how much seed it issued. And why was there copious seed sometimes and not others. She actually went downstairs the second Saturday and returned with a ruler, a pencil and a notebook.

"Thelma, it's not a science project." But since it was blatantly ram-pant, he proudly allowed her to measure it. She also jotted down the time, the date and the temperature.

"You could also include the pertinent facts that you are wearing a black brassiere, a girdle, a black garter belt and your stockings. And last, but not least, that you've been stroking it for the past ten minutes."

"Does my underwear arouse you? It's just my ordinary underwear for when I wear a dark dress. So the white won't show through. And you like the stockings too? I always think I'm so old fashioned not wearing tights like all the girls do nowadays. But I don't think they can be very healthy."

"Yes your underwear is arousing me," Geoffrey laughed, "but only when you're in it. And I also think you should get a mini skirt. Very mini. A black one. But not tights. Whatever about their healthiness, they're an eyesore."

"Geoffrey, I'm too old to wear a mini. It would look silly on me."

"Age has nothing to do with it. Legs do. And you have lovely long legs Thelma."

She bent her head and smiled to herself. Then she wrote down the details about her underwear and the duration of fondling time.

The other part of his anatomy that particularly entertained her was his bottom. She judged it to be pert like in Greek and Roman statues and she would put down her glass of wine (they had got into the habit of drinking wine in the bedroom) and pinch it unmercifully. Once when he was asleep, she bit it.

It was strange that a woman was so intrigued by his body. He had never considered that.

Not only had they grown comfortable with one another, they were also becoming more adventurous. One morning he had woken up and gone to the jax. When he returned, she was sitting up wide awake and she was studying him.

"Don't get into the bed yet."

"Why?"

"I want to watch you."

"Watch me what."

She began to blush and pulled the sheet up to her chin.

He smiled at her shyness. "What? What do you want me to do?"

"What you do when you're thinking about me. When you can't be with me...but you're thinking about me...in that way."

He paused. "I don't know if I could do it in front of you."

She blew him a kiss.

"All right, I'll try it."

He stood at the end of the bed and placed his hand on his testicles and began to rub them slowly. He could see himself in the dressing table mirror and saw what she was seeing. He began to fondle his penis and he could sense the first stirrings.

"Tell me what you're thinking Geoffrey. Like the way you told me in the kitchen last October."

"I'm thinking about you, about kissing you, about kissing you on the mouth, with my tongue. About feeling your tongue kiss me back, beckoning me, urging me, teasing me to keep going, to keep kissing you."

"Tell me what I'm wearing."

"Your business suit, the gray one. But I'm going to take it off you, Thelma." He looked at her to see if he was doing it right.

"Yes," she whispered, "tell me how you imagine undressing me."

"I'm kissing your neck, your shoulder, I'm slipping the jacket off your shoulders and I drop it on the floor. Now I'm unbuttoning your blouse, slowly, opening it and taking it off. Then I feel your breasts through your bra and I know it's driving you crazy. You're saying 'No Geoffrey, please' but I know you're as excited as I am, so I wrench both the straps off your shoulders at the same time and expose your breasts, bare and naked with their nipples jutting out."

She was watching him, watching what he was doing with his penis, watching him make it big in front of her. She was breathing deeply like at the very beginning, before her peak comes. "Tell me everything. I want to know everything a man thinks about."

"I will if you push the sheet down and do to yourself what I'm doing."

"I never do that."

"You can try."

"Oh dear."

But she complied. "Keep talking to me, Geoffrey. Tell me."

"Now you want me to take my clothes off, but I refuse. I am going to stay fully dressed, but not you. I unzip your skirt and let it fall to your feet. Then I feel beneath your panties and I find out that you're damp, no not damp, wet. And I can smell your smell, so I know you're craving what I have stiff in my trousers. So I order you to get down on your hands and knees."

He checked to see her reaction.

"What are you going to do to me?"

"You know what I'm going to do to you."

"No I don't."

"Yes you do. Now tell me."

She was still feeling 'down there' and getting red.

"Tell me," he repeated.

"You going to do it to me from behind."

"That's right. That's exactly what I'm going to do."

"You mean now."

"Yes Thelma. Get down on the floor."

"Oh. Oh dear."

***

By the third week, their routine was set. On Wednesdays and Fridays, she would collect him at the bus stop and he would stay over. On Monday she would come to Flanagan's rooms around lunchtime. Flanagan was perfectly amenable to this arrangement, especially since Geoffrey was now helping him with his term essays: 'the blind leading the dumb' as Flanagan described it. On Thursday afternoons they would meet in Bewleys Cafe on George's Street for afternoon tea.

It was all quite smooth and straightforward. Except for the dream he had that Kevin had walked in on them when they were making love, his early fears that the whole of Dublin knew he was having an affair with his aunt, faded, and he became quite relaxed about the whole business. His family never questioned the two nights out and he explained it was to be a regular arrangement. He was doing better at college too, particularly in the seminars. He sold his motor bike. Grandad Doyle had been readmitted to the Old Men's Asylum in Ranelagh, and Kevin was back in his own room. He also noticed that Kevin had actually laid off slagging him at every opportunity.

"What are you thinking about?" she asked him on their third Thursday in Bewleys.

"Just how pleasant this is, being lovers and having tea together."

She smiled. He really liked her smile and her small, pretty mouth. And despite her two front teeth being 'rabbity' as she described them, he liked them. He also thought they were part of the reason she kissed so well, now that he had taught her how to do it. He was starting to understand the 'peak' business too. The first time, when her face turned puce, it had scared him so much that he had stopped and tried to take it out, but she had gripped him so tightly inside her that he couldn't. She had said afterwards that she wasn't exactly sure what it was.

"Do you think it's a woman's climax?"

"Maybe it is. It certainly is something quite extraordinary. A little like when you put your hand down there. Or when you made me do it. But still very different—deeper. Like floating away, up into the clouds. I think I used to feel it, sort of, when I was a teenager…if I lay in bed and squeezed my thighs together very tightly."

He asked her about being a teenager and the fellas she had gone out with. She hadn't she said. She had gone to a few church dances, but hardly anyone asked her up. She was too tall, and too gawky and too shy and had no womanly shape whatsoever. The first boy to kiss her, had done it at a party when she was nineteen. And she had later discovered that he had only done it for a bet. "Imagine being so unattractive that a boy would have to be paid money to want to kiss me. I wanted to hide away for ever."

"So when did this ungainly, unattractive duckling become a swan?"

She smiled at him and stirred the teapot, three left, three right, then poured for them both.

"I believe I grew into myself during my early twenties. I also started buying my own clothes."

That weekend, Saturday morning, he noticed there was blood down there, after she peaked. Unsure, he stopped and withdrew. When she saw why, she jumped up, went into the front bedroom, then to the bathroom. After about ten minutes she came back wearing an Aran sweater and dark slacks. She brought a damp face cloth which she used to wipe him clean, while apologizing profusely that she should have warned him it was close to her time of the month.

"But I thought with the Pill, all that stopped."

"No, but it's much, much lighter and doesn't last ten days like it used to. And I don't get the terrible cramps anymore."

She apologized again and asked him to get off the bed while she removed the sheet, put it in the clothes' hamper and got a fresh one from the hot press on the landing.

He was still standing naked by the door, his obelisk now shrunk back to its base.

"I'm sorry Geoffrey, but we can't do it for the next few days."

"You still want me to stay over, don't you?"

She looked at him uneasily. "Yes, it's just that I can't...you understand...I can't let you down there."

"I shouldn't have mentioned it. I should have kept on going."

She read between his lines. "I'm sorry Geoffrey, please excuse me." She came over and stood beside him. "I just didn't want you to see me like that. I forgot you hadn't finished."

They were standing close to the full length mirror on the back of the door. He pointed their reflections out to her. She laughed. "That looks so daring. Thelma Fitzgerald and her naked lover. Whatever would my friends say?"

He positioned her hand on his penis. She smiled again, unsure. He tapped her hand indicating she should stroke it. She looked up at him. "You're still feeling frustrated, aren't you?"

"Yes."

"Do you want me to do something, is that it?"

"Yes."

"Tell me Geoffrey. Tell me what you want."

"Take off your Aran." he whispered.

She did as he asked and he watched as her breasts jiggled free.

"Kneel down, Thelma."

"Oh."

Slowly, she lowered herself to her knees. "You want me to put it in my mouth, don't you?"

"Yes."

"Right here, so you can watch me do it in the mirror."

"Yes."

"Oh dear."

***

Over the next month they each got bolder and braver. Sometimes she would ask him to tell her stories while he did it to her. Once he showed her some of Flanagan's magazines when they were in his rooms. Flanagan had a veritable cornucopia of erotic and pornographic literature neatly stacked in the corner of his bottom bookshelf. The collection spanned a wide variety of interests, from the mainstream to the bizarre to the incredible. 'Dip in and dabble whenever you've a mind to. But do so at your own risk.' Flanagan advised. He thoroughly approved of Thelma, though he'd never actually met her. And of course, Geoffrey never mentioned the familial connection, but Flanagan would probably have sanctioned that too, had he known.

"An older married woman, Sir Geoffrey, often constitutes the ideal mate for youngbloods such as we. First of all, they are already married."

Flanagan was discoursing extemporaneously over a pint in O'Neills of Suffolk Street. Geoffrey nodded wisely.

"Secondly they are experienced in such matters and so there is no need to drag, drug, intoxicate or cajole them to sacrifice their virginity to our stately and noble penises. Thirdly,—are you paying attention to these pearls, Sir Geoffrey?"

"I'm hanging on your every word."

"As indeed you should be. So, if they are interested in us, it generally follows that they are bored with their husbands' twice-weekly slam-bams. Which, Sir Geoffrey, means that they are both figuratively and literally open to suggestion. And more than willing to explore the finer points in the art of lovemaking."

Again Geoffrey nodded his worldly nod, relieved that at last it had some substance behind it.

"Nextly," Flanagan was on a roll and on his fourth pint, " for the same reason that older men are attracted to younger women, the converse or inverse—the correct usage eludes me at the moment—holds true. The older married woman becomes your sexual mentor, and like any self-respecting mentor, part of the pleasure for her is the joy of transforming a clod into a craftsman, an inept fumble-and-stumble merchant into a skilled and imaginative lover."

He lowered his glass and signalled the barman two more. "Am I right or am I right?"

Geoffrey agreed that he might well be right.

Flanagan's private collection set them off on new courses, experimenting with a wild range of positions. Some were too silly to negotiate and they gave up trying. Others suited them much better. Her straddling him was a huge success. They did that mostly in the mornings. She called it 'the rocket' because she claimed it made her see stars. Flanagan had extolled the joys of cunnilingus to Geoffrey, but Thelma was reluctant. She kind of let him try it a couple of times, but she was always too tense, and he could never seem to do it right.

Together they invented games and acted out scenes. He was the pirate, the kidnapper, the white slave trader and she the innocent helpless victim forced to submit to his sexual demands. Sometimes she was in command. Once she ordered him to remove his clothes in the hallway. Then she pulled him by his penis into the kitchen. She sat on the kitchen table, hitched up her skirt, and instructed him to make himself ready to pleasure her. Another time she tied rope around him down there and dragged him up to their room where he was to be her slave for the night.

She even bought the black mini skirt.

Then, on their sixth Wednesday night when she picked him up in the car, she said she had something to tell him. "Bradleigh's coming out next week."

It was the first time either of them had referred to him by name. They had had six weeks together.

"When next week?"

"Saturday Geoffrey. Not this Saturday, next Saturday."

And later when she peaked as they were doing it, she shouted out for the first time. She shouted out the word 'fuck'. Then she asked him to change their position so that he could do it to her on the floor, backways, to fuck her in front of the mirror, to fuck her into the floor, to fuck her because her husband couldn't and never would.

Afterwards, as they climbed back into the bed, she apologized for her obscene language.

He said it was very sexual doing it that way in front of the mirror, but he wondered to himself if what she had meant by the cursing was that she really wanted to be doing it with her husband and not with her nephew.

"We can still meet in Flanagan's rooms," he asked.

"This Monday, you mean."

"No, after next week. After he comes back."

"We'll see Geoffrey. I can't make decisions like that now." She switched out the light."

"Will you sleep with him in the front room, or in here by yourself, in our room?"

"Shussssh." She snuggled up to him, lifted his arm and wrapped it round her bare belly. "I don't want to think about next week. I only want to think about now."

***

There was one way they hadn't done it that they both wanted to try. On Monday morning he phoned her at the office from college to confirm their rendezvous.

"Be there at one. And Thelma…"

"Yes?"

"I'm the boss today."

"Oh."

"Are you wearing a bra and girdle and your stockings?"

"Of course I am," she whispered. "I'm in the office, not the bedroom."

"And panties? Have you panties on under the girdle."

"It's an open girdle," she hissed, "of course I've panties on underneath."

"What colour are they?"

"They're white. Everything's white. Except for the stockings."

"Take the bra and panties off before you leave. But not the stockings or the girdle."

He heard her gasp at the other end of the line.

"I can't do that. I can't walk through the streets in broad daylight with no underwear on."

"Yes you can. And you will."

"Oh dear."

At ten past one she knocked at Flanagan's door.

"You're late," he admonished placing his arm across the doorway.

"I was delayed at a meeting. Why are you blocking the door?"

"Did you do as I instructed?"

She made a little face.

"Did you?"

"Yes."

"Prove it."

She handed him her bag. "They're in there."

"I want to see for myself. Unbutton your coat and lift up your skirt."

"Not here on the staircase."

"Yes, here."

Her faced flushed. "Someone might come."

"Then you'd better hurry up."

She unbuttoned the coat. "This turns you on, making me do this, doesn't it?"

"Very much. Now raise your skirt."

She reached down and peeled it above her knees.

"Higher."

"Oh dear."

"Higher Thelma. Show me that my instructions have been obeyed."

And when she complied, he placed his hand between her legs, pulled her inside, shut the door and pressed her up against it.

"What are you doing, Geoffrey?"

He kissed her deeply with his tongue, while his hand explored between her legs. "I'm going to fuck you standing up against the door. And judging by your wetness and your smell, I believe that is exactly what you want me to do. Am I right Thelma?"

She reached for him, unbuttoned him, took it out and guided it up in to her.

By his tenth stroke, he could tell she was approaching her peak. Now he thrust slower, harder. The redness rose up from beneath her blouse and her eyes rolled up to the ceiling. He thrust again as hard and as high as he was able. She went rigid. Then after what seemed like minutes, she expelled all the air within her in a long single gasp.

He started again.

"What are you doing to me?"

"I'm fucking you Thelma. Up against the door."

"How long are you going to do it for?"

"As long as I want. As long as it pleases me."

"Why do you like doing this to me so much?"

"Because you want me to. Because Thelma Fitzpatrick, you crave it, you crave my penis, every inch of it. And every inch of it craves you."

"No it's not true. I don't crave it."

"Yes you do. You crave cock like a slut craves it. Stiff cock, hard cock. That's what's you dream about at night Thelma. Cock filling your cunt, filling your mouth."

"No I don't want any of those things."

"Yes you do."

"How do you know that Geoffrey? How can you say those things to me?"

"Because your little virgin cunt is sopping wet. And because I can smell its smell."

"Is that how a slut is, Geoffrey? Is that how a man can tell a slut? From down there."

"Yes. That's how any man could tell you're a slut, Thelma Fitzpatrick."

She was peaking again. Contracting. Pushing him out.

He pushed it harder against her contractions. "In, out, In, out. Stiff and hard, up against the door. That's how you like it, isn't it?"

But her redness had risen and she wasn't hearing him any more.

And after it had passed, he still kept going. This was his best. He knew this time he would last longer than ever before. And knowing it made him strong, confident, in control of his body. Like an animal. A panther. The strongest, leanest panther. The panther sexually satisfying his female, driving her beyond her wildest desires.

He began to lick her face, her ear, her neck. He unbuttoned the blouse, opened it and pushed it and her coat off her shoulders. She protested that her breasts would be exposed. He told her that was the way he liked them best. Naked and exposed for him to fondle as he chose. He ran his fingers across her outrageous nipples. Her body quivered, rippling as if he had run his fingers up the keyboard of a piano.

And still his cock surged. He pumped harder. He tugged and twisted her nipples, pulling her pointy breasts in opposite directions, inciting himself.

His legs were quaking, buckling beneath him. It wouldn't be his penis that would give out on him this time, it would be his legs. He had to hurry now. He began to ram into her.

She stared at him wide-eyed, gasping, panting.

"Yes Thelma, now."

He reached both hands under her skirt, then under the open girdle, grabbed her by the bare bottom, lifted her off the ground and plunged his final thrust into her.

She gaped at him, her expression frozen. Then she closed her eyes, and together they slid down the door and formed a pile on the floor.

***

On Wednesday she cancelled, saying her mother was sick and she had to stay over because her father was away on business. Thursday, they met in Bewleys. The waitress knew them by now and cleared the dishes from their favourite booth at the rear. He helped Thelma off with her raincoat. She was wearing a long, reddish-brown dress with no collar. She appeared even taller. It suddenly struck him, that she was in her own way more than attractive, but quite stunning. He kissed her quickly on the nape of her neck.

They ordered tea for two with an extra pot of hot water and a mixed plate of buns.

"He's home, Geoffrey."

He heard the words. He knew what she meant. But he couldn't respond.

The waitress brought the buns. "Your tea will be ready in a flash."

"He came home yesterday afternoon, when I was at the office."

"I thought he wasn't getting out till Saturday," was all he could manage.

"They said he could go early. I talked to the doctor there when I got back to the office. They had phoned when we were at Flanagan's."

The tea arrived.

"Will you come to his rooms next Wednesday?"

She shook her head.

"Ever?"

She didn't answer him, didn't do anything.

He stirred the teapot and poured her cup. Then it hit him. It hit him that never again would he be doing this with her. Never sitting in Bewleys cafe as lovers. It was over. All over. And now he was crying.

***

About three months later, two very strange things happened. First, Geoffrey received a letter from Farrell's Food Distributors in Portmarnock, informing him that he, Geoffrey Matthew Doyle had won the Mr. Perri Potato Crisp Mystery House. In a random drawing from the eight thousand, two hundred and forty-three entrants who had correctly named Wicklow as the county in which the Mr. Perri Potato Crisp Mystery House was located, his name had been selected at random. The Board of Farrell's Food Distributors offered him sincere congratulations and their solicitors would be contacting him shortly.

The following Sunday, his mother having just got off the phone and bursting with excitement, made the family guess what she had just heard from Granny White.

"That Bradleigh, now on the wagon again, has been officially elevated to sainthood," his father quipped.

"Your sarcasm is very tedious Mattie," she snapped back, "but yes, the news is about Bradleigh. And you'll never guess, but he's going to be a father. So what do you say to that now!"

"Well fair play to him, June. Not before its time, but there's lead in his pencil after all."

Part 2

Chapter sixteen

Granny White died.

It was a long, lingering death—the culmination of almost ten years of slow, but relentlessly progressing dementia, rendering her personality almost unrecognizable. The imperious, disciplined and dignified Granny White had dissipated before his eyes and her place usurped by an amoral and wanton hag.

At her funeral Geoffrey found himself wondering if there was an inverse relationship between the form a person's senility took and that person's previous behaviour. In other words, would someone who was hitherto rigid and formal be more vulnerable to becoming fluid and foul-mouthed in their senility as Granny White had.

The ironic arc of the pendulum swept broadly, very broadly.

The senility had set in shortly after her eightieth birthday and she died just before her eightieth-eighth. It had taken almost eight years to unravel the tightly knit personality she had so carefully woven over three-quarters of a century. For a woman who, rarely if ever, displayed any spontaneity of emotion, she had spent the last years of her life in childish indulgence. When Geoffrey came into her room, she would giggle like a schoolgirl, then blatantly unbutton her nightgown to expose her breasts to him. Dugs—that was the word she used. Not breasts.

She was horrible to the nurses. She would regularly throw tantrums with them, accuse them of theft and torture and refuse to let them bathe her or assist her on the commode. Only Geoffrey could do it. Geoffrey was the only person she'd allow attend to her hygiene. Only he could walk her to the commode, pull down her thick flesh-coloured cotton knickers, position her strategically and perform the necessary clean-up afterwards. When he refused, so would she. And to prove she meant business she would soil herself. The long parade of nurses—day nurses paid for by the Eastern Health Board—would tell him to have her committed to a home. His wife said the same. And once, in the early stages of her senility, he did. But Bradleigh and Aunt April and his mother ganged up against him and Bradleigh reported him to the police for abuse of an elderly person.

That was when Geoffrey and his wife upped and left for New York. That was also when Bradleigh went back on the drink and set fire to the house, and Kathleen's male companion—the one who used to be a theatrical props manager but had not been so for eight years due to an unspecified nervous condition—died from first degree burns when rescuing Granny White from her bedroom.

That was when Geoffrey returned alone from New York and knew he could never leave until they had all died. The theatrical props manager was dead and Granny White had survived. The theatrical props manager man had been offered up as a sacrificial lamb because Geoffrey had abandoned them. He would not abandon them again. God had made his point and underscored it mightily. The price of incest had yet to be paid. This dysfunctional self-destructive family was his albatross. And not until they dropped one by one from around his neck of their own or God's accord, would he would ever be rid of them.

For the next nine months, while the insurance claim was processed and a local building contractor, consisting of two brothers, rebuilt, the Doyle-White conglomerate lived in the left side of the house—Aunt April doubling up with Granny White; Kathleen and Maggie together; Grandad Doyle and Jacintha clinging steadfastly to their front bedroom; Bradleigh and Geoffrey in the living room downstairs. His wife mailed him the divorce papers from New York. He signed and mailed them back.

Two weeks later she mailed him a book entitled *Self-Analysis: how to salvage your life without spending a fortune.* She enclosed a curt note saying that at the age of thirty-four his life was badly in need of salvaging, though she suspected it might already be too late.

It was three days after the repairs had been completed and they had moved back to their original rooms when Granny White died. She had been in fine fettle the night before, had babbled on about the coming summer and ice-cream and taking off your swimming suit when it was wet and the importance of tight corsetry for young women, but when Geoffrey went into her in the morning, she was asleep which was unusual. Plus she didn't sound right.

He attempted to rouse her. He said her name, gently at first, then more loudly. He shook her by the shoulders, plumped her pillows and sat her up. But the only response was a change in her breathing which slowed down and seemed somehow to rattle in the distance as if somebody far away was endlessly stacking and re-stacking china dinner plates.

It was almost nine o'clock. The nurse didn't come on Wednesdays. Aunt April was still in bed. Bradleigh was down in the village getting the paper. Kathleen and Maggie were in Cork at an Irish music festival with the two builder brothers—they had been double dating since the reconstruction began. He'd have to ring the doctor who would probably tell him to phone for an ambulance.

Or he could just do nothing.

He was supposed to take his two senior English classes on a literary field trip to Dublin— bus leaving the school at ten sharp. It was only a thirty-five minute drive to the school at this hour of morning so he could still make it, with time to spare. And when they returned from the trip, the school secretary would have a message for him, he'd telephone, his grandfather would answer and tell him the news, that she had passed on and it was over.

He listened to the faint rattling breath and knew it would be so.

But that was a trick. He had to see this through to the end. He could not precipitate her death, and if he did, he would never be free of her.

He had to do what was within his power to prevent it. He had to make the right decisions. He could not go to New York again.

First he dialled 999 for an ambulance. Then he phoned the doctor, and told him that he had rung for an ambulance. Then he called his mother, who said to call her back when he knew what hospital she was in. Then he phoned the school and arranged for the Geography teacher to substitute as tour guide. Finally he roused Aunt April. Her arthritis was bad she said. Very bad. He helped her out of the bed and across the landing to Granny White's. As they entered the room, Geoffrey could hear the rattle, but by the time they'd reached her bedside, it had stopped. Everything had stopped. The skin rose on the surface of his body and a strange wind swerved slowly through his soul.

Aunt April reached out and unsteadily took the corpse's misshapen hand. "Aw, Mummy," she whispered, "Mummy, Mummy."

***

Initially they all blamed him. She had died of pneumonia. How could he have thought she was fine the night before. He'd obviously neglected to check on her—the implication being that he had concocted the story of her talking about the beach and eating ice-cream. He should have called the ambulance earlier. Bradleigh was irate that nobody had run down to the village to fetch him. He was the eldest son, he said. He should have been at her bedside.

"You've told me that a hundred times," Geoffrey shot back, without disguising his disgust, "but you never explained why. Did you need her to sign a cheque?" He wanted to kill this man. Right there and then. The Waterford crystal clock, presented to Uncle Brendan by the Manchester St. Patrick's Day Committee 1968 and now standing on Geoffrey's mantelpiece, would do the job nicely.

This was after the funeral and after the clergyman and guests had returned to the house to have their fill of tea and sandwiches, stout and sherry, and duly sated had subsequently departed, leaving the family to their private grief.

Not a single member of the privately grieving family reacted to his outburst. Nobody said anything. The White contingent just looked at him as if that were the kind of comment they would expect from a heartless grandson who neglected his duties. Maggie started sobbing. Then Jacintha spoke up and said she was certain that Geoffrey didn't mean anything by it and that everyone was just a little distraught, but that weren't they lucky the rain had held off and that it had been a lovely funeral. Then undeterred, Bradleigh restarted his recital about how he was coming out of Mangan's shop, having purchased *The Irish Times* and twenty Capstan cigarettes, and was about to cross the road when the ambulance roared past him and turned up the laneway to his house.

"No it didn't," asserted Geoffrey, "it turned up the laneway to my house, which you happen to live in, and in which I minded your mother for nine and a half years, the same house you almost burned to the ground, the house in which Kathleen's theatrical props manager died saving your mother's life. My house, Bradleigh."

"You won it in a potato crisp competition, Geoffrey dear," said his Aunt April, "and we do all contribute to the upkeep."

"Furthermore," Bradleigh was not to be silenced, "you persistently permitted your father's father, despite our outright objection, to cohabit in sin in your potato crisp house, under the same roof as my mother!"

Indignant, Geoffrey was about to say that first of all, his grandfather and Jacintha had more entitlement than anybody else, and that secondly, no matter how he came by it, it was still his house, and that were it not for his long-suffering charity they would all be homeless. But before he could utter a word, Jacintha had jumped out of her chair, spilling her cucumber sandwich on the carpet.

"Mr. Doyle and I don't believe in marriage," she asserted, as she reassembled the sandwich. "We are both free spirits."

"You are both geriatrics. You're sixty-seven years old and he's well nigh ninety. Your behaviour is indecent. The pair of you ought to know better."

"You're just being spiteful Bradleigh, because Thelma ran off and left you."

"Ran all the way to Australia," Grandad Doyle guffawed, "so that she and your daughter wouldn't have to live with a down-and-out alcoholic father, the kind of man who would set fire to his own mother rather than take care of her."

Maggie, who had done little else but cry since she arrived back from Cork, sobbed even louder. "Mutton, you started all this. And we were all getting on so well with each other. How could you bring up such horrible memories on the day poor Granny was buried. I don't understand such bitterness and bile." She took her builder's hand. "I don't understand you, Mutton."

Geoffrey said nothing. Thelma had not run away with Bradleigh's daughter, she had run away with his daughter. His daughter who would be almost fifteen years old now and whom he'd never seen once. Not in the hospital. Not at her christening. Not once had he set eyes on his own daughter.

Out of the blue his mother announced that she intended to write a poem entitled In Memoriam for Mother. It would be her way of paying tribute. This triggered a chain reaction of competitive tributes. Kathleen stated that she planned to paint a portrait of Granny White as an angel. Maggie's builder remarked that it must be a blessing to have that class of talent. Kathleen's builder mentioned a sculpting class at night school that he'd been considering signing up for. Bradleigh noted that in his day he was considered an accomplished pianist (the first Geoffrey had ever heard of it) and Aunt April hinted that this might be the appropriate time for her to begin a second short story if someone would transcribe it for her.

***

That night, he walked down to the pub by himself. The time had come. It wasn't that he reached his nadir, he'd reached that years ago and had defiantly remained there, but he was at a watershed within the trough. And hopefully, a turning point to boot. It was time to clear the decks of ancient clutter, to hold each possession up to the light, examine it inside out, and, based on that scrutiny, either keep it or discard it once and for all. Besides, he had to be drunk before he could muster sufficient courage to check and see how much of the albatross had fallen off.

The troll-like barman grunted a perfunctory attempt at condolence and started to pull him a pint.

Geoffrey took up position on the last stool at the end of the bar and suddenly longed for Moocher not to be in Canada, but to be taking position on the stool beside him. But nostalgia, he knew, would get him nowhere and so, quickly and efficiently, he dismissed all thought of Moocher and immediately set his mind to assessing the situation. Where did he stand now? There was a string of questions to be considered and for too long he had procrastinated and been the thief of his own time.

Did he stand at all? Or was he merely a facilitator for so many others, enabling them to stand? Had he submerged his persona to serve theirs? And if so why? Did it suit him to be like this? Was it some sort of easy way out? Was the guilt really as overwhelming as he persuaded himself it was? If so, it was very un-Protestant of him. No one else in this cast of crazies seemed touched by guilt in any shape or form. Maybe they reckoned he would carry the guilt baggage for them. Just like the way he did everything else for them. They couldn't have survived without him. Maybe, the sense of being needed provided some quirky kind of fulfillment in his life. Maybe. He'd never finished the book his wife sent him.

It wasn't a question anymore. He had willingly allowed himself to be exploited. It was his penance. Why else would he be his grandmother's nurse. If anyone should have been putting her on the commode, it should have been Bradleigh. That should have been Bradleigh's comeuppance, poetic justice at its sweetest—she had been virtually wiping his arse for fifty years. Let her expose her dugs to her eldest son and permit the oedipal urges run loose with abandon.

But perhaps poetic justice was already in play here. Perhaps she knew or suspected what had gone on between Geoffrey and Thelma. Perhaps it was the only way she could make him pay for his treachery without publicly disgracing her son.

The more Geoffrey ruminated on this, the more terrifying it became.

If she knew, even if she merely suspected, or got wind of it years later, wouldn't that alone be sufficient to put her over the edge? Was it Geoffrey's betrayal, and not Bradleigh's bankruptcy, the cause of her unravelling? And did she decide to make him pay, and pay dearly for it? Would guilt be her eternal legacy to him? Was it to be guilt and not his family that would be his albatross? If so it was an albatross for eternity.

He ordered another pint and began to reassess the guilt. Guilt for what exactly? Guilt that he had not only cuckolded his uncle, but had impregnated his uncle's wife and allowed his uncle to be deceived into thinking he had fathered a child. Amazing to think he had the balls to do all that, yet he hadn't the balls to tell anyone. And why hadn't he? The shock of it would have felled them all in one swoop. And he could have spared himself a decade of reparation and mental self-flagellation.

But would it have felled the family? This was something he had never considered till he started the book. The family were experts at denial. So the instant he declared mea culpa, they would have erected the wall of denial. Everyone would say he was delusionary. Even Thelma would have denied it.

So by owning up to his actions, those actions would in effect have been neutralized. And by this perverse logic, his grandmother would have been spared her dementia. But by holding his tongue, he had allowed suspicion to fester under cover where there was no defense mechanism to fight it.

But how could he know if she knew, if she suspected? He couldn't. He could never know. His mother, Aunt April, Kathleen, Maggie—not one of them once ever even hinted that it was Geoffrey who was the father. Sure, Maggie didn't believe it was Bradleigh and told Geoffrey so at the time, but she never indicated that she suspected it was him. Nor was there any reason for her or any of them to. A pimple-popping nineteen year old boy and his wallflower aunt. So maybe things were as they seemed. Maybe he was tormenting himself unnecessarily. The albatross was still his family, not his guilt for the consequences of his actions.

∗∗∗

Thelma. Thelma. Thelma. Had she really tricked him into getting her pregnant? At the time, he was so stunned by the abrupt turn of events that he could barely assimilate the fact that she was carrying their child and that he had caused this, that he had scarcely questioned, even to himself, her story about forgetting to take the Pill. It wasn't until months later that he acknowledged that he had never once seen her take it, or clapped eyes on the dispenser in her handbag or in the bathroom or on the bedside table. Had she really fabricated and stage-managed the whole thing with him, just as she had subsequently done with Bradleigh? Was Geoffrey her unwitting pawn, her means to the poetic justice to top all poetic justices? By hook or by crook or by both, she got a baby. And when all was said and done, a baby was her desideratum, it was the one thing she was bitter about, the one thing, more even than a decent marriage, that she felt cheated of.

Even now, Geoffrey couldn't accept that she had been consciously that calculating. Not from the start. He would have seen through it. Or were his eyes blinded to all but the physical act?

Their relationship went beyond the concupiscent. He wanted that noted for the record. True it had been hormonally initiated, but it embraced more than mere carnal cavorting. They had fun together just drinking tea. They enjoyed each other's company. They made each other laugh, they gave each other confidence, they talked, they cared for one another. He loved her. Still did. And yes, he still desired her. In his fantasies. In his dreams.

If he were to see her tomorrow, though she'd now be forty-five, one of his first thoughts would be to get her up against the wall. And she would say 'oh dear' and lift her skirt for him.

No, he still daren't check on the state of the albatross. There could be no redemption for a mind so easily given over to lust for the forbidden.

Sure he had done the deed with single women who were unrelated to him, or sometimes been incapable of doing the deed—moral retribution he thought in the case of the latter. Or worse, the revenge of the impotent—Bradleigh's revenge. Poetic justice was being flung around the family by the bucketload. But successful or no, there had never been the power between his loins to equal the intensity of the sexuality he had experienced with Thelma. And yet most other men wouldn't look twice at her from the physical point of view. But for him, homespun, skinny and virtually shapeless though she was, she was also the most exquisitely attractive woman he had ever encountered. And that included his wife.

His love for her was visceral and consequently inexplicable. It made no sense. But nothing in his pathetic life made any sense. To be more presumptuous and pontifical about it, nothing in the world made much sense. And that sweeping generalization incorporated much, including the real meaning of Granny White's death, the existence of her after-life and of course, religion.

He lit a cigarette.

Ah yes, religion—that favourite whipping boy of the Irish. He'd prefer to mull over the topic of religion, than the topic of Thelma's perceived exploitation of an eejit too goo-goo eyed to know what was happening to him. Or to his prodigious and profligate sperm.

Basically, Geoffrey never had much of a problem with religion, organized or not. It was trite to say it, but accurate nonetheless, that the problem was seldom inherent in the religion itself—he was excluding cults from this interior monologue—the problem lay in the misuse of religion. But since what remained of the Doyles, the Whites and the McNamaras was either Anglican or non-practising Catholic, misuse of religion was not a burning family issue. In fact, as far as he could determine, Anglican and non-practising Catholic registered about equal strength on any certified theological seismograph. Not a born-again, a fundamentalist or a Pentecostal among them. Not that anyone was denying God's existence, they were generally accepting and magnanimous about that, but for the most part His existence was irrelevant to day to day events. Both families were equally non-specific about the hereafter, although if interrogated they would certainly declare that there was one, but to more than that they would not commit. Nobody had said Granny White would be with God now, or with her husband. Nobody even said she would be in heaven. Jacintha had declared that she'd be at peace. And that was about as religious as it got. In times of emergency perhaps, a personal appeal might be appropriate, but otherwise a distant almost aloof relationship with the Deity was deemed preferable. And Geoffrey also numbered himself in that summary. Intense, personal relationships with God, were to be blunt, an embarrassment. And if you had one, God forbid you inflict it on others.

However inflicting your religion on others on a national scale has always been a popular global sport. The Brits had won not a few gold medals in that arena. Nor indeed were they short of stiff competition—Itch's history lessons had not been entirely wasted on Geoffrey, nor his brief college foray into philosophy, ethics and theology. He understood that none of the world religions was bad in and of themselves. In essence, Christianity, Judaism, Hinduism, Buddhism and Islam were all saying the same thing?lead a morally good life, and everything would be tickedy-boo. None of the major religions was advocating a morally corrupt life. That was the essence as far as Geoffrey was concerned. But take any religion and daub it with the politics of a few centuries or a few demagogues, and what constituted a good life and how you conducted yourself achieving it or defending it seldom dovetailed with the original idea.

Of course the communication revolution and exploding secularism of the twentieth century might have changed all that. It changed everything else. When his grandmother was born there were no cars, planes, telephones, radios, televisions or typewriters. Electricity was a novelty. And by the time she died there were spaceships, word processors and microwaves. Not that she was inordinately impressed by any of this or even ordinately. Two world wars had come and gone; Communism had risen, crested and seemed destined to collapse; and Geoffrey wondered if any of them had even noticed.

Had they lived in France or Germany they probably wouldn't have noticed the Jews being carted off to the slaughter camps either. Or if they had, would they too turn a deaf eye and a blind ear? Just like Religion had. And just like the infamous engineer from Geoffrey's ethics lectures, who repaired the brakes on the trains to Auschwitz. The same engineer who might not have stoned the Jews as they were marched through his town, who might actually have taken the rock out of his son's hand and sent him inside. And maybe that engineer didn't agree that the Jews were an insidiously evil societal disease which must at all costs be eradicated. Maybe he was convinced that although it was against their will, they were only being relocated and dispossessed. How could he know that they were in fact being gassed, and their component body parts recycled into lampshades and other decorative accessories? He probably wasn't even a member of the Nazi party. Didn't even vote for Hitler. But for all the mights and maybes, probablies and possiblies, he still repaired the brakes on the trains to the camps, and in so doing, was knowingly an accessory to a crime against humanity. He was guilty as sin. Guilty because he saw with his own eyes the Jews being herded on board, guilty because he helped enable a genocide, guilty because he did nothing to stop it. Orders or no orders.

Ah sure, but you couldn't expect the poor man to take on the Third Reich singlehandedly or even stand up against his neighbours. He and his family would be lynched within a day. Or gone missing.

But hang on a sec, didn't he have a brother-in-law in Holland whom they used to visit. Couldn't this powerless engineer have removed himself and his family from a situation of complicity to a situation of exile and protest. Couldn't he at least have done that?

But he had no guidance, or worse, the wrong guidance. From his government, his peers, and most importantly his religion. The only moral guidance he had was his conscience, but he chose instead to listen to the reasons for staying put, reasons that included his wife's rheumatism, his pension, his dislike of his Dutch inlaws; his reluctance to leave his home town and the house he had built and paid for. So he continued to fix the brakes, or oil the wheels, or drive the train, or patrol the camp perimeter, or fill out the order forms for gas pellets. He continued to do it for as long as he was told to do it. Till all the Jews were dead. Till he too was dead.

Geoffrey ordered his third pint and watched as the troglodyte pulled it with indifferent expertise.

Death. It was odd when you thought about it, but people often talked about the 'Big C' and their fear of it, but rarely did they talk about the 'Big D' itself. Beyond the burial part, that is. But the 'Big C' was only a means to the 'Big D'. A painful, horrible, long-drawn-out means, but just one of numerous means to the same end. It was the end itself, and not the route to it that Geoffrey feared more. Was it the end?

That was the trouble with Death. You could never tell for sure. When it would arrive and what it had in store. Capricious, repelling, and in the same breath, seductive, it seemed to beckon at every turn, present itself in a thousand guises, and then when someone searched for it, yearned for it, begged for it, it would turn tail and elude. Other times it would catch people unawares with their trousers around their ankles and would sneak up and wallop them over the head without them ever suspecting a thing.

Geoffrey wasn't yet drunk enough to believe he was thinking anything that Shakespeare and a host of others, thirty times more articulate and imaginative than he, hadn't considered in far greater depth before. But that wasn't the point. The point was that it was he who was thinking it, unoriginal or not, and he was thinking it now. It was also irrelevant that he required many fluid ounces of Arthur G's invention in his bloodstream to arrive at this intellectual crossroads. Furthermore he didn't care. As far as he was concerned, you could sit on the Himalayas for fifty years with a peak up your arse and be none the wiser. You might be at peace with yourself and your peak, but what could you know without having actually done it, as the actress said to the Pope. And that was the kernel of the issue. You say to a child, 'don't put your head in the fire dear, it will burn', because you know from the experience of sticking your own stupid head in places where it doesn't belong, that such is the case. A emperiori—meaning empirical or somesuch—he couldn't remember, but Hume had had a great deal to say about it once he got rolling. Not one given to idle speculation, yer man Hume.

You didn't know if death was the end or not. You didn't know because you'd never been dead. You'd never been in outer space either. But unlike the reports you've been given of what the earth looks like from the other side of its atmosphere, the reports you receive about what death is and isn't, are inconsistent and contradictory and vary widely from source to source. You knew what you hoped death was about, what you prayed it was about, what you feared and what you imagined, but going into the next world was not like going to Paris for the first time where others would have given you fairly reliable and comprehensive reports about the good and bad things you could expect to find there. Including the wonderfully suave and intellectual inhabitants and the obnoxious, arrogant shallow shites, the likes of whom would swallow any Vichy crapology to maintain their status quo. In fact, when you considered the French, or any nation and most individuals for that matter, the primary fear, despite periodical overdoses of religion, seemed to be of Life and how well you fared, not Death.

Until, that is, you realized you were on the road to Death, and knew you didn't want to be, and saw the Stop sign up ahead. And despite all your efforts at turning back, or slowing down or driving into an adjacent field, you proceeded ineluctably to that sign, to that point where the road and your journey ended. Then you would fear it.

Granny White didn't seem to be aware she was on that road, or if she was, then she was beyond caring and threw caution to the winds.

But she would know now. Whether she wanted to or not.

One down, six to go.

He had to go.

***

When he returned from the jax and reasserted himself at the bar, Geoffrey realized that the methodical appraisal he had embarked on lacked a key ingredient—method. He gazed at the undulating row of fulvous, ochre, pellucid bottles behind the bar, bottles which promised the flavours of fantasy and experiences of the exotic. But these were not for him. What he required now was a dose of mundane common sense. So he sat straight on his stool and made a concerted effort to start at the beginning.

And the beginning had started with Grandad Doyle and Jacintha.

They had moved in to his house three years before he did—it wasn't until after he had graduated and had arranged to do his teacher training in a school not fifteen miles from Kilmidder that Geoffrey took up permanent residence with them. An odd pair of old birds, Geoffrey was none too sure about having them as his tenants—it certainly hadn't been his brainwave.

What happened was that Granny White had dismissed Jacintha on the grounds of her flagrantly immoral conduct— i.e., dating his grandfather—and the family had fully expected her to return to whatever living relatives she had in Cork. Shortly thereafter, his grandfather had been evicted for the third and final time from the Asylum for Elderly Gentlemen in Ranelagh.

Geoffrey, at home with parents and unaware of this latest eviction answered the phone. It was his grandfather. He was calling from the Shelbourne Hotel in Dublin and wanted Geoffrey to come in and see him because he had an important proposition to discuss. After class the next afternoon, Geoffrey duly strolled up to the Shelbourne thinking the man had landed a position as night doorman or similar in return for a few pounds, three square meals and a room in the basement. But what he learned at the reception desk was quite different. His grandfather was a guest of the establishment, not an employee. He had checked himself in to a small suite on the third floor overlooking St. Stephen's Green. He had also checked Jacintha in with him.

Geoffrey climbed the staircase to the third floor and located the suite. They were both there, and they did indeed have a proposition.

His grandfather opened the meeting by announcing that he had 2,000 pounds sterling to his name in savings. Of that modest, but not insubstantial sum, he intended to give half to Geoffrey. Jacintha then spoke up. She had 11,000 pounds sterling and also proposed to give him half. In addition they would each pay him one third of their old age pension. Geoffrey, not anticipating what was coming, gaped at them like a typical teenage gormless grandson with his mouth hanging open.

"Now that we have your attention, Mutton," said his grandfather, "let us tell you want we want in return."

And they told him. They wanted a guarantee that he shelter them for the remainder of the natural lives in his potato crisp house. They had already seen it. Took the train to Wicklow town and a bus to Kilmidder. Located the real estate agent who held the keys and were given a tour of the premises including the garden and stable. They had picked out the room they wanted—front, upstairs double room on the right facing the hills and overlooking the driveway to the village. They had returned to the village, eaten dinner in Lafferty's Hotel, where they also stayed overnight. The next day they visited the local Church of Ireland, had morning coffee in the rectory with the minister. From there they went to the public library to check local county council planning intentions for the village. Lastly, they went to the Garda barracks, where as luck would have it, Grandad Doyle knew the father of the Sergeant on duty.

Probably once worked for a circus, thought Geoffrey.

Based on this successful and thorough reconnoitre of the house and its environs, they had mutually decided to make this offer to Geoffrey. The money could be used as Geoffrey pleased, though they predicted most of it would be invested in the upkeep of the house. Many repairs were necessary, some more urgent than others.

In addition to the bedroom, they would have full kitchen and upstairs bathroom privileges, plus a half acre plot in the back for their own exclusive use. Jacintha's nephew would drive selected items of her deceased brother's furniture up from Cork. They were fully aware that in time they would not have the whole house to themselves, and that of course Geoffrey could have friends or whomever he wished stay in the house—provided their privileges were neither revoked nor interfered with. Did he have any questions?

He had about a hundred, ranging from what would happen when they got fed up with living miles from the city to what would happen when they got fed up with each other, but all he asked was when they were planning on getting married.

They weren't, they told him.

"What happens if one of you decides to leave and I've already spent the money on the gutters?"

"You'll probably be spending it on the windows first," proclaimed his grandfather, "then the rewiring. Gutters would be way down on the list."

"If that did happen Geoffrey," said Jacintha, "which it won't," she peered lovingly at his grandfather, "then you would be under no obligation to refund the money. It is our responsibility to make this work. And we are quite in earnest."

"What if you get sick?"

"If we don't die in the hospital, we die in the house. No nursing homes, ex-servicemen's sanitoriums, or hospices for the dying. We'll take care of one another."

"What if I decide to sell the house. Which is what I've been thinking about anyway?"

His grandfather answered. "Certainly it can only increase in value, ramshackle and neglected though it is. However you're a Romantic, Mutton, and you'll marry and fill it with snot-gobblers large, small and numerous, who will not be permitted in our bedroom and who will at all times pee-pee and poo-poo in their own bathroom. You will doubt-less have to install a third. That will be long after the gutters however."

"If you do sell it, Geoffrey," Jacintha addressed the issue head on, "the agreement would be that either you re-house us in accommodation equally to our liking or you refund the capital plus the interest that would have accrued."

"Would this whole arrangement be a verbal agreement or would it be in writing?"

"Your grandfather has already approached a solicitor—the daughter of a friend of his—and she has drawn up a provisional agreement, which we'd like you to take home and study."

"Wow!" said Geoffrey and meant it. "You are both very organized and very determined."

"Yes," said Jacintha. "This is our only hope at a dignified retirement. We saw your windfall as ours too. No one would give us a mortgage at our age. And we have no means of income. And we do not want charity, or to live with relatives under sufferance."

"Not that we'd be offered any or invited to," his grandfather noted, pointedly referring to Geoffrey's parents.

"We know this is our only chance," stated Jacintha.

Geoffrey didn't say anything for a while. Then he asked, " What if I don't agree to this proposal at all? What if I sell the house without ever moving in or letting it? What is your alternative plan?"

"We would move to Cork and apply for a council flat for the elderly— the waiting list is a little over a year. We would either stay with my sister in the meantime or, try and rent, or house-sit, I think it's called. But we don't want to live in a council flat, Geoffrey. We want to live somewhere near the country. We intend to take up ornithology and gardening."

***

At the time, and given his grandfather's history in particular, Geoffrey wasn't convinced that what appeared at face value to be a reasonable, if unusual, proposal would actually pan out. But the house did possess a certain rambling character which was already growing on him. And its location and relative isolation were very appealing. Plus he was becoming accustomed to the idea of owning it.

So three weeks later, the pair of them moved in. And by and large it had worked out to the satisfaction of all parties. Apart from one or two minor issues with the constabulary concerning Jacintha's innate affinity for visiting men's conveniences—namely in Lafferty's Hotel and two of the village pubs—everything went smoothly for the next three years. In fact, Geoffrey enjoyed having them in the house. And they became well-liked in Kilmidder. An added bonus was that neither his parents nor Granny White showed any inclination to visit. In truth they viewed his letting the house to the couple as being somehow subversive. That was until Bradleigh's ignominious bankruptcy. Then all Hell broke loose.

***

It was five months or thereabouts after the bankruptcy that Granny White and Bradleigh moved in, and then Geoffrey knew for sure that his past sins had come back to haunt him. Bradleigh made it plain that as far as he was concerned, sheltering him and his mother was the least a nephew in such opportune and undeserved circumstances could do, and that he felt under no obligation whatsoever to Geoffrey. He also felt under no obligation whatsoever to look after his aging mother. And since she outrightly refused to speak to Jacintha, the task of arranging for her care, was by default, placed on Geoffrey's shoulders.

In many ways the arrival almost a year later of Kathleen and the theatrical props manager was a welcome respite. Not that Geoffrey was off the hook by any means, but at least he had two others with which to share the burden, even if only at a pinch. They also served as a distraction in the household, stealing some of the limelight away from Bradleigh and Granny White. And Kathleen did step in when one nurse or another bit the dirt and Geoffrey was out substitute teaching.

Kathleen, even more than Maggie, had been his mentor in London, his introduction to the swinging sixties and to a new Bohemian lifestyle. Kathleen—another family conundrum.

Kathleen who was now painting angels. That was her most recent theme—angels. All shapes and sizes. From the wispy and pre-Raphaelite to the muscular and mighty Michaelangeloean. Kathleen had come to him via Achill Island where she had joined an artist's colony in the company of a Tour de France cyclist from Texas who sustained a severe knee injury in the Pyrenees. She had in met him in Greece where he was recuperating. She subsequently left him for a sculptor who was one of the founders of the artists' colony. And this sculptor actually made money from his art. The city of Galway had commissioned him for a public monument and he had several private commissions in Monaco where his work was particularly popular. Kathleen, who found herself unable to paint when coupled with the crippled cyclist, discovered that the sculptor had a rich life-force which brought her out of herself. She also discovered that he had a wife who had abandoned him and six children who hadn't. But notwithstanding the brood, she painted furiously and her paintings sold well. Particularly in Monaco and to German tourists in Achill. Then her next and final discovery about the sculptor was that he was sharing his life-force with more than just her.

She confided to Geoffrey that after the break-up, she realized that she had never truly been centered so she wantonly explored the joys of self-imposed celibacy and indulgently eschewed all stimulants from caffeine to cocaine.

It was when she was in the sanitorium in west Mayo that she met the theatrical props manager. After discharging themselves, they travelled back to visit Granny White en route to London. But when she learned that both Granny White's house and Bradleigh's had been put up as collateral for one of Bradleigh's ill-conceived business expansions, and that Granny White and Bradleigh were now living with Geoffrey in his potato crisp house in Kilmidder, County Wicklow, she and the theatrical props manager decided to join them.

It wasn't quite as flip as that, but that was about the gist of it. True, there was a plan, and it seemed vaguely plausible. Kathleen was to paint and open a studio in the tumbledown stable which the theatrical props person would renovate and convert using existing materials and without incurring additional expense. He had apparently been a carpenter and a bricklayer in his day. Geoffrey was substitute teaching Economics three mornings a week in a Loreto school for girls, and his fiancee was studying at Trinity for her doctorate. The extra income to the household would be some compensation, not much, but their very presence would diminish the impact his uncle and grandmother had on his day-to-day life. And that was real compensation.

However, as with many best-laid plans, it never quite got off the paper. Kathleen did paint sometimes. And Geoffrey had hooked her up with a gallery in Dublin through a friend of Flanagan's. The gallery seemed to have no trouble selling Kathleen's work and would even ask her to paint more. But Kathleen did not create on demand, she created when inspired. So the income she generated was at best intermittent.

Now she was inspired to create angels. It was a shame she had never thought to create a guardian angel for her theatrical props man.

The props man caused something of a stir in Kilmidder. He was the first black person ever to have visited the village let alone live in it. In the potato crisp house no less. What's more, as far as Geoffrey was concerned, he did bring in money and fairly regularly, considering. He had turned his hand to cultivating the long sloping back garden and despite Geoffrey's skepticism succeeded in supplying four grocery shops in the area with carrots, peas, lettuce, cabbage, sprouts, strawberries, rhubarb, mushrooms, onions, scallions and broad beans. And in the winter he rested.

All that was gone now. It died with him. Even Grandad Doyle, who had never quite got to exploiting his own half acre, helped him work the garden. But now he hadn't the heart to keep it going. Or the strength. And, as always, Uncle Bradleigh carried on as if none of this had anything to do with him and continued to follow his daily routine oblivious to the human havoc he wreaked. Any other man worth his salt, would, on realizing the consequences of his actions, have immediately rent his garments, smitten his chest, and gnashed his teeth before throwing himself under speeding wheels of the nearest bus. But not Uncle Bradleigh.

Geoffrey sipped his pint and savoured its attempt to help him understand.

What was it about his family? His wife claimed that they lacked passion. That, with the exception of his brother Kevin, they had nothing to be passionate about and so drifted lightly and almost nonchalantly through life, pausing here and there for a little while, even staying put in one place for a long while. But whether they were nomadic or no, she was of the impression that pretty much all the places they went to and the people they encountered, were for the most part interchangeable and of little significance.

Geoffrey was still unsure as to how astute her observations really were. She wasn't saying they were merely selfish or self-centered. It was more that they were uninvolved in the world outside of their own. By choice or by inclination? Or both? Were they cold fish, passionless, unfeeling, uncaring? It seemed too simplistic a summary.

His Uncle Brendan was involved in the outside world, but like Thelma he was only family by default, and little if any of his involvement seemed to trickle through to his daughters. And his passion for all practical purposes could be best described as eclectic. The Free Welsh Army, and in later years the Free Cornwall Army, shared a common theme, but the Great Exuma Island scheme was as bizarre as it was impractical. That was no flash in the pan, no quirky one-off investment, as had been presupposed, though nobody knew that then. It wasn't until the will was read that Aunt April and Maggie learned his original holding had been considerably augmented over the years as advised by a Floridian real estate company, and was by the time of his demise, somewhat larger than anyone had imagined. Four thousand acres larger. Beautifully depicted in professionally produced literature which accompanied the will and featured full-colour photography of the aforementioned, with copy earnestly recommending an expanded portfolio in Great Exuma as a wise investment against the vicissitudes of stock, share and gold values.

From the reading of the will, it also transpired that the house and surgery had been used as collateral to pay for the protection against such vicissitudes. This forfeiting of the homesteads was a recurring motif in what the critical outsider would judge to be a poorly plotted melodrama.

Last, but not least, the will also specified that Uncle Brendan's body be cremated and his ashes distributed across his Caribbean kingdom.

So Aunt April and Maggie, not having read the will until after the funeral and burial, arranged to have the mortal remains of Uncle Brendan disinterred and then cremated. Accompanying the ashes, mother and daughter flew via London to Nassau and thence to Great Exuma Island— Kathleen was in the sanitorium at the time and was unaware of her father's death. The land was there alright and it was under his uncle's name. It was also under water twelve hours a day. Though which twelve hours exactly depended on the whim of lunar and tidal schedules. The photographs, they surmised, had been taken at low tide. So Aunt April and Maggie hired a rowing boat, distributed the ashes and then a year and a half later came to Kilmidder to join Geoffrey.

All roads lead to Kilmidder thought Geoffrey.

But there was change in the air. He could sense it. With Granny White gone, things were different. He still wasn't looking at the albatross yet but it did strike him that the fatal house fire may have had one unexpected benefit he could never have foreseen—the builders. The builders had much to commend them to Geoffrey. A: they were bachelors. B: brothers. C: regular wage earners. D: property owners. And E: they were actively courting the McNamara sisters.

Cross your fingers, stranger things have happened, say no more and ne'er a whisper.

He really wanted things to work out right for his cousins. He felt especially bad about Maggie and how they weren't as close as they used to be. And it was his fault. Of all the people he knew, Maggie was the only one he had wanted to tell about Thelma. He still wanted to tell her. That mortifying night in London—the summer he worked as an aircraft loader in Gatwick—he almost had. They were together in a tiny pub when he broached the subject by stressing he had something important that he wanted to share. But his introduction to his relative infidelity was so confidential and meandering and hesitant, that she mistook what he was trying to say for something entirely different. She reached for his hand and explained that she understood, that he didn't need to say anything more. Sometimes, she whispered, she felt the same way, but that even though they had done some silly things together as kids, it would be dangerous to go down that road now.

'And you know, Mutton, even if I took two pills everyday to be sure, to be sure,' she had laughed at the old joke, 'and you wore two frenchies so we could be doubly sure, to be sure, to be sure, you know I'd still get pregnant, and the baby would be born with two heads and a tail.'

He was so appalled that she believed he was propositioning her, that he didn't even attempt to tell her about Thelma. To make matters even worse, he had slept over the previous night in her one-room flat and had caught a glimpse of her taking off her sweater and reaching back to unsnap her bra. The effect had been such that he had had to get up and lock himself in the jax.

She was still holding his hand, but he wouldn't and couldn't talk. Maggie read his silence as heartbreak at her rejection and consoled him by saying that were they not first cousins, she would have been in his arms and in his bed ages ago.

It was a predicament straight out of Aesop. If he denied that those were his feelings for her, she would think he was being defensive and wouldn't believe him anyway. And if he kept talking and told her about Thelma, she'd think he was some sort of sicko whose fantasies were all incestuous.

Things changed between them. They were still close, but the intensity, the joy of being in each other's company had been compromised. And a few months later, in Dublin, he overheard Kathleen allude to unrequited love and to Maggie as being the sweetheart Geoffrey could never have. Then it dawned on him that this misconception had filtered through the family and was now common knowledge. She had told Kathleen. Or she had told Aunt April. And without ever saying a word to him, they attributed any criticism he levelled about her boyfriends, or any moodiness or disinterest when in her company, to the fact that he was in love with her, his first cousin. That lasted for several years.

But it was all water under the bridge now. It was high time Maggie got married and to a decent guy. Not the losers she had been living with. He had never liked any of her boyfriends— they were all sullen and cynical, and none of them ever seemed to appreciate her. The ones he'd met never laughed or had fun they way she did. They weren't nice to her. And she was so lovely. A lovely person and very pretty. She seemed to be unaware of how pretty she really was—she always turned heads. Lots of good-looking fellas, who weren't deadbeats, asked her out, but she would dismiss them as shallow or materialistic, and yet she'd shack up with these creeps who were quite content to live off her teacher's salary. Geoffrey never understood what she saw in them. He wanted to tell her she was squandering her time and her beauty on flotsam and jetsam. But it was none of his business. And he didn't want to add yet more fuel to his perceived jealousy.

He often wondered how much of it was to do with Uncle Brendan. Was he the reason she had such a low esteem of herself in regard to men? That, whether she denied it or not, she didn't consider herself worthy of anything better than the wasters she devoted herself to? Geoffrey remembered the Mark Eden story she had told him one summer. How, once when she was sixteen, there was a parcel waiting for her when she got home from school. How she was wondering what it contained, and who had mailed it to her. How at the supper table her father was chuckling to himself and urging her to open it so as they could all see. And she did. And it was the Mark Eden Bust Improvement Course. Her father had ordered it in her name. And even though Maggie was telling it years later as an embarrassing moment type story, Geoffrey felt she had been kicked in the gut. It wasn't right. Not right for a father to openly demean his daughter by judging her breasts to be inadequate. And just because he knew she was self-conscious of not having a shape like her sister did at sixteen, didn't make it right, or excusable. And anyway, it was not as if his own wife could be remotely described as being voluptuous. Yet he thought this prank was the height of hilarity. Maybe it was a dig at Aunt April too.

Uncle Brendan was a pig. Was it because he didn't have sons that he chose to belittle his daughters? If so, he didn't know his Irish history very well. He should have built them up, instead of putting them down. He could have moulded them into a Queen Maeve and an Ann Devlin instead of rejecting them for their gender. Even as women he deemed them failures—in his eyes Kathleen was a slut and Maggie androgynous. And not a husband between them.

Uncle Brendan didn't do right by his wife or by his girls. And he didn't do right by them when he died either. Even his death was saying 'the joke's on you.'

At least Kathleen had broken free of him. Geographically at any rate. When she escaped the Free Welsh Army Dental HQ in Manchester, she never went back. And if it meant the life of a nomad and relentless soul-searching, at least it was a life away from him. But Maggie returned to Manchester for every holiday, and made excuses for Kathleen, and tried to compensate by being extra attentive to her father. She always purchased and decorated the Christmas tree, sent him flowers on Valentine's Day, bought him too many presents for his birthday. She never told Geoffrey, but Geoffrey was damn sure that the man never reciprocated.

Was he, Geoffrey, more like Kathleen or Maggie? He wanted the answer to be Kathleen, but he knew it was Maggie. Kathleen had drive and a sense of adventure. He, by the looks of things, lacked both. Yet all three of them had at one point or another shaken the shackles of family and all three ended up putting them back on again.

And what was the matter with Aunt April? She had no influence on either of her daughters' or on Uncle Brendan's behaviour. Maybe she considered it acceptable for him to act like that, or believed it would toughen up the girls for the big, bad world ahead of them. But it didn't. Like their father, she had failed them too. But she did love them—there was no question about that. As to their father's love, if it indeed ever existed, then it had become so sublimated and distorted that it would have taken the combined talents and perseverance of a Sigmund Freud and a Sherlock Holmes to find it. If Geoffrey had a daughter he would...

Yeah, he would be a great father to a girl or boy. All you had to do was take a quick peek at his track record in that department and you'd know straightaway that here was a man who would do the divil and all for any child fortunate enough to be his offspring. An unparalleled paradigm of fatherhood, right enough.

No, this was not the time to travel down that road. Not yet. Change the subject.

He was starting to feel the drink at work now and that was good. He reordered and prepared to turn his attention to Bradleigh.

Get to Bradleigh and you got to the nub of things. It was Bradleigh who was and had always been the sticking point. According to *Self-analysis: how to salvage your life and squander your wife*, Bradleigh was a textbook case, the apotheosis of the self-delusional. Nothing could penetrate the grandiose and blameless opinion he held of himself. And nothing ever would. Not famine, fire, flood nor death. Except maybe this death...

The flame, the source which had nurtured and inflated his self-esteem had been abruptly doused. Would all his pumped-up pomposity turn cold and fall out of him, leaving him totally deflated. Or would he recognize the danger just in time and attempt to follow the source of his nourishment, like the Viking warrior's dog who leaped to the floating pyre to join its master? Or would he sit pitifully like the World War II bomber pilot's dog and wait forever at the end of the runway for the downed plane to return? Perhaps neither. Perhaps Bradleigh had enough arrogance in reserve to coast the rest of the way under his own steam.

Of course, 'the book' would explain the arrogance as a self-saving mask for the impotence and insecurity. Geoffrey chose to believe otherwise. Had Bradleigh been a tycoon and father of thousands, the man would have been doubly confident and reassured of his own greatness and, as a result, twice as insufferable.

He was digressing. What was he to do about Bradleigh? That was the question now! The man had been off the drink since his sojourn at St. Bridget's Hospice for the Fluidly-Challenged and the Mentally Disoriented—the first positive outcome of the fire. Would he be back drinking again by the time Geoffrey got home from the pub? If so, how willing would Geoffrey's mother and Aunt April be to have him recommitted? Geoffrey could count on the doctor, but he still needed a sibling's signature. He had learned that from experience. Or should he simply allow Bradleigh drink himself to death and just ensure that he didn't take anyone else before he went. That was assuming that Bradleigh hit the bottle. Geoffrey had expected him to, the day of Granny White's death, but to his surprise, the man remained sober. Could this be some sort of milestone? Or would it inevitably end up as another millstone to add to the albatross? The man's liver must be a medical mutant. Were Bradleigh and his liver in the process of pulling themselves up out of the mire by the bootstraps in the twilight of their years? It was highly unlikely, but Geoffrey couldn't discount it either. Maybe the dog wouldn't be sitting at the end of the runway after all.

So much time, thought and energy expended on an old drunk. So many family discussions, rows, threats, accusations and insults. And the lush was still hogging the spotlight, still the centre of attention.

There were other players on this stage, but Bradleigh seemed to view the family drama as essentially a one man show in which all the action revolved around him. And to varying degrees, the entire family colluded with this and were constantly worrying about how Bradleigh would take the news of any given development, or how he would be affected by a sudden change in circumstance. Even Kathleen and Maggie paid at least token obeisance at the Shrine of Concern for Uncle Bradleigh. Oh yeah, sure, for a few brief moments, he was forced to step aside and wait in the wings. But just for a few moments. The death of Geoffrey's father was one. The death of Kevin another.

The death of Kevin. The hardest thing in his life that Geoffrey had ever to face. And he never had. If, for an instant, Geoffrey had supernatural powers, he would put Bradleigh in the grave and bring his brother back.

It should have been his little brother he was sheltering, and well he knew it. His little brother who had a whole full life ahead of him, the airman at all costs, his little brother dead in a South American jungle.

Dead at the controls of an overloaded cargo plane shot down by the very mercenaries he was supplying.

Under whose aegis had he been placed? Where was his Guardian Angel? Where was his big brother? Too late now to want Kevin to be safe in his potato crisp house. Too late.

Kevin had passion. An undying passion, and he died in pursuit of it.

And what passion if any, ran through his big brother's veins? None. Outbursts of lust, outpourings of remorse, buckets of self-pity, but not a drop of passion. Because if there was, then where was the evidence? His daughter was fourteen, almost fifteen now and he had never seen her once. He had gone along with Thelma's cover-up, bought into it hook, line and sinker, collaborated with the whole phony facade. The child probably thought Bradleigh was her father. This was not a healthy situation. Her real father was not a healthy situation either. If he looked at it objectively, his behaviour and his actions over the last fourteen years showed neither passion nor conviction. Nor courage. He had permitted the people he held most close, to slip easily between his fingers. He accepted Thelma's rationale too readily. He should have gone. Gone to Australia after them. She would have come to terms with it. She would have taken him for her husband.

If his daughter saw his role during the last fourteen years played out on stage, she'd probably be disgusted with him. She might even choose to keep Bradleigh as her father. Geoffrey had never thought of it from this perspective before. What a choice. An impotent alcoholic or a man who hadn't the balls to stand up and tell the world 'I'm your father.'

This turn of thought, successfully sublimated for so many years, switched everything into a different light. It unscrewed the soft-glow self-pitying bulb and inserted a harsher, self-evaluating wattage. Until now he had always vaguely entertained the fantasy that when all was revealed to her, his daughter would fling her arms around him and say 'I love you Daddy' and 'I'm so glad you're my real father.' Until now.

His wretched family was not his albatross. Nor was the guilt caused by his lust for Thelma. His albatross was that he lacked the guts to stand up for what was right. He lacked the spirit, he lacked the passion. With his track record, he probably would have fixed the brakes on the Auschwitz train just as the engineer had done.

***

He was still in the pub. It was late and the troglodyte had shuttered the windows and was studying him the way you would a boxer, to see if you should bet another tenner on him going the distance. A second shift of patrons began to slip in by way of the back door. Geoffrey ordered another pint. The barman grunted.

He fumbled in the packet of cigarettes and dropped two on the floor. He'd better drink slowly, pace himself. The barman was still eyeing him but delivered the pint anyway. Geoffrey paid him, but noticed the money was swerving and twisting within his wallet like in a film when the image distorts to signal a flashback. This would be his last pint. He didn't want distortions or dissolves or different dimensions. He had trouble enough with the existing three dimensions, although it suddenly struck him that perhaps, in reality, he saw a lot of people as being only two dimensional, as caricatures. This was not good. This was a depressing commentary on his state of mental maturity. Geoffrey Doyle prided himself on being a fair-minded man, a man not prone to pre-judgement, a man who had the imagination to look at any given situation from all perspectives. But had he seen beyond the obvious caricatures of the alcoholic uncle and the grim-faced, rigid grandmother. Did he ever really put himself in Bradleigh's boots? Or in Granny White's winter coat. Maybe this was the time to do so. Before the last pint ran out.

Could Bradleigh have been totally convinced that he had fathered Geoffrey's child? The answer to the question was yes. Yes, because of the elaborate stage management by Thelma; the double dosing him with his sleeping pills and masturbating him in the night and then telling him the next morning that they had done it. Because of her insistence that she wanted to be pregnant and that she was running out of time. That this was her fertile week in her cycle and that he owed it to her. And her repeating the same rigamarole every night for seven nights. And still with all hoopla, and allowing for his enormous conceit and the self-satisfaction of having living evidence as proof of his virility, was there never a little doubt lurking in the back of his pickled brain that he had been duped? And in those rare moments when he couldn't banish this deprecating doubt or drown it with drink, how did Bradleigh handle it then. Was the whole sex thing the reason he drank? The anticipation, the pressure to perform, the embarrassment and humiliation when he couldn't. The disgusting thought that possibly he was homosexual.

Or was the drinking something more, something much bigger? When you considered how he had been brought up—Bradleigh must have reflected on it sometimes—everything had been presented to him on a platter: education, money, a career, position, respect, even a successful fertilizer business handed over to him when he was still in his twenties. Quite a platter by any standards. And he had dropped it. He had dropped the platter, not once, but a hundred times. And each time he picked it up there was less and less on it, till finally there was nothing.

What does that do to a man? The knowledge that he couldn't fit the suit that had been cut for him, that he had fumbled badly when the baton had been passed to him, that he was, though nobody ever said it, a disappointment and a failure.

His father had built up a business from nothing and he, the eldest son, had torn it down to nothing. And now that he had totally bankrupted the family, he was reduced to scrounging off his brother-in-law's son. Add to that the fact that he knew he was a chronic alcoholic whose wife and daughter had deserted him, rather than share the same roof with him, or even the same hemisphere. Considering all that, Geoffrey guessed, that even if he felt cheated by life and experienced not an ounce of self-reproach, he'd still hardly be spending a lot of time patting himself on the back and singing his own paeans for a job well done.

See. When you pushed the self-invested point of view aside and looked at Bradleigh from an impartial angle, you could almost feel sorry for the man. Almost.

Would the same procedure work on Granny White? Was her life a life of constant disappointment? Did she ever regret that she had entrusted so much faith and confidence in Bradleigh at the expense of her other children? Did she realize that she and her husband had not just made a serious error of judgement in giving Bradleigh too much responsibility too soon, but that instead of correcting the error she had ceaselessly compounded it? Was Bradleigh tailored to be the respectable man of commerce her husband never was?

Her husband. She had had a great deal to say about him in recent years, and it was rarely flattering. As a husband he had not matched her expectations. Apparently, he had fallen far short of them. Certainly he had provided her with four children, and eventually had provided for her with money and a large house, but his unconventional attitude which attracted her as a young single woman, repelled her as a wife and mother.

When his work had finally brought financial stability to the family, she hoped respectability would follow in its wake, but it didn't. His eccentric, anti-social and unconventional approach to life didn't change. If anything it became more entrenched. In the upper middle class neighbourhood where they purchased their house, he stuck out like a sore thumb. And despite being a Presbyterian as she was, he rarely attended service and quarrelled repeatedly with the minister. He had established a business, but that was only for expediency's sake—he didn't want to sell or license his patents to a competitor. Science, experimentation, discovery, invention and ammonium nitrate—these were his loves, not commerce.

And what was the final result of futtering and puttering as she disparagingly referred to it? The man literally blew himself up.

So was it any wonder she looked to her son to fill the role she had planned for her husband. The daughter of a Presbyterian minister in Antrim, she grew up a strong God-fearing, teetotalling woman, not afraid of work—she cycled twenty miles a day over hill and dale, down to the school where she taught. She met her husband on a railway excursion to Dublin with her parents. And when at last, she consented to marry him, she packed her bag and baggage and moved south to live in his country—the Papist Republic. And even though she never came to terms with the Republic's separation from Britain and refused to listen to the Irish radio station, she did enter the Dublin Gas Company Cooking competition, won first prize in the wholesome meals-for-a-family-of-six division, and gave wholesome cooking demonstrations once a fortnight at the Dublin Gas Showrooms on D'Olier Street. The Gas Company even printed pamphlets of her recipes with her byline on each. She was proud of that. She was proud of being Presbyterian. And of being abstemious. Not a lot else she seemed to be proud of. Ironic that her eldest son turned out to be a lush.

And what about the other son, the infamous Uncle Hugh, the one that got away? The one that never came back. It must have been a fight over the business, or he got some girl in trouble—Geoffrey had given up years ago trying to get to the bottom of that. And he wasn't about to start again now. Stay focussed. Return to Granny White.

Maybe when you go senile, something just snaps in the brain. Like the straw that breaks the camel's back. Putting on a brave face day after day when you know your son is constantly disgracing himself and you and dragging the family name through the detritus on the streets. Having to meet the neighbours, the shopkeepers, the delivery men; realizing that they've probably seen Bradleigh rolling drunk up the street, or that he'd tried to borrow money from them or hadn't paid his bills. And the ultimate humiliation of losing your home—that had to be the last straw. Unless it was accepting Geoffrey's begrudging charity—maybe that was what did it, what snapped the back and snapped the brain. Probably why they're called synapses in the brain—because the connections snap under the pressure of all the Machiavellian mind games we use, if not to baldfacedly deny the incoming information, then to revise it, make it more palatable, more acceptable and possible to coexist with. SNAP—we've overloaded the wiring and blown a cerebral fuse. That's what happened to Granny White. It was about to happen with Bradleigh. And Aunt April, Kathleen, Maggie and his mother were all travelling down the same path. Like a sheep, he was dumbly stumbling after them. And until tonight, until this drunken orgy of introspection, he hadn't noticed it.

***

His pint had run out.

His time had run out.

Thelma had run out.

And in duping her husband, she had also duped him. Cheated him of a say in her future, his future, his daughter's future, their future. It was not her decision to make alone, and yet she had made it. He had done nothing to encourage it.

He had done nothing to prevent it. That about summed it up. He hadn't done a damn thing either way.

***

There was no crystal clear dawn, no spectacular sunrise splitting the shroud of self-ignorance, no symbol heralding the long-awaited epiphany in the life of Geoffrey Doyle. There was just drizzle and a ditch. He had not made it back to the house, he made it only as far as the ditch that bordered the path to the house.

It was 5:30 a.m. when he woke up. He had been dreaming. Crazy drunken dreams that herded all his thoughts and played them back in horrific variations. He had dreamt about Jacintha carrying her muddled bunch of handpicked flowers up to the coffin. As she walked, the bunch became untied and the flowers fell onto the aisle one by one forming a trail behind her. And Grandad Doyle stooping every few feet to pick them up as she walked on, unaware of her loss. Over the coffin was a Guardian Angel from one of Kathleen's paintings. Sheltered by her wings was a woman and two children. The child closest to her was a little Jewish girl with the Star of David patched on the shoulder of her coat. She was Judith, Geoffrey's daughter. The woman was Thelma, but her face didn't resemble Thelma's. The third child was his brother Kevin. He knew it was Kevin because, although he was still a boy he was wearing an adult bomber jacket and sported a long white silk scarf wrapped loosely around his neck with one end slung casually over his shoulder.

Geoffrey leaned across the coffin that he might talk to Kevin, explain what had happened, but as he did so, Kevin became blurry and indistinct. He leaned back to bring him into focus again, but it didn't work. Kevin was fading, separating into a thousand wisps of mist. Geoffrey looked up at the angel and beseeched him not to let his brother disappear. The angel nodded and Kevin was reformed from the mist. Except now he was too big. And Thelma was too big. And his daughter. They were getting bigger, larger than life, too large. They were outgrowing their clothes. Then Geoffrey knew what was happening. Their bones were growing, but not their skins. Their skins were stretching, getting more and more taut. He closed his eyes to stop himself from seeing what he knew would happen. But it made no difference. He could still see.

Silently, their skins and clothes disintegrated and floated onto the coffin like strips of parchment. Only the skeletons remained.

Then the angel spoke to him without speaking and told him that it was time for it to go, time to go back to heaven and play with Geoffrey's other dead brother. Play soccer with little Michael.

That was when he woke up.

He was cold and he was wet. But strangely he wasn't tired, and he was not hung over. And he remembered everything. Everything in the dream and everything that he had thought about in the pub. He remembered the things he had learned in the pub, the one thing that he must now do, and that he knew he would do. It hadn't been the drink thinking.

Suddenly he realized how famished he was. He located his left shoe and put it on, imagined the rashers and the sausages and the blood pudding and the scalding hot tea he would consume when he got back to the house.

He stood himself upright and brushed the clots of mud off his jacket. And it wasn't until that moment that he noticed it was gone. Not partially gone or almost gone, but gone completely.

Somewhere between the pub and the ditch, the albatross had fallen off.

Part 3

Chapter seventeen

It was a chance conversation with Maggie that steered Geoffrey to the Bahamas. Fortunately he had not yet booked his ticket to Australia—the airline fare was phenomenal, and so too would be the cancellation fee—but he had already taken some preliminary steps in preparing for the trip. The Sydney telephone book had yielded nothing. The Sydney Yellow Pages, however, listed eighteen private detectives, and using his recently acquired word processor, Geoffrey wrote to each of them, requesting a cost estimate for an initial search and asking what such a search would involve.

He had still not received a single response the day he was toiling with Maggie trying to salvage a small corner of the props man's vegetable garden. They were discussing the approaching summer. As a way to set the groundwork, he tentatively mentioned he was thinking of Australia since he had two months off. She said it would be too bloody hot for her and that that was part of the problem, because the builders were angling to take her and Kathleen to some place exotic for two, maybe even three weeks. And exotic meant hot. And she didn't like the heat and she burned easily. Geoffrey asked how she had managed in the Bahamas for the ash scattering. She had been burned to a crisp she assured him, sunscreen or no. And it had been their winter then.

Which reminded her of something. "You remember after Granny White's funeral when we were all in the living room and Bradleigh and your grandfather were arguing?"

"Yes and you accused me of being petty and spiteful because I pointed out that Bradleigh was nothing but a self-centered sponger."

She stopped working and immediately protested. "I know I said that Mutton. But I told you I was sorry. We all know you shelter us and keep us from being totally dysfunctional. It's just hard for Bradleigh to accept it, to swallow his pride and admit he's a charity case."

"Whatever about his pride, which he has kept intact against all odds, he could do with swallowing his insufferable arrogance."

"Yes I know. But that's not what I wanted to tell you."

"Tell me what."

"That when Kathleen and Mummy and I were in the Bahamas, you'll never guess who we bumped into."

"Who?"

"Well remember your grandfather said Aunt Thelma had run off to Australia to get away from Bradleigh."

"Yes."

"Well she didn't stop at Australia for very long. She kept running."

He feigned only mild interest and concentrated on cutting back the rambling raspberry canes. "So where did she end up? In the Antarctic?"

"Quite the opposite my dear Mutton. That's what I'm trying to tell you. She's in the Bahamas. We bumped into her in the airport, the day we landed. She was waiting for a friend who was coming in from Australia. Of course we all nearly died of shock and hardly knew what to say to each other."

Fortunately, for his face too easily betrayed his attitude, he had turned away from her at the first mention of Thelma. Now, instantly he was overcome with the desire to ask her a thousand questions—how she looked, what she was doing, had she a job, had she a boyfriend, had she inquired about him—but he daren't give himself away.

"Was her baby with her?" he asked neutrally. Or so he hoped.

"Yes. But she's no baby. She was eight then, and that was what—six years ago when Daddy died, so she'd be a teenager now."

"Time flies when you escape Bradleigh, I guess." He had accidently uprooted a chunk of bush.

"Plump thing, cute as a button."

"Who, Thelma or the kid?"

"Hardly Thelma. She was still as thin as a rake. And as plain. Although she seemed pretty happy. She was teaching in a boarding school, she said. Probably still is. I thought we were trying to save the raspberries, not massacre them."

"Very funny."

"Kid doesn't look like Bradleigh, that's for sure. I always said Bradleigh wasn't the father."

"I know you always said that."

"So who was he? We never figured that one out."

"Don't look at me."

"Of course, Mummy said we weren't to mention it to anybody."

"You mention it every time you think of it, Maggie."

"Not the anonymous father bit. Her being in the Bahamas, you eejit."

"Let me guess. Because it might upset Bradleigh to remind him that not only had he been cuckolded in your opinion, but also dumped."

"Got it in one, Mutton."

"And no sign of her coming crawling back to him or begging him to go out there and join her, because last time I looked he was still in my house."

"His name did not pass from her lips."

And so it was that Geoffrey found himself not on a kangaroo ranch in the Australian Outback (that had been one of his fantasies), but fighting seasickness as he was sloshed up and down between reefs in a Bahamian fishing boat.

Of course, the very fact that he had suggested Australia as his summer destination trapped him in a real bind. He daren't mention that he had abruptly changed his mind and decided to aim for the Bahamas instead. Maggie would have cottoned on to that in a second. So as far everyone was concerned he was presently off the shores of Sydney viewing the Opera House, or as his grandfather intimated, posing on Bondi Beach, keeping in mind to suck his belly in while he cast the eye over the lithe line-up of indigenous females.

Fortunately the flights to both destinations were out of London so there was no possibility of confusing airport farewells or anxious examination of departure boards. Maggie drove him to Dublin airport, he boarded his flight to London and that was that. Well that was almost that. Didn't the builders have a brother in Melbourne, whom he had to look up when he was over there, and what was his itinerary anyway? Would he be having a gawk at Ayers Rock?

Enter Ms. Haberdasher into his web of deceit.

The business of Ms. Haberdasher started with his mother. Geoffrey had never actually dated her, or even asked her for coffee. But he had pulled her name out of thin air when his mother had been in her matchmaking mode and was dragging her friends' spinster daughters out from the woodwork to give him the once over. So to put an end to it, he had sort of, kind of, led her to believe that he was already dating somebody. To the inevitable 'Who?', out had popped Ms. Haberdasher. Of course that was just a nickname. Her real one was Habberish and she taught Geography. But probably because her clothes were always oversized and layered and loose, combined with her tendency to be in a perpetual hurry, she had earned herself the moniker and it stuck for good. And when Geoffrey had broached Australia to his mother, she had sighed with mild exasperation, 'Oh with Ms. Haberdasher, I suppose. And when will I get to meet her? Not till my grandchild is born I've no doubt.' Geoffrey's botched attempt at marriage and his failure to father a grandchild rankled. 'Now you'll tell me she's only just graduated and she wants to have a career before she makes any commitments.' Of course he had risen to the bait and said Ms. Haberdasher was, as far as he knew, in her early thirties. To which his mother responded that if such were the case, Ms. Haberdasher had better start baking while there was still some heat in the oven. All Geoffrey could do was hope and pray that Ms. Haberdasher's social circle and his mother's never intersected, otherwise he would have a lot of explaining ahead of him. He would have even more explaining to do if his mother ever discovered she already had a grandchild.

Kathleen had decided against the foursome arrangement proposed by the building brothers by parrying it with a counterproposal that she pursue her African agenda which centered on the study of native art in Eritrea, a heroic and victimized African country engaged in a long-standing internecine war with Ethiopia. Eritrea, she explained to them, offered an artistic purity whose likes had not been seen on this planet since George Harrison rediscovered India. Eritrea was the earth's nexus of unspoiled humanity, and provided its big-bully neighbour didn't wipe it off the face of the map, it was destined to be first Africa's and then the world's source of inspiration and cradle of renewed civilization. So multiple vaccinations later, off Kathleen went, with her charcoals, her water colours and her builder brother in tow.

Piqued, Maggie and hers had decided to tour Cork and Kerry, despite the rain and the German tourists.

And of course they had all heard about Ms. Haberdasher from one of his mother's monthly phone calls and were urging him to invite her over for Sunday dinner. However since Geoffrey decided she should be visiting relatives outside London—he would link up with her at Heathrow— it was quite out of the question. Sad to think, Geoffrey mused, that they'd have broken up by the time he returned. His grandfather was sorry Geoffrey would miss his 92nd birthday but hoped he found Ms. Haberdasher to be a good woman like Jacintha who understood a man's needs and that if such turned out not to be the case, 'A nice aboriginal lass might be just the ticket.'

Now four days and 2,500 miles later, here he was, the sole passenger in a small and uncertain fishing boat approaching a spit of an island on the outermost edge of the Out Islands.

It had only taken a matter of half a dozen phone calls to track her down. That is if his information was up to date. The first two schools had never heard of her. The third told him that a Miss Fitzpatrick had once taught there for a while, but that it was many years ago, and as far as they knew she had moved from Nassau to one of the islands, but was not sure which one. Geoffrey learned there were over 700 to choose from. The phone company suggested he contact the post-office, which put him on hold for ten minutes and then told him to try City Hall and ask for the census records department. An hour and a half later, he had the information. The last census listed a Thelma (adult female) and Judith (child female) Fitzgerald on Smidgen Cay but that was eleven years ago. The most recent census results had not yet been published.

Smidgen Cay was about 300 miles southeast of Nassau. 'Not many people there', the hotel receptionist informed him. 'And inadequate tourist facilities. Not one casino.' Everything he wanted was right here on Paradise Island, she assured him. And close to the Nassau nightlife.

Geoffrey persisted. She shrugged. "Go to Chalks seaplane. He fly you on his goose to Samana Cay or to Crooked Island. Then ask for a boat ride."

The next morning at seven o'clock Geoffrey was at Chalk's clutching his backpack and ticket. The Goose was one of a fleet of five ancient twin piston-engined high-winged Grumman Geese. Geoffrey watched it bellyflop spectacularly into the harbor throwing up a massive spray. Then it turned and waddled over to the jetty, sprouted wheels from its nose and sides and roared up the ramp to where Geoffrey and the other eight passengers sat waiting at a variety of cafe tables.

Now three hours later he had exchanged the bellyflopping goose for a sky-blue rowing boat with a phut-phut outboard engine. The boat was owned and operated by Omega, a tall and slightly grizzled Bahamian, named, he volunteered, after his father's watch.

"Do many people live on Smidgen Cay?" Geoffrey asked.

The boat was loaded with fishing pots and floats and nets and the phut-phutting was almost drowned out by the owner's transistor radio. Even though it was not yet noon, the sun was unbearably hot and the sea dazzling. And despite the sea breeze he was sweating like a pig. He had done nothing but sweat since he landed at Nassau. It did not seem physiologically possible that his body could issue such an uninterrupted stream of water.

"About a hundred or so, depending."

"Do you know of a lady called Thelma Fitzpatrick?"

A wave slapped the boat across its flank. Three more slaps followed in quick succession. Geoffrey's backpack fell off the seat and into a pool of seawater on the floor. He scooped it up and gripped the seat with his free hand. More slapping waves, and then calm.

"Bad reef," Omega pointed into the sunlight. "Makes currents."

"Omega, do you know the lady? Thelma Fitzpatrick. I'm told she lives here."

"She is the school teacher. Twenty-three children. She is a good woman. Do you come to make trouble for her?"

"No. Why would you think that?"

"Because you make it clear she does not expect you. Are you one related to the lady?"

"I knew her a long time ago. And I was here on holiday and thought it would be fun to call in on her."

"You are from Ireland also. Not Australia." It wasn't a question, it was an observation.

Geoffrey nodded.

"She does not wish to go back."

"I understand."

"Will she be glad to see you?"

"I think so," he lied.

She would not be glad to see him—he knew that. It was how she would react that he was trying to anticipate. Would she refuse to talk to him at all? Would she ask him inside? Would she call the island police-man if he persisted in badgering her? Would she even recognize him?

He had no strategy except to locate her and it was only now he real-ized how unprepared he was. He had found her too quickly. He hadn't had the time to think out his response if she shut the door in his face. It was too late to formulate a strategy. The boat was approaching a short wharf on the edge of a village. A mulatto boy aged round six or seven jumped off the end and into the boat as it was still moving. Omega motored on for a hundred yards or so and then turned the boat, cut the engine, and steered up onto the sand, transistor blaring some kind of rock-calypso.

"Take the man up to Mama," he instructed the boy.

Geoffrey wiped his face and dome with his sodden handkerchief, separated his clammy cotton shirt from his clammy skin, hauled the backpack onto his shoulder, and made a conscious point of not tripping over the nets or fish pots as he disembarked.

"Thank you Omega." he said shaking the fisherman's hand. "Your wife will take me to Miss Fitzpatrick's house, right. Or give me directions?"

"Yes to Miss Fitzpatrick's house."

As he followed the child along a botanical path overhung with palm trees and spiky-leafed plants with outsize hibiscus-like blossoms, the light coloring of the boy struck him as amusing. Must be a honky somewhere in Omega's woodpile, he concluded.

The path rose steadily and left the vegetation behind. The ground became firmer, rockier. Four girls on bicycles careened down towards them at breakneck speed, the leader shouting something at Omega's boy, which the boy appeared to ignore.

Geoffrey trudged up the hill. As usual he was sweating. And he was being eaten alive by hordes of invisible insects. Not mosquitoes. More like midges. He slapped futilely at his neck.

"No-see-ums." said the boy.

"No see what?"

The boy mimicked Geoffrey slapping at his neck. "No-see-ums. They see you. They think you tasty."

The path continued to rise for another hundred yards or so, then levelled off. Houses quickly came into view. The first, a small ramshackle affair of corrugated iron and concrete and was painted in a stunning canary yellow. They passed several more, big and small, all of mixed construction and all painted in the most amazing pastels he had ever seen. The colours weren't gaudy like in Irish villages, they were bright but somehow softened. They stopped at a bigger flamingo pink one set a little off the track. There was an adult bicycle, a man's model, lying in a fat cruciferous shrub. The boy stood it up, awkwardly mounted the crossbar and pedalled to the front door, calling Mama several times.

Uninvited, Geoffrey waited on the track for the mother to appear and speculated on how much further Thelma's house was. It was a narrow island. Even from this relatively low vantage point he realized that he could see the ocean on both sides. He even spotted Omega's boat chugging out to sea again. So wherever she lived, it couldn't be more than a mile away, two miles at the most. He wondered why Omega hadn't told the boy to take him directly to Thelma's. Probably because Omega was suspicious of his motives—he had said as much. Should he tip the boy. And what about the mother? Should he tip her also when she brought him to Thelma's? Omega had refused to take payment for the boat ride. Geoffrey mopped his head again. There was a different breeze up here, even though they were only about 300 feet above sea level. A drier breeze.

"Mama!" the boy, still standing astride the crossbar, had circumnavigated the house and was pedalling back to Geoffrey.

If she's not home, thought Geoffrey, he would ask him to take him directly to Thelma's and skip this intermediate step.

"Patrick! What is it Patrick?"

It was the first time in fifteen years that Geoffrey had heard Thelma's voice.

✦✦✦

She was wearing a loose brimmed straw hat. He couldn't see her clearly through his sunglasses, but he knew she looked surprised and didn't recognize him. She said, 'may I help you?' But he couldn't answer.

Then she turned to the boy, 'who is this man, Patrick?" The boy had shrugged. "Papa say, bring man to you." He shrugged again.

Now Thelma was studying him intently. "Geoffrey. Geoffrey Doyle?" She didn't look pleased.

He nodded and waited for her to smile.

But she didn't smile. Instead she turned to the boy. "Where is Winona?"

"On her bike with the girls."

"Go down and help your father then. And not on his bicycle. It's too dangerous."

"I want to listen to the man."

"Do as I tell you."

"Papa's out to sea. I waited for him and he brought the man for you.

"Wait for him again. Then help him with the catch."

The boy shrugged a third time. "Yes Mama."

***

They were in her living room. He was drinking a Bahamian brand of ginger beer. The brain was catching up, sifting and then assimilating the information. She was wearing a light green short-sleeved linen dress, buttons down the front. Her arms were brown but not very brown. And she was as thin as he had known her, maybe slightly broader around the beam, but only slightly. She had taken off her hat. There was grey in her hair, that was all. A few lines but no sagging chin or bagging eyes. She looked as if the last fifteen years had been her friends...she looked beautiful. And she was married. Married to Omega. And they had a son Patrick. And they also had a daughter who was older than Patrick—she had been one of the girls on the bikes.

He was sitting on a wicker couch. She came back in from the kitchen and sat down in the matching armchair. She hadn't brought herself a drink. Neither of them spoke initially. Geoffrey wiped his head again and slugged at the ginger beer.

"Why are you here, Geoffrey?"

"I needed to see you."

"Why?"

"I didn't come to see you specifically. I came to see Judith, to be introduced to her." He mustered all his resources of articulation. "Thelma, I came because I wanted to see my daughter, our daughter, Thelma."

He felt better now, more confident because he had managed to say some of the words he had yearned to say to her for so long. And yet at the same time he was almost paralyzed with nerves. The words seemed to be like bricks in his mouth. It almost choked him to get them out. And he was sweating again. He could feel the droplets erupting on his forehead. She was talking now. He had to be ready to respond to her.

"Don't you have children of your own. April told me you married a woman from New York. Did you not have children with her?"

"Judith is my own child. And yes my only child. Unlike you Thelma."

"Does your wife not want children?"

"We're divorced. It only lasted two years. She said I was still in love with you."

He waited for her to ask if that were so and would have said yes, had she asked, but she said nothing and concentrated on smoothing out the lap of her dress. Just like she used to do.

"Judith is fifteen."

"I know that. I also remember when we conceived her."

She looked up and glared at him. "Is that what you came for?" She spoke fiercely and deliberately. "To display my dirty linen to the world. Is this some sort of emotional blackmail?" Her face and chest were flaming. He'd only ever seen her flush with pleasure, never in anger.

"No, it isn't. That isn't why I came."

"Well then what's the real reason."

"I told you—it's to see Judith."

"So you just want to see her and then you'll be satisfied and leave us alone."

"To meet her, Thelma. Be introduced to her as her father. Be acknowledged, not denied."

"With a view to what. Getting custody. Bringing her back to Ireland. Never. I'll fight you every inch of the way in every court in the land. Here or there."

"For Christ's sake Thelma, I haven't come to abduct the child. Why would you even think that? What have you told her about me? That I'm the Bogey Man. That she must always be on her guard lest I steal her away. That I'm evil. You think I'm evil Thelma? Because I want to meet the daughter I was never allowed to meet." The words were coming out easier now.

"I haven't told her anything."

"Nothing. You've told her nothing about me?"

"Nothing."

"Well what then? Does she think Bradleigh's her father?"

"No she knows nothing about him, either."

"You must have told her something."

"I told her that her father and I were not able to get married."

"That's all?"

"A couple of years ago, she stumbled on the divorce papers I had filed from Sydney."

"So she does know about Bradleigh."

"She knows I was once married to a man called Bradleigh."

"And that he is not her father. Does she know that?"

"Yes, she knows that."

"Where is she now?"

"She's away at boarding school."

"Where?"

"In Nassau."

"When does school break?

"Not for another five weeks."

"Doesn't she come home on the weekends?"

"Every third weekend. She was here last weekend."

There was a clatter of metal outside and the velocipeding daughter burst into the room and plonked her long-limbed self down at her mother's feet. As best as Geoffrey could determine, she was about nine or ten years old.

"Who is the man? I want to know. And why are you red?"

"The man's name is Mr. Doyle and he is a friend of mine from Ireland. Please have the manners to introduce yourself properly."

The girl unfolded herself, stood up and extended her arm. Geoffrey stood up and reciprocated.

"My name is Winona and I am nine years old."

"Pleased to meet you Winona. Unfortunately I am a lot older than nine."

"Yes," she laughed. She folded again and leaned lazily on Thelma's knee. "Papa brought you over in the boat, didn't he?"

"Yes, he did."

"So why is Mama blushing. Did you kiss her?"

"Not yet."

"I think she's very pretty. Lots of men want to kiss—"

"Winona," Thelma interjected. "That's enough. Mr. Doyle did not come here to kiss me. He just came for a visit. Now you go out and do whatever you were doing."

Once more, the girl unfolded and stood up. "So, are you staying for dinner, Mister Doyle? Do you like grouper fish, because that's all we eat. And rice and peas."

"I like fish and rice and peas well enough, but I don't know if I will be able to stay."

"If I invite you, it would be rude for you not to stay."

"That would be very hospitable of you."

He stayed for dinner. They ate conch salad and rice and red lady peppers. Afterwards he played cards with Patrick and Winona who told him about the neighbors and about the Obeah voodoo woman and the secret pools on the north end, and the poisonous jellyfish that paralyzed you first before they tried to eat you, and how to catch a parrot and how much money "citymon" paid for one if it was the right age and the right colours and how to make sure the government in Nassau didn't know you were catching parrots, not that Patrick or Winona ever did even try but they knew the boys who did, even though the parrots belonged to the island and shouldn't be sold unless in Patrick's opinion they were old parrots with faded plumage which, as Winona quickly pointed out, nobody wanted anyway.

"Do you catch parrots in Ireland and sell them to a "citymon?"" Patrick wanted to know. "Or egrets? Big money for red egrets. More than for twenty parrots."

After dinner he sat outside with Omega and watched the sunset to the tunes of Winona and Patrick battling with Fur Elise and Molly Malone on the piano. Omega smoked a kind of cheroot and opened a bottle of nauseatingly sweet rum. As soon as the sun had dropped, it was dark. Not like in Ireland where the transition was gradual. Here God just flicked the light switch—something to do with the proximity to the equator, Geoffrey thought. But even as the light was switched off, it seemed the heat was switched on again. Oppressive, sticky heat. In minutes he was sweating like he had been in the morning. The elevation had only brought a temporary respite. He wiped his dome and his face. But already he had learned that adapting to Out Island living meant more than becoming accustomed to the Bahamian summer, it also necessitated steeling oneself for unfamiliar wildlife, specifically the insects. Endlessly biting mosquitoes and no-see-ums, cockroaches as long as oak leaves, persistently bleating hoppers and cicadas. The leaping lizards were another hazard. He had gone into the bathroom earlier and was enjoying a peak flow moment, when from inside the bowl bend, out peeked a lizard and got splashed on the head. Who was more alarmed it was difficult to tell. Geoffrey yelled 'Jaysus!' The lizard shook its head dry, scampered up the porcelain cliff and flung itself over the rim and onto the floor. Geoffrey staggered backwards, his hosepipe flailing. The lizard scurried between his legs, ran up the wall behind him and then freeze frame, it stopped halfway. And it didn't budge. Geoffrey was torn between trying to finish up, zip up, clean up, and at the same time keep one eye on the thing on the wall. And by then Patrick was banging on the bathroom door asking Mister Doyle if something bad had happened to him and if he, Patrick, could be of assistance.

He was to sleep in the living room. He didn't know if he'd able to sleep. Lizards might decide to dart up his pyjama leg. And then there was the heat. He had never experienced heat like this. New York in the summer had been bad, but this seemed even more pervasive. It was thick like New York, but it was more aggressive, more insinuating. And as if to accentuate the discomfort, it came accompanied by a soundtrack from a wildlife documentary. A multitrack quadraphonic cacophony of different ticking insects and the startlingly weird bird shrieks. And on this island there was no air-conditioned escape, no sound insulation.

Thelma came out to the porch to say goodnight—"we'll talk in the morning," she whispered to Geoffrey. "I need to sleep on things and see how I feel tomorrow." She rumpled Omega's grisly hair and kissed him on the cheek. "No trouble, now Omega. It will be all right." Then she was gone and the insects started up again.

Geoffrey unwrapped a pack of his duty-free cigarettes.

Omega poured him more rum.

"You were her lover, long time ago, yes?" said Omega quietly, almost philosophically as if this were an intriguing premiss for further discussion.

Geoffrey said nothing.

"You are the father of Judith, not Mr. White. He is dead now. That is why you have finally come."

"No, he's still alive."

Omega pondered. "But you are the father."

"Yes."

"You have come to take the girl. You cannot take Judith. You are only her father. I am her Papa."

"I have not come to take Judith. I have come to see Judith."

"Why?"

"Because I have never seen her, not even when she was a baby. And because it is my right to see her."

"Thelma didn't want you to see her?"

"She did not want me to see her. She wanted people to believe Mr. White was the father."

"And he is not dead?"

"No."

"Does he know now that you are the father?"

"No," said Geoffrey automatically. But as he uttered the word, the big hulking doubt invaded his brain yet again and joined in with the heat and the noise and the disconcerting fact that Omega knew so much about him and Thelma and that Omega was his daughter's papa.

"Does Mr. White have other children, a new wife?

"No."

"And he believes he is the father of Judith?"

"Then why does he not try to find her? Why he never try to find her. Not even one time?"

"I'm not sure."

"You have little understanding of people, Mr. Doyle. He never try to find her because he knows he is not the father."

They were silent for a while, but the turmoil in Geoffrey's head was as loud as the insect orchestra outside it. He drank more rum to drown out both the internal and external dins and allow his thoughts to settle down. The first to take coherent shape was that he needed not only Thelma's permission to meet Judith, but also Omega's. The second thought was that if Omega agreed he would be a useful ally in helping sway Thelma. If Omega did not grant his consent, then he would continue to plead his case with Thelma. If Thelma also withheld her cooperation, then he would make it clear, that with or without their blessing, he was going to make himself known to his daughter. His next thought was that he should strike while the iron was hot.

"Omega?"

"Yes."

"You are Judith's papa, I respect that. I wish I could have been her papa, but it was not to be. But I should be permitted to see her with my own eyes, to get to know her even a little bit, maybe to write to her when I return to Ireland, maybe one day have her fly over and visit me, not to take her from you and Thelma but to have me included, even if only in a small way, in her life. And her in mine." He paused, awaiting a reaction. "As her papa do you think this is a bad thing?"

Omega spat out the butt of the cheroot and lit a second. "To want to know her now so many years later—good or bad who can say? It is a natural thing that you want to see her. Is it a good thing or bad thing for Judith? She is fifteen. Part child, part woman. She asks about her father, sometimes a lot, sometimes not ever. Her mother says she does not know where he lives, or if he lives. Three years ago Judith writes letter, but she has no name to address it to, no address to send it to. So she puts it in envelope and writes on it, "To my real father" and then she licks it and locks it in her treasure box. I talk to Thelma, but Thelma says it would make trouble for all of us to tell her about you. She say it would make trouble for you also. 'Maybe later when's she's older'—that's what Thelma say."

Omega shook his head sadly. "I don't want trouble. But trouble come whether I want it or not."

"I am not trouble, Omega. She is almost a woman you say. She wants to know. Even if she decides she doesn't much like me, at least she won't feel cheated of the chance to know me. I want to do this the right way Omega."

"And if I say no and Thelma say no, what do you do then Mr. Doyle. Do you go to her against our wishes?"

"It is better for everyone if we all do it the right way."

***

When he woke up the next morning, the air was thin and clean and silent. The windows were open and the multicoloured curtains billowed like the sails of racing yachts. There was a note on the wicker table, but it was in a child's writing, not Thelma's. He found a bottle of locally branded citrus juice in the refrigerator and poured himself a glass before digging his reading glasses out of his backpack.

Dear Mister Doyle—we are in the market and will be back before 10 am. Yours truly, Winona.

Geoffrey checked his watch against their VCR. It was twenty past nine. He located his wash kit and headed for the bathroom. Before abluting he poked the toilet brush down into the bend and then initiated a pre-emptive flush as a warning to the local lizardry to appear now or forever hold their peace. By a quarter to ten he emerged, cleansed and scrubbed, ready for the day. He ate two slices of breadfruit and was just peeling a banana when he heard someone at the door. It was a neighbour, a large lady about his own age. She was calling 'Thelma, it's Jiji' and when she saw Geoffrey and the banana, she jumped. He laughed and tried to introduce himself. She seemed to understand. "I am thinking Thelma, and I find instead strange man with banana."

Thelma, Winona and Patrick arrived as she was still laughing. Thelma was wearing a tan linen dress and a colorful wooden beaded necklace. Jiji re-enacted the episode including her jumping and saying to herself 'who is this strange man eating a banana in Thelma's house.'

A little while later, at Thelma's suggestion the children took him on a tour of the island. She declined to join them because she had a project to prepare for the girl scout troop. Winona was one of the den leaders. Geoffrey expressed surprise that the island had the numbers to support a troop. He also wondered to himself why they would even be interested.

"Twenty-nine counting the two Cheemajan girls."

"I have badges in swimming, fishing, ornithology, reading, music, cooking and camping," chirruped Winona.

"Are there boy scouts too?"

"No." Patrick made a face. "There is no man Thelma on the island."

That he was being taken on a tour, Geoffrey read as a good sign; that it was Thelma's unprompted suggestion, he read as being even better. Unless of course she simply wanted to postpone confronting him. He wondered if she and Omega had talked and if Omega had communicated Geoffrey's resolve. If so it should certainly reinforce what he had said to her when he arrived.

The tour lasted almost three hours. First to the market where they looked at Omega's fish—he was out at sea, but his latest catch was in a box with his name alongside a dozen other fishermen's. An elderly Bahamian woman in a straw hat supervised the fish section. Patrick picked up a single green turtle from among the dozen or so grouper and a handful of dolphin fish in his father's box. It was a strange shade—a shiny teal—and the size of an infant. He pulled out its flippers and declared it a good catch and worth more than was being asked for it, though Geoffrey could not determine what the asking price was.

They moved on to unrecognizable fruits and watermelons, then beans, black pigeon peas and goat, bird, and lady red peppers, and by now had collected an assortment of children on bicycles and roller skates and others barefoot and in swimming shorts. At one hole-in-the-wall shop, Geoffrey tried on a brimmed straw hat and then at the audience's urging three more. A vote was taken and he purchased the second hat for two Bahamian dollars.

The heat was gathering strength again and the earlier freshness in the air was becoming moist and dank. They left the village and walked along the beach for about a mile and then travelled inland through the trees to a second high point on the island. From here they could see back down the length of the island and Patrick pointed out the blue roof on their pink house. They lay back on the rocks and ate fruit and espied Omega's boat and Patrick vainly attempted to bait a macaw which had ventured from the tree line to check them out. Then they descended to the far side and another village. It was more residential than commercial. It also seemed poorer, but nonetheless this was where the church was and the school and the school hall where the girl scouts met and where the island council meetings were held. Patrick and Winona showed him their classroom—it wasn't locked. And they entered the church, sat in their pew and said their own prayers. All Geoffrey could deduce about the denomination of the church was that it was Christian. He followed the children's example and knelt and shut his eyes. He prayed that an amicable and harmonious arrangement be reached. Maybe he shouldn't have mentioned writing to the girl, or having her visit, maybe saying those things would work against him and Omega would be convinced he would lose her to him. He had been stupid. He had let the rum do the talking. He didn't want a stand-off. He was uncomfortable in a conflict situation. And he particularly didn't want to alienate Thelma. Do that and she would never even speak to him ever. There would be no hope. What was he thinking. There was no hope. Mother of three, happily married, her own woman, her own life out here. Focus man, for your own good. Keep your eye on the ball, not on tall, thin Thelma in her linen dresses.

"Did you say a good prayer, Mr. Doyle?" Winona asked.

"I hope so. I tried to say the best I could."

He shouldn't have prayed for himself. He should have prayed for his daughter's welfare. If it was right for her to meet him, then let it be. If not, then so be it, no matter what action he took.

They followed a palm-cluttered path that paralleled the beach. The sea was calmer on this side of the island. Following the lead of Winona and Patrick, Geoffrey took off his shoes and ran down onto the beach after them. The sand was pillow-soft and wonderfully warm, but not burning hot. It was as if it had been heated to order. A pleasant breeze, neither salty nor stinging, the first breeze since they'd been on top of the hill, teased his face and banished his perpetual sweat.

And then there was the water. Waves lapped gently, seductively, teasing his hairy toes, inviting them to come in and play. Already the children were far ahead of him, but the depth of the water barely rose above their knees. In a matter of moments Patrick was calling to him to come on in, to come see the fish. Geoffrey rolled up his trousers and trotted through the water. It was exactly as described in travel brochures. If he thought the sand was heated to order, then the sea had a thermostat keyed to his physiological specifications. It was perfect, lukewarm warm and yet refreshing. Clean, clear, turquoise nectar. And swimming through it even at this shallow depth were schools of exotic fish. Skinny Marian blue fish dashed and darted, fat Kelly green ones ambled by— and all within inches of his shin bones. It was mesmerizing. He could see them clear as day. As if they were in his bath tub.

Patrick led him out to a long narrow reef on which Winona was precariously perched. When they reached her she had already scrambled up on the reef. The coral was jagged, but he'd no idea how jeopardous till he leaned up against it.

"No Mr. Doyle, it's too sharp for you. Do not touch it. Do not climb up like Winona. Instead look down and watch all the fish feed from the bottom." She was right on both counts. The coral had already scratched his arm and his sides in a dozen places and he hadn't even placed his full weight on it.

"Look down," she repeated.

At first he couldn't discern what it was he was looking at. The water, though still crystal clear was deeper. It shimmered and its images were distorted like in a hall of mirrors.

"Put your face under the water."

"In a minute Winona. Don't rush me."

On the sea bed around the bottom of the coral was a moving multi-colored ribbon about a foot wide that appeared to be constantly disintegrating and reforming.

"Take a big breath and go under, Mr. Doyle."

Just as he was about to comply, a very large pale shape slid silently towards the farthest point of the ribbon. His brain told him it was a sandshark though he'd never seen a sandshark in real life. His whole body reacted accordingly, instantly stiffening, then locking solid. He stood transfixed, the water lapping around his belly button, as the creature slipped beneath the undulating ribbon and then rose up through it, breaking and scattering it into a thousand floating smithereens. Then, as if sensing his presence, the creature turned and moved swiftly through the spangled explosion, outpacing it effortlessly. It was coming straight for him. Geoffrey could hear Winona laughing. He wanted to look over to see she was still on the reef, and to check that Patrick was at a safe distance, but he couldn't take his eyes off this ocean predator. Like the ribbon that was already recreating itself at the reef, it seemed to be polymorphous. It was closing in fast. It wasn't a sandshark, he could determine that now. And it was rolling as it swam, more like a porpoise, except it had two long trailing tendrils. And it had a mane. And they weren't tendrils, they were legs. It was Patrick for Christ's sake.

Patrick the sandshark, rugby-tackled him around the ankles and toppled him into the water where they wrestled one another before surfacing together. "I swim like a fish, yes?" the boy boasted.

"You swim like a shark."

"And I eat Irishmen with white, hairy legs." He reached out towards Geoffrey and dropped one of the fat, Kelly green fish down the front of his shirt. More splashing, laughing and falling down. He'd been in the Caribbean almost a week and this had been the first time he had actually got into the water. And was, he reflected, immediately attacked by a man-eating boy.

Afterwards, the three of them walked back towards the shore and following Patrick's example, they lay down flat on their backs in about six inches of water. Soft, warm water on a mattress of soft, warm sand. It was even more perfect than on the hill. Finally, lying fully dressed in trouble-free turquoise waters, he allowed Nature to do its work. To empty him of all his doubts and fears and fill him with the calming balm of orchid scented air and childishly simple skies with wispy white clouds. And for a long, long while, he bottled and basked, unbitten by mosquitoes, sandflies and no-see-ums; uninterrupted by the sudden scurrying of lizards. He knew he was drifting off, and he told himself that it was all right, that it was good for him to release his grip and let go.

Much later, he heard Winona's voice calling that it was time to get moving. Time to get up Mister Doyle. "Mama very angry if we late for lunch." Time to realize that the fascinating inky whorl emanating from his left hip pocket was dye from his saturated wallet.

They traced the coastline for a mile or so, then turned inland again to start the climb back. He was breathing heavily by the time the house was in sight. He was out of breath when they finally reached it. Their tour had brought them full circle. Tomorrow, they would show him the other end, they told him. That was out to the big reefs. The Obeah woman lived near the big reefs. And so did the Cheemajans. Tomorrow, he hoped, he would no longer be in suspense.

Thelma served them a spicy seafood gumbo for lunch. It had grouper in it. But no peas.

***

She was at the sink, washing the dishes, a bright, multicoloured oil-skin apron over her dress. It had a long-legged pale pink flamingo on it. He stood up from the table and asked where the towel was, but she declined the offer and bid him sit again. "I'll put on the kettle in a minute. I even have some Irish biscuits."

"Can we talk now?"

"I suppose you must. But let me wash up."

"Omega told me that she wants to know."

"I know."

"It's right Thelma. Not just for me, but for her too. And in the long run, for you, you and Omega. And Patrick and Winona as well."

"That sounds like a tired homily from a hack preacher."

"I believe it nonetheless. This is not a healthy situation and I know you know that as well as I do. If you'd no intention of telling her ever about her real father's identity, then you would have simply fictionalized me or had me killed off in a tragic car accident or something like that. So why didn't you close the possibility of discovery for her?"

"Because it would have been an outright lie."

"But what you've been doing has been even more deceitful, more cruel. You've been denying her the truth. That's lying by omission. You have to tell her Thelma. Sooner better than later. Better for everybody."

"And if I refuse."

"Don't."

"She'll hate me for this."

"Why would she hate you?"

"Because she's been asking for years. And I've postponed and obfuscated, dreading the evil day." She turned her back on him and tackled the gumbo pot. "I've been living in a fool's paradise. I've been so happy Geoffrey. So happy to be away from Bradleigh. Not just Bradleigh— everything —his mother, my mother, my sister and brother-in-law, all the conventions and phony morality and phoney concern that swamped, smothered my life there, that had me performing emotional acrobatics or aerobatics or aerobics or whatever's the right word, in order to be seen to be doing the right thing. Never asserting myself. Never breaking free. Instead, always the timid one, tip-toeing through life's thorns, always trying to keep the peace, putting a brave face, the best face on the worst situations. Always living a lie. Propagating the lie.

My lie, Bradleigh's lie, the families' lie. Timid…compliant…mousy Thelma. Thelma the good girl. Thelma toeing the party line."

Her back was still to him. She emptied the sink, rinsed out the pot, refilled the sink and submerged the four glasses they'd used at lunch.

"And then what do I do. I expand my lie, by creating a second lie and then incorporating it into the first. Having a affair with my nephew. Having a child by him. Deceiving everybody about the baby—knowing they didn't want to know the truth. Till finally, Timid Thelma plucked up the courage and did what she should have done ten years before— she ran away."

One by one she rinsed the glasses and inverted them on the dish rack. Then folded the dishrag, placed it over the spigot and turned finally to face him.

"And for me at least, it takes more courage to run away than to stand and forbear. I was familiar with standing and forbearing. I'd never run away before. Running away was the best thing I ever did."

Geoffrey wanted to ask about his contribution. Was having a relationship with him not the best thing she ever did? Surely that was her turning point? But he told himself to say nothing. Not to interrupt her now. Not to let his hungry ego and need for recognition cause her to stumble and fall and not finish the course. There would be no fight over seeing Judith now. He would get what he told himself he came for. But he would ruin it all if he attempted to fish for acknowledgement or gratitude for his crucial role in her epiphany.

He nodded to her that he understood and he saw that she was crying. Silent, silver tears. But he daren't get up from the table and take her hand as he desperately wanted to. That would throw her as much, if not more, than his seeking at minimum an honorable mention in her monologue.

"The best thing I ever did for myself," she repeated. "Having squandered my life trying to do what was best for the rest of them, for once I did what was best for myself. And yet, even here, with my own life and my own family, I'm still living a lie, just as you said."

She filled the kettle and plugged it in, then foraged in the cupboard for the crockery and set it on the table. And spoons from the drawer. And milk and sugar from the fridge.

"Sit down," he said calmly.

She acquiesced, but took her apron with its flamingo off first and hung it on its hook at the back of the door.

"You should realize that I always feared you might come. In Australia, I thought about it every day. I was like an escaped prisoner, always waiting to be tracked down, always listening for the knock on the door. That you would arrive armed with unaddressed issues, ugly truths, court orders and legal battles. That my new freedom would be polluted by your demands. But you didn't come. And I knew Bradleigh wouldn't. He didn't even contest the divorce. Then I moved here and time was passing. And I feared it less, despite bumping into your aunt and cousins —-though they never mentioned you and I couldn't ask. I convinced myself that you'd grown up and got your own life, your own wife, probably your own children. And a nice job and a house. So why would you jeopardize that to come see a child in whose life you had no involvement, none at all."

"You prevented me from having any involvement."

"Geoffrey, you were a boy. Infatuated. You would have been a child groom. You were too young. I instigated the whole affair, and when I discovered I was pregnant I orchestrated the charade to make everything look respectable. I was the cause. Ipso facto the result was my responsibility. And that included not landing you with a child you hadn't asked for and didn't want. But I wanted that child. I wanted it for myself. And of course, everybody was delighted. Bradleigh had proved his manhood. And I was his proof. His skinny anemic-looking wife was now florid-faced and full-bellied. Hurrah for Bradleigh. And I had to endure him strutting around like a stud bull, he who had barely even tried, and never once succeeded in doing it to me, let alone impregnating me. But oh no, it was hurrah for Bradleigh. And then my baby was born. And one afternoon as I looked at my tiny girl suck on my breast, he came in and sat watching. And stayed. And pontificated about bottle feeding and questioned the wisdom of nursing. And I felt my milk dry up in my pap and I knew I could not bear him any more. Could not bear having him tell me how to take care of my daughter. And that day I decided I would leave him."

She wiped her eyes quickly with her finger.

"But why didn't you tell her about me, when she asked."

"Why? Why would I? And what exactly would I tell her Geoffrey? That her mother, the woman who gave birth to her and brought her up to be straight and true and honest was in fact a tramp. A cheap slut who craved sex so badly she seduced her teenage nephew—that her mother was the female equivalent of a dirty old man looking up little girls' skirts and luring them to his house with lies about the cute little puppy dog they could play with. Isn't that a charming thing for a daughter to learn about her mother. I'd rather risk her wrath and suspicion than have her know that."

Had he read her wrongly? Was she going to fight him after all? He protested immediately. "It wasn't like that Thelma. There was nothing sordid about it. I made the first overture. And I was nineteen not nine. And you did not mislead me. If you've, over the years, decided to cast yourself as the big bad wolf, then you do us both an injustice. What we had was wild and wonderful, not cheap and sordid."

"Geoffrey. I was a married woman. I was 11 years older than you. And I was your aunt. By any definition, what we did was sordid."

"I fell in love with you Thelma. That wasn't sordid."

It was she who reached across the table and took his hand. His whole body shivered. It was the final nail in the coffin of requited love. " I know you did Geoffrey. But I didn't realize it till years later."

"It may sound corny, but you broke my heart. I never got over you. Still haven't."

This alarmed her. She withdrew her hand. "What are you saying? That you're not just here to meet Judith? What are you telling me Geoffrey?"

He was blowing it. Shooting his stupid fat mouth off. He wanted to be with her so much his whole body ached. He was harassing her. Stalking her. A crazed love-smitten buffoon. He had never moved on. His emotional development had been arrested in an adolescent crush. That's what his wife used to say to him. Move on Geoffrey. Move on. Thelma had moved on. She had moved on five minutes after their last cup of coffee together in Bewleys. Thelma had moved beyond his league, beyond his reach and he had better come to terms with that fact once and for all. Or he would truly have sabotaged his one chance to do this thing right.

He pulled himself together. "Don't worry," he reassured her, "I'm not here to proclaim my undying love for you. I'm not trying to seduce you away from your life here. Nor am I trying to bed you for old time's sake."

She relaxed and he smiled, but he wasn't quite done with the subject. On the contrary he embraced the chance to get the whole issue off his chest, or his heart. "Thelma, if you're uncomfortable with the fact that I'm still in love with you or in love with the idea of being with you then I'm sorry. But I'm not uncomfortable with it. I've with living with it for fifteen years. And I don't even have a photograph of you to fuel it. Just the memories and the what ifs. But I'm not here for you. I can see with my own eyes that you're happily married, that you've built your own life here, your own family. I see that you and Omega make a good couple, that he makes you happy, and—" he laughed to signal he was now being lighthearted, "and that he is ten times better looking than me. What hope would I have even if I had harbored evil intentions to lure you away."

She smiled. He had reprieved himself. Then he said aloud what he always suspected and now knew to be true. "I know you don't have any feelings for me Thelma. I simply and honestly just want to meet the only child I have." He was about to say more, to restate his case when he sensed he really had no more to say. So he stopped talking.

He was lying in the hammock in the garden, fitfully dozing between insect onslaughts, when she came out to him with a cold beer. "I phoned the school. You and I and Omega will go and visit her after church tomorrow. Jiji will keep an eye on the children. I phoned Captain Tom as well. He'll pick us up at the pier."

He was annoyed at the inclusion of Omega—this was not how he envisioned the meeting, but he didn't let it show. "Who's Captain Tom?"

"He's Omega's older brother. He's generally free on Sundays. Anyway he'll have us in Nassau in an hour and a half."

"Ninety minutes? Does he have a speedboat or something?"

"Better than a speedboat," she smiled, "he has a seaplane."

"I'm impressed." He wanted to ask her what she had said to Judith about him, and how she planned to introduce him, but it was she who broached the subject.

"I told her that you are an old friend of mine from Ireland and that I wanted her to meet you before you left."

"Did she ask why you wanted her to meet me."

"No. She just asked if we could go to her favorite restaurant. And I said 'yes' because I thought you would enjoy it."

"And how are we breaking the news to her?" He was suspicious. Perhaps Thelma would introduce him as an old friend and leave it at that, and they'd all stroll around town and have a lovely afternoon and bid one another farewell and Judith would be none the wiser. "We have to tell her. We have to tell her I'm her father."

"I'll be the one that tells her. But you and Omega will be with me. I'm not going to go into details. Nothing about you being Bradleigh's nephew. Or how we met. Or why it happened. Just the basic information. That's as much as I can handle. And I don't know if I can handle it. And I've no idea how she'll react. She might slap me across the face, refuse to speak to me ever again—this could be the worst decision I ever made."

Now that he was reassured, he tried to reassure her. "Thelma, even if she does those things—which I don't believe she will—it would only be from shock. It would only be temporary. Once the shock wore off, she'd come to terms with it and appreciate your honesty instead of resenting your dissembling. And remember Omega will be there. If she sees that her papa accepts this, that will help cushion the shock, or quell any anger."

"I hope so. I really hope so."

A little while later she came out to check on him and he reminded her that he still didn't have any perception of what the girl looked like—there were no photographs of any of them in the living room.

"She's in a difficult phase. Doesn't want her picture taken. Thinks it's contrived and narcissistic to pose for the camera. And of course, she's never happy with the way the pictures turn out. But I do have a family portrait in the bedroom."

A few minutes passed and she returned with a large framed photo. All five of them were in the traditional family arrangement—children seated in the front, proud parents standing behind them. Omega and Patrick had worn suits, Thelma and the girls, long dresses. "We had it taken the Christmas before last in Nassau."

"That's Judith." Thelma pointed to the one person in the photo whom he had not yet met— the older white girl in the center.

"I guessed that," he laughed.

"Her hair's much shorter now."

There was a small snapshot inserted in the bottom right corner of the frame. Judith and Omega were in the boat each holding up a grouper.

"That was when she was nine. Omega used to take her fishing."

In neither picture could he truly get a feel for her. Her looks fell somewhere between pretty and plain as if their final outcome had yet to be decided. The boat picture was the better of the two. She was genuinely grinning, very proud of her catch, very proud to be fisherman like her Papa.

"Tell me who she resembles."

"She probably looks more like you at the moment, Geoffrey."

"That's not an advantage."

"You have a handsome face. A kind face."

"Apart from looks, who does she take after?"

"That's tricky. She's an adolescent and she broods a lot. But I can't be sure if it's her nature or what's currently happening in her life. I was like that at her age. Except I was overwhelmed with shyness. She's certainly not shy or timid. Not one bit. I was determined I was not going to repeat my parents' mistakes and bring her up like I was brought up afraid of my own shadow. No Judith is an independent young woman. Too independent, I think sometimes. And she reads everything she can lay her hands on. She speaks her mind too. That's like you, Geoffrey. You always spoke your mind."

"I'm more the 'open mouth, insert foot' type of plain speaker. She can do without that."

"She wouldn't have been conceived without that, Geoffrey."

It was the first time she actually said the words, said that were it not for him, there would be no Judith. And if one followed the chain reaction, no Omega, no Winona, no Patrick.

They talked one more time after dinner. The kids were upset that he would be leaving the next day and they wanted to go to Nassau with them and go to the restaurant with Judith, but Thelma told them there wasn't room in Tom's plane and that anyway they got to take Geoffrey around the island and Judith hadn't even met him yet.

"But we wanted him to meet the Obeah lady and see the burial grounds of the walking dead," Winona protested.

"And the poisonous pools," added Patrick.

"One day," said Geoffrey, "when you're grown up, you might come to Ireland and pay me a visit and I will show you the mountain on top of a mountain where the famous Irish warrior Queen, Queen Maeve, is buried. And the massive stone cromlech rings used for human sacrifices."

"Wow!" said Patrick. "A mountain on top of a mountain. I've not even seen one mountain alone."

"Cool! A double-decker mountain," said Winona.

They walked together down towards the West beach where the sun was setting. "My sister writes to me sometimes." Thelma began. "Not often, but she's the only contact over there that I have left. The disgrace was too much for my parents. And then Omega to top it off—adding black insult to white injury."

"Do they know about the children?"

"I'm sure my sister has told my mother. But nothing has ever been acknowledged."

"Do you still want them to accept Omega and their grandchildren? They can't be getting any younger."

"It's gone beyond that, Geoffrey. If they made contact with me, then I suppose I would reciprocate. But I'm not going to waste any more of my life trying to do right by them. Instead I'm putting my energy into making what I have work."

"I think you have succeeded. You have a very lovely family."

"Thank you for saying that. But I wanted to ask you something. What I was starting to say was that in one of my sister's letters, she told me she had heard that Bradleigh and his mother were living with you somewhere in Wicklow. Was she right?"

Geoffrey explained that it was true, but that Granny White had died four months previously.

"But why were they living with you?"

"It's a long story Thelma. And the opposite of yours. You shed your family. I gathered mine closer. By default not by design. I even acquired some additional members."

"What made you decide to come here now?"

He told her about Granny White's death. About how he believed he was obligated to shelter her in his potato crisp house and how her personality had changed beyond all recognition. He explained that he felt his biggest affront had not been to Bradleigh but to Granny White. And that when she died, he somehow sensed he was freed to finally address this unresolved issue in his life.

"I had no idea you were so entangled with them. I just assumed…" She stopped. "I just assumed that my being pregnant would have minimal effect on your life. Does your wife, I mean your ex-wife, did she know about Judith?"

"No. I never told anybody. But I did tell her that I'd had an affair with a married woman and that you ended it after three months."

The sun was sinking now in a final blaze of glory. Ironic, he thought to himself, bearing in mind that he had only moments previously, complimented her on having created a happy family without him.

"What you said yesterday, Geoffrey, about me having no feelings for you—that's not true. You were a catalyst for me. Before we did what we did, it was as if my life were a car stuck in second gear. Screaming, grinding, protesting. You enabled me to shift straight through to fifth. You changed everything. And I'm sorry…Truly sorry. I never realized that it cost you so dearly."

He wasn't sure how to respond, but he was glad she had said those things. And he liked the car analogy. It also reinforced his resolve to start shifting his own gears before they fused with rust. But he couldn't resist a final, final, last ditch try, especially now when she was feeling guilty and that God had gone to the bother to provide such a spectacular sunset. This was it. Last call. Last chance.

"Thelma, are you really sure you've no feelings, romantic feelings, towards me anymore?"

She shook her head. "I'm afraid not Geoffrey."

"Or even sexual desires."

"No, my longings are well taken care of."

He had gone and done it now. Left no stone unturned. Left himself no room, not even a secret cubic millimetre in which to fantasize that she still hankered for him just a little.

"But I've no regrets either." She reached out and squeezed his hand. And then just as quickly let go again.

"You got pregnant deliberately, didn't you?"

"Yes. But I didn't plan it from the outset. Only when I got to really know you, only then did I decide that you were my one chance to be married and have a baby."

By the time they had walked back to the house, God had switched the sun off and the bug cacophony on.

***

That night he sat outside with Omega again. Omega had procured a dozen bottles of Guinness which Geoffrey read as a goodwill gesture. He drew Geoffrey's attention to the label which proclaimed it had been bottled in the Bahamas. Apparently Guinness was so popular there, it warranted a local bottling plant.

At first, jungle heat and jungle sounds seemed an incongruous match with Guinness, but by the third bottle the incongruity faded and a wonderful harmony suffused him. Tomorrow he would meet his daughter.

"We're doing the right thing Omega. The right thing for everybody."

In a way, he was almost relieved she had turned him down.

***

The note on the table explained that they had gone to church. Geoffrey poured himself the citrus juice, drank it, then washed, shaved and performed the necessary bodily functions. He couldn't tell whether it was the Guinness, the citrus or his nerves, but whatever the reason he was as loose as a goose. He was glad there was nobody in the house. He would have liked to have been invited to church with them. He hadn't attended a church service since Granny White's funeral. And he should really acknowledge that his prayer had been answered. So he formed a half-baked prayer of thanksgiving in his head with an addendum that all go well at the restaurant. Then he foraged in his backpack for fresh clothes—a white cotton shirt with pockets and epaulets and his khakis. He touched up his tonsure, pulled in his paunch and reviewed himself in the mirror. It was no wonder Thelma didn't recognize him. The last time she saw him, his hair was almost down to his shoulders. Nowadays, this was as good as it got, though he resolved to get himself into shape this year. What teenage girl wants a fat, balding father! He could do nothing about the balding, but he could shed the blubber.

It was only 10:30am. They wouldn't be back till noon. He began to pace the house. He looked in Patrick's room—it was the usual hodge-podge of boy stuff. Two giant basketball posters adorned the wall alongside his bed. And there were spaceships and model cars. With the exception of a six foot long skeleton of a fish of some sort, it could have been any boy's room anywhere in the world. The same held true when he peeked into Winona's room which was bigger and housed two beds—obviously this was also Judith's room. Lots of pinks and frills and stuffed toys and a poster of some young skinny male film star whom Geoffrey couldn't identify. The abundance of shells and sea stones strung and half strung into necklaces or hangings—Geoffrey wasn't really too sure what he was looking at—were the only clue that he was not in Ireland being shown the bedroom of the daughter of one of his friends.

He didn't want to go into "their" bedroom, but of course he did. And they did share the same bed—her white nightie (probably linen he speculated) neatly folded on her pillow. No sign of Omega's pyjamas—probably didn't wear any. All the more convenient for her, should she wake up in the middle of the night and decide she needed her sexual longings to be taken care of. No he shouldn't pursue that line of thought.

There was a biography of Eleanor Roosevelt on her bamboo table—another independent woman who knew what she was about and didn't take 'no' for an answer. So there she'd be, reading an uplifting chapter every night before going to sleep, maybe chatting with Omega about the children or about her class or her girl scouts or his catch, and then they both roll over and go to sleep serenaded by the bug symphony outside. But some nights maybe they wouldn't talk about the children or his catch, and instead they'd say other things, whisper intimate things, share lover's secrets, become lovers in the night. Maybe she still took notes in a little notebook like she had with him. And then in the freshness of the morning, with the sun slanting through the uneven bamboo blinds like it was now, she would get up and make her lover breakfast or bring him a glass of citrus juice and hop back into bed and tickle him or reach between his thighs for some early morning action before he had to go fishing and she go teaching. Maybe she even let him do it to her up against the door.

Yes, both his prayers had been answered. The answer to the first was 'yes'. The answer to the second was 'no'. No, no, never, no more.

***

The school—St. Cecilia's Academy for Young Women—was a rambling hybrid of Victorian and Bahamian architecture. The main building was a redbrick five-storey mansion that could have been imported brick for brick from the English countryside. It was flanked by adjoining pink stucco wings of different lengths and heights. These housed the classrooms. A long palm-lined driveway led to the main road; but at the back a second palm-lined path meandered between tennis courts and hockey pitches before arriving at the school's private beach. While obviously opulent, the building and its grounds broadcast a healthy overtone of dilapidation that imbued them with character. The window frames were so inconsistent they presented an illustrated history of Caribbean fenestration.

He was also intrigued by an ancient jalopy of a bicycle protruding from the top of a sixty-foot palm tree, and in one of the tennis courts a metal-framed coat-rack was inextricably entangled in the net.

They had landed at Captain Tom's wharf on the quiet side of Nassau—Thelma had knitted during the entire flight. The drive to the school (Captain Tom had loaned them the car) had been short—just two bridges and twenty minutes away.

Having announced their arrival to the crone on duty in the sentry box just inside the lobby, Geoffrey, Thelma and Omega were dismissively waved to the seating area. The crone phoned upstairs and left a message with someone to tell Judith Fitzpatrick that her guests were in the lobby. There were three other people waiting—a mother and a father, not together, and a teenage boy who was supposedly there for his sister though Geoffrey had his doubts about him.

Omega flipped through a back issue of *Maritime Monthly*, Thelma picked up her knitting from where she left off in the aeroplane and Geoffrey measured the pulse of the place by watching the varied strides and velocities of girls descend the staircase in ones and twos, and twos and threes—some in school uniform, most in shorts and T-shirts. Whether they were long or short, thin or fat, black or white, Geoffrey quickly divined that galloping, clomping or hurtling down the stairs were the preferred forms of locomotion for nearly all of the inmates. The fastest were always those in uniform because they had a chit which proclaimed them free to escape, but not until they passed muster with the crone who checked that blazers were buttoned, straw hats straightened, skirts at the appropriate length, shoes regulation, and socks pulled up. Inspection completed, she would then stamp their chits with the official seal and time.

The teenager and his "so-called" sister were the first to be reunited— the little pat she gave him on the behind belied their sibling status. Then the girls of the two other parents came and went. You could hear the thunder of hooves way before you actually saw the girl to whom they belonged turn the corner into the final stretch. Still no sign of Judith. As each new descendant triumphantly hit the linoleum floor and dismissed the three visitors with a glance, he would know that this was not her. He had memorized her face from the family photograph, but that had been taken two years ago and Thelma said she had cut her hair since then because it was a nuisance.

He was getting nervous now, sweating again. He was fully aware that Judith was a young woman, but he never really thought about the implications of that until now. He only taught boys, and his knowledge of teenage girls was limited to anecdotal stories he heard from married teachers and a couple of his friends. A lot of the young ladies at St. Cecelia's Academy seemed remarkably developed for their age and even when those who didn't have much shape had a lot of the moves and plenty of attitude. He suddenly found himself speculating that Judith probably had breasts and her periods already. He just stopped himself short of asking Thelma.

What about boyfriends? Did she think boys were interesting, or exciting? What age was Eileen when he dated her? Fifteen…sixteen. She was fifteen then. He had been sixteen. Eileen's hormones or estrogen or whatever had certainly "kicked in" at fifteen.

"Does she have a boyfriend?" he whispered to Thelma.

"No she doesn't." Omega answered without looking up from his *Maritime Monthly*.

"According to Winona," said Thelma, "she likes a boy called Richard, the one whose father works in the finance—"

"I know who Richard is. And she's not interested in him."

∗∗∗

He had missed her coming down the stairs—his attention must have been distracted at the critical moment, the moment he'd been waiting for, the moment he'd been building up to all these years. And the gombeen eejit that he was, he'd missed it. Sitting like a fool, reading the face of each girl, waiting for a reaction when she saw him, a flash of instant recognition—that he and she would know simply by making eye contact that they were father and daughter. But he didn't have any warning, not even a few seconds to brace himself. Yet he had been looking at the stairs. Two girls were clomping down them even now…so he must have daydreaming or else she had materialized out of thin air. Now she was next to him, warmly embracing her papa, asking him something about allowance money, then giving her mother a quick peck on the cheek…and all he could see was the back of her head. He still hadn't seen her face.

Her mother was talking. "We were waiting for you to come down the stairs."

"No I was outside. I just came in. I guessed it was getting late."

"You had to guess? Where's the beautiful watch we gave you for your birthday?"

"Michelle has it. It's only for today so you needn't fuss. "

"Why has Michelle got your watch?"

"She lost hers on the field trip to Bonney's Reef and Mrs. Clutcheon said if she didn't have a watch she couldn't go into town this morning even though Susan Washington has a watch and she's Michelle's pass partner for today. Of course that's just so typical of Clutcheon. Avoid logic and common sense at all costs—that's her philosophy."

"She's just being responsible dear."

"Well I'm sure you didn't come all this way to tell me how responsible Clutcheon is. So what's the occasion? And who's the mystery man?"

At last she turned and looked directly at him. "Are you he?"

Without meaning to, Geoffrey wiped his brow. Then realizing that he did not want his sweating to be her first memory of him, he attempted to obliterate it by quickly pocketting his handkerchief, standing up and proffering his hand. "Yes," he said in his strongest voice. "Allow me to introduce myself. Geoffrey Doyle, man of mystery."

She smiled. "The best kind of man to be," she quipped back, and shook his hand with gusto.

***

Between leaving the lobby and getting into the car, she ditched the tie, unbuttoned the top three buttons of her blouse and hoisted her skirt to her thighs.

"I wish you wouldn't do that dear, it's most unbecoming."

"Well mother, I've decided to become unbecoming this term. It's my difficult phase. My teenage rebellion. But don't worry, I'm sure I'll be very becoming again by the time I'm eighteen."

She was not at all even close to any of the teenage variations of womanhood he had anticipated, but he liked her immediately. They were in the car now, she in the back beside him. She talked a lot about everything. And she informed them she'd been reading more than ever. Her intake spanned from Dostoyevsky's *Idiot*, to Hemingway's *Old Man and the Sea*, Orwell's *Animal Farm* and Rushdie's *Satanic Verses*. Her teachers apparently were virtually illiterate, for she had a good deal to say about the intellectual shortcomings of a school staff whose sole goal in her opinion was to do the least amount of work to ensure an easy transition to retirement.

"Geoffrey is a teacher dear. He teaches boys."

Judith barely blinked before retorting. "No he doesn't."

"What do you mean he doesn't. That's his job, dear. In Ireland."

"He doesn't teach boys, because boys can't be taught." And she was off again. "At the very best they can only pretend to be taught. And even that only lasts for short periods. The male has only one thing on his pea-brain of a mind at any one time. And if it's not soccer, it's basketball, and if it's not basketball, it's cars. And if it's not cars, it's how they can get a girl to—"

"That's enough dear."

"Present company excluded of course."

She smiled at him again. Her facial expressions like her conversation moved seamlessly from one scene to another. Now she looked intensely jaded as she expounded on the state of the road they were travelling—it was pitted and potholed—which spurred her through the subjects of government ineptitude, endemic Bahamian complacency and political corruption—all so typical and predictable. Next year she would be the editor of *The Conch*, which was the school newspaper, and if she wasn't, then she'd damned well start an alternative school paper along with Barbara Withers, Susan Chong and Mandela Duchamps.

"Please don't curse dear" said Thelma, "there's no call for it. And the English language offers a wealth of options for expressing outrage."

Geoffrey watched her as if he were hypnotized. Yes, she talked a lot, that was for sure. And she was certainly smart. Lookswise though—well she hadn't exactly lucked out in that department. Or in physique for that matter. Thelma was right—if she took after either of them, it was him. Broad and solid, not long and lean like her mother—more like an abbreviated version of himself as an adult, but with a rounder, bolder face. But that could change, Geoffrey was optimistic. After all she was only fifteen. It could just be puppy fat—she might well shed it and sprout a few inches. His frame had filled out in his twenties. Maybe hers would stretch instead. Anyway what she lacked in looks, she had in spirit.

The restaurant was called Rum 'n' Tum's and it was situated not so much on a headland but in a headland. Converted pirate caves carved into the cliff face overlooked a never-ending parade of rollers that crashed against the rocks below them. It was a popular restaurant and the wait for Sunday seating was 35 minutes if you had failed to make a reservation. However Thelma had not neglected that detail and the foursome were ushered past reception and onto the replica bridge of a pirate ship. They were quickly positioned behind the wheel, a group photograph was snapped and they were led down the other side of the bridge and into the restaurant proper. Here they were greeted by a wax likeness of the infamous Blackbeard, pistolled and cutlassed to the teeth, his head shrouded in an intimidating miasma of blue taper smoke, much as he reputedly sported in his heyday. After Blackbeard was a line-up of lesser-knowns including one female pirate with whom Judith seemed particularly endeared, stopping to point out her listed feats of derring-do. From there they were whisked through the winding caverns of the erstwhile pirates' lair. Faux and authentic pirate memorabilia including skeletons and ships' masts bedecked the caves.

They followed the host from one buccaneeringly boisterous room to another and then to a third and then outside to a ribbon-wide cliff path and finally up two flights of steps to Read's Room where they were seated at a giant cliff opening. Now the rollers crashed unseen beneath them, but their view took in a vast expanse of azures, acquamarines, turquoises, emeralds and ceruleans. You could actually monitor black clouds of fish travelling back and forth. Presumably in pirate days you could also monitor fat, juicy cargo ships waddling into and out of port.

To underscore its name and pirate theme, the menu featured rhyming selections from the familiar 'surf 'n' turf' to the more intimidating 'shark 'n' bark', 'conch 'n' plonk', 'turtle 'n' myrtle', 'cabbage 'n' baggage', 'steak 'n' cake' and the ubiquitous grouper served in a 'stewper'. The highly recommended dessert was 'guava duff 'n' lava ruff'. Geoffrey ordered the 'steak 'n' cake' (crabcake) with a side order of baked potato from a large-breasted black woman pirate with three gold front teeth and a red bandana. Thelma chose 'chicken 'n' pick 'em', Omega also opted for the steak, and Judith the Bahama Mama which promised to be fully loaded with a bit of everything. Choosing was the best part of the meal. Laughing, reading aloud the descriptive blurbs and accompanying tales wickedness and debauchery. Omega claimed it was all Madison Avenue hocus-pocus. Judith declared that it was not hocus-pocus and that even if it was, then not all hocus-pocus was bad. Thelma confessed that although riddled with historical inaccuracies, it was somewhat amusing and that the view, if nothing else, justified the expense.

"So Geoffrey…" Judith said in confident tone.

Geoffrey braced himself for a challenge.

"…what makes you such a special friend, that I get to escape from that intellectual wasteland for a whole afternoon? And by the way, I'm sure you're a much better teacher than any of our motley crew."

Thelma answered for him. "Well dear, I've known Geoffrey for a long time. When he was a student, he used to work in the garden, two or three times a week. That's how I first met him"

"So how come I've never heard mention of him before?"

"Well I don't tell you everything dear."

Judith pulled a face and switched to a sarcastic mode. "Yes mother I am aware of that."

She was a strange mix, this daughter of his. In one breath it was all altruism and idealism and in the next it was petulance and sarcasm. This broad and highly articulate spectrum of expression in a fifteen year old was something beyond his experience. The boys he taught were by and large a taciturn bunch. Similar to Judith's earlier description of boys, his lot had much the same interests—soccer, hurling, Gaelic football, livestock, tractors and girls were the only subjects, and in that order, on which they held strong opinions. On the other hand her personality was not totally unfamiliar to him—a partial reprise of Maggie as a young girl flickered through his memory, and there was somebody else, somebody equally volatile, a girl he knew well.

Now she turned to Geoffrey again, not aggressively, but softly with a teasing smile. "So special friend of Mummy's, how is it you're so special?"

Eileen, that's who she reminded him of. Bold as brass, outspoken and outrageous.

"Do tell, Mr. Doyle," she almost cooed, "to what do I owe this privilege?"

"You shouldn't be so forthright, Judith," her mother cautioned.

Of course a substantial chunk of this behaviour had to be for his benefit. Bravado was what it was—strutting her verbal stuff to demonstrate to him, a stranger, that she was no child.

A few seconds later he was forced to revise this bravado notion. Her mother's 'forthright' comment must have been some sort of touchstone for it instantly propelled her into a vituperative monologue. Now he realized she was using his presence as a foil to keep her mother at bay so she could speak her mind.

"Apparently I'm not permitted to ask such direct questions. There are a lot of questions a fifteen year old young lady—" she placed particular emphasis on the 'young lady' for her mother's benefit— "is not permit-ted to ask. According to Mummy anyway. Who her father is, being on the top of the forbidden list. Well special friend of Mummy's, do you know who put all the spermie-wormies inside Mummy's vagina that made little me? Somebody had to have done it. And we all know it was-n't her so-called "husband", don't we!"

Omega started to talk. His voice was soft and low and described how life was not all black and white and right and wrong. That it came fully stocked with complications and grey areas.

"There's nothing grey about it, Papa. Either you do get knocked up or you don't. Either you let the boy do it to you, or he does it anyway. That's black and white in my book."

It was kind of like when he first tried learning how to dive. You were at the edge of the pool, steeled, hands outstretched, head down, all set to go, except you couldn't go. Then suddenly you were pushed from behind and in you went, like it or no. This time it wasn't Moocher who pushed him, it was his daughter.

"I did it," he heard himself saying.

He had done it, alright. He had dived in. And instantly the water swirled around his head, clouding his vision, jamming his hearing.

"What did you do?" she asked, not comprehending.

"I put the spermie-wormies inside your Mummy."

***

"What you must understand Judith…" Omega was talking, "your Mummy's husband was unable to consummate the marriage. And as a result of this, he drank heavily and became abusive towards Mummy and over time—"

"So special friend here, he was her Prince Charming and charmed the panties right off her, is that it? In the garden shed I suppose, since he was the gardener after all. Tell me Mummy, was it just a one-afternoon stand. Or did he have to charm them off you lots of times before he hit the jackpot?"

Geoffrey was still underwater, choking in his own frankness, choking with rage at this child's unwarranted hostility towards the woman he loved, trying desperately to surface, to break through the seaweed of strangled emotion, spluttering, gasping, gulping for words, then swallowing too many at once. He looked to Thelma for rescue, wanting her to say his words, to bring this girl to heel, but Thelma's hands were covering her face. How dare this precocious little bitch talk to her mother in that way. How could she presuppose to judge her mother's behaviour with him. Why should she automatically cast their relationship in the seediest possible light. There wasn't one iota of seediness in Thelma's character—romance, tragedy, passion, determination, spirit, affection, kindness, sacrifice—yes they were all present. There was nothing cheap and tawdry about her and yet those seemed to be the first things on the daughter's mind. Thelma should stop crying and slap the ungrateful punk across her stupid face. He, Geoffrey, should be slap her.

But he didn't slap her. Instead, his words all came together and poured out in a flash-flood over which he had no control whatsoever. "What do you know about it? About how your mother suffered? About how she sacrificed everything to bring you up in an environment free from petty jealousies, free from family squabbling, free from an alcoholic's endless controlling and bullying. And this is how you thank her, by calling her a slut. Why? Because she had an affair."

"Geoffrey…"

"So much for all your reading…"

"Geoffrey…" it was Omega.

"…so much for your so-called intellectual insights…"

"Geoffrey…" Omega had reached across the table and was gripping his wrist.

"An ignoramus wouldn't jump to such base conclusions as quickly as your sewer of a mind does." The grip on his wrist was now so severe, he could feel it pulling him through the seaweed and out of the flood. "Why?"

"No more talking." Omega instructed them all. "No more talking. The waitress wishes to serve us."

"Now me hearties, here be your vittles. Eat every last morsel, for there be no knowing where your next meal will come from. Now who be for the Bahama Mama?"

There being no immediate response, Omega directed the dishes to their appointed diners. Everybody served, the buccaneeress bared her gold teeth and gave them a dirty look. "I'll be back to check on you in ten minutes, and there'd better be no fighting at the table or you'll all be walking the plank."

As soon as she'd gone, Thelma excused herself and left the table. Judith shrugged and started in on her Bahama Mama. Omega gave a backward wave of his arm across her plate. "We do not begin until your mother returns."

"Lady Chatterly, you mean. Or should I say Lady Thelma."

"And I say, 'that's enough.'"

For at least five minutes they sat in silence. Geoffrey stared at his steak 'n' cake and thought desperately about what he should do. Should he try and explain to the girl? Should he get up and look for Thelma, in case she'd gone outside and not to the ladies' room. Should he ask Omega to check outside. The buccaneeress passed by with a tray for a nearby table. She paused, saw no eating happening, seemed about to say something, then changed her mind and moved on. Finally, Geoffrey saw Thelma walking purposefully towards them. She took her seat.

"Oh dear, I hadn't meant for you to wait. Please start everybody, before it gets cold. Perhaps Omega, you would say grace for us."

Having served her other table, and seeing this group now eating, the buxom buccaneeress enquired if everything was to their liking.

Judith answered. "The food is fine if that's what you mean. My mother and I and my father and my other father are enjoying it immensely."

The waitress started to respond, thought the better of it, and left.

"That's exactly how it is," said Omega. "You have two fathers. And both fathers are good and honest men, so you should believe yourself lucky." The girl started to interrupt, but he gave her such a contemptuous look, she pulled back. "As I was saying—and do not interrupt me again, daughter,—you are in a fortunate position, unusual but fortunate should you try and make the most of it. There are a lot of daughters in this world who don't even have one good father. You have known me as a good papa for most of your life and now you can look forward to the excitement of getting to know your other good father. That is not a bad thing. That is a good thing. You should think about it. You should think before you talk."

"He's just a stupid schoolteacher. I thought at least he'd be a somebody."

"And what am I—a stupid fisherman? And what does that make you? It makes you a very stupid schoolgirl. Very intelligent, but very stupid. Because you can't see or refuse to see, or do not wish to see, the woods for the trees—you can't see that this is a good thing."

"Oh I can see just fine, Daddy. I can see plain as the nose on my face that those two are disgusting beyond words, that the only thing I want to do now is vomit over the pair of them—the two fornicators. Says a lot, doesn't it, for her pious, upright life," she flicked her hand towards her mother, "pillar of the church, founder of the girl scouts, healthy mind and healthy body and feeding me the sanctimonious 'be a good girl' line and 'let dignity, duty and self-respect be your watchwords'. Easy to say after you've had your fun and frolics with the gardener. And maybe the plumber. Or how about the milkman, or the delivery boy. I mean, is this the best you could do Mummy? The latter day gardener? Couldn't you have least spread them for somebody a little more original. Like a racing car driver or a poet, or even an actor or a leading politician or a business tycoon—anything—an inventor, a guerilla fighter—anything other than a fat balding, schoolteacher."

"Have you done?" Geoffrey asked.

"No Daddy dearest, I haven't. But perhaps I should get to know you better before I jump to conclusions. So tell me, what momentous things have you done with your life apart from knocking Mummy up? Have you done anything good and noble, anything you could be proud of now that you've reached your middle age, have you composed beautiful music, written a poem, painted, invented a vaccine for some deadly disease, worked tirelessly to feed the starving, help the homeless, fight for the oppressed. Or maybe you've been too busy with the little wifey and three darling children at home in suburbia, who by the way are wondering what on earth you're doing by yourself over here. Did you come back to see if there was still fire in the old lust yet. Think you might give Mummy the slam, bam, thankyou ma'am once more for old times sake, think you could—"

"Enough!" Thelma roared. And flung a glass of water across the girl's face. "Enough of your foul mouth."

Very slowly and deliberately, the girl wiped the water off. "Enough of your foul mouth, mother, I say. Enough of all of you. Because I can't swallow any more of it." She whirled her head around to glare at each of the three conspirators. Before Geoffrey had even grasped what she was about to do, she had lifted up her plate of Bahama Mama and hurled it across the table at her mother's face.

She pushed her chair back and walked out.

"Don't any one of you come after me. I'll find my own way back."

And that was the last Geoffrey saw of her.

Chapter eighteen

The stewardess served him two miniature Scotch bottles, a plastic glass, a can of soda water and a bag of salted and dry-roasted nuts. He poured both bottles into the glass, sipped, looked out the window at the blue Caribbean and two gold-fringed islands and smiled laconically to himself. 'So Mrs. Lincoln, apart from the assassination, how did you like the play?' he thought wryly. He reached down to his knapsack, found his passport and took out the photograph he had pressed inside. They all were smiling as they posed around the ship's wheel just inside Rum 'n' Tums. Thank God he had the presence of mind as they walked to the car to think to run back and buy it. It would be a cold day in Hell before he got another family photo.

Surprisingly Thelma was the least upset. Either she was in shock or the relief at having unburdened herself far outweighed the consequences—though that was hard to imagine. All her fears, prophesies and nightmares had been fulfilled. Rage, rejection, insults, and airborne entrees aside, the girl could hardly have been described as taking the news well. Geoffrey had half expected Thelma to turn on him, to say it was all his fault, that his interloping had ruined everything. But she didn't. All she had said when they pulled up to the hotel he had stayed at during his first two days in the Bahamas, was that she was sorry it hadn't worked out, but that maybe Omega was right, and that in time, the rage and disgust would fade and she would come to accept things. He blushed now with embarrassment at his own pettiness in wanting to point out that he had said those calming words to her, not Omega.

The three of them agreed that for the time being, they would leave her alone. Judith was due to come home next weekend and that would be the first test. And yes, Thelma would let him know, one if she did come home, and two, if she mentioned the infamous get-together with Daddy. And yes, Geoffrey agreed not to attempt to initiate any further communication with the girl, but to wait and let her decide whether or not to open a dialogue. It was to be all very civilized and rational from here on in. No surprise moves on their parts. And Omega would not act as go-between. That had been his concern. He had an outsider's wisdom, Geoffrey decided. Omega's stand was that Judith buy into the whole can of worms or buy nothing. Accept her family, warts and all or reject them. There was no middle ground. The unsettling thing about Omega was not so much what he was saying, though that was scary enough, but that tears were running down his cheeks while he was saying it. And Geoffrey couldn't tell if the man was crying because of what had just transpired between his adopted daughter and the woman he loved or because of what he feared might happen as a result of it.

There was something else nagging at him. It had started at the bar that night in the hotel. It was the inconsistency of the girl's reaction— there was a mixed message throughout. It was almost as if she'd been saying that had he been on her list of top ten most desirable fathers, be he a tycoon or a 60s rock star, then everything would have been tickedy-boo. Initial offspring disgust at the discovery of parental infidelity might have been ameliorated had Geoffrey turned out to be something higher on the career ladder than boring old fart. If he'd been a cool dude Dad, then everything could have been cool. Would be cool now.

Maybe though, he was doing the girl an injustice. Maybe all she was saying without actually saying it, was that not only was their relationship disgusting, it was so bourgeois and banal that it served to underscore how trite her real parents were. A sobering thought. And at her age, who could blame her. If he, Geoffrey, had speculated for fifteen years as to what his daughter was like, whom she took after, what she wanted to do with her life, then the corollary must also hold. She had been doing exactly the same thing. Wondering, imagining, dreaming of the day she would meet him. And then finally that day comes. And she's presented with him. No warning, no chance to brace herself, to make the transition from the imaginary to the real. So she takes one look at him and clearly he doesn't even match the fantasy father or come anywhere close. If she had a specification checklist, it was very doubtful he would have passed muster on a single one. The bottom line was that he was a crashing disappointment. All her hopes dashed. All her romantic daydreams of this wonderful, exciting, powerbroker of a father smashed. Now she probably wished that she didn't know who he was. She was surely much happier not knowing.

Geoffrey downed the scotch and pressed the cabin attendant button. The stewardess served him again, but reluctantly, for he wasn't due more alcohol till dinner and she was now three-quarters way down the aisle with the trolley. But he didn't care. He wanted a drink. He wanted to sleep. So he ordered four miniatures. Suddenly it was all hitting him. The Captain announced that they had attained cruising altitude. So here he was. Thirty-five thousand feet and going back at approximately six hundred miles an hour. Going backwards at approximately six hundred miles an hour. Running away at approximately six hundred miles an hour. Running away from the mess he had made, the trouble he had caused. Running back to...back to what exactly? A life? He didn't think so. The Potato Crisp House for Geriatric Alcoholics and Other Assorted and Salted Relatives. At least he had helped the homeless, he should have claimed his checkmark from Judith for that. And of course, in addition to the house, his life also starred the schoolful of thickies. And in trying to teach them you could say he was helping the mentally challenged. Get a second checkmark on that. He smirked at his own wit. Not that he had any right to criticize them, for he was probably the greatest thickie of them all.

His was no life. Thelma and Omega had a life and he had blundered in like the proverbial bull, oblivious to the damage he could and would and did wreak.

But at least he had followed through and had done what he had said he would do—he had to give himself credit for that. He raised his glass to the Caribbean below.

He lowered his glass, for now reckoning time had arrived. Get with the program Geoffrey. Get real. Get a life. Yeah right.

But the voice within would not be silenced.

Face the facts. You were determined to find out. And you did. You found out what you wanted to know and what you didn't. Now it's time to move on. Ditch your obsession. Thelma moved on years ago. She broke with the past and you are still stuck in it. She has a life. She has forged a future. You have forged nothing.

He laughed at himself. Maybe he shouldn't be so premature in breaking it off with Ms. Haberdash. Maybe he could give their relationship a chance to develop. Even ask her out. Or not. Whatever he did, he had to do something. He could no longer use his self-imposed role as family gatekeeper as an excuse for not having a life. Nor could he use Thelma anymore as another excuse. He knew that now. He also knew something else. He knew that it wasn't a burned cabbage which rolled up to his feet the day the garden shed exploded. And he knew that he had known that for a long, long time.

9 780595 147670

Made in the USA
Middletown, DE
30 April 2017